# INVISIBLE HERO

# INVISIBLE HERO

*A Novel*

Roger K. Miller

*With best wishes.*

*Roger Miller*

iUniverse, Inc.
New York  Lincoln  Shanghai

**Invisible Hero**

iUniverse books may be ordered through booksellers or by contacting:

iUniverse
2021 Pine Lake Road, Suite 100
Lincoln, NE 68512
www.iuniverse.com
1-800-Authors (1-800-288-4677)

Because of the dynamic nature of the Internet, any Web addresses
or links contained in this book may have changed
since publication and may no longer be valid.

ISBN: 978-0-595-46183-7 (pbk)
ISBN: 978-0-595-70605-1 (cloth)
ISBN: 978-0-595-90484-6 (ebk)

Printed in the United States of America

To
the memory of
Corporal James Eugene Williams
US 51 045 415
*who knew what it was*


and to

Nancy
*who knew that it could be told*

*Because it was an invisible war, I suppose. It didn't exist. More boys fought than in World War I, but it didn't exist. Not really. Nobody cared about it. It was a war without a cause, Miss Pepperdine. And you can't be a hero unless you have a cause. So no heroes.*

—William Goldman, *Soldier in the Rain*

# CONTENTS

# Acknowledgments

First, my dear wife, Nancy, who for years never lost faith that this story could, should, and would be told, and whose love, inspiration, and—not least—support contributed the most to making her prophecy come true. The friends and extended family of Corporal James E. Williams, who made clear to me what a remarkable human being was lost in the war that so many do not want to remember. The many former prisoners of war of Korea who gave me the accounts, both horrific and inspiring, of their imprisonment, surprising me again and again with their keen insight and lack of bitterness. And Brian Felder, for the dozens of books about Korea over the years.

# Prologue: Changsong I

The cold stung, sharp, like a lash. Bob Karns stomped hard on the frozen ground twice, once with each foot, in an effort to relieve the numbness in his toes. Each time he could feel his toes jamming up against the thin canvas of his blue sneakers, but the sneakers were too flimsy and the cold too penetrating for his effort to be of any use. He looked down at them. Blue, hell. Already, just a few weeks after their issue by the Chinese, they were beginning to turn black from filth. Just like the blue quilted greatcoat, which he pulled closer about his thin body in an equally futile gesture at finding warmth. The coat was turning greasy, as well as black. No place to wash clothes here, not in this climate, not at this time of year.

He took a step away from the wall of the small house and immediately felt colder. Apparently the wall offered some protection from the wind, which was keener only a couple of feet away from it. Or maybe the house, a typical North Korean timbered mud dwelling, exuded some heat. God knows it couldn't be much, not at this hour of the morning, when last night's fire had died out almost completely. The stone-covered flues or channels in the floor that conveyed heat from the kitchen fire were cold now. The soldiers inside the house, nine other members of his American prisoner of war squad, were finishing their breakfast and getting ready to move out, grateful for the movement and the opportunity to go where it was warm, even if it was to a political indoctrination class, as it was most of these winter mornings.

Almost any activity was welcome as a break in the POWs' empty days. Listening to the Chinese yammer on about the DuPonts and the Rockefellers and Wall Street, and how American soldiers were all aggressors, could be funny, if you looked at it the right way. Political classes were mandatory, and Bob was surprised that he had been excused. But he wanted to see Tim. He'd heard that he was bad—anyone had to be very sick who landed in the camp's so-called hospital—and for some reason the Chinese had granted his request to visit him. No telling why they had, or why they had decided it was to be this morning. The Chinese were funny that way—sometimes hard-nosed, sometimes accommodating.

"Ah, Karns," the earnest Chinese interpreter had said, in his not-quite-perfect English, "this Davis. He is good friend of yours?"

"Yeah, sure," Bob had replied. "We practically grew up together."

"Karns," the interpreter said, "you know China has Lenient Policy. It is civilized nation. China does not discourage friendships among prisoners, so long as they do not threaten running of camp. You may go see this Timothy Davis in hospital. Tomorrow morning, after breakfast. Ten minutes only."

And that had been that, short and sweet. No shilly-shallying. Even the usual bullshit about how wonderful China and its policies are had been untypically short.

Bob pushed his hands down into the coat pockets and stepped around the corner of the building and headed up the dark street toward the hospital. The POW houses and huts, some with roof tiles and some with thatch, were at the southern edge of Changsong, a village that the Chinese, when they had taken control of the war and the POWs, had cleared of most of its Korean inhabitants in order to make this camp. Beyond the houses were the guards' walking posts, and beyond those were open farm fields to the south and west. Only a stone's throw north was the boundary between China and North Korea, the Yalu River, which ran southwestward, and across it the immense vastness of the Manchuria Plain. To the southeast rose high, rugged mountains, over which daylight was just beginning to crack.

The mountains reminded Bob a little bit of the mountains at home in Pennsylvania, except these in Korea were higher and had fewer trees. A lot more of them, too. GIs joked that Korea was so wrinkled with mountains that if you could iron them out the country would cover the world. Maybe not as many or as high as in the eastern part of Korea, where he'd been captured, or, from what he understood, way up in the northeastern part of North Korea. But maybe that's why they reminded him more of home—their relatively lower height and the way they ran in rows, one after the other into the purple distance, like they did in Somerton County. And that dusting of snow on their summits, which he could barely make out in the dawn's early light. It was like a morning in deer season. Different sort of hunting over here, though.

That was no lie he'd told the Chinese interpreter about him and Tim being friends, Bob thought as he puffed his way up the street. The inadequate prison diet gave him little energy, and he had to struggle painfully against the cold wind. It really was weird, if you came to think of it: Three of us from the same county in the same POW camp. And two of us from the same high school class—me and Clair Kasten, Repringer High, Class of '46. Tim, of course, had gone to Mott High, down in Black Run. When did he graduate? Forty-six, seven? But then Tim and Clair in the same outfit, Company B of the 88th, and captured together. Man, who'd ever believe the coincidence? Or the bad luck of Somerton boys? Clair said he'd heard there might be two *more* guys from the county in the camp. Five altogether. You had to laugh.

It was Clair who'd told him about Tim being in the camp, and in the hospital. He'd run into Clair soon after Clair got into the camp, even though Clair was in a different POW company. But he hadn't seen Tim. That wasn't surprising. Tim was in a different POW company still, and sometimes the Chinese let you associate and sometimes they didn't. A matter of chance, just like landing in this godforsaken hole in the first place. Besides, Tim had been in the hospital then, too. Bob remembered it, how after the first euphoria of meeting an old friend, they'd talked about home.

"Hey, do you know Tim Davis?" Clair asked.

"Yeah, I know him. I used to roller-skate with him and go to movies with him," Bob said. "Why?"

"He's in here, too. We were captured together, back around May 18th. We were in the same outfit—Company B of the 88th. We hid out for three days in an old Korean house, but it wasn't no use. The Chinese finally found us. After a while I lost touch with him on the march north. He's in the hospital."

"He is? What's the matter?"

"I dunno. What *wouldn't* be wrong with him? Look at all of us. Dysentery, malnutrition, pneumonia. Tim was bad when he come in with his bunch. They put him in the hospital. Not that it'll do him any good in that place."

That was the first time Tim was in the hospital. Apparently he had survived even that. Clair said he must have been doing OK, because Clair had even seen Tim playing his beloved basketball once the Chinese allowed them to. That couldn't have done him any good, either. Not that it could have been for very long, because that had been October, and it was already getting cold then.

Now it was, what? December 8th? December 8th, 1951, and it must easily be the coldest day since he was captured almost eight months ago, Bob thought. He was nearing his destination now. The hospital was just a few houses away, off the left side of the street. In the dark silence of the compound he could hear the rubber soles of his sneakers crunch the frozen dirt of the street. No one else was around. No guards were to be seen. None were needed. Any escape attempt would be impossible, suicidal. Even assuming that anyone could get past the guards who walked the perimeter, the nearest friendly forces were 300 miles away. The escapee would have to negotiate brutal terrain in Siberia-like weather and try and avoid millions of yellow-skinned, hostile people among whom his white skin would stick out like a dog turd at a tea party. Not to mention the lack of food. No, the Chinese had them by the short hairs.

Bob stopped. He paused at the door and wondered what to do. Might as well go ahead. He pushed open the door and stepped in. The first thing that struck him was how cool it was inside, not like a hospital at all. But then, looking around, this was like no hospital he had ever seen. One single room, and more like a hog pen or a chicken house on his family's farm. Filthy and straw-bestrewn, it contained no hospital equipment or facilities at all, aside from a few wooden beds.

Bob viewed this in the anemic glow of one light bulb. At that point he noticed the Chinese guard in a far corner. He braced for a challenge, but the guard simply nodded at him solemnly. Apparently he was expected. Why there was a guard at all Bob couldn't figure. Maybe to keep the living POWs from robbing the dead and the dying. Such things had happened, and the Chinese had a strong sense of rectitude. In a normal society what any POW possessed would not even be worth throwing away, but this society was 180 degrees off normal. Bob was about to conclude that there was no one there to steal from, but then he saw Tim....

# CHAPTER 1

▼

# REPLACEMENTS

*If you have a son overseas, write to him. If you have a son in the 2<sup>nd</sup>*
*Division, pray for him.*

—Walter Winchell

Tim had been dreaming of Helen. He felt the dream slipping away from him as
he woke up and he struggled to hold on to it. They were back at Beech Haven,
they were outside somewhere, it was warm, and she was angry at him. No, not
angry, disappointed. She was disappointed. She was chiding him for something,
something he did or wouldn't do. Her face was cast down and her voice,
reproaching him, was gentle and sorrowful. He could see her, in a crisp white
blouse with short, hemmed sleeves and a close-fitting, knee-length blue skirt. She
looked so lovely, so summery. He could even hear her: "Oh, Tim," she said, and
her voice receded with the dream. It made him feel terrible because, numbly
absorbing the soft rain of her disapproval, he knew she was right, whatever it was
she was disappointed about. He felt terrible *now*, outside the dream, which disappeared swiftly like water down a drain.

The dream was gone, leaving Tim with a sense of desolation. He opened his
eyes and couldn't remember where he was. It was strange: He saw the sky, a
leaden sky, and it was cold, very cold. He was lying on his right side, but his face
was canted upward. Why should he see the sky? Where was he? He moved his left

arm and his hand touched something cold and wet. And then it hit him, like one of those rubber balls on a long elastic cord being snapped back to the paddle: Korea.

He lifted his head up and looked about. The cold wetness he felt was snow. He was lying on the ground in his sleeping bag underneath a poncho that bore the weight of about three inches of snow. He sat up further and the snow slid down the poncho. He looked around and everywhere his gaze fell, it fell on snow. And it hit him again, this time full and complete, not a tiny rubber ball but a hundred-pound anvil: *Korea*!

Tim lay back down and watched his breath drift above him in the air. "Oh, sweet Jesus," he uttered softly, "look out for me now."

*        *        *        *

He couldn't think now what the exact date was, sometime in late February, 1951. He had been in Korea a week and a half. He had spent a day or so at a replacement depot—a "repple depple," they called it—down near Pusan, the southern port city where he had arrived in Korea.

It was chaos in Pusan. Not, from what he had heard, anything like the pandemonium of last summer, when it looked as if the North Koreans might squeeze the U.S. Army out of the stubby tube of Korea altogether, with Pusan being the mouth at the end of the tube. Then, soldiers who had been there told him, it was like some mad, murderous Keystone Kops movie. That's not how they described it, but that's how Tim imagined it: Keystone Kops in U.S. Army uniforms, driven mad with panic, everybody frantically bumping into each other in a desperate attempt to create order and stave off disaster pushing down from the north. You could cut the fear in the air with a knife.

No, it hadn't been like that when Tim was there, but, still, lack of organization ruled the day, and he was amazed that he and the hundreds of other replacements who had come over from Japan ever made it to where they were supposed to be. He still wasn't sure; he wasn't sure there *was* a place they were *supposed* to be. He thought the non-coms just pushed them off wherever was convenient, to fill quotas. It was eye-opening—and scary: You could see that neither the officers nor the NCOs cared about the soldiers in any real sense. Not there, anyway, where there was no unit pride, no comradeship. They were bodies to fill slots. "Get it off of my desk" seemed to be the principle. You were in the "pipeline" now. That's what they called it, the "pipeline," an endless stream of replacements.

But somehow, after less than two days, he and about three hundred other confused and scared GIs were hustled onto a troop train headed north.

*        *        *        *

The train ride was a slow-motion trip through a frozen hell. A blasted and denuded landscape inhabited by pitiable creatures patiently going on when any reasonable outside observer could see there was no point to going on. Once Tim had seen pictures of paintings by Salvador Dali and the scenes on this train trip reminded him of them, though the steep mountainous countryside of Korea was completely unlike Dali's lustrous settings. The resemblance lay in the sense of the abnormal being normal, illogicality being logical, like that melted watch registering time. Tim, raised on rural frugality, had never imagined, much less seen, such vicious poverty.

The train itself was something out of an old Western movie, only worse and smaller. Dirty, busted-up, unheated, it rocked along as if every turn of its wheels might be the last. The virtually stripped coaches were barely worthy of the name. Boarding early in the morning in Pusan, he grabbed a spot next to a young, sallow-faced PFC who barely acknowledged him. After stowing wherever they could their duffel bags and other gear and M1 rifles that had been issued to them in Pusan, they sat slumped next to each other in wary silence until the train finally jerked into motion and headed north. Then, the start-up of the train kick-starting Tim's natural companionability, he turned and introduced himself. The PFC said his name was Warren Goldfarb and he was from Brooklyn. And with that, the dam broken, they found each other equally garrulous and talked animatedly as they rode, each fascinated by the other's utter foreign-ness, Brooklyn Jew and Pennsylvania Protestant, but both even more fascinated by the greater foreign-ness of what was unrolling before their eyes.

The first sixty miles were uneventful, but near Taegu the nearly spring-like weather of Pusan turned to numbing cold, and they saw the first of the frozen, unburied corpses in the fields on either side of them.

Warren noticed them first. He pointed excitedly out the greasy, cracked window.

"Christ, Davis, wouldja look at that! Stiffs!"

"Yeah," Tim said, wonder registering in his voice. "What are they? They're not GIs, are they?"

"Nah. They're gooks. Lookit them, you can tell."

"Yeah, Koreans," said Tim, who hadn't yet been able to bring himself to call the Koreans *gooks*. "Maybe they're refugees."

"*Everybody's* a refugee in this goddamned country. Still, they ought to bury their stiffs. What would it cost to bury a goddamn stiff?"

"Well," Tim said, "the ground looks to be still pretty well frozen up around here."

"Yeah, well, the ground's frozen in February in Brooklyn, too, but we don't leave dead people lying around. It's unsanitary."

Tim smiled. "Maybe they're North Koreans. Maybe they don't care about burying them."

"Commie gook, southern gook, who knows the difference? Don't you remember what they told us about infiltrators, how you can't trust anybody? A North Korean could be in a South Korean's uniform, waiting to kill you. Besides, when you're dead, you're dead. I don't see how political affiliation's going to make any difference to the smell when those stiffs start thawing out in a few weeks." Warren sniffed the air theatrically. "On the other hand, it can't get much worse than it already is."

"Human shit on the fields."

"You called that right. Jesus, it's everywhere."

"You said you didn't know how it could get worse, but it can. They say it's worse in the warmer weather, in the growing season."

"Eeee-eeuw. Ancient culture, they call this. Three thousand years of civilization or however the hell long it is and what did they achieve? A latrine the size of California." Warren paused. "Not a bad comparison, come to think of it." He made another exaggerated sniff. "And to think I could have joined the Navy."

\*     \*     \*     \*

Just north of Taegu the train came to a halt. As soon as it did, dozens of aggies—half-naked, half-frozen Korean children—came swarming over, clamoring for food. They beat on the sides of the cars and thrust their thin arms upward, reaching. "You, GI, you give food?" they cried. "You give Hershey bah? You give gum?" And all along each side of the train the soldiers tossed out candy bars, gum, or whatever they had. Tim and Warren contributed. When it was clear that the rain of foodstuffs was over and that begging would achieve no more, the children ran back and huddled by their makeshift fires in barrels fed by scraps of wood and coal until another train came by and they could beg again.

Tim and Warren sat in silence. Tim tugged the collar of his GI overcoat more tightly about his neck, as if warding off not only the encroaching cold, but also contemplation of what they had just witnessed. Warren broke the silence.

"This country stinks in more ways than one."

"Yeah, little kids. That's awful, starving like that."

Further silence, broken again by Warren.

"What the hell, brooding about it won't help anything. Hey, you know any jokes?"

"No. I always like to hear them, but I can never remember them."

"I got one for you. Why does a Jewish wife do it with her eyes closed?"

Tim looked blank. "I don't know. Why?"

"God forbid she should see her husband having a good time."

Tim looked blank again.

"Well, maybe you got to be Jewish. And I know you ain't Jewish."

"No, I'm Church of the Brethren. That is, I used to be, but since I've lived in Guldwyck—I mean, when I was living in Guldwyck—I attended a Methodist church."

"Pardon my saying so, but Methodist I've heard of, but not that other thing. No disrespect."

"No, I'm not surprised. It's a pretty small church."

"My guess is there ain't many Jews out there in Palookaville or wherever it is you're from. That's all right, though. Just thank your lucky stars you ain't Jewish. Though I gotta say, thank God they sent me to Korea, even if it is the asshole of the universe, and not Germany. Germany I don't think I could take."

✳     ✳     ✳     ✳

The train sat north of Taegu for about three hours. No one knew why, and no one came through to explain. Then, just as mysteriously, it started up again. After traveling slowly for a few miles, it pulled into a siding to let a southbound train go by. The train had only a few boxcars. Some of the doors were partly open, revealing that they were filled with blood-soaked clothing removed from dead and wounded servicemen further north, where Tim and Warren and the rest of the trainload of soldiers were headed. They stared at the train wordlessly. As soon as it passed, their train pulled out of the siding and onto the main track and slowly chugged northward again.

They had traveled only a couple of miles when Tim tugged on Warren's sleeve. With his other hand he pointed out the window.

"What?" Warren asked.

"Look at that sign there."

"Where."

"There. By the road running up the mountain."

"Which mountain? There ain't nothin' *but* mountains here. Oh, yeah, I see what you mean. It's big. What's it say? 'Drive carefully. The life you save may be your replacement.'"

"Yeah, replacements," Tim said ruefully. "Us."

\*　　　\*　　　\*　　　\*

The sun was almost setting when the train stopped at another siding. Why there was a siding there none of the soldiers, looking out the windows, could understand. As far as they could see there was nothing but frozen dirt and turf, with occasional patches of snow. No one seemed to be around. Then, suddenly, figures in American combat uniforms appeared seemingly from nowhere and walked along the sides of the cars, banging on them and shouting, "Everybody off. Last stop, everybody off. Come on, come on, get up and get off. Time's a wastin'. We got important work to do for the United Nations." All the soldiers hurriedly gathered their duffel bags and M1s and other gear and scrambled down off the train and waited to be told what to do next.

It didn't take long. One of the uniformed figures stepped forward—it might just as accurately be said that the other figures made way for him—and stood looking at the new arrivals, his hands on his hips. He had on a full winter uniform, complete with cap with ear flaps, and he wore a .45 automatic at his waist. He was about six feet tall, well-built (a fact discernible even under the layers of uniform), and, as a figure, commanding. If that wasn't obvious from his appearance, it was from his voice, which could best be described as a well-modulated bellow. It got attention.

"What's this, what's this?" the figure bellowed. "Did we requisition United States soldiers and they made a mistake and sent us a gaggle of civilians?"

He ran his gaze up and down the shuffling crowd of soldiers lining the side of the train.

"Now, this is a combat area and we don't stand on ceremony in a combat area. For good reason, as you'll soon learn. But I can't believe that a group of disciplined United States soldiers—American infantrymen—would get off a train and diddle around talking and giggling like a bunch of schoolgirls sneaking a smoke outside the gym at a high school dance."

It isn't easy to bellow a lengthy comment like that, but the figure managed it with ease and authority. He stopped speaking and once again swept his gaze up and down the crowd of soldiers, who had fallen silent but were casting sheepish and questioning glances at each other.

"What I'm saying, gentlemen, is that I want some semblance of a military formation here. I can't talk to a disorganized rabble. It's not fitting. It's not proper. What is more, it is not military. So what I would like is, I would like four ranks of swingin' dicks in front of me, and I would like them *now!*"

The soldiers quickly shifted into motion, stumbling about and bumping into each other but eventually forming themselves into four long ranks. Once lined up, they continued to twitch about and cough and mumble. The figure in front of them waited patiently in silence until they realized that he was waiting for their silence in return, and they stopped talking.

"Good," he bellowed "Gentlemen, welcome to Wonju, for the moment the combat operational area of the 2nd Division—the Indianhead Division, Second to None. My name is Master Sergeant Tasker, and I am first sergeant of Headquarters Company of the First Battalion of the 88th Regiment of the 2nd Division. I have been chosen by the highly scientific process of drawing of straws to welcome you and explain a few things.

"The first, which maybe some of you have already noticed, is that I am not wearing any insignia of rank. As you can see, none of the non-commissioned officers with me here"—he gestured toward the group of men standing nearby— "are wearing insignia of rank.

"This is because we do not wish to be needlessly shot by the enemy. Enemy snipers dearly love to pick off commissioned and non-commissioned officers, and we don't want to give them any help by advertising who we are. So you will rarely see any officers or NCOs wearing insignia. That is what I meant by not standing on ceremony. But that is all I meant. You will quickly learn who your officers and NCOs are.

"As you may have heard, the 88th Regiment and the 2nd Division took a hell of a beating from the Chinese in the last couple of weeks at Chipyong-ni, Hoengsong and here at Wonju. It was in all the newspapers. We gave them much more than we got, but we took a lot of casualties. You have been brought here at great expense to the American taxpayer to replace these brave men. Please do not disappoint the great trust reposed in you by screwing up.

"If you follow the orders of your officers and NCOs and do as you are told, you will do all right. Please note that I did not say *be* all right. This is a highly dangerous situation, as your status as replacements should tell you. Despite what you may have been told, the enemy is extremely competent and formidable, as each of you will personally learn.

"In just a minute or so, the NCOs here are going to march you up that hill behind me and there you will be told which companies you have been assigned to. Your orders have been—"

A small voice from the first rank in front of him interrupted him.

"Sergeant Tasker, I think there's been a mistake."

The sergeant stared at his interrupter in disbelief.

"Sergeant Tasker, I'm supposed to be a postal specialist."

Titters broke out in the ranks.

"There's been some mistake. I've been trying to explain this ever since I got to Pusan, but nobody seems to be able to do anything. I'm supposed to be a postal specialist. I don't think I'm supposed to be here."

The titters grew louder and more extensive. Tim and Warren glanced at each other furtively and rolled their eyes.

"Well, now, son," Sergeant Tasker said, "I think I can safely say that none of us thinks he is supposed to be here. But if what you say is true, then we in the First Battalion are especially lucky today, because we have been without a mail clerk ever since the last one got his head blown off. Someone said incoming and he thought they meant the mail."

The assembled ranks broke out in laughter.

The voice persisted, "But Sergeant—"

"Son, don't talk while I'm talking. It's not polite. You go off with the nice sergeants here and I'm sure they'll get it all straightened out."

*     *     *     *

The sergeants let the soldiers proceed route-step up the steep hill because of all the gear each of them was carrying and because hardly anyone ever marched anywhere around there. It was too dangerous. Tim and Warren, sticking to each other's company for support, hefted their duffel bags onto their shoulders and trudged uphill together.

At the top of the hill they entered a big administrative tent where a corporal read off their assignments from a mimeographed list, one company at a time. Tim and Warren held their breaths until they learned, happily, that they were assigned to the same outfit: Company B, First Battalion, 88th Regiment. They grinned at each other.

As the corporal started to read off the names for the next company, a voice piped up. It was the PFC who had interrupted Master Sergeant Tasker. He had been assigned to Tim and Warren's company.

"Corporal, there's a mistake here."

The corporal looked up, glowering, irritated at being slowed in his task.

"I'm not supposed to be on your list. I'm a postal specialist. I've been trying to explain that ever since I got in Korea, but I just keep getting sent on."

"What's your name?"

He hesitated, glancing around him, prepared for the inevitable response. "Aldrich, Henry, PFC."

"*COM*-ing Mother!" someone shouted from the back of the tent, and everyone laughed.

The corporal ignored the laughter. He held his clipboard with its sheaf of orders toward Aldrich and, with a grimy thumb pressed next to his name, said, "That's your name, right? Aldrich, H.J., private first class?"

"Yes, but—"

"Then you're assigned to Company B, 88th Regiment, 2nd Infantry Division. I ain't the Pentagon. I don't make the assignments, I just read 'em off."

By this time the soldiers in the tent were growing restless, some of them a little indignant at the continued protestations. "Hey, mailman," one yelled out, "tell your troubles to Jesus, the chaplain's gone to chow."

"C'mon, let's get movin'," another said. "We're all goin' to the same place, anyway." And the man next to him said, "Yeah—hell."

Aldrich looked so dejected that Tim felt pity for him, though he, too, had been annoyed at his persistent objections.

"Never mind," Tim said, moving next to Aldrich. "Tell the first shirt when we get to the company. Maybe he can do something."

But neither he nor Aldrich believed that at all.

*     *     *     *

It was pitch dark, once they all pushed outside the tent, and growing colder by the minute. The men milled around, grousing, bitching, wondering where they were going next. "Hey, buddy," someone would say every now and then, "you got a smoke?" or, "Christ, it's cold," until several of the NCOs who'd marched them up the hill came out of the tent and stepped around to what was vaguely the front of the mob and explained what was to happen next.

They told them they wouldn't need all of the gear they'd brought with them. Just a blanket, sleeping bag, poncho, web belt with mess kit and entrenching tool, steel helmet, M1 rifle or carbine. Any clothing they wanted to take had to fit into their backpack, and the poncho and blanket or blankets had to be rolled up and bent around the backpack. Anything they didn't take could be put in their duffel bags and left in the administrative tent, from which they would be taken to be placed in storage. They were told to be sure, if their names and service numbers weren't stenciled on their bags, to identify them in some way, otherwise they'd be SOL—shit out of luck—when it came time to find them again. *If* they came to find them again. Grim Army humor again.

After that they were sent off to the mess tent for their first hot meal of the day. Tim and Warren lined up with the rest outside the tent, the only warm place around, and waited with their mess kits in their hands. Most everyone in line was talking and joking apprehensively, as young men in the Army always do when standing in lines leading to uncertainty, which so many do. After getting their food, Tim and Warren walked out the other side of the tent and sat on a couple of five-gallon jerry cans to eat.

"So it's too late, we're not going to our companies till the morning," Warren said, spooning up a mess of roast beef and gravy that steamed in the cold. "Typical Army fuck-up. Where we supposed to sleep tonight?"

Tim smiled at the sight of his new friend bent over his aluminum plate/pan, just barely distinguishable in the light seeping out of the mess tent.

"Didn't you hear?" Tim said. "Right here. Find a warm hole, they said, and curl up."

"I'd like to find a warm hole, all right, but not in the ground." Warren looked up and shot Tim a wolfish grin. "Oops, I forgot. You're a Methodist or something. I probly shouldn't be talking like that."

"Church of the Brethren," Tim said, still smiling. "That's all right. I've heard a lot worse, and I'm not a saint."

"That's what I figured, you weren't exactly cherry. All them milkmaids in the haymow down on the farm."

"I didn't live on a farm. I don't know where you got that idea. I *worked* on enough of them, but I didn't live on one. And I never saw a milkmaid in my life. You don't know much about farms, do you?"

"Me? I'm a Jew from Brooklyn, what would I know from farms? But I just figured you country boys and girls were always going at it like rabbits. Effect of all that healthy country air and all."

"Dream on," Tim said. "And I always figured in the big city you could get it at the drop of a hat."

"Dream on. You'd have a pretty dirty hat and nothing to show for it if you figured that."

Both men fell silent. The sounds of their spoons scraping against the aluminum broke the cold night air.

Warren broke their wistful reverie. "I got a girl, actually. But she's in Brooklyn and I'm over here, that's why I made that comment about—well, never mind."

Warren looked at Tim pointedly, as if eliciting response. "Her name's Rachel. I got her picture here." He put down his mess kit and reached into his pants pocket and pulled out a wallet from which he took a photo. He handed it to Tim.

Tim took it. In the dim light from the tent he could see it was a cracked and chipped snapshot of a very pretty girl in her early twenties with a broad, smiling face from which thick hair was pulled tightly back, apparently in a bun or otherwise tied in the back.

"Very pretty," Tim said, and handed it back. "Warren and Rachel, very nice."

"Yeah, well, she's a year older than me, to tell you the truth. But that don't mean anything. She's nice. Her old man's a tailor. He's nice too, I guess."

Warren looked at the photo, then tucked it lovingly back into the wallet and put the wallet back into his pocket. He looked at Tim. "You? A girlfriend, I mean?"

Tim hesitated, then spoke carefully. "No, not really. I went out with a few girls in Guldwyck, but nothing serious. Well, there was one girl. Two girls, really, but one I really liked."

He hesitated again, and something in the engaging openness of this friend he had made scant hours ago made him open up, too.

"There was a girl I was pretty serious about when I still lived in Pennsylvania, but that was three years ago."

"Really? Still carrying the torch?"

"No, no. She was from Ohio, and she went back to Ohio, and I haven't seen her since."

"Sounds like it *was* pretty serious, the way you're talking. Or avoiding talking, I mean. What was her name? Got a picture of her?"

"Her name? Her name's Helen Booth. Yes, I guess it was pretty serious. I don't know, maybe it was a mistake, breaking up. She was ... she was ... real nice." Tim looked at Warren absently, as if trying to remember something. "No, sorry, I don't have any picture of her."

But that wasn't true. Tim did have a photo. A half-hour later he went looking for a depression in the ground to bed down in. In it, he spread out his poncho, placed his sleeping bag on top of it, stuffed an extra blanket inside, and crawled in, wrapping the other half of the poncho over it all. After shifting about a bit, and using his combat boots as an unsatisfactory pillow, Tim settled down for the night. Why had he mentioned Helen? Why hadn't he said Peg? He thought he might even be in love with Peg. Why not Lynn? He had photos of them both. Before letting himself fall asleep, he took out his wallet, and from it the photo. It was virtually impossible to see anything in the dark, but it was Helen, all right. The next morning when he woke up, dreaming of her, there was three inches of snow on the ground, and Warren was curled up in another small hole nearby, snoring softly.

# CHAPTER 2

▼

# ANCESTRAL SOMERTON

*That the mountains may bring prosperity to the people, and the little hills bring righteousness.*

—The Book of Common Prayer

If you were a hawk, or maybe a low-flying angel, soaring over Somerton County, Pennsylvania, keeping an eye out for this thing or that person, you would see a landscape not totally unlike that of northern North Korea. Maybe not so ancient, nor in winter so cold, but old enough by American standards and cold enough for most tastes. And mountainous—several low ranges that slash across it from northeast to southwest. Mountains whose continuous folds from that height look like a scuffed rug, but that create unpredictable updrafts and downdrafts to keep the most experienced hawk, or angel, on its figurative toes. Far down below you blue-gray ribbons of road wriggle through those folds, connecting communities with names like Frawleysburg and Bright Item and Port Arthur and Black Run. The roads are two-lane, mostly, the chief exceptions being the Pennsylvania Turnpike, which snakes east-west across the county on its way from and to places of greater prominence, and U.S. Route 220, which, starting 'way up north on the New York border, shoots southward like a seam holding together the state's rural center. But 220 only clips a corner of Somerton County before veering off into the neighboring county, so it almost wouldn't count if it weren't such a main road for getting in and out, mostly out.

At most times in your angelic or accipitral flight you would pass over a peaceful, unhurried scene, for hardly more than 45,000 souls toil within its 1,000 square miles of territory. At that it's not by any means the least populous county in the state, but it's rural for a certainty. In summer green foliage blurs the roughness of this extension of the Appalachians, and the hills and valleys and broad flat areas that here are called "coves" take on a masquerading softness. And in the fall, for a brief shining moment, the roughness is hidden by the dying foliage's shimmering luminescence. But in winter, when hawks are not likely to be out and even angels would not dare to tread, the roughness of the land is laid bare, until a snowfall provides a coat of white to hide its edges again. But all those coverings don't matter, except possibly to strangers passing through. Whether covered or laid bare, the plainness and the roughness equal a rare beauty perceivable only by hawks and angels—and by people many of whose families have lived here for generations.

That's what you'd see today. What you would have seen when Tim Davis, who was one of those people, was born here in 1928 would have been different. Not terribly different, but different. The Turnpike, for instance, was a decade in the future, and Route 220 only a feeble beginning toward getting country travelers out of the mud. There were fewer houses and smaller, but, paradoxically, more people, or at least the appearance of more people, because families had more children and less money to house them with. And more farms but fewer and poorer roads to get to them by. Tim was born in Somerton County and spent his most formative years here. He was born in one of those folds in the hills, in an extra-wide spot in the road called Manley, east of the borough of Horton. Don't look for it on your standard road map, because that's one of the small differences. It faded away with the tannery—one of the last of many that once dotted the county—that gave it life. Tim's parents were born in the county and his grandparents and some of his great-grandparents, and generations back further than most Americans want to bother to go. His family had strong and deep roots in Somerton County and does still, despite the tremendous centrifugal force in American life that flings people far from their birthplace. Being from a family that has been in one place for generations doesn't make you any more American than someone who arrived yesterday, but the place and the family do form the individual.

Somerton County, a ragged-edged cartographical trapezoid, sits on the Maryland border in west-central Pennsylvania. The county is older, in fact, than the

Republic, though this is not a unique distinction; many counties in the thirteen original colonies/states can boast of that. At the time of original creation, the county encompassed much of the southwest corner of the province. When the Revolutionary War began, it took in six present counties and a little left over. Today it is much smaller. Its largest municipality, also called Somerton, the county seat, is a pleasant community of about 3,500.

Groups of Welsh immigrants came into the area at various times, many of them in the 19th Century, and it's possible that Tim is descended from one of them. The other side of his family is somewhat clearer. The great revolt of the South had ended just two years before when Tim's maternal grandfather, Lawrence Leland King, was born on April 11, 1867, in Stanfield Township. Lawrence King lived all of his long life in and around Stanfield Township, one of the older political subdivisions of Somerton County, having been formed in October 1774. He was one of six children, four girls and two boys, of Henry and Martha (Geller) King, who came from Germany. Or at any rate Henry did, where he might have been Hans, or Heinrich, Koenig. As Henry King, he became a farmer in Stanfield Township, and served as a private in Company C, 205th Pennsylvania Volunteers, during the Civil War when he was in his middle 30s. Lawrence King's future wife, Naomi Wentley, was born in Horton, not far from Stanfield, on November 23, 1878. Horton was a relatively new political entity at the time, having been incorporated in 1860 as Point Deadly, a name it retained until it was changed to Horton in 1873. Naomi had one sister and six brothers. Some of her Wentley ancestors, too, were from Germany, and Switzerland, where they were known as Wentli or Wintli, though both her mother and father, Israel and Rose (Krug) Wentley, were born in Somerton County. The Wentleys have been in this country since at least the early 1700s and in the county long enough to have generated two or three separate branches whose members often are barely related to, or on speaking terms with, the others.

When Lawrence King married Naomi Wentley on July 9, 1897, she was 11 years younger than he and one of his former pupils in the series of one-room schoolhouses he taught in around the county. Lawrence and Naomi raised twelve children, five boys and seven girls, of whom one, Anna, would become Tim Davis's mother. A thirteenth child died in infancy.

Lawrence taught school for twelve years until his father died and he took over the family farm. He started each school year by drilling in his younger pupils a time-worn bit of life-(and afterlife-) affirming grade-school doggerel:

*So-and-so is my name*
*America's my nation*
*Black Run is my dwelling place*
*And Heaven's my destination*

After leaving teaching he remained a farmer until he retired. Never wealthy, nor even well-off, he was a respected member of the community for all of his 86 years. He served as a school director in Stanfield Township for twenty-five years and for four years in Welland Borough, as well as assessor for Stanfield. He was an elder and Sunday School teacher in the Evangelical and Reformed Church, where he worshipped in that dutiful and accepting way that people did when evangelical Christianity was setting out to be our national ethos. Everyone who remembers him, decades after his death in 1953, remembers him as one of nature's gentlemen, kindly and soft-spoken. At the age of 95, Elva, his oldest child, said she was always proud of her "Daddy."

By all accounts the King household was an unusually warm and child-friendly, if rather crowded, one. Lawrence rarely had to resort to the use of the strap, and if Naomi raised her voice to the children it was not out of anger, but out of a feeling of harassment virtually constant in a woman in a household with more children than money or time. Lawrence and Naomi were an unusually amiable couple— and vigorous, to say the least. Their youngest child, Bertram, was born when Lawrence was 58 and Naomi 46. In fact, he was born *after* their first grandchild was born to Elva and her husband, Archie Flanders.

From 1921 to 1927, life got even more crowded, for in those years Lawrence and Naomi shared a farmhouse and property known as the Packer Farm with the family of Naomi's brother, Mitchell Wentley, and his wife, Winona. Lawrence and Naomi and Mitchell and Winona engaged in a sort of communal living not at all uncommon in rural areas early last century. All over the state you could find two families sharing these tiny wood frame houses, typically three rooms up and two or three down on each side, cold in winter and hot in summer, with few amenities other than an outside privy and little means of blocking out the other family's noise.

To just this sort of situation at the Packer Farm Lawrence and Naomi brought seven children and Mitchell and Winona two, and both couples added to their progeny after moving in. Everyone's reserves of courtesy and goodwill were constantly tested, for while the house never had more than nine rooms, including five bedrooms, at one point it had eighteen occupants. It helped that the two families were related.

The place fairly bulged, and in April 1927 Lawrence and Naomi decided it was time to move on. Lawrence sold his interest in the property and they moved to the red-brick house known as the Flanders Farm on State Route 23. They took with them the eight children who remained at home, the older ones having moved out.

It was around this time that Anna, their fifth (living) child, married Hugh Davis. In later years the King women tended toward either a fine-drawn slenderness, like Jean and Eileen, or a slight plumpness, like Harriet, but as young women they all displayed a cool and composed prettiness, if not indeed beauty. So it was with Anna. An early photo shows her standing in the snow, a cloche hat over her ears, dark hair spraying out, and a fur-trimmed coat that comes to her knees, revealing shapely legs. She looks at the camera with calm assurance, traces of a smile at the corners of her mouth. Hugh, like most grooms or young husbands, is just there, an agreeable, good-looking, dark-haired young man only slightly taller than his bride. They were married April 25, 1927, when she was not yet nineteen years old and he was almost twenty-three.

Married couples tend to gravitate toward the family of one or the other spouse, and Anna's own soon-to-be family gravitated to the Kings. Hugh Davis was born May 29, 1904, to Alonzo and Judith (Chester) Davis. Hugh was a twin. Years later Anna would tell her children how their father and his brother, Morgan, would play tricks on people who couldn't tell them apart. She said that once they "switched girlfriends," and even the girlfriends were fooled for a time. But she would never tell whether she or someone else was one of the tricked girlfriends. Hugh's parents lived in Manley and ultimately had five other children, two boys and three girls.

Hugh and Anna immediately moved in with Hugh's father (Judith, the mother, had died a few years back) on the family farm, which Alonzo had bought before the twins were born because even then the tannery he worked for was beginning to be a shaky proposition. There Timothy Arthur Davis was born on January 21, 1928, almost exactly nine months after their wedding. What Hugh did for a living no one in the family is sure. Some think he tried to make a go of the farm from which his father had largely retired, though it had never been much more than a subsistence operation. There wasn't much work in an overwhelmingly agricultural area like Somerton County in the best of times, and these times were becoming something decidedly other than that. Though much later Anna's younger sister Jean, a teenager at the time, would say, "I didn't realize we were having a Depression that much until I read about it, because we had the food and everything down in the country in Pennsylvania. My father could afford to send me to high school. We had to pay to go to high school even, because we had to go outside the district, outside our area." The King children, and children of other families in the Stanfield area who could scrape together the fees, went to Repringer High School in West Linton until the Leander P. Mott High School was built in Black Run, a section of Stanfield Township. Construction on the buildings that would eventually include that school began the year Tim was born, but he wouldn't enter it for eleven more years, because sometime around this period Hugh and Anna felt the lure of Guldwyck, New York.

# CHAPTER 3

▼

# UPSTATE SOJOURN

*Fair weather cometh out of the north.*

Psalm 37:22

Why members of the King and Davis families, in seeking work, chose to leap 400 miles from Somerton County to Guldwyck, in an era of barely adequate roads, rather than to go to, say, Pittsburgh, which was much closer, is lost in the twists of time. Probably Hugh went because his brother had preceded him. Morgan Davis had found work at General Electric in Schenectady, a sister city to Guldwyck in Upstate New York, and Hugh and Anna followed him there.

Guldwyck, hugging the Hudson River, then a far cry from the bombed-out shell it, and hundreds of other small American cities, became after the 1960s. It was a vibrant, bustling community, as full of industry, or the promise of it (shirts, shoes, tools, business machines), as it was of history. The Battle of Guldwyck has been called a pivotal point of the Revolution—though, admittedly, practically all of its battles have been described that way; the Revolution must have been pivoting like a veritable dervish. Though the story of the King family, and of the families it married into, is intimately connected with Guldwyck, Hugh and Anna never lived there. Mostly they lived in either Schenectady or Albany.

In any event, in March 1929 Hugh and Anna (and Tim) moved into an apartment on Pleasant Street in Schenectady. This was not long after Herbert Hoover was inaugurated president on March 4, to preside over the start of the national Great Depression. But just as much of the nation was beginning to lose their jobs, Hugh, with Morgan's help, found one, as a punch press operator at GE. They lived on Pleasant Street when their second child, Richard Hugh, was born on September 30, 1930, becoming part of a national population of 122,775,046, according to that year's decennial U.S. Census. He was delivered by a midwife. Country ways die hard.

While they lived in Schenectady, misfortune struck, the first in a series of misfortunes that would befall Anna and her family. One day when he was three, Richard—known as Rick—was playing outside with another, older boy who had an air gun. The boy brandished it smugly, lording it over his younger, awestruck, gunless playmate. Of course, the gun went off when he didn't want it to, and the pellet struck Rick in the right eye. The injury would leave him blind in that eye and give it a slight cast. That's all—if "all" is the word for it—there was to it in those days: a terrible accident.

*     *     *     *

All the while they lived Upstate, Hugh and Anna kept close ties to Somerton County. Hugh loved to hunt—a love that both Tim and Rick would inherit—and, though he hunted Upstate, he preferred to hunt in the familiar hills of Pennsylvania. Whenever he could get time off work in deer or turkey or small-game season he and Anna and the boys went back there for a few days to visit the family, traveling in the same car that Hugh had bought used in 1929 to bring them north, a purple-and-black 1926 four-door Dodge sedan. However, some of the family were coming to them now. Harriet, the younger sister closest in age to Anna, followed her sister and brother-in-law Upstate, and Jean came not long after, upon her graduation from Mott High School. Both of them got jobs as maids or kitchen help or other service work at Alma Blaine, the exclusive girls' college in Guldwyck, as did a younger sister, Eileen, who made the trek north still later.

In 1936, the Davises moved to Albany. There were six of them now, two girls, Barbara Ann ("Barb") and Constance Mary ("Connie"), having been born in 1933 and 1935. The lingering Depression had caught up with Hugh's job at GE. At the time Connie was born he was out of work and they were living out in the country in Altamont, southwest of Schenectady and northwest of Albany. After a time he found other work, as a mechanic, but nothing solid or lasting, and he kept looking for something else. Luck came to his aid again—though, considering later developments, luck may not be the word. In any event, he landed a job as a mechanic with a trucking company in Watervliet, just north of Albany. To be nearer his work they moved to Albany. To Albany Street in Albany, in fact.

On a hot June morning they pulled up to the house in that '26 Dodge with all of the kids—except Connie, who was too young—goggling out the windows at their new home. A tall maple grew at the curb in front of it, one in two lines of maples that stood as sentinels on either side of the street, their immense green bushes forming an incomplete arch across the street through which shafts of sunlight shot down. This was something different from the multi-apartment building they had lived in in Schenectady. This was a two-family house, and they had rented the top floor. The house was sided in big, dark-blue, cedar-like shingles, and was divided equally in two, the top floor mirroring the bottom. Each floor had a porch running across the full front of the building facing the street, the porch closed in by a solid railing on the lower half and by a screen on the upper, the only difference between the two being the steps that ran to the front walk on the ground floor. The ground floor was already occupied by another family. A big family, by the looks of it. Kids, mostly boys, spilled all over the front yard and the porch railing. The yard was pretty scrappy looking, the result of all those young, running feet.

"So, kiddo, what do you think?" Hugh asked, slouched over the steering wheel and scrunching to look out at the house. Somewhere in all those trees cicadas were making their high-pitched miniature-sawmill buzz.

Anna, holding not-quite-one-year-old Connie asleep in her lap, looked up at the house from the passenger side. She had, of course, seen and approved of the house before. Hugh was only seeking reassurance. She turned to him and smiled. "I like the house fine, Hugh. I think we'll be happy here."

"Mom, is this where we're going to live?" Tim asked. Anna turned to look at him in the rear seat. There was no apprehension on his eight-year-old face, only curiosity. He was taking on more and more aspects of his father—the narrow face, the thick shock of dark hair, the perpetual grin. That grin. What was so amusing all of the time?

"Yes, sweetie," Anna answered, ruffling his hair and running her hand softly down the side of his face. "This is our new home."

"Will I have to go to a different school?"

"Yes, you will. Albany is a different city and so you'll have to start a new school." A murmur of silent concern twisted in her. She and Hugh had held Tim back; he hadn't started first grade until he was seven. She wondered now if this had been the right thing to do.

Rick asked, "And I'll go to the same school as Tim, right, Mom?"

"That's right, Rick. You'll go to school with Timmy." Rick was six. Almost monthly, like a slowly developing photograph, his features grew more to resemble his brother's. Maybe they would do things differently with him; maybe they would enter him in first grade this fall.

By this time the children in the yard and on the porch had noticed the car, and a couple of them had shyly approached it. One, a boy about Rick's age or slightly younger, was hanging by both hands from the car window, peeking up at Anna with the left side of his face pressed against the door.

"What's your name?" he asked.

"Mrs. Davis. What's yours?"

"Frank Connell Clay Junior." He popped up and looked in the car. "Are these your kids?"

Before Anna had a chance to reply, a young woman, under thirty, came bustling out the front door of the house, drying her hands on a large kitchen apron while heading toward the car.

"Frankie, you get away from there! Stop bothering those people." The woman stooped to look in the window when she got to the car. Thin and of medium build, she had the eager-to-please manner of a woman with too many responsibilities to want to run the risk of adding to them by offending the world. She pulled her hands out of the apron and thrust her right into the car. "I'm Ruth Clay. That's Frank Junior, my oldest boy. Are you the new upstairs folks?"

"Yes. I'm Anna Davis. This is my husband, Hugh." Hugh smiled and nodded to Ruth. Anna started to enumerate the children, but Hugh, getting out of the car, stopped her.

"It's hot and we might as well get started before it gets any hotter," he said. "We'll have to make a lot of trips, and the truck will be here with our stuff anytime now. Besides, I'd like to get the radio plugged in and see if I can find out what's going on at that convention."

It was June 10, a muggy pre-summer day, and the Republican National Convention was taking place in Cleveland. Hugh had uprooted his Republican loyalties from Somerton and replanted them in the less hospitable soil of Upstate New York. He swung open the door and stepped out. Standing by the fender, he pushed his fedora back on his head and with a sigh contemplated the house and the long hot job before him.

*       *       *       *

In such manner began a three-year stretch in the Davises' lives, one of the happiest times any of them can remember. Hugh and Anna and the Clays, Frank Senior and Ruth, became the fastest of friends. Their lives revolved around their families; their families *were* their lives. Anna, like Ruth, worked at that most ancient and venerable of trades, housewife, and Hugh went off every day to the trucking company. Frequently he would bring something home from work for the kids to play with—ball bearings, or a wooden freight box.

The Davis and Clay children played together constantly. The Clays eventually had thirteen children, although—shades of Lawrence and Naomi King—one of the thirteen died in infancy. Tim and Rick and young Frank, who was between Tim and Rick in age, attended Albany School District School No. 20 on North Pearl Street. In the back of the house was a huge field where Frank and Hugh parked their cars and the kids played, either basketball or whatever pick-up games kids from large families with few toys could devise. Sometimes they took big pieces of cardboard ripped from boxes and sledded down the hill on the tall, slippery grass. Other times they went back to the gravel bank maintained by the Albany Gravel Company and had themselves a little cookout.

Once in that first year some smartass bigger kids came by their play area and they teased Rick. They kept asking him, "Ricky, are you happy? How do you feel, Rick? Do you feel happy?" And Rick, confused and daunted by the older boys, said, Sure, he felt happy. And one of the older kids said, "Well, put your hand in your pocket, you'll feel nuts," and they all laughed uproariously. Fell all over themselves with merriment. Rick, not knowing what was going on except that he was the object of ridicule, looked to Tim for help. Tim, just as clueless but assuming the role of older brother, quickly scurried Rick and their friends away, saying they had to go home now, while the big kids jeered.

They had a lot of good times, the two families together. In the summer the Clays and Davises camped out at Half-Moon Beach on the Mohawk River. Frank bought what he called a "circus tent," about twenty-by-forty feet, for his large and growing family and pitched it on a lot he rented at the beach. Hugh pitched one somewhat smaller. They stayed out there on weekends, and sometimes the wives and children remained there during the week and Hugh and Frank would commute to and from work. Each spring the men and boys spent a Saturday or Sunday caulking a rowboat Frank built for use on the river. Most Saturday nights the parents went down to the roofed-over, wooden-floored dance pavilion and danced away the cares of the lean times underneath the cones of buttery light and the moths that flitted around them. This was an exciting time for the kids, lurking at the edges of the pavilion, because it is always amusing to see adults at play, and an adult unbuttoned and in high spirits was likely to spring for a rare bottle of soft drink. Then, on Sunday morning, the fathers cooked breakfast, throwing potatoes up in the air and catching them in the frying pan, just having fun.

Having fun. If personalities can be inherited, Tim inherited his from his father. No one now can speak of Tim without mentioning his eternally cheerful, easy-going, and happy-go-lucky nature. Just like Hugh's. It could be maddening, the way he was so hard to rile.

The same year they moved to Albany, Hugh bought a new car, a tan, 1936 Dodge sedan. His previous car, also a Dodge, he had bought used, but this one was new, and he was proud of it. On the first Sunday afternoon after he bought the car, Anna and Frank and Ruth and a couple other neighbors and some of the kids were standing around helping him admire it. The men walked around it with Solomonic mien, conscious that every new car owner wants approval but not approval given in haste that indicates insufficient appraisal. The women stood at the curb, arms crossed on their breasts, happy that their men were happy. The kids jumped up and down, simply because here was a fresh occasion to jump up and down.

"Real nice, Hugh," Frank said finally. "How do you like it?"

"I like it fine, Frankie. The thing is, though, I don't much like the color. I wish it was green."

Much discussion followed about the great deal Hugh had gotten, which was why he'd bought a car whose color he didn't particularly care for. That part of the conversation wasn't heard by young Frank and Tim, whose eyes locked and ears stopped listening when they heard that Mr. Davis preferred his car to be a color of which Mr. Clay had a can of paint in the cellar. To which they repaired immediately.

After a few minutes the adults drifted indoors to continue the discussion over coffee. Shortly after that, the two boys, ascertaining that the coast was clear though not conscious that that's what they were doing, popped out of the cellar doorway, a gallon can of green shutter paint in Frank's hand.

By the time Frank Senior came back outside, they had that car almost completely painted in Hugh's preferred color. Including the windows. Seeing the two boys, one on the hood, the other on the roof, Frank gave a whoop, stuck his head back inside to summon Hugh, and ran outside to stop the painting. Frank was steaming when he hauled the mystified youngsters—what had they done but satisfy a wish?—off the car, so angry he could barely contain himself.

But not Hugh. "We'll get it washed up," he said. "Don't worry about it. We'll get it cleaned off."

And so they did. Frank had a fifty-five-gallon drum of kerosene from which he fed a space heater in the house. He and Hugh filled pails with kerosene and washed down the Dodge, which came out relatively unscathed. Rather better, in fact, than the kids, who had done as complete a painting job on themselves as they had on the car—in the process ruining brand-new suits they had worn home from church. Ruth, silently containing her anger, got out a galvanized wash tub and half-filled it with kerosene. She made the boys strip. It didn't matter that one wasn't her son, and Anna was not inclined to intervene at that point. When they didn't move fast enough to suit her don't-mess-with-me mood, she helped them, jerking the clothes off in a way that bobbed the boys about. They didn't complain, because it had finally sunk in that they had done something really bad. Then she had them get into the tub and she scrubbed them down briskly. The kerosene stung, but again, they didn't complain, and when she was done they were as clean as the Dodge.

*     *     *     *

The Albany interlude came to an end on July 13, 1939. It was a Thursday, the middle of the afternoon, and Anna was working in the kitchen. Music came softly from the table-model radio on the linoleum-covered counter, a silly little, white plastic Majestic with Charlie McCarthy on its front that they had recently bought so Anna could listen to the soap operas without having to turn the volume way up on the console model in the living room. She liked a number of them and tried never to miss them, though it didn't matter if she did, because their stories progressed slowly and recapped themselves consistently. That was the main thing she liked—their constancy and dependability, heralded each day by the same theme music and the same opening announcements.

She especially liked "The Romance of Helen Trent": Its theme, "Juanita," thrummed in the background as the announcer promised once again as he promised every day, "that because a woman is thirty-five … or more … romance in life need not be over." She'd listened to that for years. And there was a relatively new one that she'd grown attached to in the last couple of years, "Our Gal Sunday," with its opening question that comedians on the night-time shows had begun satirizing: "Can a girl from a mining town in the West find happiness as the wife of a wealthy and titled Englishman?" The vague melancholy of its theme, "Red River Valley," like the softly yearning "Juanita," caught at something inside her each time she heard it. There were others, like "Just Plain Bill," the story of a barber in the small town of Hartville that concluded each episode with "Polly Wolly Doodle." She knew they were silly and dwelt on misery, but they were anchors in her life, and she was a person who could not have too many anchors.

But her soap operas were over for the day, and Anna was humming to the music as she worked. Barb and Connie were downstairs playing with the Clay children, Rick had been out and in and now was out somewhere again, and Tim was putting a kite together in the living room. Anna was peeling potatoes at the sink when there was a knock at the door. She dried her hands on her apron as she went to answer it.

A man in a blue policeman's uniform stood in the doorway. Immediately Anna's chest constricted. She was vaguely aware that Tim had come in from the living room and was watching her, his kite trailing from his left hand.

"Mrs. Davis?" The policeman touched the visor of his cap. "Anna Davis?"

"Yes. What's wrong? Something's wrong, isn't it?" Something had to be wrong. Policemen didn't come to your door in the middle of the day. The children were all here. Except Rick. No, but Rick was just here, it couldn't be Rick. "Has something happened to Hugh?"

"Mrs. Davis, there's been an accident. May I come in, please?"

Anna backed away from the door into the room, her hands at her throat, appalled at this tall, broad-shouldered, blue-clothed messenger of probable doom. She couldn't look at his eyes, and instead focused on his tightly buttoned, lapel-less tunic with its high collar like an Army uniform from the Great War. The officer stepped apologetically into the room. Tim watched, his gaze shifting from his mother to the policeman.

"There's been a terrible accident, Mrs. Davis." The officer was visibly uncomfortable at these melodramatic words and actions. "Maybe you'd better sit down. Is there a place to sit down?" His desperate glance caught sight of the living room. "In the living room?"

Anna looked into the living room, too, seeming surprised to find it there. Then she looked down at Tim, who stood between them, open-mouthed, wide-eyed. "Timmy," she said almost sharply, "you go downstairs to the Clays."

"But Mom, I—"

"Timothy, do you hear me?"

And Tim went downstairs, and Anna and the policeman went into the living room, where he told her that her husband had been killed at work earlier that afternoon at the truck terminal. It was a horrible death. Hugh had just filled the fuel tank on a tractor-trailer. Exactly what happened and how were matters that were, and always would remain, unclear. Whether Hugh had signaled the driver to back into the freight terminal, or whether the driver had misunderstood another command, the result was that the driver did back up, and Hugh, having for some reason stepped in between the side of the truck and the building wall, was pinned and crushed. The driver didn't realize what was happening until he heard some other workers shouting. When they got to Hugh, he was lying mangled, an electric lead light in his hand, possibly indicating that he intended to check the truck's oil when the driver completed backing up to the loading platform. A doctor was summoned and gave emergency treatment before Hugh was rushed to Memorial Hospital, where he was pronounced dead on arrival. By the time the policeman finished telling Anna this he was sweating profusely, Anna was in a state of chalk-faced disbelief, and Ruth Clay, alerted by Tim's frightened report of a policeman in his house, had rushed upstairs to give aid and comfort to her friend and neighbor.

It proved difficult to get word of the accident to others. Her sisters Harriet and Jean were visiting a friend in Wynantskill. Harriet was married by this time, to Freddie Farrell, and had a two-year-old son of her own, Ralph. When Harriet got back to her house, the phone was ringing, and when she got on the phone, she recalled later, "I said, 'No, no, don't tell me that.' I couldn't believe it." Frank Clay, meanwhile, took Anna down to the truck terminal and then to the hospital. When they got back, Harriet and Freddie and Jean were there, along with a crush of others, prepared to help Anna with this sudden and immense sorrow.

"I'd tell her, 'Let me do this, let me do that,'" Jean remembered. "And she'd say, 'No, no, I've got to keep busy.' Oh, she was a state."

She *was* a state. When she was in a crowd of people—and there were constant crowds in the next couple of days—she did keep busy. She maintained her composure, completing with precision the myriad bizarre and cruel tasks required of a grieving person. But when she was alone, or with one or more of her sisters, she let go and cried uncontrollably and crazily. She sobbed with such abandon, with such awful shaking ferocity, that it frightened Harriet and Jean, who had never seen such raw emotion of any kind in their sister before. Little wonder. She and Hugh had achieved, as few do, the biblical injunction of two becoming one, and now half of her had been ripped away. Her chief anchor was gone.

But she wasn't the sort of person to keep herself in a state for long. Her life had just been set dangerously adrift, and she took hold of the only other anchor she knew: Somerton County. Though she had family over in Guldwyck, Pennsylvania was home and they had to head back.

Hugh's remains were taken to Horton, where, on the afternoon of Sunday, July 16, with a huge, sorrowing crowd of friends and family attending, funeral services were held at the Church of the Brethren, the Rev. D. K. Riemenschneider officiating. The day began hot and then turned threatening, with huge thunderclouds building up and an occasional peal of thunder rolling out, but the rain held off until after Hugh was interred in Horton Cemetery.

Few memories and fewer artifacts of that emotion-shaking time remain. One that does is a letter from Anna's brother Guy, dated July 13, the day of the death, and written from Camp Tom-o-Hawk near Au Sable Forks, New York, where Guy worked as a counselor in the summers away from his teaching job at the exclusive Barrett School in New York:

My dear Anna:—

The news of your tragedy has left Essie [his wife, Esther] and me distraught. Please know that we love you and that you are in our constant prayers at this terrible time. You have always been so thoughtful of others and brave in difficult situations. When I think of Richard's eye accident and Barbara Ann's recent bout with polio (which thank God was not severe), I wonder that you have the strength to bear this still greater sorrow. But your disposition has always been an example to others. It makes our own heartfelt sympathy seem feeble indeed.

That you and Hugh always seemed so perfectly matched makes the loss all the greater. Hugh, like yourself, was always so kind and cheerful, and I can see those traits already emerging in Timmy especially. You both have been wonderful parents. Your children are *very* nice.

We wish you did not have to go through this suffering, but remember, Anna dear, that we will always love you.

Guy & Esther

# CHAPTER 4

▼

# THE LAND OF THE
# MORNING CALM

*The combat deepens. On, ye brave,*
*Who rush to glory or the grave!*

—Thomas Campbell

Tim and Warren and the rest did not get to their companies the next day as they had expected. It turned even colder, and the trucks to transport them didn't arrive, or something. It was all pretty vague and no one seemed to know what was going on. After the highly structured existence of training, Tim was surprised at the looseness of everything in Korea. He supposed it was only to be expected— you can't really organize war one, two, three—but he found himself just hanging around with little to do except try to keep warm.

Not that he'd seen any signs of war yet—no noise of battle or anything like that. It was just cold and empty and bleak where they were. Nor had he met his company officers, though he had met his platoon sergeant, who had come up to this site to collect the replacements. He was a guy not much older than Tim, a staff sergeant named Thomas Paden, also from Upstate New York, and he seemed all right, looked like he knew what he was doing. Sergeant Paden explained that their platoon didn't have a platoon leader, a lieutenant. The lieutenant had been killed last month and they hadn't yet got a replacement, so for the time being he was acting platoon leader. Tim was to be a rifleman, and so was Warren. Aldrich, who already had been tagged "Mailman," was in the weapons squad. He was not well pleased. Paden found an old heated wooden structure for them and some of the other replacements and so they slept inside and fairly warm that second night.

The next morning as they were eating breakfast outside the mess tent the trucks arrived and suddenly it was Army turmoil again. NCOs went scurrying around, hollering, "C'mon, c'mon, let's get going. Don't want to miss the war. It'll be over before you get there if you don't haul ass." It was just like when they were ordered off the train the day before yesterday; the NCOs seemed imbued with the spirit of pointless hustle. It was the Army's Principle of Serial Aggravation: Somebody made my life a misery so I'm damn well going to make yours one, too. So the replacements all quickly gobbled down what they could and swished their mess kits in a garbage can of what was supposed to be steaming hot water, though the morning cold had rapidly cooled it, and clambered aboard the trucks.

It wasn't the war they went to, however. After about an hour and a half the trucks stopped in a secluded valley with a stream, now frozen, running through it. A couple of hundred yards from the stream a score or so squad-size tents were set up. The trucks stopped in a kind of street that ran between rows of tents and they were ordered off. This was where they were to get some training. And this was where Tim met Clair Kasten.

The training was a joke, Tim thought. They were given lectures on front-line duties, dangers, and responsibilities. It was no different from training in the States, except colder and more primitive. The main difficulty was in trying to stay awake during the lectures, though they were constantly punctuated by the instructors' fiery warnings to Pay Attention Because This Could Save Your Life Someday. Rifle practice consisted of seeing if they could knock over empty C ration cans set up in a field.

They stayed there a week. Late in the afternoon of the second day, his naturally outgoing personality reasserting itself after a few days' acclimation to Korea, Tim decided to go through his company's area and see if there was anyone from Pennsylvania. He simply went through the tents, in his hearty way, calling out, "Anyone here from Pennsylvania?" He met a guy from Pittsburgh, and another from up near Grove City, and talked with them for a while.

And then, while he was striding through a tent, someone responded to his question by saying, "Yeah, I'm from Pennsylvania. Where 'bouts you from?"

Tim stopped in front of the canvas cot the man was sitting on and stuck out his hand. "Hi. I'm Tim Davis."

"Clair Kasten," the man said, and shook Tim's hand. "Like I said, where you from?"

"Oh, it's so small, you probably never heard of it."

"Try me. The place I'm from is pretty small, too."

"A place called Black Run. North of Horton. But Horton's not very big, either. You probably never heard of that, either. Somerton County, southwest part of the state."

"Heck, yes, I've heard of Black Run and Horton. I ought to of—I'm from just up the road from you. Ainsley."

"Ainsley!" Tim shouted. "No kidding! Ainsley. I can't believe it."

"Well, Ainsley is where I was living when I was called back in. I'm from near West Linton, originally. Went to Repringer High."

"Repringer, yeah, of course. I went to Mott, graduated in '47. Well, well, am I glad to meet you. How long have you been here? Korea, I mean."

"Oh, I got to Korea just after the first of the year, but I didn't get to this outfit until but a couple weeks ago. I come into Korea at Pusan, same as you, I guess. They put me to guarding trains between there and Taegu. But I only did that a little while. They begun to need infantry replacements bad after all that fighting in December and January. So next thing I know I'm a passenger on the train instead of a guard. They sent me to Taegu by train and then to Chunchon by truck, and from there I went by shank's mare to wherever Company B was. They got me in the heavy weapons platoon. I ain't exactly an infantryman by training or temperament. But it hasn't been too bad so far."

"You said you got called back in?"

"Yeah, that's a good one on me. I first enlisted in '48. Figured I was gonna get drafted anyway, might as well get it over with. I was in ordnance, in Japan. That was good duty. But I was only in a little over a year because they offered me early release because they didn't need so many men. Only thing is, I'd have to spend a few years in the reserves. Heck, I didn't mind, I took it. Then the war come along and not much more than a year after I got out, I was back in. Last October. They give me a six-week refresher course in infantry tactics at Fort Campbell, Kentucky, and shipped me over."

"That's rough," Tim said. He looked at Clair's plain, bluff face topped by a crop of stiff brown hair. It seemed naive, almost innocent.

"Heck, it's nothing to some of the things I've heard. I was talking to a guy in A Company, a guy a few years older'n me. He enlisted toward the end of the war, in early '45, instead of waiting to be drafted. Same as me, in a way. But he put in just about two years and got out in '47. Didn't have to serve in no reserve unit or nothing. He'd completed his service, or so he thought. Bango, last August he gets called back in. Turns out that precisely *because* he had enlisted rather than waiting to be drafted, he was eligible to be called back in. He had some critical specialty, supposedly. But his specialty right now is carrying an M1 rifle. You figure it out."

"It's a royal screwing," Tim said. He had sat down on the ground and was toying ruminatively with his boot laces. "But I guess it's happening to a lot of guys. Seems like half the NCOs I've met have been called back in."

"Yep, re-treads," Clair said. "How about you? You enlist, or what?"

Tim gave his boot lace a decisive final flip and said, "Well, it's like this." And he proceeded to tell Clair about being drafted from Albany and before that how he had moved from Black Run up to Guldwyck in Upstate New York and how he had worked there for two-and-a-half years. He was still talking when they got up to go to chow together.

✳    ✳    ✳    ✳

Next started what seemed to Tim a strange journey to get to the front lines. Maybe the idea was to toughen their bodies to the rigors of outdoor living, or more likely it was simply the Army's usual half-assed way of doing things, but at any rate one day shortly thereafter their training abruptly ended. They were ordered aboard trucks and transported to the base of a mountain range. They arrived there about three in the afternoon and immediately started climbing. The lower areas had melting ice underfoot. The climb was so steep and difficult that they had to use bushes and rocks to pull themselves up. They each were carrying not only their own gear, but various pieces of additional equipment, and before long they were all sweating despite the cold.

"Boy, we could sure use the A-Frame Army now," Tim gasped, looking back at Warren, struggling upwards just behind him.

"The A-Frame Army? What's that?" Warren paused in his scrabbling at rocks and dirt.

"Ain't you never heard of the A-Frame Army?" Clair asked, pausing next to Warren and leaning against the hillside. "How long you been in Korea? I thought you knew everything." In the last few days Tim, Warren, and Clair had formed an unlikely trio and stuck together whenever their being in two different platoons didn't make it impossible.

"They never tell the Jews anything. The whole Army is full of anti-Semites."

"What do you mean?" Tim said. "How can you say that? I'm in the Army. I'm not anti-Semitic, am I?"

"Who knows? Ask me again after I've known you ten years."

"Besides," Clair said, grinning wickedly, "what about Eisenhower? He's one of the biggest generals the Army ever had, and he's a Jew, ain't he? Lookit the name."

"My friend, if Eisenhower's a Jew, then Moses was a Presbyterian. I'm telling you, it's just like under the czars: They all hate the Jews and they'll keep me in the Army twenty-five years. Anyway, what's this got to do with the A-Frame Army, whatever that is?"

"The A-Frame Army, young PFC, is all these Koreans that the Army hires to chogie things up the mountains for us on their idiot boards. Like they should be doing here." Tim looked upward at the heights yet to be scaled. "They lash stuff to an A-frame that they carry on their backs. The Korean forklift, you know? They pay them about a dollar a week and a couple of balls of rice a day. I heard the 9th Division had about five thousand of them."

Warren started to say it was just like under the czars, where the Jewish conscripts did all that, except without the dollar a week, but at that point a sergeant below them shouted to them to cut the grab-ass and get moving. The three turned their faces to the side of the mountain again and continued their half-crawl, half-climb upward.

They arrived at the snow-covered summit at eleven the next morning. They had stopped their climbing at ten the night before to eat cold rations and sleep where they fell. Once on the summit, they were ordered to spread out with about a half-dozen men in each group and go down the other side.

Clair looked at Tim as if to say, Is this the Army, or what?

Tim's raised eyebrows expressed his sarcasm. "Yeah, I mean, what was wrong with the other side of the mountain? One seems as good as the other to me."

They got ready to head down. Tim looked around him and saw abandoned equipment strewn about on the ground. It reminded him of a training film during basic, the moral of which was that soldiers who are careless of their equipment suffer as a result. If the officers and NCOs were concerned about the waste, they were too busy organizing the downhill movement to do anything about it.

After several cautious steps it all came apart. Nearly everyone took the easy way out and slid most of the way down on their rear ends. They ended up at a plateau where they lined up single file and began walking north. Despite their downhill slide, they were by no means in a valley. They were still on relatively high ground. The enemy, it was rumored, held the low ground.

*       *       *       *

And so they marched north. At night they would stop, sometimes in a rare grove of trees. After setting up a watch rotation, two or three men to each hour, they would spend several hours trying to dig foxholes in the rocky, frozen ground. For their efforts they produced holes at most a foot and a half deep. One night as Tim was stabbing at the ground with his entrenching tool and mumbling softly, even letting out the occasional curse—his language had coarsened considerably in just the few weeks he'd been in Korea—Sergeant Paden came by checking on his men's efforts.

"No chance of digging a bunny hole in there to get away from the mortars, is there, Davis?" Paden was a short, stocky, conscientious fellow with an inno-cent-looking face. His question was an honest bid for contact with the fellow human beings he was responsible for, most of them, like Tim, in their early days of combat service. Tim could barely make out the sergeant's face or form in the darkness, but he responded in kind.

"You're right there, Sarge. No wonder they call this country the Badlands."

"You ain't seen nothing yet, young trooper. Wait'll you're standing neck-deep in mud with the rain pouring down and dust blowing in your eyes. It can happen in the Frozen Chosun, yes it can. The Land of the Morning Calm, my sweet fanny." And he moved on to the next cursing soldier.

Some days instead of marching they patrolled lower areas looking for signs of the enemy. One afternoon a plane flew overhead and dropped supplies and ammunition for the rifles, carbines, mortars, machine guns and 57 mm. recoilless rifles. So that meant twenty-five or thirty pounds extra each had to carry in addi-tion to their normal gear.

"I said it before and I'll say it again," Warren groused to Tim as he puffed along with his load of 57 mm. rounds, "I shoulda joined the Navy when I had the chanct. What do sailors have to schlep around? Nothing."

"I don't know about that. Do they have Jews in the Navy?"

"Sure they got Jews in the Navy. Whattaya think? You got your prejudices mixed up. It's *schwartzes* they don't got in the Navy. Except stewards."

It was while they were still in the mountains that they first came under fire. The Chinese began shooting at them in the dark after they had bedded down. Small arms fire came screaming over their heads. Tim, who had just come off watch, tried to jam his entire body into the bunny hole that this time he had managed to scratch into the back of his foxhole. He could hear some of the men returning fire, but he couldn't bring himself to turn around and face forward and begin firing himself, and by the time Sergeant Paden came puffing into view to rally the troops it was all over. It hadn't amounted to much and there were no casualties on their side, but when Paden got to his hole Tim was sitting facing forward with his rifle between his knees, both of which were shaking uncontrollably.

In mid-March they left the mountains and hiked until they came to a well-traveled, gravelly mud road. It was still cold, and frequently they marched into squalls of snow pellets that stung their faces. They were miserable: hunched over, dejected, cold. Tim looked up at the file of men in front of him and the file clumping along on the other side of the road like figures in a Bill Mauldin drawing of grimy, sodden GIs marching and marching forever. Soon the road began snaking into a valley that housed a few pathetic, apparently deserted farmhouses. The files halted, and the NCOs walked back along the line saying they would stay there that night.

Immediately the men began pulling straw from the roofs to burn to keep warm. Someone, Tim wasn't sure who, rounded up a stray ox and killed it and then cut out a large chunk of meat and attempted to cook it. But after several hours of cooking it was still too tough to chew, and some of the men were saying it's no wonder the goddamn thing was a stray: Even the gooks didn't want it. The men had been issued beer and were growing garrulous.

"I wouldn't eat any of that," Tim said.

"Me neither," Warren said, "you don't know where it's been." He held his steel beer can in his right hand and twirled it around in a circle. "You think it's wise to issue this stuff to armed men?"

"Armed and *desperate* men." Tim took a swig of beer and looked at the can. "I don't drink much but this tastes good, cold as it is. I mean, cold as the weather is, not the beer."

"You got that right. What's going on over there?" Warren indicated the fire that had been started. A Korean man was bustling about among the soldiers, gesticulating and speaking rapidly. The soldiers were laughing. The fire and the shadows it cast gave their grinning faces a fearsome red-and-black look, like Halloween masks

"I dunno. Looks like he's telling them to stop using his house for firewood. Can't say as I blame him, poor guy."

That night, after they had arranged themselves in several of the houses for sleep, they heard for the first time the distant noise of war. It sounded dull, but big and menacing, far bigger and more menacing than the sharp little firefight that so far had been their single taste of combat.

\*         \*         \*         \*

Not long after, on a spring-like day, the first that year, they stopped near the crest of a hill amid a pear orchard and a few houses. The officers and NCOs huddled in a group studying a map. There were several battalion vehicles there, including a jeep with an Angry Nine, the AN/GR radio. The radio took up the entire back-seat area of the jeep, but it was valued because it could transmit and receive over long distances. Someone was talking into it. Tim, watching what was going on, figured it must be the battalion CO.

The huddle broke up and Sergeant Paden came back to the platoon and said there were Chinese in some dry rice paddies about a mile away and that platoons from A and B companies would engage them. Engage them, Tim thought when he realized he would be involved, that's a neutral-sounding term for going off to possibly get yourself killed. He listened intently and with a mounting sense of panic as Paden told the squad leaders and the men what they would be doing and what they should take with them. Paden was brisk and businesslike, but looked worried. Through his field jacket Tim rubbed his chest; it felt tight, constricted. He took a deep breath, as if that might clear the constriction, and his chest hurt. Maybe he was having a heart attack? No, he realized, it was fear, the knowledge of danger. He hadn't had time to develop this heavy sense of dread in the firefight; it had happened too fast. Now anticipation was almost unmanning him. He had lost track of what Paden was saying when he heard him slap his thigh and snap sharply, "OK, let's move." The lounging, squatting, kneeling GIs got to their feet and moved toward the assembly area.

Clair, as a member of the heavy weapons platoon, stayed behind. This was to be mostly a rifle squad affair, though for some reason his platoon leader, a second lieutenant, was going along. He watched as the force of men, including Tim and Warren, moved out of the assembly area and off toward the rice paddies. It wasn't long before they were over the crest of the hill and out of sight.

Clair waited, sitting on a .50 caliber ammunition box, smoking, staring at the ground. He heard the chug-chug of an artillery shell passing overhead from the rear, heard it hit in front of him. Then another, then another. Each time they hit he could feel the ground shake. It was quiet for a while, and then he heard the crackle of small arms fire and the occasional swoosh of a mortar round. Ours or theirs? he wondered. He couldn't tell. And then it was quiet again.

Nearly two hours passed before Clair saw the men come back. They straggled, some limped, some were being assisted. Two were being carried, on pieces of clothing or shelter halves it looked like from Clair's vantage point. He stood up to see better. When they got close enough to identify he saw that Tim and Warren, who were in front, appeared to be OK, but even from that distance they looked exhausted.

When they got to the company area, Tim and Warren slumped to the ground without saying a word. Clair squatted next to them and waited for them to say something. Both were grimy, their faces smudged with sweat-streaked dirt. There was blood on Tim's field jacket and pants. Other returning soldiers trudged past them. Clair hesitated, then spoke:

"How was it?"

Tim swiveled his head and stared at his friend in silence. "How was it?" he slowly responded. "It was, it was—" Tim turned both of his hands, resting on the ground, palms upward, expressing inexpressibility. "I think I could sleep for a week."

"Anybody—?"

"Get killed? Yeah, your platoon leader, Lieutenant Perreault. Bought the farm. One of our artillery rounds fell short. I think it landed practically on top of him. I don't think there was anything left to bring back. One of our own fucking artillery rounds. Friendly fire, they call that."

Clair looked at Tim, silently asking the next question as soldiers continued to move past them.

"The Mailman and three or four others wounded, I'm not sure how many. All from that artillery round. Funny thing, I don't think any got wounded by the Chicoms. Just by that artillery round. I don't think the Mailman's gonna make it, if he's not dead already. They had to bring him in slow, he's hurt so bad. They gave him a couple syrettes of morphine out there, but that's all. They didn't have anything else. They should—wait, there he is now."

Tim pointed to three men about seven or eight yards away who were carefully lowering a body slung in a makeshift litter to the ground and yelling for help. As they did so another figure, a medic, rushed over to them.

Clair stood up again to see better.

"Is he alive?" Tim asked.

"I don't know. He looks, he looks—white."

The medic was kneeling next to the body and swiftly slashing with a knife at the jacket and shirt sleeves covering the Mailman's right arm. As soon as it was exposed he took a container of plasma and inserted the needle expertly into the heavy vein.

"How's he doing?"

"Not too well, it looks like. I've heard sometimes if you're wounded and you get a jolt of plasma it can bring you right around. But it don't look like this did."

"Poor Mailman. All he wanted was to be a postal clerk."

*        *        *        *

That night they heard that the Mailman died before he got to the MASH unit that a litter jeep had driven him to. They stayed that night on the crest of the hill.

It began to rain. Tim formed his poncho into the semblance of a tent and managed to keep fairly dry inside. He lay listening to the *pock-pock* sound of the rain striking the poncho and remembered the crude witticism about "incoming" that Master Sergeant Tasker made at the Mailman's expense when they first got off the train. Now it had all but come true.

The events of the day, his first real day in combat, began coursing through his mind. The confusion, the shouted commands, the plaintive cries for help, the horrible screams of pain, his own abject terror. Lying prone, he had fired wildly, insanely at anything that came into his sights, scarcely aware of anything but the continuous roar of noise. The clip bounced from his M1 and without thinking he snapped up the spare clip that he had placed just in front of him and continued to blaze away, frantic to keep the enemy from coming any nearer. But he was bone-weary and, despite the excitement of the most extraordinary day of his life, before long he fell fast asleep.

At 4 a.m., when the squad leaders went through rousting everyone, Tim woke up dreaming of Helen again. Again he could recollect no details, this time not even where they were or what they were doing, only a disturbing sense of unease. And he had no time to try and recapture anything of the dream: They were being told to hurry up.

As they marched to a road where half-track vehicles were waiting to transport them to another location, Tim mulled over the significance of the previous day's events. I could have been killed, he thought, and no one outside would have known it. Hardly anyone would even care, not until they told Mother and the family. Into his mind came words from Lincoln's Gettysburg Address that he had had to memorize years ago at Leander P. Mott School: *The world will little note, nor long remember.* Would anybody note, he wondered, would anybody remember?

It was light now and they could see a brace of low-flying F-51 Mustangs pass overhead. As they roared past the pilots wagged their wings in recognition and the men on the ground cheered. It gave Tim a small feeling of comfort, as if it were a sign that they hadn't been utterly forgotten.

# CHAPTER 5

▼

# SOMERTON BACKGROUND

*All men become brothers under your tender wing.*
—Friedrich von Schiller, *Ode to Joy*

Anna and the children moved back to Pennsylvania almost immediately. She received a pension through the New York State Workmen's Compensation Board, a small pension for the children until they reached legal age. She also received a small settlement that allowed her to buy a house in Black Run, in the northeastern part of the county, named after a stream that runs into Hacketts Creek. The house Anna bought (it is still there today, owned by the son of a man who used to be a schoolmate of Tim's)—a small, two-story, bungalow-like structure on Route 23—sat almost on the banks of Black Run. Just to the west of it was the Church of the Brethren the family would attend. It, too, is still there. And just to the west of that, still within easy walking distance, was the high school, the Leander P. Mott Vocational High School, the children would attend. That building also is still there, but it ceased being a school in 1986. The man it was named for was a native of the county who went to New York and made good and became a longtime benefactor of the school and the area. The school, and the church nearby, would be a center of Tim's and the family's lives for years to come. It was, in fact, Anna's livelihood, for she got a job there as one of the cafeteria's three cooks—the first year the school had a cafeteria.

With this move back to Somerton County, this house, and this school, Tim Davis's story begins to come into its own.

\*      \*      \*      \*

War had come to the world again when Tim started fifth grade in the attached grade school. He was eleven years old, older than most of his classmates. It was shortly after Labor Day, which was shortly after war broke out in Europe.

It is difficult to get a handle on those early days back in Pennsylvania except through reminiscences. And it is odd, but when Tim's old friends and former classmates talk about their school days, World War II doesn't often bulk large in their memories. Historically, this may seem a puzzle: What else was there? Rick said that, when he was growing up then, he wondered what they used to put in the newspaper before there was war news.

"We were aware, but I think it's something like you lived *away* from it," is the way Betty Stishin puts it. She was Betty Ruppertal then, a member of Tim's high school class of 1947. "'Course, I think as kids you don't think a whole lot. You just live day by day." The thing that she remembers most, probably from before she entered high school, is that some boys went into the service before they finished high school. Maybe it was only a couple of weeks or a couple months before.

That sort of thing almost happened to Clark Bace. Clark was two years ahead of Tim in school, in the class of 1945. Clark's class graduated on May 29, and the day after that, at six o'clock in the morning, he was on the bus for the Army. Clark had already turned 18, and they were drafting young men as soon as they were 18, but a woman he knew had a brother on the draft board in Somerton, and she persuaded her brother to postpone the call-up of Clark and two other 18-year-olds until the day after graduation.

Donny Barber, another member of Tim's class, remembered picking apples at an orchard in West Linton. "During wartime you got credits or certificates for helping out with the labor because of the labor shortage," he said. High school boys could go out on orchards or farms and pick potatoes or apples or husk corn. For apples they got between five cents and seven cents a bushel. One time he and Tim and three other guys went and picked potatoes "where they'd plowed them out on the ground," and they got ten cents a bushel.

Donny lived about three miles from Tim on his father's farm, which, like a lot of farms in rural areas around the country, had no electricity. "We didn't have electric in my home until about 1943 or '44. And you had a battery radio. So you didn't play the radio just to hear music. You played the radio, you stayed in front of it and listened to it. And if you got up and left, you had to turn that radio off. Because Dad and Mom wanted to hear the news. The radio played off a car battery. Every so often I used to haul that battery to Elmer Wentley's garage in a wagon to get it recharged and then haul it back again. First radio that we had, we had to run a long wire out to a tree to get the signal. Although where Tim's home was they had electric. They got electric back there probably in the '30s. 'Bout '36, '35, because Penelec went through there and put electric in. Bein' as I lived in a rural area, why, till the rural electric associations become effective, that's when we received electricity. I can remember going to Tim's home—boy, how nice it was just to walk in a house and flip on a light." Donny still has his parents' first plug-in radio, an old Philco.

It was the same for Ray Jones, a good friend and classmate of Tim's. Ray lived about a half-mile from the Davises. His father was a stonemason, had 12 acres of land with a garden, and kept a pig, a cow, and some chickens—"just typical country living. We didn't even have a radio, we didn't have any electricity, and Tim had electric lights and all that. That was kind of fantastic to me.

"And Tim? He was something special as a kid. I don't know. We just grew up together. It's something you never thought about. He had nice curly hair. If it had been 'Happy Days,' he'd have been the Fonzie of Black Run. Tim had more Teflon than Ronald Reagan. He had a very nice personality, very likable, very athletic, easy to laugh, just easy to be with. I mean, he'd get in trouble, he'd get out of it. Just that type of person."

✳     ✳     ✳     ✳

An incident with bullets:

Rick and Tim liked to go over to the Friedles' and play with their cousins. Anna's sister Cassie was married to Clyde Friedle, and they had eight children, but Tim mostly palled around with Ron and Bill, who were closest to him in age. One of the Friedle girls, Isobel, later would marry one of Tim's best boyhood friends, Jim Calder. Clyde drove a milk truck for the dairy, picking up the cans of milk from the farmers. If you wanted a ride into Horton or Somerton, you'd catch a ride with Clyde. In exchange for the ride, you helped him do his route.

One wintry but sunny weekend afternoon shortly after they moved back to Pennsylvania—Tim was not yet in his teens—they went over to the Friedles' and ended up outside because it was fairly warm. Clyde had shot a big buck and hung it from a tree in the driveway. The kids were running around in the yard playing cowboys and Indians or nothing in particular, and after circling the deer several times the thought began to creep into their minds, individually and collectively, that somehow this fascinating object could be incorporated into their play. Spontaneously, the way it happens with kids, one of them—Ron, probably, since he was the oldest Friedle boy—said, "Let's pretend we're hunters, deer hunters, and we'll pretend that deer's running around the corner, and we'll shoot it." Then he, or someone, went into the house and came out with a .22 rifle, and they took turns taking shots at the buck. They peppered that dead deer with .22 bullets. The tree and buck were a considerable distance from the house, and it took a while before anyone inside realized that something was going on outdoors. When Clyde came out to investigate, the kids grew silent, instinctively realizing that something—who knows what, with grown-ups?—was wrong.

"What's going on?" Clyde said. "What you kids up to?"

Silence.

"What're you doing with that rifle?" Silence. "Here, gimme that." He took the rifle and looked at the boys, all of whose faces were half-downcast and apprehensive.

"Say, what's going on?" Then, with an instinct as keen as the kids', he looked over at the buck, probably because he could tell they were avoiding it. "You been messin' around with that deer?" And he walked over to it.

One quick look told him the awful truth. The deer had more holes than a cheese grater. "Jee-sus Kee-rist!" He looked up, and whether he was more horrified than angry, or angry than horrified, was impossible to tell.

"Who did this?" Steely, level, cold voice.

Silence.

"WHO DID THIS?"

At that barked command, they admitted in a gabble of confessions and justifications that they had all taken part. The deer meat, of course, was ruined. Clyde took them inside and gave each a good swift whack on their bottoms. They all took it pretty well.

*     *     *     *

Everybody liked Tim. On the face of it, his personality is impossible. No one can be this nice. You could take a shelf-full of thesauruses and copy out all the synonyms for cheerful and sunny, and still not exhaust the ways people describe him, over and over again. It clearly goes beyond a desire of people to speak well of a friend. Apparently it goes straight to the truth.

"Yeah, a happy-go-lucky guy as a kid," Rick says. "He couldn't sit down. He always had to be doin' something."

Donny Barber says it, too: "Tim had an attitude of happy-go-lucky. He just didn't seem to have any care in the world."

Clark Bace thinks Tim was sort of half-clown. Whenever you were around him he was always "cutting up, doing something. When he was growing up he didn't have any enemies around. You know, you always get one guy as soon as he walks in the room he becomes the center of attention. That's about the way Tim was."

Tim's Albany friend, Frank Clay, cannot think of a time when Tim was ever discouraged or down-hearted. "He was just upbeat all the time. There aren't many people like that. In my lifetime I can only think of three or four that were anything like Tim."

He rarely complained, had a bad day, or spoke ill of anyone. When asked whether Tim, after he was drafted, resented men who didn't go into the service, either by draft-dodging or for other reasons, Rick says flatly, "I don't think Tim ever resented anybody."

✳    ✳    ✳    ✳

An incident with a bell:

On the road toward Tim's house was an old house owned by a part-time farmer called Pasquale who kept baby chicks in a still older and smaller shack. His name actually was Anthony, but he had been born in Italy and spoke with somewhat of an accent, and in that overwhelmingly Anglo and Teutonic region anyone with a different heritage automatically got tagged with a stereotyped moniker. Out in front of both these structures, in the front yard by the side of the road, was a big old bell with a four or five pound clapper, sitting up off the ground in a kind of bell housing. The bell once had been destined for a church in West Linton but never made it. Why it sat there in the yard everybody had long since forgotten, but almost nobody forgot to give it a ring whenever they went past it. Especially kids, especially at night. This raised the ire of Pasquale.

One evening four or five of them, including Tim, were coming home from fishing. As they went past the bell, one of them ran up to give it the obligatory ring when Tim caught him by the biceps and said, "Wait, I got a better idea." He dug into his pocket and pulled out some fish line. "We'll take this line and tie it to the clanger and go down the road with it and pull. When Pasquale comes out he won't know what's going on because he won't be able to see us."

Which they did. They sneaked up and tied the line around the clapper, ran down the road fifty yards or so until they came to a big rock by the road, hid behind it, and pulled on the string.

Clang! Clang! Clang!

After about a minute the farmhouse door slammed open. Silhouetted in the yellow kitchen light was Pasquale, yelling. "Damn you, you kids, you better stop that, or I'll fix you good."

Slam! went the door.

Giggle giggle, went the rock.

Clang, clang, clang! went the bell.

This time Pasquale was at the door and out on the porch in even less time, with a shotgun in his hands. He raised it in the air. "Goddamn it, I warned you!" *Blam*! "Stay away from that goddamn bell!" *Blam*!

Slam.

Giggle giggle.

Clang clang clang!

This time he was out the door and off the porch instantly, running down through the yard in an effort to catch the miscreants in the act. He pulled up short at the bell, surprised to find no one there nor anyone scampering off into the darkness. After a few moments of circling the bell and muttering fearsome imprecations, he turned back toward the house, and his foot snagged the fish line. He looked down, bewildered. He stooped over, picked up the line, looked at it, looked at the bell, looked back at the line. He tugged at it. *Clang*! Then he tugged at the other end. Nothing. He pulled at the long end, then began following it until he reached the rock, where it ended. No one was there. He swiveled in four directions in a vain search for a way out of this ridiculous situation.

"Yah, you som-a-ma-beeching kids! I know who you are. You, Jimmy Calder. You, Timmy Davis. I'll tell your Mama on you. Such a nice lady, and you doing such a thing."

But by this time Tim was home laughing into his pillow.

\*      \*      \*      \*

Those wartime school years are a jumble of activities, impossible to nail down as to exact date, except in rare instances. It was a perennial round of school, church, movies, roller-skating, ice-skating, hunting, fishing, trapping, working. It was a pleasant if restricted life.

Anna worked as cook at the school, and during the summer she worked at other jobs. The children helped out at home, and the five of them kept the little place going at cruising speed. In the first year they did not have an inside bathroom, but an outhouse. The kids didn't like that. Even when they had a bathroom put in upstairs, they didn't have hot water. They always had a bath on Saturday and carried hot water upstairs. They didn't have radiators upstairs. Any heat there drifted up from the radiators on the first floor. Newspapers came in handy: They stuffed them into the windows to keep the cold air out and wrapped them around heated bricks to put in the beds at night. In the beginning, before they installed an oil furnace, Tim or Rick had to get up early to tend the fire in the coal furnace. Every once in a while they got a load of wood, and the boys chopped it up and put it in the cellar, mostly for use in the Kalamazoo kitchen wood stove. Barbara and Connie kept the house clean.

"She was really good," Rick says of their mother. "That's why we liked to help her out as much as we could. We raised pigs, and all that money went to the house." Leander P. Mott was an agricultural-vocational high school, and students had practical projects to do, such as raising animals. Tim raised pigs, which later they sold for slaughter. He fed the pigs with waste food thrown out from the cafeteria, which he hauled down the road from the school in a wagon.

They mostly always got along, the four siblings. "We were too busy to fight," Barbara says. Rick says, "I can't ever remember arguing. We were always trying to make a dollar. Tim would say, 'C'mon, we gotta go trappin'.' So, I'd follow him, and we'd go down and he'd show me how to set the traps. I don't know where in the world he learned all this stuff." They went up along Black Run, which ran beside their house, in the evening to set the traps. They could see where the animals, muskrat and mink, would slide along the bank into the creek. "Tim'd say, 'Now, we'll set the trap below the slide inside the water.'" They caught about three minks and twelve to fifteen muskrats a year, plus countless rats. The mink and muskrat pelts they sold.

But then, as Betty Stishin says, "Nobody had very much money. And I'm sure that Anna didn't earn a lot of money, and she had to work to keep it going. But, you know, it didn't take a lot of money, and still they lived good enough. I don't mean rich things. We lived differently than people in cities maybe in that era. So I don't know how Anna did in spending, but I know still they were comfortable enough, it seemed like."

Or Ray Jones: "I can't remember them as being particularly hard up. Nobody had anything, so nobody knew what hard up was."

And, of course, family helped family. Tim stayed with his cousin Bill Friedle's family for a short time that first summer until Anna bought the house. Anna's brother, Guy King, sent Tim and Ricky the cast-off clothes that the well-off boys at the Barrett School, where he taught, no longer wanted.

They did just about everything to bring in money. Tim was always the spark plug, initiating things—like trapping—and then bringing Rick in. "Tim, he encouraged me a lot," Rick says. "He was always getting jobs, and he'd get me to help him. We were pretty good workers, even with the farmers. The farmers all liked us. They always called us." They cut corn, made hay, cleaned barns, hauled manure, whatever there was to be done.

Sometimes they sold the fish they caught—suckers, mostly—to farmers. And turtles. Rick and Tim would lie on the bridge over Black Run near their home and "wait for *hours* for this dumb turtle to stick his head up above the water. And when he did we'd shoot 'im. And then we'd pull him out and take him up to this farmer and he'd pay us for the turtle."

Nearly all of the kids picked blueberries to sell. There was a man who came out from Pittsburgh to buy them. They knew him only as "Shakewell" because of his habit of shaking down their pails of berries to pack them in more tightly and get more for his money.

The summer Tim was seventeen and Rick two years younger they worked at the cannery in Martinsburg in Blair County. They worked outside, breaking the corn off and throwing it on a slow-moving truck. At the end of the day their arms were all cut up from the corn. Anna, who normally worked as a cook at resorts in Glens Falls in Upstate New York in the summers, also worked there one summer. It was probably early in the 1940s, because the children's older cousin, Audrey Flanders, who was a young teenager then, took care of them in the evening. Anna worked second shift at the cannery so she could be with the children during the day. The next July, 1946, when he was 18 (but still not graduated from high school), Tim worked at a bakery in Altoona, where he boarded for the month.

Ray Jones and Tim had a little business going for two years, painting metal roofs. Their work was primarily for farmers, though they also did the roof of the Reformed church in Black Run. It was a wonder they didn't break their necks. The tar-like material they painted with was extremely slippery, and they didn't use ladders or other supports to get around with.

Then there was Beech Haven, a resort that was a kind-of second-string White Sulpher Springs just south of the borough of Somerton. Seemingly everybody worked there, tending to the vacation needs of affluent city folk—Tim, Betty Stishin, Bill and Ron Friedle. Even Anna worked there for a time. Tim did everything—caddy, bellhop, room service, kitchen work. As usual, he got Rick in there too. They often stayed overnight at the resort, bunking together in a dormitory.

\*     \*     \*     \*

Tim's school was small. Stanfield Township, where they lived, didn't establish a consolidated school until 1929. That closed down the several one-room school-houses in the area in which Tim's grandfather once had taught. At first there was only a grade school; if Stanfield students wanted to go to high school they had to pay to attend in another district, like West Linton. The next year, 1930, the school board authorized a high school, and classes were held in various buildings around the township until a separate high school building was constructed adjacent to the grade school in 1931.

Tim's Class of 1947 had twenty-seven graduates. Even at that, when they entered as freshmen in 1943 their class was unusually large because it was joined by students from nearby Green Heights Township whose school building had burned down. The smallness made for a feeling of closeness, and the school was a central part of their lives, academically and recreationally.

Tim was not a world-class scholar.

"Well, poor old Tim would study and study and get up the next day just as dumb as he was the day before," Ray Jones says. "Oh, I don't mean dumb. He passed his classes and all, but he was just too busy with other things to retain what he'd learned. He wasn't dumb, but he was just too busy living to really apply himself, that's all."

Betty Stishin agrees: "He probably wasn't the best student the school ever had because he was too silly, or crazy, or having a good time."

He was one of those people who can get away with things, things that he just to keep the atmosphere stirred up, to see what the reaction would be. He painted his shoes different colors and wore them to school that way—one day blue, one day yellow, and so on. He particularly could get around Miss Sanford—Sally C. Sanford, whom he referred to as "the nylon kid" because of her black stockings (which probably weren't nylon). Once he had to give a book report in her class, and hadn't read the book, so he got up in front of the class and made up his own story—not the first student in the history of education to pull such a stunt, but one of the few able to do it with aplomb and with the assurance that he would be forgiven.

He liked music; he liked to sing. He was in the school chorus. He was in the junior class play; they did *Our Town* and Tim played the Stage Manager. Also in his junior year he was in the school forensics society. He and Walter Wight, a fellow class member, were in a runoff at Mott to decide who went to the state forensic finals, and Tim won. And he was an enthusiastic athlete, both baseball and basketball, but particularly basketball. In his senior year he was on the Mott team that went to the district playoffs at St. Francis College in Loretto, though they failed to win the championship in the category for their school size.

\*     \*     \*     \*

An interlude at Elmer Wentley's gas station:

"We loved to go down there," Rick says, "Tim and I and Jim Calder and a lot of us. In the back of the garage there was a big-bellied stove. They'd put wood in there and that thing would get red *hot*. In deer season we loved to go down there. And they'd have these chairs—cushions from cars—sittin' around the stove. And we used to listen to the older people about their deer hunting. They'd sit around that stove and tell you they missed this buck and they missed that buck, and they shot the other one. Tim liked that. He liked to get his deer, and he figured he'd use any advantage he could get, so he'd listen to the older guys. And they'd be workin' on the cars around there while we'd be shootin' the bull about hunting and everything else. We'd spend a lot of time there just sittin' there listenin' to 'em."

\*     \*     \*     \*

Tim was a faithful and active churchgoer. He went to Sunday School, even as a young man. The family worshipped at the Church of the Brethren just up the road, in between the house and the school. So did many of the people they knew—Tim's Friedle cousins, Betty Stishin, Herb Wentley, Donny Barber. Also known as the Dunkers, the Church of the Brethren as a denomination had been in Pennsylvania since the early 1700s, one of several German pietist groups that flocked to American shores in that century.

By Tim's time the church, while still distinctive, had evolved along more mainline Protestant lines. Tim was in the church's choir as well its youth group, which organized many activities. The group met usually once a month, each time at a different member's house. There would be a meditation, refreshments, and often games—including "spin the bottle," a kissing game mildly daring for its time. Occasionally they'd have a taffy pull. There was little dancing, but always, whether done under the aegis of the youth group or the school, or individually, there was roller skating. Tim loved to roller-skate as much as he loved to play basketball. Nearly every other community or crossroads had a roller-skating rink, but one of the most popular was at a place called Bagtown. Herb Wentley says, "That place would always be jammed on Sunday nights."

If it wasn't roller-skating, it was the movies. Again, movie houses were virtually everywhere—in Horton, West Linton, Bright Item, Port Arthur, Somerton. People occasionally went as far as Altoona to the movies. "That was maybe the only thing we had," Betty Stishin says. "If you went out anywhere, it was the movies. Movies or roller-skating." When Tim and the rest of them went to a nearby activity, such as a basketball game at the school, they often walked. To the movies, it was by car. But either way, it was usually a gang of them, maybe a couple of carloads. Clark Bace wasn't in the crowd Tim ran with, but he remembers, "As a class, the Class of '45 and the teachers all got along real well together. We might decide sometime during the day that we was going to see this movie tonight. And the whole class, teachers and all, would go. That's just the way it was. Barney Ford—he was one of the school's most popular teachers—used to go with us. One time we were at the Capitol Theater in Altoona whenever V-E Day was announced. They announced it right there in the theater, that Germany had surrendered."

Tim didn't take one particular girl to these activities. He liked all the gals. Ray Jones says, "Tim was a ladies man. He was just likable. Everybody liked him. But I can't think of him as having a special girlfriend. He went with this one and this one and this one." Alice Anne Wentley, one of Tim's classmates and a distant cousin, agrees: "He had a great personality, very outgoing. Everybody liked him, especially the girls. He didn't have a particular girlfriend, though Betty Ruppertal really liked him. She had a crush on him I know." Betty Ruppertal Stishin, after the passage of decades, is inclined to demur, but then turns girlishly bashful and admits, "That's probably true, rather than the other way around, because I don't know whether he had any special girl. He just was going here and there."

✳    ✳    ✳    ✳

An incident over the airwaves:

Anna was amused, but appalled, at what she had just heard on the radio. It was November 15, 1945, a cold, dark Wednesday night, and she was ironing in the quiet warmth of the house, all alone. She had been half-listening to *Rogue's Gallery*, a detective show on Mutual Broadcasting starring Dick Powell as private investigator Richard Rogue. It was some sort of mystery in which a woman was accused of murdering her employer. Powell was pushing the plot along, telling what was going on: "Assorted and unrelated facts were whirling around in my massive intellect like neutrons around an atom," when it sounded as if he stumbled over his lines: "They were—they were just as—as much explosive in them—as if I could get—if I could get them properly under control." And then did she hear right? Did he say, "… if I could get them properly under control. Holy Christ"? Yes, she did hear right. He did say it: "Holy Christ."

It was funny. He had obviously blown his lines. But still, blaspheming over the air. What was the world coming to?

\*       \*       \*       \*

Radio was king in the 1940s. Network radio was *the* mass medium. By the time Tim graduated from Mott High, nearly every one of the 38 1/2 million households in the country had at least one radio receiver, and that's not counting the ones in cars and in stores and other institutions. Tim loved listening to the radio, all of it—music, comedy, adventure shows—though, like most people he knew, he did not normally sit down and listen to an evening of radio the way people now watch an evening of television. Nor did they do it evening after evening after evening. Radio was a warmer, friendlier medium; it fit into lives rather than dominated them.

Life was too full to sit indoors in front of a mass medium, life made up of dozens of little daily and weekly activities and concerns. Shopping, for one. The family usually shopped on Saturday. Sometimes they would drive as far as Altoona, that was a treat, though usually it was Horton. In the early days Anna still had the '36 Dodge, though later she bought a new Frazer (which Rick subsequently rolled over and wrecked). They all had chores to do, and after that they went shopping. Anna would treat the kids to a movie. Barb and Connie often went with their older cousin, Isobel Friedle, and then Anna took her children home. Barb says, "We got so upset because Isobel always got to go out Saturday night to the town and walk up and down the street. That's all they had to do, just park in Horton and walk up and down the street to see the people. I remember Isobel always had extra money because Clyde always made pretty good money."

Herb Wentley met Tim shortly after Anna and the kids moved back to Somerton County. Herb was out riding his bike on a Sunday when he came across this other, strange kid riding a bike. They approached each other warily and gradually began talking and Herb learned that Tim was related to the Kings, whom he knew, of course. One of the things Herb and Tim used to like to do that late summer is ride their bikes out and watch the cut being made east of Horton for the new Pennsylvania Turnpike. It was called the Point Deadly Cut, after the old name for Horton, and it was awesome to two country boys: a half-mile long and 150 feet deep, from which workers removed more than a million cubic yards of material.

Herb, along with Jim Calder and Bill Friedle, became one of Jim's best boyhood friends, but neither he nor they ever knew what, if anything, Jim felt about the death of his father. They can't recall him ever mentioning it. So either it didn't affect him, or it was, to him, a secret to be kept.

Ray Jones thinks he first met Tim about a year later, in the sixth grade. Though he didn't pal around with him as much as Herb and Jim and Bill did, still he was at Tim's house many evenings. They'd walk home from school and Ray would stop in, maybe help Tim with his homework.

"You know," Ray says, "you get to looking back, and you think, 'What the heck *did* we use to do as kids?' I think we played Chinese checkers a lot, up there to the house." Or they flew kites. "I don't know, maybe it was windier then than it is now. We used to fly a kite in the evening, tie it fast there in the ground, and go to school the next morning and it'd still be flying." In the fall, get in fights with corn stubbles. "Pull the corn stubbles up and fight with 'em, throw 'em at each other. Just kids, livin'."

In the summer, swimming in Black Run, on the lower side of the bridge near Tim's house where there was a deep hole. "Crazy Timmy'd stand up there on the top of the bridge and dive in," Ray says. "I was afraid to try that. There was a big rock in there and you had to miss the rock and you had to dive shallow." Or play baseball. Every town had a ball team, the railroad had a ball team, factories and other businesses had ball teams. Or basketball over at the school.

\*        \*        \*        \*

Interlude, with bats:

"There's another thing we used to do that was kind of dumb," Rick says. "Bats used to fly up along Black Run. I don't know where they came from. They probably stayed along the banks. In the evening they would fly up along the creek. And we'd get boards and practice our swingin'. And every once in a while we'd get one. Tim would get one and he'd say, 'Boy, I did pretty good.'"

\*          \*          \*          \*

People used to just drop by. In Guldwyck in the 1950s, when the women of Tim's extended King family were establishing their own families, family used to drop by unannounced on Sunday afternoons. Aunts, uncles, cousins of all degrees, shirt-tail relations and their friends, any and all would show up with nothing more on their minds than to shoot the breeze. If they didn't show up at one house, it was because they went to another. "We thought you'd be home," they'd say. Chances are you would be home, and not a bit inconvenienced by the visit. Bologna and bread and mayonnaise would be put out on the table, and coffee on the stove to perk, and another Sunday afternoon would be pleasantly passed without the aid of televised major league sports. Telling the fascinatingly banal things that had happened to you during the week, or the little triumphs and defeats your spouse or children had experienced, was the point. Getting a modicum of consolation or advice, however inappropriate, with a problem was the point. The point was connecting.

People were always just stopping by Anna's, too, either during the week, like Ray Jones, or on weekends, when she almost always had someone over for dinner. This was a continuation of her parents' practice. Rick loved to go to his Grandmother King's for dinner. His grandparents lived in several places around the county at different times, but they always had a big Sunday dinner. For good or ill, family lived with family. Few people lived alone—less than 8 percent of households in 1940, government statistics tell us.

Barney Ford, as Clark Bace said, was one of the most popular teachers at Leander P. Mott High School. He was there when the first class graduated in 1931 and when the last one graduated in 1956. He used to drop by Anna's house a lot. Some people think they were romantically involved, though they probably were not, at least not to the extent that it was serious. Actually, it was Anna's sister, Harriet, that he had his eye on, back in the early 1930s before she moved to Guldwyck. One reason he was at the house so much was that they both worked at the school. Barney, in the ill-recompensed, many-dutied way of teachers of the time, was head of the cafeteria committee and had been responsible for hiring Anna as cook. Clark was a good friend of Barney's, even when Clark was Barney's student in high school. Later, when they were both taking courses at Juniata College, they ran around together much of the time. "Many a night we'd have nothing to do, he'd stop by and we'd end up at Anna's place," Clark says. "We'd go down and get some ice cream and bring it back. Most people thought Barney was going with Anna, but he wasn't. They were just good friends."

Barney never married. If he ever had thoughts of marrying Anna, he would have had to put them on hold, because she had determined not to marry again while the children were at home. She didn't want to take a chance on the disruption a stepfather might cause in their lives. Not till 1954, a year after Connie graduated from Mott and was married, did Anna marry again, to a local man her age named Del Frace.

"Yeah, Anna was a nice lady, always laughing and friendly like," Clark says. "For the amount of trouble she probably had in her life, she did real well."

# CHAPTER 6

▼

# LEAVE-TAKING

*Bliss was it in that dawn to be alive,*
*But to be young was very heaven!*

—William Wordsworth

Tim, on the brink of graduation from high school, was nineteen years old—he was born in January and had started school a year late—and five feet, ten inches tall. Not especially tall as we measure men today, but tall enough to make him a standout among the runty farm lads he went to school with as well as on the basketball court. His good looks are almost of movie-star standard: even, white teeth displayed in a perpetual grin; a well-shaped face, more thin than broad; soft blue eyes; and a shock of light brown, slightly wavy hair combed back in a low Pompadour. Even his ears are reasonable. Movie star? To compare him to someone well-known of his era, he looks like a less intense Farley Granger or a more intense Robert Walker. Someone said he looks like James Dean, and so he does, and in fact Dean and Tim are almost the same age. But Dean's is another era as Hollywood measures eras, and Tim as a teenager had nothing in common with the sullen rebelliousness that Dean represented. Anyway, Tim's smile is nicer than any of theirs: It melted girls' hearts and lowered men's guard.

Nineteen forty-seven, the year he turned nineteen, opened with a snowstorm in Somerton County. It snowed all New Year's Day and into the next, yet, though it was drifting in places, school opened on the 2nd. He played basketball for Mott just about every third day or night that month against schools both within and outside the county. Losing upset him terribly. Sometimes it was hard to travel to away games because of the snow. It snowed on his birthday, January 21, and it snowed four days later when Al Capone died, his brain riddled with by syphilis, in Florida. There was much sniggering in school the day after Rev. Riemenschneider at the Church of the Brethren used the infamous gangster's death in his sermon as an illustration of the wages of sin. Donny Barber said the wages of sin didn't sound so bad, it was those killer taxes you wanted to avoid. To which a gaggle of girls chorused, "Oh, *you*."

It was a miserable late winter. When it didn't snow, it was damp and cold and foggy. Tim did the things that people in rural winter isolation did to entertain themselves and ease cabin fever. Early in February the Juniata College Choir came to the Methodist church in Horton for a concert and the music lover in him found the performance exhilarating. He was elected president of the student council, on the basis of his charm and personality. In the middle of February it snowed and the drifts were so high that school was canceled from Thursday through Tuesday. The mailman didn't get through, but the basketball teams did, and on Friday night the junior varsity beat Repringer at Mott High. On March 4 he fell ill—fever, sore throat, chills. On March 5 he was still feeling bad, but with the help of aspirin played a big playoff game, which Mott won 25-24. The next day he was still feeling lousy so he stayed home from school, remaining in bed and going out only to feed the pigs.

That night, about quarter to one, when they were all in bed, there came a loud and furious knocking at the door. When Tim, woozy from sleep and the lingering effects of his illness, went downstairs to see what was going on, he found his mother and his aunt, her sister Cassie, in the kitchen. Anna, wrapped in a dressing gown and her hair mussed from the bed, was bending over her sister, who was distraught, sitting in a straight kitchen chair.

"Oh, Anna, Anna," she moaned, rocking back and forth like a Jew at prayer, "I'm so afraid it's serious. I'm so afraid Clyde's going to, going to...."

"Cassie, please. Stop a minute." Anna laid her left hand consolingly on Cassie's shoulder. "You haven't told me what's happened."

"Hey, Mom," Tim said, running his hand through his hair and blinking in the bright kitchen light. "What's going on?"

"I don't know, Tim." Anna turned her face toward him to speak. "I can't get a straight sentence out of her. She's too upset. Something's wrong with Clyde."

She turned her attention back to her sister. "Cassie, pull yourself together for a minute. Tell me what's wrong."

"Oh, Anna, Tim. They took Clyde to the hospital in Somerton. The boys did, Ron and Bill." Cassie paused, as if to gather strength to keep from wailing again, and went on. "He woke up with these pains. He went to bed early because he said he wasn't feeling well. Then about two hours ago he woke up complaining of these terrible pains. In his left arm and chest, he said. It hurt so he couldn't stand it, he said. Thank God Bill was home. He took his father to the hospital in his Ford, him and Ron. I came over here in our car. I couldn't bear to go there by myself, I mean, with just the boys. I didn't wake up Isobel. I didn't want to worry her. I came over here to see if you would go with me, Anna. God help me, I couldn't face it by myself if it's...." She broke down in sobs.

Anna and Tim got no sleep that night. They went to the hospital with Cassie and waited until dawn. The night staff at the hospital, a small, inadequately equipped community facility, was able to do little that night beyond sedating Clyde and making him comfortable. The next couple of days they did some tests and found nothing seriously wrong, and sent him home with the recommendation that he quit smoking. "He refuses to do that," Cassie said. "He always has. He says smoking doesn't do anything worse than cut your wind."

✳     ✳     ✳     ✳

Tim saw a lot of Betty Ruppertal that winter and spring. They played cards at her house or his house or someone else's house, or they went for rides in Anna's car—still the '36 Dodge—or went to the movies. In the afternoon of March 16, a Sunday, they drove over to Ainsley, about 18 miles from Black Run, to see *The Jolson Story*, a hugely popular movie from the previous year that was being shown in second run. It was a rare nice day, almost warm, and still light out when they left the theater, so they decided to go for a ride. They drove around a while, stopping at Schott's restaurant in Stanfield where Anna worked part-time—but not this day—and ended up by pulling off to the side of a dirt road that overlooked Herb Wentley's father's farm and parking and talking. The Dodge had no radio, but Betty had brought along her family's lunky old Zenith portable with the lighting-shaped Z on the front and the long, red-and-black U-shaped aerial trailing out of its back. Because of its size they had placed it in the back seat, though the reception in the car was poor. They had it turned low, and Elmo Tanner was whistling zippily away in Ted Weems's crazy half-rhumba version of "Heartaches," the current rage.

"I really like Larry Parks," Betty said, sitting leaning against the passenger-side door. "This is a different kind of role for him, playing Al Jolson. I saw him in *Counter-Attack* with Paul Muni. He was good in that, too, but this is really different."

Betty was a pretty girl, with a heart-shaped face framed by short-cropped blond hair. She had muscular but shapely legs and a comfortable bosom, both of which were seen to advantage, as she well knew, in her Mott High cheerleader's uniform, which her farmer father did not like her to wear. Today she had on a pleated skirt and plain white blouse and red cardigan, and her legs ended in black-and-white saddle shoes. She had a crush on Tim, but she kept both feet on the floor, both figuratively and, as today, literally.

"Yeah, I like Larry Parks, too. I saw that *Counter-Attack*. I don't know about those war movies. The vets all say it wasn't anything like that."

"I guess it was pretty horrible, what they went through." Betty looked at Tim and couldn't help thinking, God help her, that he would look handsome, even more handsome than he was, in a uniform. "What about you, Tim? You'll have to go into the Army, won't you? I mean someday?"

Tim stared out the windshield and rubbed the side of his nose with his thumb, thinking. "I suppose so. I don't know. I hear they're thinking of doing away with the draft. I sure hope so. I got better things to do with my life than spend two years of it in the Army."

Betty looked down at her left hand resting in her lap, her fingers curled over into her palm, and flicked her little fingernail with her thumbnail, meditatively. "Have you heard it going 'round that Sally Hough is going to have a baby?"

"Yes. I heard Tony Pepko's left the county. They say he's the father."

"Tony Pepko?"

"Yeah, over to West Linton. Goes to Repringer. Went, I guess I should say."

"Well, I think it's terrible for her." With her right index finger, Betty traced absent-mindedly in the condensation on the side window. It was growing cooler, and darker, and she could see her face reflected dully in the misted-over glass.

"Terrible? Huh. It's what she gets for being a slut."

"A slut? Of course, Tony Pepko had nothing to do with it. Tony Pepko's a perfect angel."

"I don't know that he's a perfect angel, but everybody knows Sally Hough goes out with anything in pants."

"And the boys hanging 'round her like a, like a"—Betty could not bring herself to say "bitch"—"like a female dog in heat, there's nothing wrong with that? And why doesn't Tony Pepko live up to his responsibilities instead of skipping out? Oh, Tim, don't be so stupid." Betty turned her head to look out the window. She hated to argue with Tim, she didn't want to make him angry with her, but she couldn't let him get away with this.

"You talk about responsibilities? Seems to me it's the girl's responsibility to—" but he thought better of that line of reasoning. "Anyway. Say, talking about this— how about what's going on between Mrs. Wayne and old Springer?" Laura Wayne taught English and Carl Springer taught shop at the high school.

"I know. I think it's disgraceful. And to think that his wife teaches second grade right next door. Have you ever noticed how Mrs. Springer goes around? Like she hasn't a friend in the world. Alice Anne Wentley said she heard Waynie and Springer were seen together at a motor court over near Johnstown. Everybody knows what's going on, but everybody acts like nothing is going on. It's just disgraceful. Why, they've both got children. They must be in their forties."

"Yeah, I know. That's my mother's age, for Pete's sake." Tim had a brief flash in his mind of Barney Ford and his mother, but quickly pushed it aside. They sat in silence a few moments, then he slid out from under the steering wheel and moved next to Betty and put his right arm around her shoulders. "Well, you know, they just weren't careful."

"Who wasn't careful?" Betty said as Tim nuzzled his face softly down to the back of her neck, a procedure she did not find totally uncongenial. She arched her neck slightly to accommodate him. "Sally and Tony?"

"No. Waynie and old Springer. You got to, you got to ... just be careful," he said dreamily and meaninglessly as he moved over her halfway recumbent form.

There followed a period of what can only be called restrained abandon, and the condensation inside the Dodge built up to near precipitation level. Hands went here and there with no hindrance. Until.

"Tim! No! Stop that!" Betty sat bolt upright.

"What? Stop what?"

"You know very well what. Don't act the innocent." Betty pulled her blouse together and began pushing her hair back into shape. "I'm just being careful. I'm just taking the"—she said it tauntingly—"*girl's* responsibility."

"You mean Sally and Tony? That's different. I *like* you."

"Well, I imagine Tony liked Sally. *Then.*"

"What do you mean? I like you, period." Tim's frustrated, painful ardor got the best of him, and he flung out the first sarcastic riposte that came to mind. "I guess that shows how really concerned you are about me having to go into the Army."

"Oh, Tim," Betty said, smiling while cupping his face softly in her hands. "You're pathetic. What's that got to do with Sally Hough being pregnant? Anyway, don't you know the war's over? You're terribly sweet, and sometimes I could eat you right up, but right now you're pathetic. And so obvious."

*     *     *     *

The military draft ended on March 31, 1947. It had been in continuous operation since its establishment under the Selective Service Act of 1940, the first peacetime draft in American history. President Truman was not entirely happy with either the draft or its ending, but problems with it had given him fits, so, on March 3, at the urging of the War Department, he recommended that the draft be ended as scheduled on the 31st. One of his first acts after becoming president on April 12, 1945, was to sign a one-year draft extension. He did this on May 9, one day after Germany surrendered, in the face of calls throughout the country for an end to conscription. When Japan surrendered, the calls intensified, not only for ending the draft but for bringing the boys home—though the boys still in uniform, realizing that their chances of going home would be affected by the availability of other boys to replace them, didn't necessarily clamor for the draft to end. The huge demand for troops for occupation duty, such as Clark Bace was doing in Germany, required that Selective Service be continued. The fact is, because of restrictions placed on who could be inducted, there weren't enough young men of the right age. Troops in Germany told the press it seemed funny that Selective Service could find soldiers speedily enough during the war, but it couldn't in peacetime. In the Pacific soldiers rioted. With the draft scheduled to end in May 1946, Truman signed a six-week draft extension. On June 25 Congress authorized a further extension to March 31, 1947. The objections to the draft in Congress were so numerous that it became obvious to Truman and others that another extension beyond that seemed impossible. And so conscription passed, briefly, out of the lives of young American males.

*     *     *     *

In Somerton County they took all of this much the same as the rest of the nation did—if anything, a bit more bellicosely, in the way of rural regions throughout the country. Polls showed that in the months after the end of the war the mood changed—people might distrust the Russians, but not a large standing army, which they thought should be manned through the draft.

Tim and his classmates were of different opinion and were not sorry to see the back end of the draft. Life was good in this carefree time when school was almost over and responsibilities were few. A golden future spread before them, and not simply because they would soon be free of the routine, however pleasant, that had formed their lives for the last twelve years. The country, if not Somerton County, was growing prosperous, and jobs not only were plentiful, they beckoned. Now they could look forward to what they saw as their real existence as independent beings who would get things, or most of them, right.

The whole month of March was windy. On the 24th wind blew off several roofs in Black Run. The day before, a Sunday, their heating oil ran out and they had no heat in the house until they could get oil the next day. Fortunately, Anna was working at Schott's that Sunday, so she was all right, but the rest of them had to go off to friends or relatives to keep warm until nighttime when they could crawl under the covers. On the 31st, the day the draft ended, six members of the class, including Tim, met at lunchtime to plan the class trip. One person lobbied for someplace "different," like Hollywood or Havana, but everybody else knew it had to be the traditional choice between New York or Washington, D.C., and Washington won. That same day after school Tim went out for baseball, trying out for second base.

Second base was as far as he got with Betty, try as he might as they continued to go out together. He also continued doing farm chores for Bayard Wentley, Herb's father, to earn money—hauling manure and firewood, mainly. On April 3 he practiced for the Easter service at church. He saw no contradiction in his attempts on Betty's presumptive virginity and his attendance at services of the church that proscribed such behavior. Tim was a young man who loved church—indeed, he loved Jesus—and he loved pretty young women. Where was the problem?

Life went on in its variegated pleasant and cruel, peaceful and violent, way for Tim and his fellow Americans. On April 7 Henry Ford died, and on April 10 Jackie Robinson signed with the Brooklyn Dodgers. Among some in Somerton County there was much regret over these events, both the passing of an American icon and the signing of a Negro player in the major leagues, though not on Tim's part, for he was an open-hearted and tolerant young man who believed in America while sharing much of the casual racism of most Americans, 42 percent of whom would tell a Gallup poll next year that they favored segregation in public transportation. On April 16 a ship explosion and its aftereffects left 500 people dead in Texas City, Texas. On the 20th Tim quit baseball, and on the 25th he along with a few others made up a committee that met at Betty's house to decide on a class motto. Each year's class had one, and they were all without exception pretentious or grandiloquent, or both. The Class of 1947 was determined to be original. Donny Barber, always the clown, wanted "Thank God That's Over." One of the girls, Gladys Tasmin, a pointedly plain young woman from a farm in the outer reaches of the school district who fairly quivered with religiosity, thought they should honor their Lord with "We Go Forth Into His Service." Everyone, while professing admiration for the sentiment, quickly dumped cold water on that, which left Gladys silent, indignant, and nursing a satisfying feeling of moral superiority for the rest of the meeting. They kicked around a few more ideas, including alterations or variations on traditional American slogans, such as "Give Us Liberty or Give Us Death" (Donny's: "Give Us a Job or Get Out of the Way"). Finally, no one could be sure who first suggested it, but they settled on "An End Is But a Beginning," and considered it both clever and becomingly modest.

The first part of May was unusually cold. Tim dug a hole by the side of the house to bury a new oil tank. On the 8th it snowed, leaving more than two inches of snow on the ground. The following Saturday it was still on the ground, all churned up and brown and gray, when Tim and Rick drove into the gravel parking lot of Schott's restaurant shortly after noon. Stones spattered up against the underside of the Dodge's bulbous fenders as Tim brought the car to a bobbing halt near the entrance of the shining, railroad-car-shaped diner. It sat on Route 23 just outside Stanfield Borough on a narrow stretch of gravely, cindery ground, so narrow that the diner backed right up against Tanners Mountain, which loomed over it. Anna was working there as a cook that Saturday. Tim had driven her over early in the morning so that he and Rick could have the car to go and paint the roof of the Reformed church, but the day turned out too cold for that, so he decided to go into Horton to shop for things he needed for the class trip to Washington, for which he needed money.

The diner was abustle with a large, noisy crowd of Saturday lunchtime customers when Tim and Rick pushed open the second door, the one that opened into the diner and that led off from the little added-on box-like foyer, sitting on the concrete steps, that jutted out from the diner's aluminum front. The atmosphere, coming in from a cold, damp day, was almost thick. Every booth along the front and the two ends was taken, as well as most of the stools at the counter. The owner, Benjy Schott, was working the counter wearing a freshly washed white apron bearing the faded stains of a thousand spilled and spattered foods. Atop his curly, salt-and-pepper hair sat a paper cap and tucked behind his right ear was a pencil for writing out orders. His jowly face radiated weariness. There was a lot of day left before he could let his barking dogs lie.

Tim and Rick walked to the counter. No two stools in a row were unoccupied, so they stood behind the diners.

"Hi, Mr. Schott. Is my mother here?" Tim asked.

Benjy looked up from writing an order. "Yeah, sure." He pointed over his right shoulder with his pencil "She's in the back. Pretty busy. I'll let her know you're here soon's I go back there, Timmy." Tim hated to be called Timmy.

The diner seated directly in front of Tim and Rick half-turned in his stool and looked up at them. Wesley Kohl, a farmer with three days' worth of white stubble and a wide grin on his face.

"Hiya, Timmy, Ricky." Rick didn't like to be called Ricky, either. "Here, sit yourselfs down. I'm finished." He rose and scooped up his white-and-green bill from the counter in his big meaty fist and turned toward the cash register. "Two stools free now," he said, indicating the one he had just vacated and the open one next to it. Rick and Tim sat down.

"Two coffees, please, Mr. Schott. Black," Rick said. He looked at Tim. "My treat."

"Coming up," Benjy said.

Rick fiddled with the jukebox selector mounted on the counter in front of him, flipping the metal-bound cards inside its bulging semi-circle of glass, looking for something he liked. Finally he dropped in a nickel and punched the buttons for "Ole Buttermilk Sky." In a few moments the bouncy brass and strings of Kay Kyser's orchestra came booming out of the jukebox at the end of the diner and the three speakers spaced along the top of the walls.

"Did you see the movie this is from?" Rick asked his brother.

"What? This song? No. Did you?"

"Yeah. Last year, I think it was. Down to the Horton Theater. Pretty good."

"Yeah? What was it?"

"I don't know. I can't remember the name. Some Western. 'Canyon Something,' or 'Something Canyon.' Dana Andrews was in it. Hoagy Carmichael, too. He wrote the song."

"That's not Hoagy Carmichael singing now, is it?"

"No." Rick peered at the song selector. "Some guy named Mike Douglas."

"Never heard of him."

"Me neither."

Benjy brought over their coffees in two thick ceramic cups and saucers and placed the bill next to them. "Your mother's coming right out," he said, just as she came through the double swinging doors at the center of the diner.

"Hi, Mom," Tim said when she approached the counter. Anna had on a small-patterned, gray work dress covered by a huge kitchen apron. She didn't wear her school cafeteria uniform in the restaurant. She smiled at her sons. They were so fine; she could see their father in their faces. At thirty-eight, Anna's not-quite-plump, unlined face always bore a genuine, inviting smile, and her dark hair, reaching to the nape of her neck, contained but a few strands of gray. The years and four children had added a decided ridge line to her hips, yet she was buxom, like all the King girls grown to maturity, and shapely. Little wonder that many men in her part of the county considered her comely, especially those whose own wives weren't.

"What're you two doing here? You didn't paint the church roof?"

"No," Rick said. "Too cold."

"So what do you want? I can't stop long." Her tone was not impatient, merely businesslike, as she years ago had learned she had to be. With her left hand she pushed back a few strands of hair that had crept out from under her hairnet, and with her chin gestured in the direction of the diner, as if that explained every-thing. "It's real busy today."

"I know, Mom," Tim said. "I stopped in to see if you had any money. I have to buy some stuff for the class trip to Washington."

"What kind of stuff? What'd you do with the money you earned helping Bayard?"

"Well, I kinda need that to pay for my bus fare and the hotel room, and to spend there. I really need to get a new dress shirt and a pair of shoes and some new underwear. If I'm going to be rooming with a bunch of guys in a hotel...."

"All right, that's fine," Anna said, laying her hand on top of her son's. The need for clean underwear wins over many a mother's heart. "Wait here a minute and I'll go get my purse. I have a few dollars in there." Anna didn't begrudge Tim the money. She knew he was being square with her. She knew all her children were; they were diligent workers. She simply had to know the situation; there was no one else to assess it.

\*     \*     \*     \*

The class trip was a lightning one: down on a Friday afternoon and back on a Sunday afternoon. Tim almost missed the charter bus that took them. He got up late and rushed in Anna's car to Elmer Wentley's garage, where the bus stopped, and left it there for Rick to pick up. Someone would give Rick a lift to the garage. Rick didn't have his license yet, but Tim had been teaching him to drive and he had been driving solo, with a cautious eye out for the sheriff or state troopers.

The students and two teacher chaperones stayed at a dingy but decent seven-story hotel and ate their meals in a self-service restaurant. They scurried from museum to White House to Potomac boat trip to Lincoln Memorial and a few other stops in between. The students slept three or four to a room, and on Saturday night somebody got the bright idea to get a little liquor to celebrate. After they returned from the trip, Ray Jones related the story in school to some girls and the boys who hadn't been in on it.

"Everybody chipped in something," Ray said. "A quarter, half-dollar, whatever they could. We couldn't raise enough in our room, so we asked the guys in the room next door if they wanted to be in on it, and they said yeah. Anyway, we got a few bucks together and then we had to decide who was going to go get it. Nobody wanted to do it, everybody was too nervous, being in a strange city and all. But finally Walt pipes up that he'll do it. And so he goes downstairs looking for a liquor store, and before long he's back. No whiskey. They wouldn't sell it to him. You had to be eighteen. They made him show his driver's license, and of course he's not eighteen. None of us is, except Jim Calder, and he refused to go. Too nervous about getting caught by old Barney Ford. So then we all look at Tim. He's not only eighteen, he's nineteen. And ol' Tim, he says, 'What the hell, fellas. Why not?' And he takes the money and goes out, and before you know it he's back with a fifth of whiskey in a brown paper bag. I don't even know what brand it was. Something cheap. So we took paper cups from the bathroom and we each got our share. There was seven or eight of us, so none of us got very much. But it was enough to make ol' Tim happy, I'll tell you. After about his third cupful, which is the most I think any of us got, he got real happy. Hopping around from bed to bed and just carryin' on. Then he starts acting scheming, like, and says we all ought to go raid the girls' rooms. Talk about getting in Dutch with Ford! He was real insistent, but we managed to restrain him. But he kept on giggling and acting crazy until he finally fell asleep. I never realized a few swigs of liquor could have that effect on anyone."

The next day they had their picture taken as a class on a patch of lawn in front of the Capitol. There they are, all twenty-seven of them plus the two chaperones, posing in front of a scraggly line of bushes and smiling confidently at the future. The girls are standing, nearly all of them in cloth coats with wide sleeves, and their hair comes down to their shoulders. An occasional cloth bow or ruffle graces their chests, but most are in plain blouses or sweaters. Aside from one or two dour or quizzical expressions, they look hopeful. The boys, sitting cross-legged on the ground in front of them, are in shirtsleeves or suit coats or two-tone sports jackets. Tim is the only one sporting a tie. From the ground, they squint upward at the camera slightly. Like the girls, they exude that special appealing quality of youth—not carefree exactly, since we all have cares at any age, but the ability not to be constantly fussed by them. A snapshot of a semi-generation—post-World War II, pre-Vietnam. Shortly after that they boarded the bus for the four-hour trip back to Somerton County.

*     *     *     *

No one did much school work after they got back. It was all but over. They had to take exams—high school exams and county exams. Tim did all right, the "C" work that had been his achievement all through school. The weather was fine; the cold of the early part of the month had disappeared entirely. The warm weather was a kind of liberation. Everybody seemed to be driving around in cars, either their own or someone else's, and attending "socials" and dropping in for visits. Tim and Herb and Jim Calder drove up to Altoona a couple of times, just for a place to go, just because they couldn't stand not to be in motion. Despite the bravado of their class motto, a sense of an end that was simply an end was setting in, and people were eager to touch the familiar for what they feared might be the last time. Even in a farming area, where at the time fewer people tended to drift away once out of school, some did, and in any case a phase of their life was coming to a close. Tim spent several days writing and practicing his speech. Back in the first half of the school year, around the time he was elected president of the student council, he was also elected president of his class, and as such he had to give a speech at the high school commencement. On the last day of the month a big party was held at Kenny Ruppertal's house.

Ken Ruppertal was Betty's cousin and a member of the class. He lived with his younger brother and two sisters in a big white frame house on Route 33 just past where it branches off of Route 23, heading toward West Linton. Ken's father, Ken Senior, was a carpenter and, like Ray Jones's father and many others, kept a few animals and did a little farming on the side. Ken planned to let his father's influence get him into carpentry, too.

The party was well under way when Tim drove the Dodge into the grass-and-dirt driveway alongside the Ruppertals' house. A half-dozen cars were already parked here and there on the scraggly grass a few yards from the house, and Tim pulled in among them. The weather was fine, cloudy and slightly windy but warm. People were milling around the big stone fireplace in the back yard, some cooking hotdogs, others just talking, still others playing volleyball. Tim got out of the car, reached back in to pick up the potato salad, made by Anna, and bottles of root beer that were his donation to the party supplies. As he backed away, his hands full and closing the door with his left knee, he could hear music wafting down from the yard. Someone had brought a record player.

"Hey, squirt," Tim said to Ken's thirteen-year old sister, Sarah, who was running by, chasing one of her friends. "Help me with some of this stuff, willya?"

Sarah stopped. "Help yourself, goon. Who was your nigger servant last year?" She smiled to show she didn't mean it and took some of the soft drink bottles from him.

"Hey hey," Tim admonished. "Nice talk. Where'd you learn talk like that?" He looked down at her head of yellow pigtailed hair as they walked up toward the fireplace.

"Probably listening to you and my idiot brother."

"Well, just make sure you don't use it in polite company."

"Where would I meet any polite company around here?"

"You know what I mean."

They had reached the fireplace. Small tables, covered with oilcloths and piled with food, were set up here and there. Tim and Sarah placed the potato salad and bottles on one of them.

"There, think you can manage by yourself now?" Sarah looked around the yard. "I don't know where my dear cousin Betty is. Probably up in the haymow with Wesley Rogan." She glanced at Tim sidelong to see what effect her remark might have had.

It had none. Tim knew that Betty wasn't up in the Ruppertals' haymow with Wesley, nor was anyone else up there with anyone else. He looked at Sarah. She had an intelligent face, fronted by a chipped front tooth and eyeglasses with pale pinkish frames. He could see that breasts were beginning to blossom beneath her knit shirt.

"You're pretty smart, aren't you? What do you know about haymows?"

"I know enough not to go up in them with Wesley Rogan. Or any other stupid boy." She shot him another inquisitive glance, and then turned and ran back down through the yard, just as Ken came up to greet Tim.

"Buh-rother, Ken," Tim said. "Your sister's got a real smart mouth on her, you know that?"

"She's just trying to get your goat. I think she's got a thing for you."

"*What*? How old is she? Twelve, thirteen?"

"Yeah, well, puppy love, you know?" He looked at Tim and grinned. "Must run in the family."

Tim gave him a sarcastic, drop-dead look. Ken took hold of Tim's upper arm and said, "C'mon, get yourself a hotdog," and motioned him toward the fireplace.

On a little stand next to the food table, Caroline Ollinger was manning the record player, a small, Leatherette-covered RCA Victor plugged into an extension cord running from the house. She had just put on Count Basie's novelty tune, "Open the Door, Richard!" Caroline was a shy little fawn, the only child of Arnie and Bessie Ollinger, who owned the Horton Pharmacy but lived in Black Run. The store put them among Black Run's well-to-do, and they had the money to indulge her passion for popular music. Caroline bought nearly all the new records when they came out. She went often to the music store in Altoona to listen to them and buy. Tim liked going there, too, but he didn't go very often and he bought even less. He just liked going in there and asking for a record he'd heard and taking it into the booth and listening to it. That was nice. You were by yourself with the music, yet the glass-walled upper half of the wooden booth let you feel like part of the crowd swirling around outside. Like being in a fishbowl. You could see the rows and rows of record racks lining one wall behind the class counter. All those records, thousands of them. If they should come smashing down, what a mess. There were several booths, and you could see into them, too, of course. Some were jammed with three or four kids, and that irked the fussy little store manager, who skittered around the store with one eye nervously on the booths like a hen clucking after her chicks.

The record came to an end. Caroline lifted the tone arm and set it down on its rest and carefully picked up the 78-rpm record by grasping its rim with her fingertips and placed it back inside its paper sleeve.

"You sure take care of your records, Caroline," Tim said while putting mustard and relish on his hotdog.

"I know. I'm fussy. It's silly, I know," Caroline said, kneeling down to place the record on the bottom shelf of the stand. From her kneeling position, she looked up at him. Most of the girls in the high school yearned to a greater or lesser degree for Tim, and Caroline was not an exception. Like them, she wondered what it would be like to be his, not in a carnal or sexual sense, necessarily, but just to be *his*—two together, them alone. He simply had that effect, and the nice thing, from the girls' perspective, is that he was but dimly aware of it. Caroline heaved an inner sigh, and thought of giddy Shirley Temple in the presence of dreamboat Cary Grant in *The Bachelor and the Bobby-Soxer*. She stood up.

"Where's Betty?" she asked. "Didn't Betty come with you?"

"No, she didn't," Tim replied, irked. "Why does everybody keep expecting I've got to be with Betty?"

"I'm sorry, Tim. It's just—it's just I thought you and she were going out a lot."

"Maybe we are," Tim said, still heated. "But that doesn't mean we're going together or anything. We just go out sometimes. It doesn't mean we have to go everywhere together."

"Well, OK, Tim." Caroline was for the moment nonplussed by Tim's comments. Normally he acted and reacted to everything so equably. To regain her composure she turned to her records. "Is there anything you'd particularly like to hear?"

"I don't know. What've you got?" Tim said, taking a bite of his hotdog, which had remained in his right hand during their exchange. With his left hand he began sorting through the records. "Oh, hey, 'Bongo Bongo Bongo!' Play that. I like that; it's really funny."

He handed the record to Caroline and she set it down onto the turntable and, as Danny Kaye was telling the Andrews Sisters that bongo bongo bongo he would never leave the Congo oh no no no no no, Tim said to Caroline, "I guess you'll be leaving Black Run to go to college in the fall."

"Yes. Up to State College. To Penn State."

"Will you take all your records?"

Caroline laughed. "I don't know. Maybe. I'd like to. I suppose it depends on what my roommate's like." She paused, pretending again to sort through the records.

"Are you going on to post-secondary education, Tim?" Caroline talked like that sometimes, "post-secondary education." She knew he wasn't. Caroline was one of only three students out of the twenty-seven in the Mott High graduating class going to college.

"No," he said. "There's no money for that."

"Do you know what you'll do?"

"No. Get a job, I guess. Seems like there's plenty of work around now. Maybe not in Stanfield or Horton or Somerton County, but in general, in the country. Maybe I'll go up to Guldwyck. York State, you know? I've got family up there. We used to live up near there."

"Yes, I know. That's where—that's where your father died, isn't it?"

"Yes. In Watervliet, actually. That's right nearby."

"I hope you don't mind my mentioning it." Caroline, unsure of herself, tended to apologize too much. "Does it still bother you? Your father's death?"

"No. That was a long time ago. Though maybe it isn't for my mother. I think she still misses my Dad." That thought did seem to bother Tim, and now it was his turn to use the records as a crutch. He picked one up. "Here, put this on. 'Feudin' and Fightin'; it's funny too. Dorothy Shay, the Park Avenue Hillbilly. Boy, there's sure a lot of nutty songs lately."

∗       ∗       ∗       ∗

No, there wasn't any money for college. There wasn't any desire, either, on Tim's part. Veterans, taking advantage of the Servicemen's Readjustment Act of 1944—the G.I. Bill—were flocking to campuses, more than one million of them in the year Tim decided not to go. Their fecundity peaked in 1947, too, showing that they were getting busy on more than just their studies: The national birth rate reached 25.8 per thousand, the highest in decades. Times were flush. Postwar prosperity was building up a good head of steam and young men—young white men, anyway—could walk out of high school, or military service, and into good jobs.

Tim's high school commencement was held June 2, a gorgeous pre-summer Monday evening. The weather was so delectable that the commencement could have been held outdoors, but the planners couldn't be sure of that, so it was held in the high school auditorium. Besides, everyone wanted to try out the new auditorium, which had been built only in the past year.

Before that commencements had been held in the nearby Black Run Church of the Brethren. Separation of church and state and academia was an issue that did not overly trouble the minds of the farmers, shopkeepers, and artisans of the day. And so, after the Class of 1947 marched in for the first Mott High commencement under a secular roof, a minister gave the invocation: the Rev. Jack Calder, father of Tim's friend Jim Calder and pastor of a different Brethren parish, turned what were supposed to be brief remarks into a mini-sermon taking the hymn "Lead On, O King Eternal" as his departure point. After that Gladys Tasmin, thrumming with evangelical fervor like a plucked bowstring, sang "Take My Life and Let It Be"; Caroline Ollinger spoke on "Life's True Heroes—Our Parents"; Walter Wight spoke on "Education for Life, Not Just for a Living"; and the high school band played "Stars and Stripes Forever." Then, with the other twenty-six members of the class seated on the stage behind him, Tim got up to give his speech as class president.

He was not nervous, even facing that scariest of audiences—people who have known you all your life. He looked out at the faces. In the front row, next to Principal Bambarger, sat Leander P. Mott, namesake benefactor of the school and of Stanfield Borough, who came to nearly all the commencements. Tim picked out Anna sitting with Rick and the two girls. She looked proud and happy—and tired. No, he was not nervous, but as he stood at the lectern, slightly uncomfortable in his new blue graduation suit, he felt uncertain of his speech, which by tradition had to be on the topic suggested by the class motto. At the time he and the others had adopted the motto, he had paid no attention to this requirement—the speech was too far off, all of two months. Now he was not at all sure that an End Is But a Beginning. He hoped what he had written made sense. Barney Ford had helped him, smiling indulgently over some of its sentiments but not suggesting that Tim change them. Now Tim cleared his throat, took a sip of water from the glass sitting in its well in the lectern, and began speaking.

"Principal Bambarger, Mr. Mott, members of the school board, teachers, parents, and fellow students: Welcome to the graduation exercises of the Class of 1947, the best class ever to graduate from Leander P. Mott Vocational High School."

A few muted "yeas" and hand clappings from the students behind him were brought to a guilty halt by a fierce glare from Principal Bambarger that said such tomfoolery had no place at Leander P. Mott, especially not when Leander P. Mott himself was in the place.

"The tradition at Mott High, as most of you know, is for the class president to give a commencement speech on the topic of the class motto. I was privileged to receive the honor of being elected class president by my fellow class members. I am glad they had that confidence in me. I wish I had the same confidence in the speech I am about to give. [Laughter.] In fact, I wish now we had chosen a different motto. [Louder laughter.] But I promise you I will make my speech short, even if it turns out not so sweet. [Diminished laughter.]

"Our class motto, as you can see by the banner behind me, is 'An End Is But a Beginning.' Now, what does that mean? We today are at what we call a commencement. A starting out. A beginning, in other words. We have ended our school lives and are beginning our working lives. Our childhood has ended and our adulthood begins. We have all heard similar comments at other graduation ceremonies.

"But I would like to turn our attention to an experience that I think is a better example of the truth of our motto. It is an experience we all shared, in one way or another. I refer to the great world war that now is almost two years behind us and that disrupted all our lives. It *ended* the lives of many of our fathers, uncles, brothers, and schoolmates. It was a terrible ordeal for people on both the war front and the home front.

"But it ended. And at the same time it ended, a new life began. Out of the ashes of war a shining future can arise. We here can see but dimly into the future—as the Good Book says, in a glass darkly—but the signs we are given at this place in our lives point to a future possibly more prosperous and peaceful than any the human race has ever seen. As we look out over the world, we see few instances of warfare. Our own country, significantly, has ended the draft, for which my own generation is immensely grateful. The guys, anyway. [Laughter.]

"It probably would be too bold and foolish to say with certainty that our world has learned through this terrible worldwide conflict to do without war and militarism. We know, for one thing, that Soviet Russian Communism looms over the world like an international menace, and we must be ever vigilant against it. It can never be taken lightly, because Joe Stalin is as big a dictator as Adolf Hitler ever was. But other than that, looking out we see a world learning to put itself back together, and mostly without warfare. And that is why I say—or maybe I should say I *hope*—that the end of a long war will prove to be the begin-ning of an even longer peace.

"Thank you."

Finished, Tim folded his speech in two, stepped away from the lectern, wiped a thin film of sweat from his brow, and walked back to his chair in the front row of his seated classmates. Enthusiastic applause broke out, along with a whistle—that was Rick, but it was glared into silence by Principal Bambarger. Who then, saving the best for last, rose to introduce Leander P. Mott, who of course needed no introduction. A self-made man who worshiped his creator, Mott then gave a few appropriate remarks about the need to study hard and work hard and follow what he hoped he could modestly say was his own example and then they, the assembled graduates, might be able to come back to Leander P. Mott High School in thirty or thirty-five years and give inspiring talks to assembled gradu-ates.

And then, modestly apologizing for taking up so much of the audience's valu-able time, Mr. Mott said it was time for what they all had come for, the handing out of diplomas. Which he did. As Principal Bambarger read out each name, the boy or girl rose and crossed the stage, receiving from Mr. Mott a handshake, a smile, and a diploma. After all twenty-seven had received one of each, the Rev. Riemenschneider of the Black Run Church gave the benediction. Following that, the band struck up "Onward, Christian Soldiers," and the Class of 1947 of Leander P. Mott High School recessed out into the peaceful new world of which Tim had spoken so hopefully.

# CHAPTER 7

▼

# LOVERS, BROTHERS, AND OTHER STRANGERS

*When things are bad, it is not as important to find a way to improve them as it is to find someone to blame them on.*
—Giovannino Guareschi, *The Little World of Don Camillo*

It was a peaceful new world, perhaps, but not one without incident. That summer, while Tim and Ray earned money painting roofs, the world continued its manic spin, throwing off events both momentous and minor. Of most of them, Tim and his friends were sublimely unaware, being more concerned with immediate events. It was summer, the weather was gorgeous, the country was prosperous, and they were as free as they would ever be in their lives. He dressed, like his friends, casually in jeans—or dungarees, as they were more commonly called—with the bottoms folded up several times. His sisters and all the other girls he knew put their hair up in rag curlers, though later in the year they got a Toni, the home permanent that millions of women took to, swayed by the convincing advertisement asking, "Which Twin Has the Toni?," unaware that, while one of the identical twins with identical hair-dos in the ad had indeed given herself a home wave, both of them had subsequently gone to a hairdresser. It didn't matter: If you were a girl, it was something fun to do for yourself or for a friend.

Momentous events. The week that Tim and his friends graduated from high school, Secretary of State George C. Marshall took himself up to Harvard University to propose the plan for the reconstruction of Europe that subsequently became known as the Marshall Plan. That didn't mean much to Anna, though the ending of sugar rationing six days later did. Out in Idaho, a businessman flying a two-seater plane saw nine saucer-like objects streaking through the sky, but, despite continued sightings over two weeks throughout the West, most Somerton Countians, being level-headed, agreed with the official reports that such "unidentified flying objects" were the result of mass hallucination or suggestibility. The inauguration of the first round-the-world airline service, on a Lockheed Constellation, by Pan American Airways on June 17, now that was something more like, though no one in the county could possibly have afforded the $1,700 fare. Down in Washington, they showed that they could move fast when they wanted. On July 25 Congress passed the National Security Act of 1947, reorganizing the armed forces, including a new, separate Air Force, into a national military establishment headed by a new official of cabinet rank, the secretary of defense. It also established the National Security Council and the Central Intelligence Agency. President Truman, who nominated Secretary of the Navy James V. Forrestal as the first secretary of defense, signed the act the next day, and the day after that Forrestal was confirmed by Congress. Some of this was to affect Tim profoundly.

For now, though, nothing affected Tim except for the weather and thoughts of women and work. A week after graduation he went with his cousin, Bill Friedle, out to Beech Haven to see about a job. With Ray and sometimes Rick he painted three roofs. It grew hot and he went swimming and slept out on the porch. He played baseball. He took Betty Ruppertal to the movies in Somerton city to see *The Farmer's Daughter*. On the trip back, despite his most adroit maneuvers, she proved as obdurate about her virtue as ever. "No luck," he told Rick, who was thrilled with these confidences, when he got back and flopped down disconsolately on the bed in the room they shared.

Then, less than two weeks after he applied, he and Bill were called out to Beech Haven for jobs.

Beech Haven, resort and hotel, was quite a big deal. It's not in operation any more; it's been shuttered since the early 1970s; at one point some local business and government leaders formed a committee to see about cranking it up again, to no avail. It was the sort of resort behemoth that was well past its time when it finally closed. It had a pretty good run, having been started in the early 19th century as a watering hole for westward travelers and expanding from there into a resort. Mark Twain once made a flying visit to Beech Haven in 1870 to scout it out as a place of recuperation for his brand-new and desperately ill father-in-law, Jervis Langdon. But it quickly became clear that Langdon had stomach cancer and he died shortly thereafter without ever making it to Beech Haven. Presidents stayed there—Taylor, Polk, Garfield—and less famous though often wealthier guests came from Pittsburgh, Philadelphia, Baltimore, and Washington, D.C. Its greatest claim to fame was for being a hidey-hole later in the 19th century for Henry Adams when he needed a quiet place to concoct his pessimistic views on the United States and everything else. Nowadays, of course, it would be hard to explain who Henry Adams was, though anyone climbing the hotel's sagging, wide wooden steps to the front porch can still read about him on a bronze plaque affixed to the wall near the main entrance.

But in June 1947, when Tim went to work there, Beech Haven was still a going concern: a huge, rambling, four-story, wood frame hotel, painted white with green trim, encircled by a deep, commodious porch. No one knew exactly how many rooms it had, though it could accommodate at least eighty to ninety guests. There were also outlying guest cabins. Set on a small lake, with an eighteen-hole golf course, tennis courts, squash courts, swimming pools (indoor and out), weight room, steam room, gymnasium—everything for the businessman of the first half of the 20th century who told himself he wanted to get in trim. All set on more than 2,000 acres. There were even some locally famous springs, though there was a reason they were only locally famous, because the only thing the guests knew them to cure was excess amounts of cash.

"So what're you gonna do there?" Rick asked when Tim came home after interviewing with the personnel director.

"I don't know. Everything and anything, I guess. They're starting me out on room service, nights. That should be OK. Chance for some tips." Tim lay on the bed on the porch where they slept when it was hot. He folded his arms behind his head and stared at the porch roof. "Boy, Rick, you should see the women out there."

There was silence for a few moments, then Rick, reacting to the reverence in his brother's voice, said softly, "Guests, you mean?"

"Yeah. Running around in swimsuits and those little tennis skirts that show those white panties. And not just the daughters of the guests, either. The mothers, the wives, too." Tim's throat went dry as he spoke. He turned his head and looked at Rick in the deepening twilight. "But I noticed some good-looking women working there, too. There's girls and men working there that aren't from around here. They come in just for the summer, even from different states. Like Mom going to cook up at Lake George, I suppose."

"Yeah, but what about Betty?" Rick said.

"What do you mean, what about Betty?"

"Well, I mean, you and her...."

"What about me and her?"

"Well, she's real nice and all. And you like her and she really likes you."

"Yeah, I know she's real nice and all. And I know I like her and I know she really likes me." Tim kicked out with his right foot and rattled the low metal frame of the foot of his bed. "But this is 1947 and I'm not ready to settle down, not by a long shot. You know?"

So Tim went to work that summer at Beech Haven. Anna went up to Lake George to cook in one of the resorts there. The girls, Barb and Connie, fourteen and twelve years old, went with her; they would sometimes wait tables there. But Tim and Rick, nineteen and almost seventeen, stayed in Black Run—alone in the little house, but surrounded by family. When he could he came home to play ball for Black Run, playing against Horton and the other towns' teams. He didn't have a car—Anna had that, of course—so he had to hitch or catch a ride with someone else. Sometimes he took the mail bus. Just before the Fourth of July he got Rick on at the hotel, and they stayed out there much of the time. Rick's work was less steady, mostly caddying and washing dishes.

Tim worked at anything and everything at Beech Haven on practically every day and shift—bellboy, caddy, dishwasher, even substitute switchboard operator. But mostly bellboy and room service. He was continually catching hell from the head bellman for being late and not having his tie tied, but he never cared. He worked hard and the guests liked him. What were they going to do, fire him? If they did, it was their loss.

Rick was trying to get his driver's license, and Tim went out with him to practice driving. Since Anna had the family car up to Lake George, they had to borrow Bill Friedle's '39 Ford or someone else's car. Because of his blindness in the one eye, Rick had had to get a form signed by a doctor attesting to his eyesight. Tim sent money to Connie for her birthday—a dollar. It wasn't much, but it was a considerable sum from the small amount he made, and Tim was good that way; he always remembered birthdays. Sometimes he would even draw up his own crude birthday cards. Both he and Rick went fishing whenever they could, especially in the morning, either at Beech Haven or back home in Black Run. They went to a lot of movies, often in a group, in Somerton or Horton or wherever they saw something playing they thought they'd like. Movies didn't stay in theaters for long stretches, so they struck while the iron was hot. Tim liked *The Sea of Grass*, with Spencer Tracy and Katharine Hepburn, so much that he saw it twice, once with Rick and Bill, and once more when he took out a girl from Chardon, Ohio, who was working as a waitress at Beech Haven. For the moment Tim had given up on Betty Ruppertal. The summer was too pleasant and she was too frustrating. And distant.

\*     \*     \*     \*

One day in midsummer—it was August 8, a Friday—Tim was stretched out on his back in his bunk in the dormitory reading a copy of the *Altoona Mirror* that someone had left lying on the floor. Not the speediest reader or quickest study in the world, he was engrossed in an article when Rick came hurrying in and, though he noticed his brother, he failed to notice his agitation.

"Hey Rick," Tim said, not taking his eyes from the newspaper page. "Did you see this about this Norwegian guy who sailed with a five-man crew in a balsa raft from Peru to the Polynesian islands? What's his name? Hard to pronounce. Thor Hey-, Heyerdahl. That's unbelievable. He called his raft the Kon-Tiki. It says here he left Peru April 29 and just now landed on a reef. He wanted to prove that ancient Inca Indians sailed from South America to settle Polynesia." Tim lowered the newspaper to his chest and looked up inquiringly. "That's fantastic. I didn't know anything about that, did you?"

"Tim, Uncle Clyde's dead," Rick said.

"WHAT?" Tim cried, bolting up and hitting his head on a cross-support on the head of the bunk bed.

"You all right?" Rick asked.

"Yeah. Ouch." Tim rubbed his forehead and looked at Rick through pain-squinted eyes. "What do you mean, Uncle Clyde's dead? I just saw him a couple days ago."

"I mean he's dead. It was a heart attack."

"Yeah, but I mean, when? And where? Jeez, this is awful. Poor Aunt Cassie."

"It was just this morning. They found him slumped over in his milk truck. He had just picked up the milk at Thatcher Mason's farm and climbed back in the cab. Thatcher found him. When he noticed Uncle Clyde's truck just sitting there and not moving on, he went out to see what was the matter. That's when he found him."

"Oh my gosh, this is just terrible," Tim said. "Where's Bill? Is he here?"

"No, he wasn't scheduled to work today. He's out to the house, to Aunt Cassie's. So's Ron and Isobel and the rest of them."

"What about Grandpop and Grandma King? Do they know?"

"Yes. They're both there. Bill went to get them. Aunt Cassie's place must be chaos about now."

"How about Mom? And Barb and Connie?"

"They're trying to get hold of them. And everybody up in Guldwyck, too—Aunt Eileen and Aunt Jean and Aunt Harriet and the rest. I guess it's not easy with the long-distance calls."

Tim and Rick stood in silence.

"When was it that we took Clyde to the hospital that night?" Tim said after a while. "Just a couple of months ago? I guess it was more serious than we thought. Think what'll be going through Mom's mind when she hears. First she loses Dad, and now her sister loses *her* husband. 'Course, Uncle Clyde is—*was*—older than Dad was, but he couldn't have been fifty."

"Yeah," Rick said. And there was more reflective silence.

"Hey, guess what?" Rick said. "You know that thunderstorm we had yesterday afternoon? Well, lightning killed one of Lyle Calder's cows."

"Really?"

"Oh yeah. Deader'n a doornail. I saw it on my way out here. It's still lying in the field. On its side, legs sticking out like four pokers. Funny. But Jim says his Dad's not laughing. It's one of his prize Holsteins."

"I wouldn't mind seeing that."

"Maybe it'll still be there when we go in," Rick said. "C'mon, we gotta see about getting time off. Oh brother, it's gonna be mass confusion."

Which it was—mass, but compassionate, confusion. A huge funeral was held, with the Rev. Riemenschneider officiating as usual. The King and Friedle clans and their various in-laws came in from hither and yon for a period of hearty and gregarious grieving. Everything was stiffly somber except for one moment at the gravesite. Clyde's eighty five year-old father, whose mental ship had slipped its moorings a couple of years back and who had too long been a devotee of gangster movies, was heard muttering over and over, "Don't worry, Clyde, I'll get the bastards that did this." Clyde's brother, Garland, gripped his father's left bicep and whispered fiercely, "Dad! It was a heart attack. Clyde died of a heart attack." But it was no use. The old man, wandering lonely as a cloud, did not comprehend a word—was, indeed, wondering at that point why all these people were gathered there. Other than that, it was what Somerton County society called a lovely funeral, and when it was over everyone went back their regular lives. Tim went back to Beech Haven, where he continued to date the girl from Chardon, Ohio. Her name was Helen Booth. They went to see *Life With Father*, which had them laughing even as they left the theater.

*     *     *     *

While Somerton County and the rest of the country was grieving and working and going to movies, down in Washington, D.C., the Joint Chiefs of Staff was cooking up a memorandum. Responding to pressure from Secretary of the Army Robert P. Patterson, who was looking for ways to cut costs in a shrinking Army, they sent to Secretary of Defense Forrestal a memorandum in which they stated that "from the standpoint of military security, the United States has little strategic interest in maintaining the present troops and bases in Korea."

Couched in the orotund language of bureaucrats secure in the knowledge that they will never have to be personally inconvenienced by the consequences of any recommendations they might make, the memorandum went on to say that "in the event of hostilities in the Far East, our present forces in Korea would be a military liability and could not be maintained there without substantial reinforcement prior to the initiation of hostilities. Moreover, any offensive operation the United States might wish to conduct on the Asian continent most probably would bypass the Korean peninsula."

Furthermore, reversing at top speed from most previously held views, they confidently asserted that "enemy interference from Korea could be neutralized by air action, which would be more feasible and less costly than large-scale ground operations."

Three days later, as if to put the cap on it, Secretary of State George C. Marshall said that "ultimately the U.S. position in Korea is untenable even with expenditure of considerable U.S. money and effort."

*     *     *     *

By this time Tim and the girl, Helen, had been what Anna would have called "intimate" on several occasions. There was a lot of dating among the young staff members at Beech Haven, and both he and she had gone out with others, but she was clearly gone on Tim and Tim was all but snorting over the frequent and enthusiastic sex. Anna and the girls were back from Lake George and so he had regular use of her car to get back and forth from Black Run to Beech Haven. Rick was back home and in high school, but Tim—and Helen—were still working there.

Helen was, again in Anna's terms, a lovely girl. Tim thought she looked and acted like Cathy O'Donnell, the soft-voiced, demurely curved actress who played paraplegic Harold Russell's girlfriend in *The Best Years of Our Lives*, which both of them had seen the year before. He told her this and she was pleased, because she liked O'Donnell's hesitant yet supportive manner toward Russell in the movie. And Helen did rather look like her—five-foot-four, with dark blond hair down to her shoulders, a soft yet somehow almost severe face in which dark brown eyes were widely set. Her modest bust was well-rounded, as were her shapely legs. She was nearly nineteen years old, just slightly younger than Tim, and a sensible young woman who was working as hard as she could this year to save money to go to college the next.

They had, in the trade jargon of the movies they loved so much, "met cute." It was one of those days when the planets are not in alignment and everything was going wrong all the time for everyone at the resort. Waiters were crashing through swing doors in the wrong direction and busboys were spilling carafes of ice water into the crotches of distinguished elderly gentlemen. Helen's portion of this disaster was to be pressed into service as switchboard operator because the regular operator had called in sick and none of the substitutes or anyone else experienced was available. She was sitting at the furiously blinking switchboard, ready to pull out her hair in desperation if her hands had not been so occupied pulling switchboard wires, when she spied Tim scurrying by.

"Hey you!" she hissed from her little alcove off the main lobby.

Tim stopped on a dime and turned, caught off balance by this sudden, rude greeting.

"Who, me?"

"Yes. Do you know anything about this damned switchboard? I've seen you working here. They put me here and I don't have a clue. Look at this," she wailed, waving a fistful of switchboard plugs at the blinking red lights.

Tim was in a black mood from being rushed off his feet in the shambles of the day and from having had yet another argument with the head bellman and was not happy at being given another problem.

"I wish they'd give this job to someone who knows what they're doing," he said, standing just inside the alcove.

"Oh do you?" she replied, in a tone as frosty as his was testy. "So do I, believe me. Thanks so much for your help." She turned her upturned face from his and began pushing plugs into sockets in mad abandon.

But it was unlike Tim to be unhelpful, and his irritation quickly melted. Besides, this girl, as he had noticed on earlier occasions, was terribly pretty.

"Ah, what the heck. Here, let me sit down there, I'll show you how. I'm mad at that head bellman, anyway. Serve him right if he can't find me for a while. Sorry I popped off at you."

So Tim sat there for a half-hour, showing her how to run the switchboard and getting acquainted. By the time he left to confront once again the wrath of the head bellman, he had made a date for them to go swimming the next evening at the section of the lake set aside for employees.

And their relationship developed from there. Where Tim was concerned she lost her wonted sensibleness completely and was anything but demure. After going out somewhere on one of their dates they would often end up making love—sometimes in Anna's car, sometimes in a remote room in one of the Beech Haven buildings, once even out of doors. They would lie down and Helen would swiftly ruck up her skirt, pull down her panties, draw up her legs and blissfully fit her body to his. At the outset they had both been virgins. Throughout it all she was the coolly competent one and Tim was simply dumbstruck at her beauty and his good fortune.

They did many things together. A couple of times they got into an argument and to teach each other a lesson they dated other people, but they quickly reconciled. They went to the movies often, as everyone did. They went roller-skating. They went to church—Helen was a Methodist—because Tim genuinely liked church and especially a good sermon, as long as it wasn't too deep, which was rarely a problem. Once they even went dancing, despite Tim's two left feet and consequent aversion to dancing. Helen insisted on it.

"Tim," she said one Tuesday when they both happened to have a break in the resort's kitchen, "we both have this Friday night off. Let's go dancing over to Altoona. Harry James is going to be there."

"I don't like dancing. I never learned how."

"I know you don't. But I do and I did. I'll show you. We don't have to do anything fancy. No jitterbugging, just slow dances."

"Why do we have to go this week? Besides, we probably won't be able to get in. It's probably sold out, this late date. Harry James is big."

"Not so big anymore. That's why I want to go. All the big bands are folding—Benny Goodman, Tommy Dorsey, Les Brown, Jack Teagarden. I read about it in a magazine, *Time* or *Newsweek* or somewhere. Harry James is probably going to do the same. I want to see him before he's gone."

"Are you sure? I never heard anything about that. I hear their music all the time. You know, what's his name's, Francis Craig's, orchestra, 'Near You.'" Tim leered and leaned toward Helen. "That's what I want to be, *near* you." Helen pushed him playfully away. "And that one I really like, Freddy Martin's 'Managua, Nicaragua.'" Tim jigged a little Latin step on the kitchen floor.

"See? You *can* dance. But it's true. I guess all these jukeboxes and disc jockeys on the radio are driving the bands out of business, from what the story said. I really want to go. *Please*, Tim?"

"Well, OK, why not?" Tim gave in. "What the heck, maybe Betty Grable will be with him."

And so they went to Altoona that late summer Friday in 1947 and danced to the music of Harry James and his orchestra. And afterward they did what Tim— after they did it—called the horizontal two-step, and Helen giggled.

$$* \qquad * \qquad * \qquad *$$

George F. Kennan, chairman of the State Department's Policy Planning Staff and one of Secretary of State Marshall's top advisers, summing up the department's position on Korea in October 1947: "There is no longer any real hope of a genuinely peaceful and free democratic development in that country. Its political life in the coming period is bound to be dominated by political immaturity, intolerance and violence. Where such conditions prevail, the communists are in their element. Therefore we cannot count on native forces to help hold the line against Soviet expansion. Since the territory is not of decisive strategic importance to us, our main task is to extricate ourselves without too great loss of prestige."

$$* \qquad * \qquad * \qquad *$$

That month, October, Anna bought a new car to finally replace the old '36 Dodge, a midnight blue 1947 Frazer, which had been introduced earlier by Kaiser-Frazer, the first new company to make American cars in more than twenty years. Tim wrote a letter to Governor Duff of Pennsylvania, urging him to lift a ban on hunting. On October 4, Beech Haven gave a big Saturday-night close-of-season party for its remaining employees. Bill Friedle had already quit, and Rick, of course, but Tim and Helen were still there. They were somber amid the surrounding festivities, because they were parting. Helen was going back to Ohio to work in a shirt factory until next September, when she would go to Ohio State. They moved off to stand along a far wall by themselves and talked all evening, making promises that were more fervent and earnestly meant on Helen's part than on Tim's, which Helen fearfully sensed and Tim shamefully admitted to himself.

"Tim," Helen said, gripping in her moist right hand a glass of pink-colored punch and looking dolefully into his downcast face, "I don't want to go back to Ohio. I'll miss you terribly. I miss you already."

"I know, Helen, I know. I'll miss you, too. But your plans. College. You know."

"Oh, to heck with college. It's you I want now, not college. No, that's not true. I want you *and* I want college. Oh, I wish it was easier."

"I do too, honey, but it's not. And think, what would you do if you stayed here?"

"I don't know. Am I the only girl in Somerton County? What do girls from Somerton County do when they're through school?"

"Not much. What is there? They work here at Beech Haven. They work on the family farm. They go to Altoona to work, or someplace else. They get married."

"They get married," Helen said, evenly.

Tim examined the tops of his shoes even more intently than before, if that was possible, and said nothing.

"I'm sorry, Tim," Helen said. "That wasn't called for. We've never brought that subject up, either of us. But you must know how much I care for you." There was in Helen's voice a sense of something further unexpressed.

After a pause Tim said quietly, "You know I care for you, too, Helen."

"Do you, Tim Davis?" For all her softness and sense of play, Helen had a spine. "You know I've never done, well, what we've done, with anyone else."

"I know that," Tim said, a hint of abjectness in his voice. "You know that you—you're—you're my—."

"First? Meaning there'll be more? You hope?"

Tim said nothing, merely swirled the remaining punch in his glass and listened without listening to the blaring of the record player. Some people were trying to dance to Margaret Whiting's caressing strains of "Come Rain or Come Shine," but were finding its rhythms awkward.

"Well, there's no point in us going on like this. We're going to do what we planned to do. I've got my plans, you've got yours. Will you come out to Ohio and visit sometime? We do have some kind of a future, don't we? These last two months have been special. I came to Pennsylvania for a summer job and found a pretty nice guy."

Smiling wanly, Helen took her forefinger and poked Tim gently on the point of his chin. "Sometimes I think you don't know how nice. You've got your faults and your weaknesses, but there aren't many like you, Tim."

It flustered him. "Sure, I'm gonna try and make it out there to Chardon, Helen. And yes, of course we've got a future, some kind. It's just, I don't know now, what I'm going to do, where I'm going."

Helen looked at him squarely and blankly, as she had several times that evening.

"I think I love you, Tim."

Silence amid the din.

"I know you do, Helen," Tim said.

Behind him, Margaret Whiting finished singing "Come Rain or Come Shine."

By the end of the evening Helen couldn't stop weeping and Tim couldn't stop apologizing for anything and everything. The next day, Sunday, Tim saw Helen off on a Greyhound bus. It was drizzling, from the skies and in their hearts. With the other passengers watching out the rain-and-dirt-streaked windows, Helen gave Tim a dry, soft peck on the lips at the bus door before boarding. He watched as she found her way to her aisle seat, then lost sight of her. He waited until the bus pulled away, blasting blue smoke, and then he went back to work his last day at Beech Haven to help close it up for the winter.

✳　　✳　　✳　　✳

That fall Tim was at loose ends. He took Betty Ruppertal out in his mother's new car, but he wasn't really interested in her and she was frosty toward him for neglecting her all summer. "Hear anything from your Ohio friend?" she asked in the car on their way home from the theater in Ainsley where they saw *Angel and the Badman*, with John Wayne and Gail Russell, which neither of them could enjoy though both of them liked it. He had, in fact, heard from Helen. She wrote nearly every day, plaintive, desperate letters, to which he replied with a couple of terse, badly spelled letters in his schoolboyish hand. Anna sensed that something was wrong. He was curt and snarly toward Barb and Connie, which was totally unlike him, and he seemed to avoid Rick, which was contrary to the pattern of their entire life.

He worked at odd jobs. He hauled manure for Bayard Wentley. Late in the month he spent an afternoon helping to fight a brush fire in a field near Bagtown, for which he netted a princely $2.50. He went hunting almost every day, usually with someone else, either Jim Calder or Bill Friedle or Bill's brother Don. On November 15 he drove over to West Linton with several others to see *Forever Amber*. He didn't like it. It was too long and the way it treated immorality as humorous made him uneasy.

✳    ✳    ✳    ✳

*The Edgar Bergen and Charlie McCarthy Show*, with guest star Lana Turner, was on the air. Mortimer Snerd had just told Bergen that he had fallen in love with a store window manikin—"girlikin," he said.

Bergen: "My advice is to be cautious."

Mortimer: "Yuh, yuh, that's right, yuh."

Bergen: "Remember, a clever girl can make a fool out of you."

Mortimer: "Well, well. [Pause, sucking sound.] Well, what have I got to lose?"

The studio audience roared with laughter, but Tim, slouching in a stuffed chair in the living room, scarcely heard it. Sunk in despondency, he missed Charlie's description of taking a New York City bus for a joyride and trying to drive it through a tunnel too small for it.

Charlie: "I hollered low bridge, but the bus forgot to duck."

Bergen: "You tried to sandwich your way through?"

Charlie: "Exactly, sir. The bus went in a double-decker and came out an open-face."

Again the audience howled and still Tim sat motionless in the chair, mindlessly fiddling with one of the doilies that his Grandmother King had crocheted for the arms. He stared at the console radio's cloth-covered speaker, with its curlicues and whorls of wooden fretwork, as if it were an arabesque that had him mesmerized. Outside the pitch black November Sunday night was frigid and alive with tiny dancing snow pellets that ticked against the windows. Inside it was bright and warm with steam heat that dribbled from the radiator and dead with the heavy hand of misery that lay upon Timothy Arthur Davis.

The sound of the kitchen door opening and closing broke in on Tim's depressive reverie. That knob's loose, he thought; I keep meaning to fix it. He could hear Rick walking around, putting his coat into the closet, coming toward the living room.

"Mom home?" Rick asked, stepping in from the kitchen.

"No, she's still at church. Her and the girls. Some kind of meeting to decorate the church for Thanksgiving."

"You didn't go?"

"Yes, I did. This is just my ghost sitting here."

"Very funny, wise guy." Rick walked over to Tim's chair. "Hey, you OK? You look kinda down."

"I'm fine."

"Really?"

"Really."

"Yeah, fine, my fat fanny. Something's bothering you."

"Well, if you want to know, you can waddle your fat fanny over there and turn off that radio. That's what's bothering me."

"Whoa, don't bite my head off. I was just asking." Rick went over to the radio. "Hey, it's Charlie McCarthy. I thought you liked Charlie McCarthy."

"I hate and despise Charlie McCarthy. It's the stupidest fucking program that ever came down the pike. A ventriloquist on the radio. Next it'll be mimes for the blind. Christ!"

Rick looked back at Tim in amazement. Tim rarely used profanity or blasphemy. Even with the callowness of his seventeen years, Rick could recognize on Tim's face fear and bitterness and worry.

"Hey, man," Rick began, softly.

"Hey man what?" Anger, undiluted anger.

"What's wrong?"

"Helen broke up with me, that's what's wrong."

Rick looked at him quizzically. "This is a problem?"

"Hell, yes, it's a problem. Oh, I don't know, not a problem, exactly. It's a blow, like. It's so unexpected."

"What I mean is, were—*are*—you so attached to her that it's a problem?"

"Yes, I am, it is. I mean, I thought we understood what we were supposed to be doing. When she left we had an understanding. Kind of one, I thought, anyway."

"How'd you find out?"

Tim reached down into the space between his thigh and the side of the chair arm with his left hand and pulled out an envelope. He smacked it with his right. "I got this Wednesday. I've talked to her on the phone twice since then. She means it."

Rick stood with his hands tucked into his pants pocket and observed his brother. "And you're all broken up about it?"

Tim looked up. "What kind of a snide remark is that?"

"What I mean is, that letter is probably the latest in more than a dozen she's sent you. I know, I've seen the mail. Now, I'll admit that's maybe kind of excessive. But how many have you written to her?"

Tim glowered. "I'm not a letter-writing kind of guy."

"Neither am I. But I'll bet I'd write more than you have to a girl who, if I thought she'd break up with me, it would break my heart."

"You're just a fountain of compassion, aren't you?"

"What, compassion? I'm just telling you what I see. Did you write her? Hardly. Did you plan to go see her? I don't think so, not right away. Did you call her? Only when you got this letter. I know we're not the kind of family that makes expensive long-distance calls, but still."

"You seem to see a lot for a green high school kid."

"Look who's been so long out of high school himself."

Tim smiled. "It didn't take her long to dump me. Less than two months."

"Oh, dump, there's a choice word. Maybe she's a smart girl."

"Is there no end to your wisdom? A smart girl?"

"I mean maybe she's smart enough to recognize quickly a road going nowhere."

"And yet she said she cared for me. More than that."

"And what did you say to her?" Rick asked, sitting down on the hassock near Tim's chair. He sat with an elbow on each knee and his hands joined, looking down at the floor through the thus-formed triangle of air. He looked up. "Look, I don't know about love and all that stuff. I'm just a high school kid. But to her it could still be a road going nowhere, no matter how much you care."

Tim sighed. "Well, I guess you're right, Mr. Lonelyhearts. But you're wrong, too. I did—I *do*—care for Helen. But it's just that—I'm nineteen years old. I don't have a steady job. I want to do things. I want to go places. For that matter, she wants to do things. She plans to go to college."

"Her going to college next year doesn't stop you from writing her letters now."

"What are you, my conscience?"

"No, just my brother's keeper." Rick grinned.

"Well, keep it to yourself, little brother." Tim grinned back.

"What about Betty Ruppertal?"

"What *about* Betty Ruppertal?"

"I asked first. In fact, I remember asking you earlier this year, when you started at Beech Haven. You said she really liked you and you really liked her. And now you really like Helen."

"And a guy can't like two women?"

"I'm just wondering, since you seem to be in such a sweat about Helen."

Tim let out another sigh. "I don't know, Rick. Helen's special. If you want the truth, I think I might even be in love with her. But I can't get serious about it now. I just can't."

"Well, it's not for me to tell you what to do. Like I said, I'm only a high school kid. But you're right, Helen is special. She's really sweet, but she's, well, she's got a streak of toughness in her, too, from what I've seen. She's nobody's fool. Heck, maybe I'll go after her. She *is* a pretty hot number."

"I don't think she's interested in robbing the cradle. And she's not a hot number. She's a nice number." Tim thought for a couple of moments, then smiled with the memory. "Well, maybe kinda hot, sometimes."

"Does Mom know?"

"What, about the break-up?"

"Yeah."

"No, she doesn't. At least, I don't think so. I'm sure she suspects something's wrong, though. I haven't exactly been the soul of peace and harmony around here. I hope she thinks it's just because I don't know what to do with my life."

They sat in silence, listening to the snow hitting the windows and the creaks of the small house as it strained against the gusts of wind. After a couple of minutes there was the low growl of the Frazer coming into the driveway and then the sound of car doors slamming and women's voices.

Tim stood up. "That's another thing."

"What's that?"

"I've decided I've got to get out of here. I'm going up to Guldwyck and look for work. I can stay with Aunt Harriet. Or somebody. There's nothing for me here. I've got to get off the dime."

From the porch came the sounds of feet stomping and scraping.

"Now c'mon," Tim said. "Turn that radio back on. Act happy for Mom and the girls. Let's make this place seem less like a funeral parlor."

\*          \*          \*          \*

But, of course, Tim didn't leave right away. He hung around Black Run for the next few weeks, doing this and that. If it seems that he took the break-up with Helen relatively casually, it was simply in keeping with his make-up. He was cheerful and happy-go-lucky, as his friends said. Right now was important, not the past or future. And there was just a little bit of Helena as well as Helen in his attitude. Goethe's Mephistopheles told Faust: "Every wench is Helena to you." A girl might start out as Helena, but becomes less attractive by becoming available. If Tim was honest with himself, as he usually tried to be, he would have admitted this, if he would ever have thought of it, which he wouldn't, never having heard of Goethe, Faust, Mephistopheles, or Helena. Instead, his conscience simply twinged him that his behavior toward Helen was a little weasely and that what they had done was a sin.

The week after his conversation with Rick he went bear hunting. Three carloads of men went up toward Du Bois and spent a couple of days looking for bear, but none of them got anything. When he came back, he spent a lot of time checking his traps. And when December arrived, he went deer hunting every day for two weeks. One day he crippled a buck, but it got away and he never found it. Toward the middle of the month he went looking for a job at a sawmill, but there was nothing available. The next evening, the 17th, a Friday, he told his mother about his decision to leave for Guldwyck.

"Well, I can't say I'm surprised," Anna said, sitting with her hands clasped at the kitchen table. The bright, cheery light from the overhead lamp created soft shadows in the soft folds of her face. "You've been pretty antsy the last couple of months. I thought maybe it was over that Ohio girl."

"Who? Oh, you mean Helen?"

"Is there another Ohio girl?" A wry smile betrayed Anna's amusement.

"No, of course not. I mean, you're right. That is, about me being preoccupied with what I'm going to do. I guess I haven't been the best of company around here."

"Oh, Tim, that's not a problem. But I hate to see you go, even though I know you've been thinking about it. It does bother me that you have to go. Our family has been here in Somerton County for such a long time, and so many are still here. But so many have had to go away. Your father and I, and Morgan. And all the girls—Harriet and Eileen and Jean. It just seems so hard."

"I know, Mom, but what else am I going to do? There's nothing here, unless you want to be a farmer, and you can't be a farmer unless your father was a farmer. Not that I want to. I've hauled enough cow shit for Bayard Wentley and Lyle Calder to last me a lifetime."

"I wish you wouldn't use that vulgar word, Tim."

"When you've shoveled as much as I have, Mom, there's no other word for it."

Tim filled the remaining days of the year with a flurry of Christmas activities and preparations for his departure. Several nights he went to the Horton Methodist Church to practice for a Christmas Eve cantata. One whole day he spent playing basketball at the high school. He took Betty Ruppertal and two other girls—that did not please Betty at all—to Ainsley to see Betty Grable in *Mother Wore Tights*. Christmas Day much of the family came to their house to celebrate, as they often did, and the little place bulged. Amid the crush of familiar people, Anna could not help but think of Tim's imminent departure and was stricken by another attack of sorrow, which always seems to ride in tandem with joy.

"Oh dear," Anna said when she and Tim were for a moment alone in the overheated kitchen. "All this happiness going on and all I can think of is that you're going to leave in a few days." Tears welled in her eyes and she seemed to shrink within herself.

"Cheer up, Mom." Tim gave her shoulders a squeeze. "It's not that far away. And there's plenty of family in Guldwyck. Even Grandma and Aunt Elva are up there now, staying with Aunt Eileen and Dave for Christmas. You'll be up there to visit, I'll be down here to visit. It's not like I'm being drafted into the Army or anything."

"Oh, don't mention the draft."

"Mom, there's no draft."

"*Now* there's no draft. Who knows what the government will do? During the war they drafted boys as soon as they turned eighteen."

"Mom, there's no war."

"*Now* there's no war. I've lived through two world wars and I'm not quite forty years old. I know forty sounds ancient to you, but it's not a long time."

For reply, Tim pulled a long, demented-looking face at his mother, to indicate that the subject was getting out of hand. Anna smiled.

"I hope when you're up to Guldwyck you'll continue to go to church."

"I will, Mom. You know I like church."

"You could go with Harriet or Jean or Eileen or any of them. They'll introduce you."

"I will. Don't worry."

"We've always felt church was important, even your father did. You know your name means 'honoring God,' don't you?"

"No, really?" Tim jumped backward, as if jolted by startling news. "'Davis' means honoring God? Gosh, why didn't you ever tell me that before?"

"'Timothy' does. You know better. I've told you. I'm just reminding you. It doesn't hurt to be reminded."

Two days after Christmas a severe snowstorm slammed the Northeast, stalling trains and stranding commuters all across the region. It left the whole county isolated for two days. Tim didn't mind. During the day he went sledding with Barb and Connie, and at night he listened to the radio and pulled together the things he wanted to take with him to Guldwyck.

# CHAPTER 8

▼

# IT ONLY TAKES ONE

*Old soldiers never die, they just fade away.*

—General Douglas MacArthur

Eddie Fisher entered the U.S Army the same day that General MacArthur effectively left it. The singer—born Edwin Jack Fisher in 1928, only a few months after Tim's birth—was drafted April 11, 1951, as President Truman was recalling MacArthur from his imperial post in Japan for being an arrogant, preening, insubordinate son-of-a-bitch who thought he should be president, if not God, and who wanted to take nuclear war into China. If those were not Truman's exact words, that was his attitude, though officially he said he relieved MacArthur of his command because he was "unable to give his wholehearted support to the policies of the United States government and of the United Nations" and designated Lieutenant General Matthew Bunker Ridgway as his successor. Tim and his comrades didn't hear about Fisher until some days later, but they heard about MacArthur right away, and it caused a stir.

Tim's squad leader, a big corporal in his late twenties named Sbarra, said, wryly, that it was no big deal; MacArthur was just being rotated.

"I mean, the guy's been out here, what, six years? Twelve or more, if you count since the beginning of the last war. He's way overdue to go back to the Land of the Big Round Eyes and Off-the-Floor Beds," Sbarra said. He plopped a chunk of chocolate bar from a C-ration into his mouth and rolled the wrapping paper into a little ball and flipped it into a corner of the bunker in which they were sitting.

"Hey, corporal, watch it with the littering," Warren said. "I just vacuumed this place. But I think I forgot to hang up an Air Wick. It smells like mold and burnt heat tabs in here."

"And a few other things. Do they make Air Wick in a ten-pound size?" Sbarra said. "Actually you're right, soldier, though as usual you don't know it." Sbarra leaned out from his perch on a grenade crate and, stretching, picked up the paper ball. "No reason to provide more temptations for rats in our lovely home away from home."

"Yeah, like one piece of paper is going to make a difference. The rats got this place staked out as rodent paradise." Warren let his gaze sweep the bunker's small interior, ending with the 8-inch-by-8-inch pine beams of the ceiling, above which were layers and layers of sandbags. "I should write my congressman. I wonder what he'd say if he knew about this dump?"

"The thing is, how many times has he crossed the 38$^{th}$ Parallel?" Tim asked no one in particular.

"Who? My congressman? He ain't been out of Brooklyn since 1943, except to go to Washington to pick up his paycheck. He wouldn't know the 38$^{th}$ Parallel from 42$^{nd}$ Street."

"No, I mean MacArthur. He's the one who made this into a yo-yo war." Rumors had circulated that the first contingents of veteran troops were soon to be rotated back to the States, and the joke going around the first battalion—indeed, around the 2$^{nd}$ Division and the entire U.S. Army in Korea—was that eligibility for rotation would depend on the number of times a man had crossed the 38th Parallel that divided North and South Korea. Communist and U.N. troops had chased each other up and down the Korean Peninsula so many times in the past ten months that GIs were calling it the yo-yo war, ping-pong war, the seesaw war, the accordion war.

"And we're the biggest yo-yos of them all for getting caught in it," said another member of Tim's squad, a 19-year-old PFC from Illinois named Jansen.

"Jansen, you never had it so good. You found a home in the Army." Sbarra turned his attention to Tim. "Thing that got MacArthur in trouble was, it was the Yalu that he wanted to cross, not just the 38$^{th}$ Parallel. Harry S wasn't having any of that. The Wet Roadblock was just that as far as Harry was concerned, and Goonyland is off-limits to U.S. Army personnel."

"How do you think Ridgway will do?" Tim asked.

"Old Iron Tits?" Sbarra said, using the GIs' nickname derived from Ridgway's practice of wearing a grenade on one front strap of his webbing and a medical pack on the other, so that they hung on each side of his chest. "We'll be fine with him. Look how he brought 8<sup>th</sup> Army back from the dead. Look how Operation Killer took the initiative away from the Chicoms, in February, about the time you joined the company. We'll be fine with Matt Ridgway."

\*        \*        \*        \*

Tim had missed Ridgway's Operation Killer, a counteroffensive aimed at driving the North Koreans and Chinese Communists out of South Korea, but he made its successor/subsidiary, Operation Ripper. Not long after, military PR specialists sensitive to the savage implications of words like Killer and Ripper—however appropriate they might be to the situation—began giving operations more high-sounding names like Courageous, Rugged, and Dauntless. But it was a fire-fight in Operation Ripper, which had taken the life of the Mailman and Clair's Lieutenant Perreault, that had given Tim his baptism of fire.

After that Tim's battalion and regiment endured a grueling slog northward in weather that alternated spring thaws with rains and sub-zero freezing. Starting from the Arizona Line, which stretched roughly east-west south of Changbong-ni and north of Wonju, 2<sup>nd</sup> Division soldiers moved northward past a series of lines whose familiar names accumulated in their heads—Phoenix, Albany, Reno, Idaho, Texas, Maine. The enemy was slowly pushed back toward Yudong-ni, despite enjoying easily defensible terrain, but not without inflicting casualties through increased use of land mines and booby traps. U.N. forces, including Republic of Korea (ROK) Army units, crossed the Han River south of Seoul to outflank the capital to the east, seeking to advance to the 38<sup>th</sup> Parallel along a fifty-mile front. The enemy abandoned Seoul, and by the first of April, 8<sup>th</sup> Army's front-line divisions, including the 2<sup>nd</sup>, had moved forward seventy miles and reached the Parallel.

It was while the 88th Regiment was moving forward to the Reno line to relieve a regimental combat team that the first official word trickled down that a rotation system was being worked out. The effect on morale was electric, even though actual rotation would not happen for some time. The Navy and Marines already had rotation plans in place and the fact that the Army did not had left troops grumbling.

"Not that it'll mean anything to us," Warren said to the back of Tim's head as they walked in single file along the side of the road. "We just got here. We'll be here till 1956."

"You think we'll get home that soon?" Tim replied. He turned his head to glance back at Warren. "Did you see that roadside sign, I think it was the day before yesterday? It was like Burma-Shave signs, you know? Four in a row, one right after another, with a poem. It said, 'Slow Down, Joe/Curve Ahead/No Rotation/If You're Dead.'"

"I guess we're safe, then, going everywhere on foot. Our speed ain't likely to get out of control. No, I didn't see that, but I saw a poster. It showed a GI driving a jeep glaring at one of our Little Friends, an old gook all bent over under his idiot board, who was blocking the jeep's way. It said, 'Keep your shirt on. After all, it's *his* road.' I had to laugh. Where does the Army come up with these ideas? Not only are we supposed to get shot at on their behalf, we're supposed to be polite about it. *His* road? You know what? He could keep his road and I could tell him where."

The two men fell silent. They trudged past Sergeant Paden standing by the side of the road, his head down talking into the Prick-6, the PRC-6 walkie-talkie, but apparently getting no response. Behind them they heard Jansen softly humming the "Bugout Boogie," the alternative version of Hank Snow's "Moving On," which had become an unofficial anthem of the war after the 2nd Division's disaster at Kunu-ri in northwestern Korea at the end of November. As Jansen passed Paden, the sergeant told him to knock it off. Jansen protested, but Paden said the song was bad for morale and disrespectful to the division. When Jansen tried to protest further that he wasn't even singing words, just humming, Paden warned him he'd be in deep kimchi if he didn't cease and desist.

"You hear that, Davis? You can't even sing in this man's Army anymore," Warren said, but not loudly, because he didn't want to get in trouble with Paden, whom he respected.

The sergeant was in no mood. Still acting platoon leader, because no officer replacement had yet been found, he was daily harassed by the responsibility of dozens of pesky details he was growing weary of taking care of. In one respect things had grown better. Division had received intelligence reports that the North Koreans and Chinese Communists were withdrawing to a Main Line of Resistance (MLR) north of the 38th, so that the threat of combat was reduced. On the other hand, B Company and other companies in the regiment found themselves increasingly being ordered to send out patrols, which had a wearying and dispiriting effect.

"Luke the Gook and Old Joe Chink are still out there, trying to find a chink in our armor, no pun intended," Paden told the men at a platoon meeting. Regimental headquarters encouraged briefings as often as possible, because in an absence of information, rumors and complaints ballooned. "The only way to find out what they're up to is patrols, so we go out on patrols. I know we've been getting them UTA, and I don't like it any more than you do, but that's the way it is for now." Finished, Paden set his mouth in a grim line, registering I Don't Want to Hear About It.

"UTA, up to the ass, *my* ass," Warren said. "We been getting them UTE, up to the eyeballs."

"I don't know, I don't mind patrols that much," Tim said. "It's something to do. You get away from things."

"'Get away from things?' What d'you think a patrol is, two weeks in the Catskills?"

"Well, you have to admit, we've been lucky in B Company. We haven't had any casualties on patrols."

"Well, you know the Rifleman's Creed."

"'*It only takes one to kill you.*'" Tim, grinning, chanted the well-worn saying in unison with his friend. "Still, it's true. We haven't even come across any Chinks or gooks. No one's been hurt."

"I'll give you that, aside from freezing our fingers off, and other things. Which makes me think, you got any jerkoff lotion left? I'm all out."

Tim smiled again. They used Jergen's hand lotion to relieve cracking and soreness from the bitter cold, and almost the only way to get it was in the mail from home.

"No, I don't. In my next letter I'll ask Mom or Peg to send me some. I'd like to know what they'd think if they knew what we call it."

"Rachel would slap my face if I told her. Jerkoff lotion, ha! You know what my uncle told me they used to say back in the big war? 'I used to think of my wife as my right hand. Now I think of my right hand as my wife.'"

\*     \*     \*     \*

On one of their night patrols at this time, Tim's squad came across sixteen American soldiers who for a short time had been prisoners of the Chinese. It was a fairly warm night in late March, but fortunately cool enough that they were traversing hard earth and not mud; the moon was up but not very bright because of scattered cloud cover. They were creeping along the southeastern edge of a ridge, being even more cautious about noise than usual because Chinese were believed to be in the area. They were bent over, trying to keep their heads below the ridge line as they moved along when Russ Caldwell, the point man, frantically waved back at Sbarra, the squad leader, motioning him to hold up the line. Tim was crouched directly behind Sbarra. Caldwell scurried the few steps back to Sbarra.

"Hold up, corporal, I think I heard something," Caldwell whispered.

"It's probably your own goddam rifle sling. I heard it. I told you and told you about that."

"No, no. This was right on the other side of the ridge. Like someone moving around."

"You sure?" Sbarra stared fiercely into Caldwell's 20-year-old face. "Don't clank up on me now."

"Yes, I'm sure. Maybe voices too."

"Right." Sbarra turned around to Tim, preparatory to ordering the squad to fan out, when they heard definite voices on the other side of the ridge.

"Jesus." Sbarra looked questioningly at Tim.

"Don't shoot," a voice said from other side of the ridge. 'Don't shoot. We're Americans."

"Jesus," Sbarra repeated. "Caldwell, give them the password."

"Old Ironsides," Caldwell croaked. He pulled his M-1 up close to his side, ready to fire. The response was to be "Constitution"—for USS Constitution, the formal name of Old Ironsides, the Revolutionary War and War of 1812 U.S. warship docked in Boston Harbor.

"We don't know the password," came the voice, sounding frighteningly loud in the clear night air. "We're prisoners of war. The Chinks let us go. Help us, please. We've got wounded, some of 'em bad."

Sbarra looked at Tim again. "What do you think, Davis? The goonies let POWs go? That doesn't sound right. Could be a trick by the goonies themselves."

Tim didn't know what to say. Weirdly, scenes from war movies came into his head. Should they ask them which league the Red Sox are in? He realized how absurd that sounded.

"Please," the voice said. "Help us. A couple of us won't make it if we don't get medical help hyakoo, and I mean it."

"I think they're legit, corporal," Tim said. Somehow the Japanese word hya-koo—hurry up, pretty soon—convinced him they couldn't be Chinese; it was just too common among American troops. "I think you ought to tell them to show themselves and we'll hold fire. A Chicom's not going to stick his head over that ridge and get it blown off."

"Maybe you're right." Acting on Tim's suggestion, Sbarra barely could get the words out before the members of the 1$^{st}$ squad, 1$^{st}$ platoon, Company B, 1$^{st}$ Battalion, 88th Regiment, 2$^{nd}$ Division found themselves staring up at the haggard, bewhiskered, pain-lined face of an American prisoner of war looming brokenly above the ridge.

When they brought the sixteen POWs to the battalion area, it was discovered that four were so badly injured they required immediate evacuation by helicopter. The remaining twelve were preliminarily interrogated by intelligence officers before being evacuated by a deuce-and-a-half. All were medically unfit, either by reason of wounds or malnutrition or both. The sixteen had been captured during the Chinese advance on Hoengsong in February and were part of a group of 800 prisoners being marched northward.

The next night, as they strolled off by themselves after watching the movie *Harvey*, which had been set up for B Company in the mess tent, Clair asked Tim if he had had a chance to talk with the POWs.

"Not really," Tim replied. He had trouble focusing on what Clair was saying, because he couldn't get the vision of one of the actresses, Peggy Dow, out of his mind. "On the way back we observed silence, of course. Anyway, they were all in such bad shape it was about all they could do to walk, let alone talk."

"Did they say anything about how they was treated?"

"Yeah, they did. Most of what I know, though, isn't what I heard from them but what I picked up from what I heard of their interrogation."

"How was it? Was it bad?" Clair's voice expressed fearful concern, because they all had heard stories of savage treatment of American prisoners of war, and capture was nearly as frightening a prospect as wounding or death.

"It was bad enough, I guess. It sounds like they were on a real death march."

"It was the Chinks?"

"Yes. There were North Koreans with them"—Tim still only reluctantly used the term "gooks"—"but the Chicoms were definitely in charge."

"That's a blessing." Clair laughed bitterly. "Blessing! What a word to use. But I've heard old Luke the Gook is a real bastard with POWs."

"Well, you have to say it was a blessing they were let go, and it was the Chinese who did it. What happened was, they were marching north—this was a whole bunch of guys, hundreds, even some British—and they had stopped to rest in some village. Mostly they traveled by night, to avoid our planes. But they got caught in a daytime bombing raid. It was our own planes that wounded them, that's the awful part."

"I know. That's happened before. But I love to see them planes go over. I wouldn't want them to stop. Every time I see one of them Mustangs or F-86s, the Sabrejets, I wave."

"So what happened," Tim continued, "the Chinese couldn't handle wounded on the march. They told them they would have to be left behind. They gave them letters to show to any other Chicoms or ... or gooks they came across, letters ordering them not to be molested in any way."

"Right." Clair's sarcasm was thick. "I'll bet them pieces of paper did a lot of good."

"No, apparently they did. The POWs remained in the house where they got hit by the planes, and in the next couple of weeks both Chink and gook units came by and questioned and threatened them, but after reading the letters, left them alone. It makes me think of the brutal way our guys were treated by the Japs. No pieces of paper from them. The Japs would've marched the wounded till they died."

"And beat them with their rifles if they didn't die quick enough. Still, it couldn't've been no picnic. How'd they end up where you found them?"

"After a while they decided they were pressing their luck with those letters, that sooner or later some enemy unit would come by that wouldn't honor them and they'd be on the march again to probably a POW camp or worse. No one wanted that. And some of the wounded would never have survived it. Since no American unit had found them in that time, they all agreed to take a chance on going out to find one. And they did. Us."

"That was pure luck. They could as easily have stumbled onto the goonies or gooks. How'd they get captured in the first place?"

"I'm not sure. These sixteen were from among I don't know how many units that got overrun by the Chinese, so they had a lot of different stories. They weren't all captured by the same group of Reds. Several of them, though, said there was a Chicom major who ordered their hands tied behind their backs with wire. Then he interrogated most of them, I guess you could call it, right there on the spot."

"What'd he ask them?"

"Oh, all kinds of things. More than just name, rank, and service number. Things like the name of their outfit, where it was located, their hometown. Some of the guys admitted they told more than they were supposed to—name, rank, number."

Clair cleared his throat, looked off to the side, and spit on the ground. "Well, I won't judge them, not from here. I don't know what I'd do in that situation. Shit my pants, first thing, probably."

"They also asked personal and political-type questions. What did they think of communism? Why were they in the Army? What were they doing in this country? They were smart enough to give noncommittal answers—they didn't know anything about it, they were drafted, and so on. A couple, though, said something like they were here to liberate Korea. I guess the major slapped them around for that, said they'd need re-education.

"There was a ROK officer, a captain, with them, too. He didn't fare so well, if you can call what happened to them faring well. The Chinks despise the ROKs, of course. And the North Koreans—there were North Koreans with the Chinks—and when they got done with the ROK captain...."

"They killed him? Right there?"

"Not before they really worked him over. The Chink major spat in his face and slapped him. Then the gooks started jabbering away at him. One of them smashed his rifle butt right in his face. When the ROK was on the ground, they stabbed him in the legs with their bayonets. They laughed when he tried to scurry away from them, blood spurting all over from his leg wounds. This is one of the things I did hear from a POW himself. He couldn't believe what he was seeing. The gooks beat him with their rifles some more, and when he tried to get up, one of them kicked him right square in the temple with the toe of his boot."

"And the Chink major didn't do nothing?"

"Yeah, he did. This POW said he pulled out his pistol, leaned down, whispered something to the gook who was on all fours on the ground, put the pistol against the back of his head, and blew his brains out."

Neither man said a thing for a long spell. The momentary silence in the company area was, for a war zone, unearthly. It was cool and damp out; night dew hung in the air.

Clair sighed. "That's just like your Oriental, Tim. They got no respect or understanding for the sanctity of individual human life. No wonder they can withstand pain a lot better than we can. They've had to learn to. Hell, I heard that ROK medical officers have performed amputations in the field without anesthesia. Myself I *seen* ROK officers discipline soldiers with slaps and punches, and once I saw a ROK general dress down a colonel by cuffing him up side the head. I heard too that sometimes generals don't even bother with court-martials—just go ahead and try, sentence, and execute all in one go."

"Efficient."

"You got that right." Clair could not see Tim's wry smile in the dark. He lifted his rifle, which had been resting against his leg, butt-down on the ground, preparing to go back to his own platoon. "Say, Tim, what'd you think of that movie tonight?"

"*Harvey*? I liked it. I liked it a lot. Very funny. That old lady, Jimmy Stewart's sister, fluttering around. Made me forget the war for a while, anyway."

"Well, maybe. But I don't know. Invisible, six-foot-tall rabbits. Kind of silly. Give me a good Western. We had *The Gunfighter* before you came to the company. That was *some* movie. And *King Solomon's Mines*. That wasn't a Western, but that was OK."

# CHAPTER 9

▼

# INDEPENDENCE,
# DEPENDENCE

*Nobody who has not been in the interior of a family can say what the difficulties of any individual of that family may be.*

—Jane Austen, *Emma*

Tim arrived at the Albany train station shortly before midnight on January 4, 1948, a Sunday. It was bitter cold and there was twenty-five inches of snow on the ground, some of it remaining from the storm that struck the East Coast at the end of the year.

His last few days at home he hung out with Ron and Bill Friedle, Jim Calder, and a few others, soaking up as much as he could of relationships that were about to be sundered. It rained all New Year's Day, and the next day it turned to snow, but only three inches—not enough to keep them from driving to Somerton city to see Clark Gable and Ava Gardner in *The Hucksters*. The third he spent by himself or with his family, going into Horton only long enough to do some last-minute shopping for his trip.

On the fourth Tim got up before daylight and finished his packing. Rick woke up too and sat in the room watching him move about as he picked up this thing and that and asking if there was anything he could do, which there wasn't. The whole family ate a silent and gloomy breakfast together, and when Tim couldn't bear it any longer he said he guessed it was time they drove over to Altoona to catch the train. Barb and Connie burst into tears and refused to go, so Anna and Rick took him themselves.

He was met at the Albany station by Dave Burnham, who was married to his Aunt Eileen, Anna's younger sister. The Burnhams had lived in the Albany-Guldwyck area for many years, having moved down from the Adirondacks before Dave was born. Dave had met Eileen after she had made the move north from Black Run to Guldwyck to do service work at Alma Blaine College like her sisters. They married in 1941, and in 1943 their first daughter, Arlene, was born, and then eighteen months later their second daughter, Dorothy. Eileen gave up her job when Arlene was born. Dave, who drove a bakery truck when they got married, now worked as a tool and die maker at the Watervliet Arsenal.

"How's Aunt Eileen?" Tim asked after they had stowed all his luggage in the trunk and back seat of Dave's black, two-door 1940 Ford. Though many of their aunts and uncles were only scant years older than they, Tim and Rick and the girls sometimes still called them Aunt or Uncle, particularly when sensitive or formal issues were at hand. It was a family habit.

"Not too good, Tim," Dave said, pulling the car away from the station and entering the thin dribble of midnight traffic. Since the end of the war Eileen had been seriously and it seemed progressively ill with a lung ailment, which eluded both exact diagnosis and treatment. At times she was confined to bed.

"Gee, I'm sorry to hear that, Dave." God, Tim thought, did that sound lame: *Gee, I'm sorry to hear that.* I'm almost twenty years old and I'm always saying "gee" or "gosh." In the faint light from the dash he observed his uncle as he drove. He's only—what?—seven, eight years older than me, and look what he has to contend with: a beautiful wife who's bedridden and can't properly take care of their two lively young daughters.

Dave had turned onto Lattimer Street, which led out of Albany into Guldwyck. Lattimer ran into one of the main streets of Guldwyck, Raleigh Avenue, where the Burnhams lived in an apartment.

"Do they know any more what's wrong with her?" Tim asked. Man, was this difficult to talk about!

"I don't think so, to tell you the truth. The latest thing is they're calling it bronchiectasis. That's kind of an enlargement of the bronchial tubes. That's just to give it a name, if you ask me. I don't think they know any more than they did two, three years ago, when all of this started. We're seriously asking ourselves if we shouldn't try moving to the Southwest—Arizona, maybe—to see if the dry climate might be better for her."

"Is that what the doctors recommend?"

"Oh, it's like everything else. They're never certain. It might help and it might not. At least it couldn't hurt, they say."

"That's a long way to go on the strength of only, 'At least it couldn't hurt.'"

"You're telling me," Dave said, a hint of anger in his voice.

"Well, go—"—Tim swallowed the "gosh" and continued—"I sure appreciate you letting me stay with you a while, at least till I get a room and a job. I hope it won't be too inconvenient. I hope I won't be in the way. I mean, in a small apartment with Au-, with Eileen not feeling well and the girls."

"Oh, no. Don't even think about it, Tim." Dave turned onto Raleigh Avenue and glanced quickly at Tim for the first time since starting to drive. He smiled, and the smile's warmth came through the ghoulish cast given it by the dim glow of the dash lights. "My mother helps take care of Arlene and Dorothy, that's no problem. And it'll be company for Eileen to have you around. Besides, you know how tight knit this whole family is. They were fighting over who would have the privilege of having you stay with them—Eileen and Jean and Harriet, even my family. Gosh, it almost came to blows."

"Gosh." Tim relaxed into the seat back. What a family. Gosh.

⚹    ⚹    ⚹    ⚹

Was there ever a more delightful time to be alive in the Republic than this year of 1948? Relative peace and far-less-relative prosperity continued to reign. Strikes were few, labor-management relations fairly mellow, and increased defense expenditures and foreign aid programs helped keep the national engine running. Auto workers received about $1.60 an hour and construction workers—the highest hourly wage earners in the U.S.—about $2.10. A new Ford sedan sold for $1,236 and a Chevrolet convertible for $1,750.

A ferment of postwar ideas and activities roiled the nation, some of them serious, many of them goofy. The day after Tim arrived in Albany, President Truman announced his Fair Deal program in his State of the Union message. It was also the official publication date of Alfred C. Kinsey's *Sexual Behavior in the American Male*, a nominally dry and professorial tome by a Hoosier zoologist that might in the normal academic way of things be expected to sell a respectable couple thousand copies but that by the first week of March had passed 200,000. Kinsey and his work would continue all that year and for years to come to be the subject of conversations, jokes, and cartoons. ("Is there a Mrs. Kinsey?" asked a cartoon in *The New Yorker*. Yes, there is, answered a headline in *McCall's*.) Whatever controversial things people were telling Prof. Kinsey they were getting up to, they were telling Dr. Gallup something different and more traditional. An eleven-nation poll at this time revealed that 94 percent of Americans professed belief in God. Tim certainly numbered himself among them.

Radio was still the dominant medium—900 new stations in the last two years alone—but 1948 was the springboard year for television's eventual supplanting of it. Albany had one of the country's 37 stations and a few hundred of its 350,000 TV sets. Many long-running programs or performers made their debut. Ed Sullivan's very first program included as guests Dean Martin and Jerry Lewis, an emerging comedy duo whose frantic antics, silly and at the same time sophisticated, would capture the postwar years perfectly. Tim spent a lot of time watching TV—particularly another favorite on the new medium, Milton Berle—at the home of old friends, the Nicholses, whom his parents had known in their days Upstate and who now were one of the few families willing to shell out the stiff price of $300 for a set.

Alexander Aberle, a self-styled yogi from Brooklyn who called himself eden ahbez and thought that only deities' names should be capitalized, left a song for Nat King Cole at the stage door of a California theater and it became one of Cole's signature tunes, *Nature Boy*. Walt Kelly's comic strip *Pogo* debuted in the New York *Star*, but it was too sophisticated to be picked up by the prosaic Guldwyck evening daily, the *Standard*, which did, however, run another brand-new strip that became Tim's favorite, *Rex Morgan, M.D.*

Communism blew into the year and the country just as snow blew into January and Upstate New York. The country, with the help of Whittaker Chambers, reacted strongly against this alien ideology threatening its highly unusual stability and prosperity. Even the astronomers seemed to prefer stability. For the first time since the 1920s they began seriously disputing the "big bang" theory of the formation of the universe, arguing instead for the "steady state" theory of a universe expanding at a constant rate.

But most of this was in the immediate future, and though some of it was pushing Tim toward his own future, for the moment his personal universe was quite small, consisting of a few streets around Raleigh Avenue in Guldwyck, New York.

*        *        *        *

Tim discovered for himself just how terribly sick Eileen was. She was asleep when he and Dave got to the apartment the night of his arrival, a small, two-bedroom apartment on the second floor at 613 Raleigh Avenue. Dave and Eileen had one bedroom, Arlene and Dorothy the other. Tim bunked down on a frayed pull-out couch in the living room. He didn't see his aunt until the next morning, Monday, after Dave had left for work, taking the girls with him to drop off at his mother's. After finishing his breakfast of corn flakes and coffee, he went to the bedroom where Eileen spent many of her days.

"Eileen?" Tim cautiously peeped around the doorjamb, as if reluctant to disturb her.

"Tim!" she exclaimed, joy animating her thin face. She sat propped up in pillows in the bed, constructed of a kind of fat, brown-metal tubing with an elaborate design painted in dull yellow on the headboard. A pink bedjacket covered her ample King-family bosom, which illness had done nothing to diminish. She extended her arms, inviting an embrace.

Tim walked over to the bed, leaned down and accepted the hug, at the same time bussing her lightly on the left cheek. When he pulled back and she looked up at him, he could see the paleness of her face and the frailty of her frame. Despite that, she was a strikingly pretty woman, particularly her eyes, which, oddly, were both bright and soft, an appealing quality that seemed to exude understanding. Her sincere smile expressed her delight at seeing him. It occurred to Tim, not for the first time, how filled his life was with pleasant, lovely women.

"Tim, how wonderful to see you." With her right hand Eileen lightly kept a grip on Tim's right hand as he stood at the bedside.

"It's great to see you, too, Eileen. Awful nice of you to let me stay here. It'll just be for a little while, till I find a room or something."

"Nonsense. Stay as long as you want. A new face is a nice change. I'm stuck in here too much. How's Anna?"

"Mom's fine. She starts back to work today after Christmas vacation."

"I'll bet she hated to see you leave."

"Yeah, she did. But she also understands. I've got to find work and there's no work in Somerton County, at least not anything I want to do. Seems like everyone in our family comes up here. Mom and I were talking about that." Tim slipped his hand out of Eileen's grasp and slid his hands into the tops of his hip pockets. He looked at Eileen determinedly, as if this were the way to show deep interest in a topic he really wanted to avoid. "So how are you feeling?"

"Pretty well. You know. Some days good, some days not so good. I just wish they knew what was wrong with me. Sometimes it leaves me with no strength, like the last few days. Other times I'm almost normal, up and about doing things. But there are others worse off than me. Polio, for instance. I worry about Arlene and Dorothy during the hot weather. Polio's a lot more widespread now than when your sister Barbara got it. Though *that* was a scare. It's a blessing she got off as lightly as she did. Does she still limp?"

"Yes. A little bit. Not too bad."

"Actually, it's Dave I feel bad for. I feel my illness must be such a strain on him."

"He doesn't seem to let it bother him."

"No, he doesn't. He's such a sweet guy. Look how he indulges me." With her right hand she indicated a small portable record player sitting on the chest of drawers. "He shouldn't do it. We really can't afford it, and I have the radio. But he knows I like music. He buys me records all the time." She swung around in bed and sorted through a small stack of 78s until she found what she was looking for, a record with an RCA label.

"I especially like this one." She handed it to Tim.

Tim read the label. "I Wish I Didn't Love You So." Vaughn Monroe. I've heard it. I like it too."

"Sometimes I think it expresses the way I feel about Dave. Or maybe the way I wonder if Dave feels about me. If he didn't care about me so, maybe he wouldn't feel like he had to be saddled with this burden." She shook her head to shake away the melancholy tendency of her thoughts. "Oh dear, listen to me going on to my nephew about love. It's from a movie that's nothing like the sadness of the song. *The Perils of Pauline*. Very funny. Dave took me to see it. Betty Hutton's in it."

"I know. I saw it. Betty Hutton's good." Tim looked at Eileen quizzically. "This is the strangest thing. I know another girl who's got a record player almost a copy of this one. She's got quite a record collection also. Caroline Ollinger. Well, you probably remember her father, Arnie Ollinger. Owns the Horton Pharmacy."

"You probably know a lot of girls."

"Not so many."

"Go on. A good-looking young man like you. I heard from Anna there was a special someone you met at Beech Haven. A girl from Ohio."

"That's over with."

"Oh?"

"We broke up." Tim looked away. "It just didn't work out."

Tim was uncomfortable talking about such matters with Eileen. Despite their being family, he didn't know her all that well. When she was growing up with her sisters and Grandma and Grandpa King and the rest of her family in Somerton County, Tim and his family were living in the Albany area. Then, about the time that Anna and the children moved back to Black Run from Albany, Eileen moved up to Albany.

But there was something else besides the lack of familiarity that troubled him. Was he attracted to her? His own aunt? His *sick* aunt? But sick as she was, she was still darn pretty. And she was—what?—seven or eight years older? Same age as Dave, was Tim's guilty thought. Good grief, he thought after left the apartment, what was wrong with him? "Heartbreaker," she had called him.

*     *     *     *

The next day, Tuesday, Dave Burnham took off from work and drove Tim around to view the Albany-Guldwyck area and visit relatives. Harriet, Tim's aunt, went along, and so did Grandma King and Elva, who were staying with Harriet. Like her sisters Eileen and Jean, Harriet had lived in the Albany area since the 1930s. That night they had supper at Harriet's and Tim took a short walk around Watervliet, where Harriet lived.

The day after that, Tim settled down to look for work. He looked through the want ads of the Albany *Times Union* and the Guldwyck *Standard* and put his name in at the union office in Guldwyck. When Dave came home from work that night, he told Tim that a co-worker had told him about a job possibility at the box factory that was only a block from Dave's house. So on Thursday morning Tim went over to see about it and the personnel guy told him to come in on Monday, which made him feel good.

But he never went to work there because that night he decided to look up the Clays. He was having supper at his Aunt Jean's when the subject came up. Jean was married to Leon Kammer, a naturally sour young man of intellectual inclinations made even sourer by the low-level clerical job he held in the state government in Albany, and they lived in an apartment complex in Guldwyck with their son, Anthony. The three of them had already eaten and Anthony was in his room and Leon was sitting in an easy chair reading the *Standard* in the living room part of their combined living room-dining room. The radio, sitting on top of a bookcase, was on low and Tim could hear a bouncy singing commercial: "Use Wildroot Cream Oil, Cha-a-a r-lie, it keeps your hair in trim." Jean was serving Tim warmed-up pork roast when she mentioned that she had happened to run into Frank Clay a few days ago when she was over in Albany shopping and she thought that was probably only the second or third time she had seen him since the terrible time of Tim's father's accident.

"He's such a nice man," Jean said to Tim. "You knew Ruth, his wife, passed away, didn't you?"

"No, I didn't," said Tim, who hadn't really thought about the Clays since moving from Albany. But Jean's mention of them brought a flood of memories to his mind and a spurt of excitement to his chest. Suddenly he remembered young Frank with great clarity and fondness.

"Yes, she did," Jean said, as if the fact of death were after all in dispute and needed affirmation. Her tone was typically calm and soothing. "I'm not sure what she died of. But that poor man. All those children to raise on his own. Twelve. Of course, some of the older ones are grown now, but still."

"Where do they live now?" Tim asked.

"I'm not exactly certain. Somewhere out on Albany Shaker Road, near the airport."

"I think I'll try and look them up. I remember I used to play all the time with young Frank when we lived upstairs from them in Albany."

"Twelve kids?" said Leon, rustling the opened newspaper that separated him from his wife and nephew-in-law. "It's obvious what the poor woman died of. Exhaustion."

Jean was silent for a couple of seconds as she stared a hole in Leon's newspaper. "My mother had twelve children, you know, and she's perfectly all right."

"Are you sure?" Leon said, without lowering his paper shield.

"Oh Lee," Jean said.

*     *     *     *

Tim located them the very next day, Friday. They did live on Albany Shaker Road, in a not-small house that nevertheless bulged with Clays. They took to him immediately, as if not nine years but only nine days had passed, and he to them. Especially with Frank's older sister, Stella. She was so lively and flirtatious she was able to persuade Tim to get up and dance to songs on the radio. They even tried to dance to Vaughn Monroe's "Ballerina," which was stuck at the top of the charts and stations constantly were playing, but it was impossible and they ended up in a fit of giggling. Tim stayed there overnight, sleeping on a sofa, and the next morning at breakfast Frank Senior said he'd try and get Tim into the Allegheny Ludlum Steel plant in Watervliet, where he worked.

\*       \*       \*       \*

Jan. 31 (Saturday)

Dear Mother,

Thank you for the birthday card and the $10, but you didn't have to do that because I am doing all right now. It arrived right on my birthday, the 21st——how did you make that happen, what with the mail? Also thanks for the clothes you sent before that. I am making good use of them.

I'm sorry I didn't write sooner but you know me and writing letters. Probably Grandma and Aunt Elva told you about me here when they came home, but I'll try and fill you in on what's happened. At least until I get sick of writing, which could come soon, like I said.

Speaking of what's happened, did you read the news about that Ghandi fellow in India yesterday? Somebody assasinated him. I think that's terrible. I always kind of liked him, what I read anyway. Funny, Orville Wright died the same day. Two great men.

The news here is that it's <u>VERY</u> cold. It said on the radio this morning that it was minus 40 degrees in the Albany area. Some kind of record, I guess. It's been cold for almost two weeks now. I'm glad I didn't have to work unloading freight cars today, I would have froze my tail off. I worked cleaning the grinding rooms, the dustiest job in the plant but at least it was inside.

Working at the steel plant is pretty good. The hours are kind of crazy but that's okay—I'm a new guy, that's why, and I'm greatful to Frank Clay for getting me in there. I've been seeing a lot of the Clays, I've stayed at their house a couple of nights. They've changed a lot from the way I remember them, Mrs. Clay passed away, did you know that? But they're a lot of fun, especially Stella, who is full of pep (and good-looking!), but she's going with a guy who's no good, that's what Frank Jr. says anyway.

I've also been spending a lot of time with Aunt Eileen. They're <u>so</u> nice. They all treat me just like family, which I suppose I am in a way because of Eileen. Dave's sister Pat has had me over to her place for supper and his brother Henry has had me over to play cards. I always have a good time.

You know I'm rooming now with Dave's grandmother in her house on Peach Avenue. She charges me $4 a week for a room on the first floor, the second floor she rents out as an apartment to someone else. Her name is Mrs. Altschuler (I think that's how you spell it) but she tells me to call her Grandma, so I do. She's my second "Grandma" up here. Dave's mother Alice, Mrs. Burnham (Mrs. Altschuler's daughter), tells me to call her Grandma, too. Probably because I'm Arlene and Dot's cousin, even though I'm a lot older than the girls. They're really cute kids, they like me to play with them. If I ever have daughters I'd like them to be just like them.

They spend a lot of time over at their grandmother's because of Eileen's illness. In fact she just went in the Guldwyck Hospital again, she had another spell or relapse or something. Poor Dave. So he leaves them with his mother a lot, but I guess she has her own troubles with her husband Perry who Dave tells me drinks something awful. He don't have anything to do with his father because of that. He has another sister named Peggy who lives with her mother and helps take care of the girls. Dave says she has a pretty good job in the state tax department.

Mom you'll be glad to know I've been going to church. I go with Dave and the girls to Raleigh Avenue Methodist around the corner from where I'm staying. They are a pretty nice bunch of people there and they have a young people's group that I might join. Nicer anyway than the ones I met ice skating last night at Belcher Pond. They weren't very sociable, but maybe it was me.

Well, Mom I think I'll sign off now. This is already way longer than I thought I would ever write. Don't worry about me, I'm doing fine. I've had a couple paychecks now and I've paid off the money I borrowed from Leon and I've paid Jean for the lunch she packs me everyday. And I even have some money to spare. So you can see I'm okay. Kiss Barbara and Connie for me and tell them I miss them.

With love

Tim

\*     \*     \*     \*

"I just don't know what to do, Tim. I've begun looking at trailers."

"Trailers?"

"Yes. You know, to go to Arizona in. I don't know what else to do. Nothing the doctors do seems to be working. Maybe the Southwest climate will help her."

Tim and Dave were returning home from Guldwyck Memorial Hospital, where they had visited Eileen. She was to come home the next day; her condition was improved over the time of her admittance, but it was clear she wasn't getting better overall. Dave was uncharacteristically glum, slunk behind the steering wheel as he drove through the slush of Guldwyck's streets. Tim reached forward and clicked off the car radio, cutting announcer Norman Brokenshire's deep voice right in the middle of its trademark "How *do* you do?" For a brief moment Tim wondered what the program could be.

"Trailer?" Tim repeated. "Why a trailer? Why not just get an apartment down there?"

"I just thought it would be better. A place of our own, like, even if it's small. The trailers I've been looking at aren't any more than thirty feet long. We'd have to sell our furniture, anyway. I couldn't afford to haul it out there. Not to mention buying all new. Plus a trailer would be cheaper than paying rent."

"How would you get it down there?"

"Pull it with the Ford here." Dave gave the steering wheel a light thump with the heel of his right hand.

Tim cast his gaze around the darkened interior of the car, as if gauging its pulling power. It didn't seem like much to him. Here they were in the car again, talking about Eileen's illness. He was sorry for Dave's dilemma and guiltily glad it wasn't his own.

They were sitting at a red light. Dave drew himself up straight and took a deep breath. "How're things going with you? Still comfortable at Grandma's?"

"Yes. I've been getting up better in the mornings when I work the day shift. She was getting a little put out with me, how hard it was to wake me up. I know because she mentioned it to Eileen and Eileen told me. I've been better about it lately."

"How's work?"

"Pretty good. The different shifts drive me a little crazy, and the different jobs. Rolling mill, finishing department. I think they're going to have me recording soon."

"Allegheny Ludlum's a good place to work."

"Yes, it is," Tim said, his voice betraying a slight plaintiveness. "But I sometimes think I'd like to have some other goal besides going to work each day."

\*       \*       \*       \*

"What's the matter with *him*?"

"I don't know. He's been like that ever since he got home from work and opened the letter from his mother. Sitting there in the living room, silent. It's almost like he's in shock."

Peggy Burnham and her Grandmother Altschuler were in the grandmother's kitchen preparing supper. It was a cold Saturday toward the end of February and snow was coming down heavily past the kitchen windows. The furnace fan was blasting hot air and a whirring noise into the kitchen as the two women moved around the table. Tim normally didn't eat at Grandma's; it wasn't part of his rent. He usually ate his breakfast or dinner or both, depending on his shift, at Jean's or sometimes Harriet's or at a diner. But Peggy, scraping carrots and casting a pitying glance at his figure slouched in the living room chair, thought this night ought to be an exception.

"What could be in a letter from his mother to cause a reaction like that?" Peggy said.

"I don't know. I'll tell you, though, I don't think it was his mother's letter that caused it. The envelope was thick. I think there was another letter inside it."

"Oh?"

"Yes." Grandma Altschuler put the knife she had in her hand down on the table and looked meaningfully at her granddaughter.

"From who, then?"

"Well, I don't know for sure, but I'll just bet you it's from that girl that his grandmother and aunt and the rest were talking about. The one in Ohio that he broke up with and they said it troubled him so. Who else could cause him such agitation? I'll bet she didn't know his address here and sent it to his mother's."

"You could be right. Grandma, you're quite the snoop. Anyway, he looks pole-axed. What could she have written?"

"That's the sixty-four dollar question."

"Well, whatever it is, he looks like he could use a friend or two tonight," Peggy said, and, wiping her hands on her apron, she walked toward the living room.

# CHAPTER 10

▼

# FAINT HEART NE'ER WON FAIR LADY

*Peg o' my heart, I love you, don't let us part.*
*—Peg o' My Heart*, popular song of the 1940s

Peggy Burnham sat in an easy chair in her mother's living room. The day was miserable outside, windy, wet, and cold. Rain blasted against the clapboards of the house. Inside, in the second-floor apartment, it was stuffy and fuggy.

Peggy felt drowsy. She sat in the chair with her feet, clad in white socks, resting on an ottoman. Her black-and-white plaid skirt had slid slightly up her outstretched legs, which were covered with an almost invisible downy fuzz. She stared at them in disapproval: She hadn't shaved them for a couple of days. Tim, stretched out on the sofa across from her and reading the Sunday paper, had glanced at them, too, she knew, and not with disapproval. Her mouth twisted in a small, wry grin. Men, she thought, they're all alike. And quickly told herself, No, not this one. He's really nice. I'm glad he likes my legs. In her happiness she gave them a wriggly little twist, as if to authorize their viewability.

She and Tim had been dating with increasing frequency, ever since that snowy Saturday afternoon when she had gone into the living room at her grandmother's to try and cheer him up. Peg could not believe the depths of his despondency. It would have been terrible with anyone, but for a person of what she knew to be Tim's usual exuberance and cheerfulness, it was startling. He would not tell what the trouble was and she didn't press him on it because at that point she knew him only casually. He did not allude to the letter—it wasn't in sight when she got into the living room—though it was obvious to anyone that his dejection sprang from it. He even tried to act as if nothing was wrong, though that was even more obviously untrue, but she let him have his little charade and merely asked him to come to supper.

They did not start going out together immediately after that. The opportunities for him to ask her out were few because their paths did not naturally cross very often—until she found herself turning up at her grandmother's more frequently than she used to. On one of those visits she happened to mention that she liked Spencer Tracy and Lana Turner, both of whom happened to be in *Cass Timberlane*, which happened to be playing at the Ritz in Guldwyck, and Tim asked if she'd like to go see it. After that they began going out regularly, often to the movies because the weather was cold and there wasn't much else to do. Though he did take her with him ice fishing at the reservoir in the 1928 Ford that he had bought for $60. She did not especially like that—it was too cold, both on the ice and in the drafty car—but women long have been enduring their men's pastimes and so she put up with it patiently. And, on the Sundays he did not have to work, he took to escorting her to church, which she suddenly began to want to attend more faithfully than she previously did.

Tim did not have far to go to pick Peg up. She lived with her mother in a three-bedroom apartment just up the hill on Peach Avenue from her Grandmother Altschuler's house, where Tim roomed. One of the bedrooms was Peg's, another was pretty much reserved for Arlene and Dorothy when they had to stay with their grandmother because of Eileen's illness, and the third was for Peg's mother, whose name was Alice but whom Tim called "Grandma," of course. Peg, who was a year younger than Tim, found that amusing.

What she didn't find amusing was her father, Perry Burnham, who was a falling-down drunk. One evening when Dorothy and Arlene were younger and staying with their grandparents, Dorothy saw her grandfather come home staggering drunk. After clambering noisily up the stairs, he stood on the upstairs porch and unbuttoned his fly and, weaving left and right with his penis in his hands, took a piss over the porch railing. When he finished and turned around, he saw his granddaughter staring at him, fascinated, through the window. Embarrassed, he mumbled, "Sorry, honey," and brushed roughly past her into the living room. Finally his behavior grew so disgusting and disagreeable to his wife and humanity in general that his sons, Dave and Henry, forced him to leave the house and move into a small apartment of his own. Still, occasionally he would show up, deep in his cups, cursing his thankless family and his miserable fate. Peg lived in dread of these appearances, but fortunately none occurred when Tim was around. To Tim, the hatred that the children—Peg, Dave, Henry, and Pat—held for their father was inexplicable. Though it became less so one Sunday evening when Peg and Tim were walking home from having seen *Killer McCoy*, with Mickey Rooney, and, as they rounded the corner from Raleigh Avenue onto Peach Avenue, they saw her father getting out of the rear seat of a cab. He stumbled against the curb and rolled into the gutter. Tim bolted to go help him up, but Peg grabbed his arm and said sharply, "No, let him lay there."

But thoughts of her abhorrent father were far from her this raw but pleasant Sunday. The thoughts of youth are not only long, long thoughts, they are frequently wandering. She was thinking of *Oklahoma*.

"Hey, know what I heard on the radio last night?" Peg said.

"Hmmm, what's that?" Tim said while continuing his reading of the Albany *Times Union*.

"They said on the news that *Oklahoma* closed after 2,248 performances. Yesterday, I mean. It closed yesterday. They said it was Broadway's longest-running show."

Tim lowered the paper into his lap and looked over at Peg. "Now how would you remember that?"

Peg cocked her head and knitted her brows in confusion. "What do you mean, how would I remember it? It was only last night. I'm not going senile, you know." Peg smiled.

"No, I know. I mean, how would you remember the exact number of performances?"

"Because they said it on the radio, dope."

"Yes, but most people wouldn't remember an exact figure like that. They'd probably say something like, 'Two thousand performances' or something like that."

"Well, I'm not most people, as I hope by this time you realize." Peg turned her smile into an exaggerated, flirtatious grin. "Maybe it's from working all day every day with all those figures at the tax department."

Tim returned to reading the newspaper. Gusts of rain slapped against the house.

"It would've been nice if we could've gone to see it," Peg said.

"What, *Oklahoma*? Your mother'd have a conniption fit if we stayed overnight together in New York City."

"So would I. I meant we could have gone to a matinee. Down and back the same day on the train."

"Yes, well, maybe." Tim tossed the newspaper onto the sofa and swung his legs down onto the rag rug on the floor. He faced Peg. "Know what *I* heard last night? At work?"

"You're getting a raise."

"Ha, I wish. No, some guys are joining the National Guard because Truman's going to revive the draft and they want to beat it. Better a Ready Freddie one weekend a month, they say, than a couple years in Uncle Sam's Army."

"Are you thinking of joining too?" Apprehension registered in Peg's voice.

"Me? No. I figure I'll take my chances. Maybe they'll never call me."

"That's good," Peg said, and took a plunge into cautious audacity: "I'd hate to see you go, even for a short time."

"Not as much as me," Tim said, and meant it. Peg was nice, pretty: Short, slender, good figure, very fetching face framed in medium-length dark hair. And clever and a sharp dresser. And passionate, too, up to a point, he had learned.

"Speaking of doing things," Tim said, "you want to do something tomorrow? It's Decoration Day. You have it off, I have it off."

"Sure, I guess I would. But I don't think we can do much of anything if this weather doesn't improve."

"Well, what I thought was, if it *is* nice, that we could drive out to Saratoga Lake. I was talking to Frank Clay, he's taking his younger brothers and sisters out. You might want to bring Arlene and Dorothy along."

"What? All of us in your old car? It would scrape the road."

"Now now, let's have no disparaging words about old Betsy. No, Frank's going to drive, too. I just thought we could all have a picnic together. Maybe go swimming, too, if it's not too cold."

"I'd like that, Tim. And it's nice, your thinking of the girls. Especially since their mother hasn't been well again."

✳       ✳       ✳       ✳

On June 24, 1948, President Truman signed the Selective Service Act providing for the registration of all men between the ages of eighteen and twenty-five to guarantee enough inductees to man an Army of 837,000, a Navy and Marine

Corps of 666,882, and an Air Force of 502,000. The draft was to be reactivated August 30, and service was to be for twenty-one months.

✳    ✳    ✳    ✳

Earlier in the evening Peg and Tim had been at Tim's friends, the Nicholses, watching Joe Louis defend his heavyweight championship against Jersey Joe Walcott. The Nicholses, who lived on the Albany Shaker Road not far from the Clays, had one of the few television sets in the area and they invited Tim to come out and watch the championship bout being telecast from the Bronx. Louis had knocked Walcott on his rear, winning the boxing match in eleven rounds.

Now, in the semi-darkness of Peg's living room, Tim and Peg were engaged in a slow-motion wrestling match, lying on the sofa and pressed together tightly. They kissed lingeringly and explored each other's bodies with swift, light touches. They did not speak. Tim, lying on his side with his back to the back of the sofa, moved his right hand down to the small of Peg's back. Peg, also lying on her side, shifted her body in sympathetic concert with his move. The shift pushed her green print dress further up her legs, exposing the dark bands at the tops of her stockings. All was warm silence save for their breathing and Margaret Whiting's low, wistful crooning of "The Tree in the Meadow" coming from the radio. Peg cocked her left leg infinitesimally, involuntarily, which Tim took as a signal and began to move over her. Peg's body stiffened.

"Tim, get off! Come on," she said, pushing him away and beginning to work herself into an upright position. "Come on. This has gone far enough."

"What? Oh why?" he said, attempting to keep a hold on her back and catching a flash of her thigh, which was somehow more alluring than when he saw it revealed by her swimsuit at the lake. He did not get up.

"Come on," she persisted. She was sitting up now and gave him a playful punch to encourage him to do the same.

"Oh, all right." Slowly and reluctantly, in an attempt to give an embarrassing condition time to relieve itself, he pulled himself up and sat alongside Peg, who was smoothing down her dress. Tim leaned forward, his elbows propped on his knees, and buried his face in his hands. He rubbed his hands over his face and groaned.

"What?" Peg said. She ran her right hand over his hair, soothingly.

"I was just thinking." Tim rubbed his face again and sat up straight.

"About what?"

"Oh, I don't know." In fact, he had been thinking about Betty Ruppertal. "What's today? The date, I mean."

Peg thought a moment. "June twenty-fifth, I think. Well, by now it's the twenty-sixth. Why?"

Was it about this time last year he had been necking with Betty Ruppertal in his mother's '36 Dodge? No, that was way earlier, in the spring. Why did things in his life seem to repeat themselves? Even that insignificant incident with Eileen, her having a record player and all those records like Caroline Ollinger. Why did they always have to do with women?

Peg moved her hand down to Tim's neck and massaged it lightly. "Why? What's so important about the date?"

"Nothing, really. I was just thinking, I read once about a French word, dayjah voo or something like that. It means you remember something you've experienced sometime before."

"Deja vu. And it doesn't mean recalling something you've experienced before. It means feeling that you've experienced something before that you're actually experiencing for the first time." Peg leaned forward and looked in Tim's face and smiled impishly. "Why? Have you experienced this before? Or do you only have the *feeling* you've experienced it before? Not very flattering to me either way, I must say."

Tim sat stock still, not knowing what to say. The radio had shifted to Kay Kyser's "Woody Woodpecker Song," whose silly lyrics seemed to mock the awkwardness of the moment.

"Tim, I'm teasing." She paused, still gazing at Tim, her fondness for him obvious in both look and voice. Maybe this was her opportunity. "What was it you were thinking of? Was it that girl in Ohio? Was that what made you so sad that day at Grandma's?"

Tim said nothing, but only stared blankly into the middle distance.

"Well, if you won't talk about it...."

Tim shook his head, as if visibly shaking himself out of his reverie. He slapped both knees with his hands decisively. "You know what I want?"

"I think I've got a pretty clear idea what you want."

Tim looked at her, embarrassed, irritated, grinning slightly. "No, what I'd really like is a new car. That old Ford just about conked out on us coming home tonight."

"Not too long ago you told me you wouldn't hear any disparaging words about old Betsy."

"Well, old Betsy hasn't been any more dependable than the other women in my life." Immediately Tim realized his mistake, the potential significance of words casually thrown off and meant to be humorous. He darted a glance at Peg, whose reaction indicated that he was right, because she looked as if this was the perfect opening to probe. "Present company excepted, of course," he quickly added. "No, what I'd like is one of those new '49 Fords they just brought out a couple weeks ago. Boy, what styling. Nothing like the prewar cars. Not that I could get one even if I could afford one. I hear there's a long waiting list."

"Yes, I've seen pictures of them. In *Collier's* or someplace. They're lovely." Lovely: a car was a car to Peg.

"'Course, the person who could *really* use a new car is your brother Dave, going out to Arizona and all."

"I thought his car was in good shape."

"I suppose it is, for being eight years old, but it's got to pull a trailer all that way."

"It's a pretty good sized car, isn't it?"

"Yes, but he really ought to have something heavier. Like a pickup truck."

"Well, I can't see Dave buying a pickup truck. I doubt that he has the money, for one thing. And I can't see Eileen traveling in one, not in her condition. Then there's the girls."

"I suppose not." Tim stood up and stretched, locking the fingers of both hands together and pushing them out away from him, making his knuckles crack and Peg wince. "It's nice your mother is going out with them to help."

"No nicer than your sister Connie going out to help. After all, it's her son and daughter-in-law and grandchildren Mom's helping. Anyway, Mom's not going to stay all that long."

"After all," Tim retorted, in conscious repetition, "it's her aunt that Connie's helping. Remember, Eileen is my mother's sister. And Dorothy and Arlene are Connie's cousins."

"Still, Connie's—what?—twelve years old? It's a big thing to uproot a girl of that age. It's nice of her and your mother to do it. Is your whole family this nice?"

"Everybody except me."

"Now you're fishing for compliments. OK, you've landed one: A good-looking, personable young man who's hard-working and a churchgoer and good to his family. No, now, don't go all false modest on me. I know about the stuff you've bought and sent to your brother and mother since you've been here. That all sounds pretty nice to me."

"What you've said is no different than anything Dave does, *and* he's got the extra burden of this trip to Tucson. What he's doing for his wife sounds like a real love story."

"Plus the wonder boy recognizes a real love story when he sees one. Oh, Tim, are you for real? It's late and you'd better go. A girl only has so much strength."

✳    ✳    ✳    ✳

The sun, a molten coin in the sky, blazed down on Dave and Tim as they worked around the car and the trailer alongside Dave's apartment house, getting it ready for the trip. It was a Friday, July 16, and Tim had taken off from work to help his uncle. The trailer was a new, twenty-five-foot Pacemaker that Dave had bought for $2,500, which represented practically all the money he had in the world. It was aluminum-sided with a green Masonite-like material in the window areas. The aluminum like a magnifying reflector threw off the sun's rays with increased intensity, and the two men sweated. Tim's white T-shirt was soaked, and sweat dripped from his forehead as he bent over the trailer hitch.

Tim straightened up and gave the hitch a friendly kick. He raised his face to the bone-white sky and wiped his forehead with his right forearm.

"Man, it's about as hot as I've seen it in a long time," Tim said. He gave the hitch another kick. "I'm glad you put a helper spring on the car. I'd hate to've seen you go all that way with it the way it was."

Dave came around the front of the trailer. He had been working on a balky door latch.

"Yeah, I put in a truck clutch, too. That ought to get us over the mountains." Ray held up for Tim's inspection the door latch mechanism he had been working on. "Doesn't seem to me I ought to have this trouble with a brand-new trailer. If I can't fix it easy, I'm calling 'em and telling 'em to come over here and fix it themselves. It's not a big deal, but my gosh."

"I don't blame you. You shouldn't have to fix something on something that's new."

"Oh well." Dave set the latch mechanism down on the hitch. "Say, did you catch any of the Democratic convention yesterday?"

"No, I didn't. I guess since I'm not old enough to vote yet I don't pay much attention. I suppose I should. If I could vote I'd vote for Dewey anyway." Tim knew his Republican sympathies, inherited from the King and Davis families, were safe with Dave.

"That's how I'm voting. Dewey's been a good governor for New York. He should have gotten it the last time, in '44. No disrespect to Roosevelt, but four terms? We were way overdue for a change."

"Looks like we'll get it this time for sure. Everybody's been saying Truman doesn't have a chance."

"Not with these splits in the Democrats. What do they call them? The Dixiecrats? And that nut Henry Wallace. Progressive Party my left eye. He's a Red if you ask me."

While Dave was talking Tim's attention had been diverted by activity in front of a house down the street. A number of people, one of them in Army uniform, were going up and down the front steps, in and out the door.

"Hey Dave," Tim said, touching his uncle's left arm. "What's going on down there?"

Dave peered to where Tim was pointing. "Oh, they're bringing another poor boy back from Europe. That guy in uniform is a military escort or something. I don't know the family, but I heard. Their son. Killed right after the Battle of the Bulge. I guess he was buried in France or Luxembourg but now they've brought his remains back home for burial."

"I've read about that in the papers, but never come across it," Tim said. He watched as a middle-aged woman in black dress and black veil was helped down the steps in the sweltering mid-July mid-afternoon by a middle-aged man in a dark fedora with a black band around the left sleeve of his suit coat. "It's the right thing to do.

"Yes, it is. I hope it makes the war over for the family at last." Dave picked up the door latch and returned to his labors. "I hope it's the last war."

✳     ✳     ✳     ✳

On a Monday at the end of August, Tim received a letter from his mother, dated two days before and mailed from Lake George, where she was working again for the summer.

Saturday

Dearest Timothy,

This will be a short letter because I am so rushed what with all the things I have to do to finish up here for the Labor Day wrap-up of everything so that Barbara and I can head on back home. We are leaving tomorrow. They do not like me leaving before Labor Day but that is too bad because I have to get back to my regular job at the cafeteria and I told them about that when I first got here in the summer. They knew that, they are just being stinkers.

Well by now Connie must be settled in in Tucson with Eileen and Dave and the girls and Dave's mother Alice. Imagine that, six of them in a 25 foot trailer. I don't know where they'll all fit, that's even smaller than our little house. Ha ha. But I suppose they'll make out fine. I just hope that climate proves to be beneficial to Eileen.

I was so sorry not to be able to come over to Albany with Connie and put her on the train myself. But I had to be here and she had all of the family there to be with her, you and Eileen and Jean and Harriet. And Dave's wonderful family of course, they couldn't be nicer, especially Dave's mother. It's funny you call her 'Grandma.' But nice. Barbara and I had a nice little going-away party for Connie here. She probably told you. I know Alice took good care of her on the train trip. I don't know, sometimes it all seems so sad. I hope it does turn out that Connie will be a help with Arlene and Dorothy, she's still so young herself.

Well Tim I trust that you are well. You don't write often but I suppose no news is good news and I admit I don't write much myself. I see that they are going to start up this draft again in a couple of days. I thought we were done with all that business. Maybe if Dewey becomes president? Do you have to do anything or are you still registered with the draft board down in Penna? Just so there's not another war. I don't know, these Communists causing all that trouble with the Berlin Airlift.

I will cut this off now because it is getting late and I still have things to do before I fall into bed. Be a good boy (I know you hate to hear that) and please take care of yourself.

Love,

Mother

*        *        *        *

The world, meanwhile, was continuing its relentless roll toward everyone's destinies. Earlier that month Congressman Richard M. Nixon and others on the House Un-American Activities Committee grilled Whittaker Chambers and Alger Hiss about their Communist Party backgrounds, which Chambers admitted to and Hiss didn't. Hiss's condescending demeanor irritated the hell out of Nixon, who rather liked Chambers. Congress adjourned its special session, having done nothing Truman wanted, thus allowing him to call it the Do-Nothing Eightieth Congress. On August 15, the day Dave and Eileen and the kids set off for Arizona, taking Peg along, 73-year-old Syngman Rhee was elected president of Korea in a U.S.-sponsored election and proclaimed the Republic of Korea in Seoul. Twenty-five days later the Soviets established the Korean People's Democratic Republic under Kim Il-sung in Pyongyang. Tim missed Peg, who- -in a last-minute decision made among all of them—went along to help take care of Arlene and Dorothy on the car trip. Shortly after her mother and Connie arrived by train, she went back to Guldwyck by train.

*        *        *        *

Tuscon, Ariz.
Sept. 3, 1948

Dear Tim,

Gosh, it will soon be Labor Day and I will be coming back home. I will be glad to get there. I am glad I came along to do what I can and that work gave me the time off, and I guess it is nice here, but I don't care for this heat! and sand.

The car trip went okay without any major troubles. A couple of times when Dave couldn't find a trailer park to stay in overnight he pulled into a gas station and asked if he could hook up to their electric, and usually they let him for a dollar or so. One guy got kind of snotty and told us to buzz off, only not that word. I guess he thought we were Okies or something. The only time it got scary was going over the mountains. It looked like the old Ford might overheat. Dave got out and put a couple of blocks of wood under the hood to prop it up and let more air through, which helped. Eileen survived the trip fine and the girls were simply wonderful. They are so darling and are so good for their mother and me, and now for Mom and Connie.

The place we are staying is called the Princeton Trailer Park. It's really quite nice, the people too. Nothing trashy. A lot of them have come by to introduce themselves and ask if they can help. Dave and Eileen have already started trying to make things homey. Dave has blocked off part of the ground just outside the trailer door with large stones to make it look like a little yard. Most of the other trailer park residents have done the same thing, in the area underneath their awnings. In a way it looks a little pathetic, because of course it's just sand, not a real yard, but I would never say that because they are just trying to make things the best. I took some pictures. I'll show them to you when I get home and get them developed.

I have to hand it to Dave, with all he has to contend with. He never lets up and he never complains. As you know he came out here with no job or prospects. He said he would do anything, even wash dishes. Fortunately, he doesn't have to do that. He just landed a job at Davis-Monthan Air Base as a "stored aircraft servicer helper" at $1.01 an hour. He didn't tell me the pay, of course. Eileen did. She is glad it is so much. She was afraid he'd have to work for 75 cents an hour or even less. He hopes eventually to get into the motor pool and maybe the machine shop, work more like what he did at the arsenal. Like I said, I really give him credit.

It's too early to tell if this move will help Eileen's lungs. Right now she seems in good health and is able to do work around the house. Mom helps, of course, and so does Connie. I still think it's marvelous that your sister would do this for her aunt. She has registered to go school here, and so has Arlene, for kindergarten. Dorothy is still too young. You should see the sleeping arrangements here. Well, maybe it's better you can't. Poor Dave! One man and six women in a trailer!

That will ease up soon when I leave. Mom, too, but I'm not sure when she will leave. She is fine but I do think the heat gets to her. I know it gets to me. Right now it is 4:00 in the afternoon and 99 degrees. But as they say here, it's a dry heat. Wet, dry, I say it's hot!

So I will be happy to get back to good old green upstate New York. And to see you and all the rest. I wrote a letter to my sister telling her the news, but other than that you're the only one I wrote to, since my mother is here, of course. Tell everyone I said hello, and see you soon!

Fondly,

Peg


        \*        \*        \*        \*


Not long after Peg got back from Tucson, she began to suspect that Tim was seeing other women. Not that he wasn't free to, strictly speaking. They weren't engaged. They weren't even, strictly speaking, "going steady," even though they in fact had been going out pretty steadily. And she had even gone to the movies once with another guy, someone from the tax department who had asked her, though she hadn't had an especially good time. All through the date she couldn't shake the notion that this wasn't right—not in an ethical sense, but that it wasn't right for her. Just as now she couldn't shake the notion—the *fear*—that Tim was probably not troubled in the same way. She wondered if she was allowed to bring the subject up with him, and, even if she could convince herself that she was, how in the world it could be done with a guy who resisted being pinned down. And with whom, because he was so gosh-darn sweet about everything, it was impossible to get angry over his resistance to being thus pinned. But then why did he act like he missed her when she was gone, if now he acts like this?

She thought these melancholy thoughts on a golden, hazy Saturday afternoon in late September, encouraged by Bing Crosby's lugubrious lowing of "Now Is the Hour" drifting softly out of the radio. It was one of those impossibly perfect Indian summer days when dust motes float in honeyed sunshine and the scarcely moving air intoxicates like a cool white wine. Perfect for feeling pleasantly blue about her woes as she moodily drifted with the music around the empty apartment, adjusting picture frames that needed no adjusting and straightening doilies that could get no straighter. And a perfect target for being rudely shattered. By a noisy car. Tim's new car.

Not new. New to Tim. While Peg was gone he had got rid of old Betsy, the '28 Ford, and moved forward chronologically to a 1933 Chevrolet coupe that he bought from the Nicholses for $100. It was in good mechanical condition, except for the muffler, but its appearance left something to be desired—such as a paint job to cover up its fading black. Peg went out to the porch and looked down and, seeing Tim stick his head out the driver's side window, smiled, despite her mood. It was almost like Andy Hardy come to pick up Polly in the old heap.

"Hey, kid," Tim said, grinning up at her. "What ya doing?"

"Not much," Peg replied, her arms crossed over her breasts, prepared if she could to do a little resisting of her own. "Not much going on. No one here. Mom and the girls in Arizona. I miss them." Especially now it struck her how much she missed them.

Tim got out of the car and walked to the stoop and looked up at Peg, who had come down to the first-floor porch. "Want to go to the movies?"

Peg's impulse was to respond, "Are you sure you don't want to go with someone else?" But she said, "I don't know. Where? What's on?"

"I thought we'd go out to the Menands Drive-In. One more time before it closes for the season. It won't be long; getting late in September."

"You thought we'd go to the drive-in." Peg repeated, and her smile assumed a mischievous cast. "What's playing? Wrestling?"

"What?" Tim said, truly not getting it. Then, "Oh," and he smiled too. "No. No, really. I thought we'd take the Clay kids. *I Remember Mama* is playing. They'd like that. I'd like it too."

Peg dropped her arms. Her defenses were breached. She stepped down onto the top step.

"That's a nice idea, Tim. Yes, let's go." A sudden vision of her nieces, Dorothy and Arlene, came into her head. "Those Clay children, raised by their father and Frank Junior and the other older sisters, I don't imagine they get to the movies much. Let's do it. Will they all fit in your car? The back seat's not very big."

"Not all of them. I thought we'd take maybe four, five of them. They can sit in the back, or in front, on our laps if they have to. Just before we get to the drive-in we'll stop and put them all in the trunk. Sneak 'em in for free. Then when we get in they can get back into the car."

"Tim! They'll die from the exhaust. I'll pay their way."

"What? For two minutes? No they won't. It's not the money, though why you have to pay by the head to get into the drive-in I don't understand. It's not like you're taking up extra seats. Anyway, I just want to see if we can do it. You know—just for fun."

∗      ∗      ∗      ∗

The Indian summer came to an end and the drive-ins closed and Tim and Peg and all of Guldwyck and the Albany area steadily buttoned up tighter and tighter for another Upstate winter. Tim wrote to his mother, enclosing some money, not for any special occasion but simply because he was earning good money and felt flush. Anna wrote back, telling him the news and worrying whether the mysterious and deadly smog that had settled over Donora, Pennsylvania, would drift eastward and kill them all. It was in all the newspapers, she said. Until it got too cold, Tim and Frank Clay, and anyone else they could get, usually played basketball a couple of afternoons a week out at Frank's house. Tim went roller-skating a lot, usually at Mid-City Park, sometimes with Peg, sometimes with other young women. They would skate singly or together, holding hands, twirling around and around to Ken Griffin singing "You Can't Be True, Dear" or the Andrews Sisters' "Toolie Oolie Doolie." Then he would take them home, or elsewhere, and sometimes matters would grow amorous to a greater or lesser degree, and afterward the young women would wonder about this cheerfully mixed-up young man they had met at church or at work or someplace else. And Tim would wonder what he was doing and where he was going and about Peg and about Black Run and Horton and Betty—and Helen. And Peg would wonder about this young man, who to her had something more working in him than mixed-up cheerfulness, and whom she both missed and found herself avoiding by not visiting her grandmother's, where he roomed, as often as she used to. It looked like being a long winter.

✳     ✳     ✳     ✳

"I don't know what Dad's going to do now."

"Jean, if you've said that once, you've said it fifty times now. For Christ's sake, you know what your father's going to do. Eventually, anyway. Soon. He's going to move in with Anna, when they get a room built on her place."

Jean looked at her husband and sighed. She hated his using profanity. She didn't know why he did it, a smart man better than such vulgarity. But she no longer said anything.

"I know, Lee. I just meant, Dad always depended so much on Mother, and vice versa. It's so sad." Sad because it's so nice, Jean thought, that closeness, that need. And sighed again.

"And your father's a hale and hearty man for someone his age," Leon said, a hint of apology in his voice. He turned away from the dining room window he had been peering out of, at the snow streaming by. "He'll do fine."

They were in Jean's apartment, she and Leon and Tim, getting ready for dinner. It was Armistice Day, the evening after they had come back from Pennsylvania for the funeral of Jean's mother and Tim's grandmother, Naomi King, who had died a few days before less than a month shy of her 70<sup>th</sup> birthday. They had all gone down to Pennsylvania, the King women and their husbands, and Tim. Peg went, too, out of respect for Tim and as sort of the Burnham family representative to a family to which they had close marital and emotional ties. Other King family members came in from other parts of the country, of course, along with what seemed like half of Somerton County, and the crowded funeral service, if it didn't completely overwhelm the little Reformed church, did threaten to overwhelm the confused and grieving 80-year-old widower.

"It was a wonderful service. Such a large turnout," Jean said. She moved around the dining room table, placing plates and utensils. She turned to Tim. "I'm just sorry that Eileen couldn't be there. Of course, I know it was impossible. But it was nice of Peg Burnham to go. She didn't have to, taking time off from work."

Tim had moved over to the window to look out at the storm. "Yeah, well, she wanted to. Felt it was the right thing." He and Peg had driven down together in his car, avoiding any important subjects on the trip. He drummed the backs of his fingernails against the window pane, tick-tick-tick-tick-tick. "I'm glad we didn't get this kind of weather for the funeral or for the drive down and back."

"She's certainly a lovely girl." Jean twisted a dry dishtowel in her hands and smiled the slightly beseeching smile of the King family women that said it hoped everything could be well with everyone for once. "Wouldn't it be funny if you— I mean...."

"If I what?" Tim tried to sound stern, but was smiling.

"I just meant, well, another member of our family and another member of the Burnham family.... You two go out together so much."

"Not so much." The uncomfortableness in Tim's voice was almost palpable. "We just both like the movies and roller-skating."

"You take my advice, young-fellow-me-lad," Leon said, advancing toward the table, "and grab that fine figure of female flesh before someone else does. Why, she'd even make this idiotic New Look fashion look good. Except that, among her other qualities, she has too much taste to wear it. A zaftig wench, that Peg Burnham."

"Lee."

"What, Lee? You're always saying 'Lee.' What'd I say so terrible? A zaftig wench. You don't even know what zaftig means."

"I can imagine."

"Well, don't. It's not that. Anyway," Lee said, pulling out a chair and sitting at the table, "it's Armistice Day and here's one Navy veteran who's famished. What about you, Tim? This Truman government going to make you a veteran eventually? That's one thing I'll say: If your mother, God bless her, hadn't died, Truman's victory would have killed her. That surprise win was a real vindication of the New Deal, which all you rabid Republicans don't like to hear, I know."

Lee looked at his wife. Her lips parted, but she didn't say it.

\*        \*        \*        \*

"There's one," Tim said, braking the car.

"Where?" Frank Clay, sitting next to him, peered out through Jim's window.

"There," Tim said. He rolled down his window and pointed to a large Scotch pine, one of a pair flanking the end of a long gravel driveway of a rather stately looking, pillared, colonial-style house on the road to Wynantskill. It was eleven o'clock, a cold and clear night, and they were looking for a Christmas tree.

"Oh, jeez, Tim, I don't think we should do that. That's someone's tree," Frank said, meaning, That's the tree of someone well-to-do and important. "Besides, look at the size of it."

"No no, not the whole tree. We just climb up it and take the top out and we don't hurt the tree at all."

"And the owner doesn't notice that one of a pair of perfectly matched trees on their perfectly maintained lawn in front of their perfectly gorgeous house is eight feet shorter than the other?"

"No, they'll never notice. Anyway, we'll be long gone and no one will know who. C'mon, we used to do this all the time in Black Run."

"What, steal Christmas trees?"

"No, top out trees. You get a perfect shape that way."

"Like I said, steal trees." Frank grimaced in the faint light of the dashboard dial. "Why don't we just go and buy a tree? I'll buy it. Or chop one down in the woods somewhere?"

"Because we're here and I want this one. It's perfect. Grandma Altschuler said she didn't want a tree, she never had a tree. I'm going to surprise her. Grab that saw in the back."

Frank sighed and turned and reached into the narrow back seat area of the coupe. "Okay. Here."

"No, you keep it and climb up the tree. I'll tell you where to cut."

"*Me* climb it? Why don't you climb it? You're the mighty goddam woodsman."

"Because I can stay down here as a lookout."

"Lookout. I like the sound of that." Frank sighed again, opened his door, flipped away the cigarette he'd been smoking, and stepped out into the snow. "Jeez, and me with no boots on." He took a couple of careful, mincing steps toward the trees, shaking snow off his feet as he went. "Which one you want? This one?" he asked, placing his hand on the tree to the right of the driveway.

"Yeah, that's good. Go ahead, scoot up."

"Scoot," Frank mocked. But he tied the saw to his belt, grabbed hold of the lowest branches, gave a grunt, and scooted.

Five minutes later Frank was sawing away about thirty feet up. Tim stood under the tree looking up at him and whispered loudly, "How's it going?"

"OK, I guess," Frank whispered loudly back, continuing to saw. "'Course, I'm not used to cutting down trees in the air one-handed in twenty-degree weather, so you'll understand if I'm a little slow. How's it down there?"

"OK, I guess." Tim paused. "I don't know. I think I hear something."

"You hear something?" Frank stopped sawing, alarm in his voice. "What?"

"I don't know." Another pause. "Wait, it's coming from the house. I think it's a dog."

"A *dog*?" Oh, God, you're right. I hear barking."

"Yeah, it's coming this way. Forget about the tree. Quick, come on down."

Frank had acted before Tim's warning and begun scrambling down the tree, still holding on to the saw, which flopped wildly with each handhold. Bits of branches and bark rained down on Tim's upturned face.

"Hurry up, hurry up," Tim pleaded, but beginning to laugh at Frank's frantic scrambling. "Let go of the damn saw."

Frank did. The saw landed next to Tim's feet. Then, a couple of seconds later, so did Frank. He had lost his grip and, with a soft yelp and flailing arms, he fell about twelve feet into a low snowdrift.

Tim was bent over, laughing. "Jesus God, that was funny. You should have seen yourself. You all right?" He extended a hand to Frank.

"Yeah, I think so," Frank said, taking Tim's hand and pulling himself up. "Thanks for caring. Where's that dog?"

"Coming down the driveway, and I'm not sure he's friendly. C'mon, let's skedaddle."

And with that, grabbing the saw at the last instant, they leaped into the Chevy, started up, and took off, both of them laughing now and leaving a perplexed boxer staring down the road at their taillight and exhaust.

The next night Tim bought a tree from a Rotary Club stand.

✳      ✳      ✳      ✳

"That surely is a beautiful tree you and Frank Clay cut down," Grandma Altschuler said to Tim, as she watched Peg put ornaments on. "I shouldn't have let you bring it in. I don't have a tree, normally, you know that, and the dear Lord only knows if you took it from someone's property." The look she gave Tim was full of forgiveness for any possible misdemeanor. "But it is beautiful, I will give you that."

Tim looked at Peg, and they smiled at each other. He had told her about the tree-cutting misadventure, and she had advised him to maintain that he had cut the tree anyway, to forestall her grandmother's certain protests at Tim's paying for an unwanted tree to bring into her house. Grandma's indulgence of Tim, like that of all the women in his life, had its unique limits.

It was three days before Christmas. The tree had stood several days, "settling," in Grandma's living room, which faced Peach Avenue. Grandma, mildly opposed to the Christmas tree as a concept, was not going to let one in her house be decorated until shortly before Christmas Day. But now it stood, fully decorated by Tim and Peg, twinkling its multi-colored lights out through the living room curtains and the porch windows to any passersby on Peach Avenue. They were pleased with their efforts, and stood next to each other in the gloaming, not touching, admiring the tree as "All I Want for Christmas Is My Two Front Teeth" played on the radio.

"Will someone please turn that damn song off?" said Henry Burnham, Peg's younger brother, who had come by the house with a couple of boxes of ornaments. "I've heard it a thousand times since yesterday. Don't they play any other songs on the radio at Christmastime anymore?"

"Henry Burnham," Grandma scolded, "I don't know where you learned that language, and I don't know, and don't *want* to know, where else you use it. But I do know I don't want you to use it in this house."

"Well, sorry, Grandma. But the song is enough to drive you nuts."

"Here, let me take a picture now," Peg said to Tim. She pointed the telescoped extension of a camera at the tree and looked through the view finder.

"Hey," Henry said, "you got one of those new instant cameras. What're they called?"

"Polaroid Land camera. Don't jostle me," Peg said, and snapped the shutter.

"How's it work?"

"I'll show you in a minute." Peg held the camera stiffly in front of her. "You have to wait sixty seconds for it to develop in the camera, then you pull it out here." She pointed to a small flap extending out one end of the camera. When a minute had gone by, she gave the flap a tug.

Everyone gathered around the curling piece of paper. As they watched, the image completed its emergence from chemicals and darkness into a fuzzy Christmas tree that blinked and sparkled gaily in gray and white.

"I think maybe I was standing too close to the tree," Peg said.

"No, the picture's great," Tim said. "What'll they think of next?"

\*     \*     \*     \*

About the time that Tim and Frank were in a stranger's driveway in Wynantskill, New York, attempting to cut off the top of his Scotch pine, Whittaker Chambers was in his strawberry patch in Westminster, Maryland, hiding microfilm inside a pumpkin that overgrew the patch, hoping thereby to discredit communism by using the skills that his failed faith had taught him. On December 15 Alger Hiss was indicted on charges of perjury, behind which lurked the greater charge of espionage, not prosecutable because the statute of limitations had run out. On December 20 one Laurence Duggan leaped or was thrown out of sixteenth-story offices in Manhattan. Chambers testified that Duggan was one of six who had provided confidential information to Soviet intelligence, and when a reporter asked Representative Karl Mundt, a member of the House Un-American Activities Committee, who the other five were, Mundt replied, "We'll release the others as they jump out windows."

In response to the growing communist threat, RCA released a new seven-inch, 45-rpm record, assigning a different color for each type of music. And Maurice and Richard McDonald opened a hamburger stand in San Bernardino, California, serving precooked food rather than preparing to order. Hamburgers were fifteen cents (four cents extra for cheese), soft drinks ten cents, milk shakes 20 cents, and coffee a nickel.

Only 30,000 American men were drafted in the late months of 1948. At the end of the year, the United Nations General Assembly recommended, 48-6, that the new government of South Korea be recognized as the only legitimate Korean government, but North Korea ignored the resolution and claimed sovereignty over the entire country.

# CHAPTER 11

▼

# DRIFTING AND DREAMING

*"[Emmeline's] father, like all men, did not understand romance as women did. Romance was when you fell in love with someone or something which was denied to you. Romance was not marriage."*

—Brian Moore, *The Magician's Wife*

Early in 1949, just when the draft was suspended for a short period and President Truman announced the first major civil rights bill since Reconstruction, Tim decided to move out of Grandma Altschuler's house. He decided—though "decided" is too strong a word for the process by which he reached that point—to move for a couple reasons, neither very clear to him. The clearest, perhaps, was that it was somewhat closer to where he worked, and since he still found it hard to get up, no matter which shift he worked, any time saved was a plus. Less definite but more significant was the distancing of his relationship with Peg, which he felt he could deal with better if the physical distance were greater, too. Neither of them—Peg in particular—seemed to want it, either the physical or emotional distance. Neither of them could explain why it was happening, especially Tim, who was doing most of the apparently unwilled distancing. And neither of them could stop it. The tinge of moodiness that had begun to color his personality—almost undetectable in a young man so outgoing but all the more affecting for that—probably joined with his usual restlessness to spark the move.

He found the room through Norm Artzahl, a friend at work. He and Norm were sitting in the Jenkins Diner in Watervliet eating a late supper on a Monday night and watching a puppet show on the seven-inch television set at their end of the rounded counter. The diner catered mostly to workers at the Watervliet Arsenal and offered meal tickets: pay five dollars and you got a ticket for meals worth five dollars and fifty cents. Since fifty cents would more than pay for one meal, Tim bought tickets frequently. The reception on the television set was lousy so they had begun talking with the counterman, Barry Jenkins, who helped out at his father's diner, about the recent snowfall in San Diego, the first one ever recorded there, the newspaper had said. Barry's family owned the house in which Norm roomed.

"Aunt Cissy wants to rent out another room," Norm said to Barry. Aunt Cissy was an elderly woman who rented the top floor of the Jenkins house and sublet a room to Norm.

"Yeah, that's what I heard," Barry replied as he restocked napkin dispensers. "Pop said it was OK with him."

"Tim here is interested," Norm said, cocking his head toward Tim. "He wants to move out of where he is now over in Guldwyck. Tim Davis, this is Barry Jenkins. Barry's Dad owns the house."

"Glad to meet you, Tim," Barry said, shaking Tim's proffered hand across the counter. "Well, you're welcome if you want to move in, but you'll need a shoehorn to do it. The only room left in her floor is more like an outsize closet. I don't know why Aunt Cissy wants to rent it. She's got more money than God."

"Aunt Cissy, she's your aunt?" Tim asked.

"Nah, she's no relation. That's just what everyone calls her, 'cause she's also *older* than God."

"I think she just likes having people around, makes her feel safe," Norm said. "She lets you have kitchen privileges," he added, as if that helped explain Aunt Cissy's rationale.

"That's another thing I don't understand," Barry said, clearing away Tim's and Norm's dishes. "She's got a brother and sister-in-law over to Menands, and a son in Guldwyck. But then, I guess I wouldn't want to live with my brother and sister-in-law, either, or son, if I had one."

Tim and Norm got up to go. They gave their meal tickets to Barry to punch, and while he was doing so Norm pointed to the snowy TV screen.

"That's dumb, that new program. What's it called? 'Cuckoo'? Good name for it."

"'Kookla,' I think it was, something like that," Tim said, pulling on his coat. "I don't know, I kind of liked it, what I could see."

"Naaaa, it's dumb. Who wants to watch a lot of dumb puppets?"

✳    ✳    ✳    ✳

And so, apparently fated to live with ersatz elderly relatives—first Grandma Altschuler and now Aunt Cissy—on the evening of the day that Harry S Truman and Alben W. Barkley were inaugurated, and the eve of his twenty-first birthday, Tim moved into his new digs. Grandma Altschuler was sorry to see him go. Peg stayed away. It was good that he had few things, because, as Barry had said, there was little space to put them. He had a single bed, a nightstand, a dresser, a narrow space between them, and no window to look out of. His room at Grandma's had been much nicer, but he was happy with the move. Prompted by the consciousness of this new stage in his life and by an unconscious desire to put some order into his irresolute existence, he bought a five-year diary and started keeping it. It was, in keeping with its keeper, a hit-or-miss affair, sometimes effusive but mostly mundane jottings.

Feb 1 (Tues) At Ludlum Steel, it has been cold this week so far, as much as 28 below sometimes; been putting in easy days.

Feb 2 (Wed) Only worked 15 minutes because of snow; went to Guldwyck Dollar Days, spent $4

Feb 4 (Fri) Unloading freight, electrodes, etc., on an easy day, then payday—$43.50 for 5 days. Went with Henry Burnham to the city to buy rubbers and a Valentine's Day card for Mom. Should I have got one for Peg too? Went skateing with her tonight, she still seems funny.

Feb 5 (Sat) In the rolling mill all day, 14" and 9". Worked 5 hours overtime; to bed as soon as I got home as I was tired.

Feb 6 (Sun) Got up and went to church over to Guldwyck with Grandma Burnham. I have continued to go with her like we all used to do together with Dave and Eileen when they were here. Peg came too. Very pretty in a pale blue suit. Church was nice; lasted an hour and a half. Went to Nichols in Albany; they were glad to see me.

Feb 7 (Mon) Got home from Nichols about 3 a.m.; watched television there for 4 hours.

Feb 8 (Tue) Got up at noon, left for work at 2:30—the finishing department; it was warm and easy, not tired.

Feb 11 (Fri) A south wind blowing, bringing snow and seeming to be cold. Went to store for Aunt Cissy. I talked for a while with Barry Jenkins' sister Lynn. A very pretty girl. About Peg's age I'd say. She lives downstairs with her parents, like Barry.

Feb 12 (Sat) Got up at 10, paid Aunt Cissy $5. Went to Jean's for breakfast, paid her $7 for lunches and other things. Went to Ward's, bought shotgun for Rick, $67. Got 2 Valentine's cards from Betty R. and Peg and a letter from home.

Feb 13 (Sun) Very cold, snowy, wind getting stronger. Was restless all day but managed to go to Harriet's and spend the night. Bought overcoat from her husband Freddie; almost new but it doesn't fit him so that's why he was selling it.

Feb 14 (Mon) On the 12-8 shift it's the graveyard shift, if you can manage to stay awake. We fix the salamanders, then sleep till morn.

Feb 15 (Tue) Slept till one in the afternoon. The weather has been warm, the snow is going fast.

Feb 17 (Thu) Was at church last night, stayed for chorus practice. I believe the voice is better. Listened to Duffy's Tavern after getting home from church. It was hilareous; Archie was scrapping with a friend from grade school who had been voted most likely to succeed.

Feb 18 (Fri) Got paid this morning, $43.65/40 hours. Went home, slept till noon.

Feb 19 (Sat) Went to Mont. Ward's, bought a baseball glove and fishing net, going to send them to Rick.

Feb 20 (Sun) Didn't get up in time for Sunday School but went to church, Laymen's Sunday. Ate a good dinner at Jean's. Leon is an odd duck. When I got there he said to me "f—k you." At least that's what I thought he said. It turns out what he was really saying was "fug you." He said he was reading a novel and that's how they said that word in the novel, to get around the censors, I guess. He thought it was funny. It's a good thing Jean didn't hear him. I guess it's a big best seller war book, The Naked Dead or something.

Feb 22 (Tue) Washington's Birthday, the Father of Our Country. I was stopped at the main gate and told I was now drafted on the new 9" mill till bumped, starting on nights this week.

Feb 23 (Wed) I bought a dictionary and a song book at the five-and-dime.

Feb 24 (Thu) I caught a cold somewhere. I've been sleeping till 11 a.m.

Feb 25 (Fri) Today is payday. I drew $44.43 for last week's work on 12-8 shift. I very much feel the urge to study hard for some goal but don't know what it is.

Feb 26 (Sat) Went to do some shopping for Grandma Altschuler. Peg was there. Played a basketball game at Sacred Heart; we won. Took Peg to a movie, A Letter to Three Wives. With Jean Crane & Linda Darnell. Quite the story; we both liked it. Peg's a great girl.

Feb 27 (Sun) Went to Sunday School and church afterward. Dinner at Jean's. Leon has not been feeling well the past week; he is on a diet. A basketball game in the afternoon, young people's meeting, church again, met a girl.

*    *    *    *

Of course he met a girl. Tim was always meeting girls. It was harder for him to avoid a girl than for the moth to avoid the flame. But who was the moth, who the flame? And was the flame ever all-consuming? He continued to go out occasionally with Peg, and visited with members of her family and his own relatives every week, but increasingly he dated Lynn Jenkins, Barry's sister.

After talking to her in early February he found he liked her. She was his age, twenty-one, five-foot-three, with short-cropped, truly honey-golden hair, green eyes, an almost plump face and a figure that was fuller than that of most of the young women he knew. The funny thing was, she worked for the state government, too, like Peg, but for the department of motor vehicles, not the tax department.

All that late winter and into spring they did a lot of things together, went to movies and roller-skating and bowling and, when it got warmer, miniature golf. On one of their dates, on a Monday just past the middle of March, they played canasta, the rummy-like Argentine card game whose popularity was raging through the country. They went out with Frank Clay and his date, a woman named Cynthia, who was the true enthusiast for the game. They played on a card table in the living room of an Albany apartment Cynthia shared with a roommate, who was working second shift that evening. After playing a couple of hands, Frank called for a break so that he could listen to Suspense, which he didn't like to miss. Cynthia, joined by Lynn, went to the kitchen to make coffee and cut up a coffee cake. The two men sat for a half-hour and listened to Gregory Peck in "The Lonely Road" plot with his girlfriend to kill his wife, of whom he had tired, only to have a change of heart when it was too late. The women, bearing coffee and coffee cake, came back into the living room just as the announcer was signing off, telling the audience that Suspense was sponsored by Roma Wines, "made in California for enjoyment throughout the world," and broadcast on CBS, "from coast to coast and to our men and women of the armed forces overseas, by short wave and through the worldwide facilities of the Armed Forces Radio Service."

"It's nice they have that," Cynthia said as she and Lynn set cups and saucers down on the card table. "Was it a good program?"

"Yes, it was great. Gregory Peck. They knew what they were doing when they called it *Suspense*," Frank said. "It's nice they have what?"

"That Armed Forces Radio thing they just mentioned," Cynthia said. "If our boys have to be overseas away from home and all, at least they should have some entertainment they're used to."

"Uh-huh," Frank said, stirring sugar into his coffee and taking a sip. "Great coffee, Cyn. I've been thinking of joining up."

"What?" Tim said, incredulous. "Enlisting?"

"Yeah."

"Why?"

"Why not? You might as well, they're going to draft you sooner or later anyway. Unless you've got flat feet or are queer or something."

Cynthia giggled.

"What draft?" Tim asked. "The draft's suspended."

"Now it's suspended. Tomorrow it'll probably be on again."

"I think I had this conversation with my mother over a year ago," Tim said. "But you're right about that—on-again, off-again."

"Well, I hope it stays off," Lynn said, hitching her chair closer to Tim's and hooking her left arm through his right, tenderly. "I don't know why they need the draft anyway. The war's been over almost four years."

"Well," Cynthia said, scooping together the scattered playing cards, "I'm drafting you for one more hand of canasta, at least, before we have to call it a night."

✳    ✳    ✳    ✳

Apr 2 (Sat) I have been trying to read the newspaper more. I should know more about what is going on in the world. I see it says they turned the street lights and advertising signs on in London for the first time in 10 years. That seems like a long time.

Apr 3 (Sun) Good old Sunday. I do not like to get up but Grandma Altschuler made me and that was all right because they're my real friends and I did have fun at the Young People's meeting. I stayed at Grandma's Saturday night because we were playing pinochle and it got late and they said why not stay. Peg was there. It was nice to see her.

Apr 4 (Mon) Got up at 10:30 a.m. It was raining out. Got a letter from Mother, everything OK back home. The paper says America, England, Canada and some European countries have started up a group for defense called NATO, but I forget what that means.

Apr 7 (Thu) Got a letter from Mother and Jim Calder today; he got the baseball glove OK that I sent him. Work 4-12 this week.

Apr 12 (Tue) I like days better because I have the night to run around in and I went to the show, saw The Hasty Heart about an English army hospital with Ronald Ragan. Very touching.

Apr 15 (Fri) Got paid today, $55. Paid Aunt Cissy $5. Have a date tonight with Rosemary, a girl from church. Going to Guldwyck High play.

April 16 (Sat) Went to work, came home, played basketball till 5:30 and went to American Theater in Guldwyck with Frank Clay, met some girl.

Apr 17 (Sun) Got up about 5:30, read a little, then ate breakfast, shaved and cleaned up for Easter Sunday.

Apr 19 (Tue) Afternoons this week. This is our last night on the new 9" mill, we go down to the old 9" mill on Monday 12-8 of next week, so we won't be laid off.

Apr 20 (Wed) Went down to Albany, got 16 gage double barrel for $42 and a box of shells for Jim and a box of shells for my gun.

Apr 22 (Fri) Shot 4 shells in my new gun to try it out. Got paid $62.14 a large check.

Apr 24 (Sun) I didn't get up till 10:30 and didn't go to church and don't care either because I felt as though they didn't care. I was too late for the Young People's meeting.

Apr 29 (Fri) I have been packing my own lunches, sleeping most of the day too. My boss, Ernie, took me fishing this week, bullhead. $63 was check this week.

*        *        *        *

It was a lovely, warm evening in mid-May. The city was already beginning to take on the aspects of summer. Noises were brighter, warmer, cheerier, more abundant: car doors, car horns, cars racing away from traffic lights, house doors, kids playing on the sidewalks. Lights that were not noticed or not there in winter were suddenly back: neon signs in their garish red and orange and green, car headlights, store windows throwing trapezoids of dazzling light onto the sidewalks. Now and then a mother could be heard calling for her son to get in the house this instant. A light breeze was blowing and all was right with this little part of the world.

Lynn and Tim sat at an outside table in the small paved lot adjoining Chris's Diner, which proclaimed on its door, We Serve Everything From Hotdogs to Hamburgers and Everybody From Him to Her, Ha Ha, The Prop. Because of the warm weather a few customers, like Lynn and Tim, had ventured to eat outside. He and she had come from Tim's softball game at Congress Park in Watervliet. Tim played third base for his Allegheny Ludlum team, which had won 11-6 against an Albany team. The enticing aroma of onions and French fries and hot grease wafted out the diner's raised windows, along with the strains of "Cruising Down the River."

"I like this song, but it's beginning to get old," Tim said. "Seems like it's been running forever."

"Mmmm, me too," Lynn said, working her jaw around to keep a fried onion from sliding down her chin. "But this is Russ Morgan. I prefer the Blue Barron version."

"Huh. I couldn't've told you the difference. I didn't know there *were* two versions."

Lynn, holding the remains of her hamburger in two hands before her mouth, smiled at Tim, and he, viewing her grease-smeared chin and tousled hair in the shadows created by the dim, softening light from the windows, thought she looked lovely. This is like a movie, he thought, Jimmy Stewart and Dorothy McGuire or somebody. The unaccustomed image pleased him, and the sound of the cars rushing by on the avenue and sucking away the last thumping notes of "Cruising Down the River" couldn't have been more like a movie if he had directed it himself.

"What're you reading?" Lynn, her arms propped straight up and still holding her half-eaten hamburger in her two hands, had her head canted away to the left, squinting in the semidarkness to read a copy of the Guldwyck *Standard* someone had left on the table.

"Huh?" she said, glancing at him and then turning back to the newspaper. "Oh, I was just reading this story about Rodgers and Hammerstein's *South Pacific*, what a hit it's been in New York. They say it might be as big as *Oklahoma*. It had a million dollars in advance ticket sales when it opened April 7." She returned to eating her hamburger and looking at Tim. "I wouldn't mind seeing that. I missed *Oklahoma* and I've always regretted it. Maybe I'll get to see a road company version."

"I seem to keep having these conversations over and over."

"What?"

"Oh, nothing," Tim said, and smiled. "You remember that draft discussion I had with Frank a couple months ago that I said was like one I had with my mother?"

"Vaguely."

"Well, it's just I had a similar conversation about *Oklahoma* with someone else once."

"'Someone else,'" Lynn mocked. "Someone female, I imagine?" she said with a sly smile that she hoped both indicated she was joking and masked her desire for a full and complete answer.

"Aaaaah, women," Tim said, sipping his Coke and setting the glass down on the table.

"I know. You can't live with 'em and you can't live without 'em, right?" The sly smile, somewhat broader, remained on Lynn's face.

"No, it's not that. It's just, I don't know, it seems somehow so hard to get along. I mean, with girls I really like."

"Oh. We're not getting along? Or maybe you don't really like me?" The same smile.

Tim was embarrassed. "No, no, I like you. See? It's starting to happen again. It's probably me."

"It probably is. I mean that in a nice way." Lynn cocked her right ear toward voices and laughter coming from the radio. "You know what you're like, Tim? You're like that Mr. Boynton there on *Our Miss Brooks*, kind of a divine dope. You don't know what a great guy you are. And that's your charm. I think you pick women you know you can't get anywhere with, which I also think is what you really mean by 'can't get along with.' And so women, the poor saps, are all the more attracted to you. Maybe they all secretly hope they're that kind of girl—even when they are."

"See? I told you I keep having these conversations."

"What? People have told you this before? And by people I mean women?"

"Well, yeah, stuff sort of like this. Once."

"And yet, imagine that, you're not the least bit conceited." A big smile.

"I didn't mean to sound conceited. You're the one who said that stuff."

"Tim, you're *not* conceited. I'm kidding you. See? Big smile." And she produced a forced grin that displayed all her teeth. "Maybe you ought to try sticking with just one woman. I'm not advertising for the job, understand"—she hoped it wasn't too obvious that in fact she was—"but it might simplify things for you."

"I don't know what you mean."

"Oh, please. I know you go out with Peg Burnham and with other girls. And you have a perfect right. But you don't then also have a perfect right to moan. Some people say you're still carrying a torch for a girl from Ohio." She cocked an inquisitive eye at him.

"Some people don't know what they're talking about. That's over long ago."

"Um-hmm. Well, this is getting too intense. Let's talk about something else. What do you think about the Russians ending their blockade in Berlin? That's good news, don't you think?"

*        *        *        *

The Soviets did end their nearly yearlong blockade of Berlin on May 12, but the Americans and British would continue their airlift of supplies to the city until September 30. Ending the blockade by no means meant ending of tensions. Less than two weeks later, on May 23, the Federal Republic of Germany—West Germany—was established, with Bonn as its capital and comprising two-thirds of the old Germany. A month after that the last U.S. forces were withdrawn from Korea, the southern portion of which they had been occupying since the end of World War II, leaving only a military mission. The Soviets also continued to pull their troops out of North Korea while strengthening the North Korean People's Army. President Truman, calling Korea a testing ground for democracy "marched against the practices of communism," called on Congress to appropriate $150 million in economic aid for South Koreans, which would be approved later in the year. None of this did anything to ease tensions, either.

*        *        *        *

Jun 2 (Wed) Changed shifts with Eddie Roebler. from 4-12 to 12-8 so I could be in a play at church and it turned out OK. We cleared $25.

Jun 3 (Fri) Stayed off work today. Freddie Farrell was drinking and his work is on strike at the Valve company. I took him to get his check and get their groceries, he and Harriet are having it tough. Took Nancy T. to Guldwyck High prom & enjoyed it very much. Nancy is a divine dancer. Took her and another couple in my car.

Jun 11 (Sat) Went to Albany and met a little Wop girl, made a date for Wednesday night. Home at 1:00 and didn't have any girls out.

Jun 12 (Sun) Today is children's day and you ought to have seen the kids at church. Everyone said a little rhyme and most of the small babies were baptized. Peg was there.

Jun 13 (Mon) Went to Nichols and had breaks put on car and left it there.

Jun 15 (Wed) The Wop is no good.

Jun 18 (Sat) Took Nancy T. to the movies. Saw an older one from last year I think, The Snake Pit. About a loony bin. Don't think Nancy liked it.

Jun 19 (Sun) Crystal Lake with Nancy. Battery broke on car.

Jun 21 (Tue) I'm having a fine time getting someone to help me with the car. Just like Penna, no one will help you unless you kiss their ass.

Jun 26 (Sun) I joined the church today. Mr. Grundon's idea, the Methodist preacher, but it was a good move, I'm sure.

Jun 27 (Mon) Last night was Fred Allen's last radio show. That is kind of sad, though the program was funny. I've been listening to F. Allen a long time. Jack Benny, his life long "enemy," was his guest.

Jun 29 (Wed) Boy was I tired. This 12-8 shift is a killer but it's something that goes with the job so that's that. What I think I would like is a small trailer so I could be by my work.

✳     ✳     ✳     ✳

At 8:30 on a warm night in July, a singing voice came bouncing out of the television set in Peg's mother's apartment:

> *"It pays to be ignorant!*
> *"To be dumb, to be dense, to be ignorant.*
> *"It pays to be ignorant*
> *"Just like me!"*

"Hey!" Tim shouted, "it's *It Pays to Be Ignorant*. I loved that program on radio. I haven't listened to it in a long time. I didn't know it was on TV. Wizard!"

"Wizard?"

"Yeah, wizard. Isn't that what the kids say these days—*wizard*? You know, like *terrific*."

Peg laughed. "I don't know. I'm not up on the latest slang." She knelt in front of the recently acquired set, a 15-inch Majestic, peering at and twiddling the knobs to try and adjust the vertical hold, then the horizontal hold, then the vertical hold again. Finally she gave up. "I'm not sure this is a regular program. It might be on just for the summer." She moved back to the couch and sat down next to Tim.

"I wish the picture would come in better," Tim said. Poor reception was causing the faces on the screen to twist grotesquely to the left, like in a funhouse mirror. He got up to fiddle with the rabbit ears, to no success. One of the panelists on the show told a bad joke, and in reply one of other panelists, Harry McNaughton, hooted his trademark, "Hoo, ha ha ha. Hoo, ha ha ha. Hoo, ha ha ha"—a pause, then, deadpan: "I don't get it."

"It cracks me up every time he does that." Tim sat back down on the couch.

"You really like this show? It's not really a quiz show."

"I know. It's not supposed to be. It's hilarious."

"There are many sides to your personality, Tim Davis."

"That sounds like less than a complete compliment."

"Oh, no," Peg said, smiling fondly at the back of his head as she stroked it with her left hand. "I'm really tickled at the range of your interests."

"I mean, I know the program's silly." He added, defensively, as if it explained his interest: "I was just surprised it was on television."

"Tim, it's OK that you like the program." She changed the subject: "Do you still like where you're living?"

"It's OK. Well, you know, sometimes I wish I was back at Grandma's. She used to get on me about not getting up for work on time, but that was all right and I guess I needed it. Now Aunt Cissy does it. Aunt Cissy—she's the woman I sublet from. Me and Norm Artzahl."

"I know. You've told me you or Norm sometimes drive her to visit her brother in Menands. That's nice of you."

"That's right, I'd forgotten I told you. We tease Aunt Cissy a lot, but she doesn't seem to mind it."

"That must be a pretty full house. The three of you upstairs, and the Jenkinses have grown children living with them, don't they?"

"Yes. Barry, he helps out at the diner sometimes." Tim turned his attention back to the TV screen. "And their daughter, Lynn."

"Oh yes, Lynn. I think you've mentioned her."

They both listened to the faint, distant wail of a train whistle over the laughter from the television. Peg flipped through a magazine and came across an ad that, it struck her, she had been seeing a lot recently. It showed a haughtily beautiful woman dressed in only a skirt and a bra and said, "I dreamed I went shopping in my Maidenform bra." It seemed to her daring and she wondered how men reacted to it. Were ads for women's things meant to attract men, or women? She wanted to show it to Tim and ask, but didn't.

Tim broke the silence: "You're probably glad to have your mother back from Arizona."

"Yes. And I imagine your mother is happy to have your sister back." Peg's mother and Tim's sister Connie had come back from Arizona together on the train. "But you never know. Mom might have to go out again. I'd like to go out there again myself, but I really couldn't ask them to give me more time off work."

"Any news about Eileen?"

"Well, you know, the usual thing, just like when they were here. Sometimes it looks like the Arizona climate is doing her good, sometimes not."

Tim hesitated, as if not sure whether to pursue the line that thoughts of Eileen had evoked, but continued anyway: "Not to add to the gloom or anything, but I wonder what the Clays are going to do now? With Mr. Clay gone, I mean." Frank Clay's father had died of a heart attack the week before, and Tim had gone to the funeral.

"All those young children, you mean? And with their mother passed away— what?—less than two years ago. Who'll take care of them?"

"Frank and the older sisters, I suppose. I don't imagine he'll be enlisting now."

"Who? Frank, enlisting? What do you mean?"

"He and I were talking, I don't remember when, exactly. Earlier this year, any-way. He said he was thinking of enlisting. Might as well, he thought, since the draft will get us anyway."

"*Ooooh*, the draft," Peg said, damningly, dismissively.

From the television set came *It Pays to Be Ignorant* quizmaster Tom Howard's sign-off:

"Good night … and good nonsense!"

\*　　\*　　\*　　\*

Aug 5 (Fri) The clutch broke on my car and that is about the fourth time it's let me down. Have to get it fixed and right before my trip home.

Aug 12 (Fri) Pulled the car up to Clays today so we can work on it, it's been hot weather. Read in the paper that Margaret Mitchell the author of Gone With the Wind was hit by a car yesterday and is in bad condition. I never read that book, I should.

Aug 13 (Sat) I've been looking around for a clutch for my car, no find.

Aug 14 (Sun) Went swimming, Watervliet pool. Some nice girls over there.

Aug 17 (Wed) Gave Aunt Cissy $6, room not worth it but she takes it anyway. I see that Marg. Mitchell died from that car accident.

Aug 19 (Fri) Went down to Ward's, met a girl, her name is Connie, just like my sister. I have a date Friday night next week.

Aug 20 (Sat) Down to Ward's again to see Connie again, got to know her better.

Aug 24 (Wed) Down to Clays. Found a clutch and we got car fixed. Rick arrived on the train, he's staying at Harriet's till we go home.

Aug 26 (Fri) Grossed $71 last week, after union dues, etc., made $57.

Aug 31 (Wed) I've been out till 1:00-2:00 every night this week and boy I'm tired too. I've not made out so good either.

∗     ∗     ∗     ∗

"So, is this a very special girl, then, Tim?" Anna Davis asked her son.

Anna and Tim were sitting at the table in the kitchen of her small house in Black Run. It was the Sunday before Labor Day and she was cooking and baking for a big family gathering to be held there on the holiday. Tim and Rick, who had come up to visit Tim earlier in August, had driven down from New York on Friday night after Tim got off work. The purpose of Rick's visit north had been to scout out the possibility of work, now that he was out of high school. It was not the first time Tim had been home—he had visited three or four times in the year and a half since he moved to New York—but this was the first time he had brought a woman along.

"Lynn?" Tim said in response to his mother's question. "No, not special. She's just a friend."

"Young men don't usually bring young women to meet their mothers when they're 'just friends,'" Anna responded, the quotation marks around "just friends" almost visible. "I don't remember you doing that with that Ohio girl, Helen. Peg Burnham was here for mother's funeral of course, but she's almost family. Nice girl. But then, so was that Helen, so I gather."

"Mom, will you lay off Helen? That's ancient history. And so is Peg. Well, not ancient history—I mean, Peg's just a friend, too."

"And so is this Lynn, from what I can tell so far—nice, I mean. The girls love her." Lynn, who had been wedged in with Barbara and Connie to sleep, was getting along famously with Tim's sisters.

"Mother," Tim said slowly, as if with superhuman patience, "she's *just* a friend. We both had the time off from work for the holiday and we thought it would be a fun trip to come down here, the three of us together. And it was fun—is, I mean."

"Except for the part about the speeding ticket, I suppose?"

Tim looked startled. "Oh, you heard about that."

"Yes." Anna smiled impishly. "From your 'friend.'" Again, the quotation marks.

"How's Grandpa doing?" Tim asked, eager to steer the conversation away from where it seemed to be heading.

"Your grandfather is fine. He misses Mother, but he's doing very well. I don't believe he's eager to move in here, but he really should be living with someone. He's over eighty, you know. I've had a couple estimates to add on a room, but, really, the costs." Anna paused, hearing a sound outside the door. "Oh. Here's your friend now."

Lynn, coming in to the kitchen, let the screen door close behind her without banging.

"Did you have a nice time in Horton with the girls, dear?" Anna asked.

"Oh yes, very much." Conscious of both Tim's and Anna's eyes on her, Lynn ran her hands through her wind-blown hair. "It's a lovely town. Barb and Connie showed me all the places you go on Saturday night."

"Used to go," Anna said. "Not so much anymore. Everyone's scattering. Soon it'll be Rick, too, from the looks of it." She rose from the table to get the coffee-pot from the stove. "Coffee, dear?"

"No thank you. We had Cokes in town."

"You, Tim? More coffee?" She waggled the coffeepot in his direction.

"No thanks, Mom." Tim shot a mock-fierce look at Lynn. "I understand you told Mom about Rick's speeding ticket."

Lynn giggled. She was not unaware that a girlish demeanor suited her just-shy-of-plump physique. "Yes, I hope you're not mad. I thought it was funny."

"Funny? There's nothing funny about a thirty-five dollar speeding ticket."

"No, but you were so angry at Rick." She giggled again. "Tim, you *never* get angry. At anyone."

"Well, going forty-nine miles an hour in a twenty-mile zone in Tyrone is enough to make anyone mad." Tim turned to explain to his mother: "It was late and I was tired from working, so I let Rick drive when we got into Pennsylvania.

I fell asleep. He should have known the cops would be out on a holiday week-end."

"That was the funny thing," Lynn said to Anna, who had sat back down at the table. "You could tell the policeman was wondering what this girl was doing in a car with two guys at one o'clock in the morning. I think he thought Tim and Rick were white slavers or something. He had this big old potbelly and he kept asking us questions. But he let us go, finally."

"Yeah, he asked almost as many questions as your mother," Tim said.

Anna looked at Lynn questioningly.

"My mother." Lynn smiled broadly. "She didn't want me to come. That is, not that she didn't *want* me to come, but she thought it wasn't right. That nice girls don't go traipsing off into the night to another state with two guys. Even though my mother knows Tim and Rick are great guys. It's just not done. I finally told her, 'Mother, I'm free, white, and twenty-one, and I can take care of myself.' I'm sure she worries that *you* think it's terrible."

"Not at all. I understand your mother's concern, but I'm awfully glad you came." Anna pushed herself up from the table with both arms. "Now, if you'll excuse me, I should get back to my baking."

"Can I do anything to help?"

"Oh, no. You enjoy yourself while you're here."

"No, but really, I'd like to, if there's anything."

"Well, if you really want to, there's some apples need peeling for the pies." Anna looked at Tim. "But I should put him and his brother to work on them, rather than have their guest work. Isn't that Rick I hear outside, singing?"

"Yes," Lynn said. "'Riders in the Sky.' He's been singing it since we left Guld-wyck. I think he thinks he's Vaughn Monroe."

"I hate to think of him going up to Guldwyck, too. But it's inevitable, I sup-pose. And he does have Tim there, with all his friends. It's nice Tim has so many friends."

*     *     *     *

But Rick, like his brother before him, did not act immediately on his plans to move to Guldwyck; that would wait until next year. Tim and Lynn drove back to New York late in the afternoon of Labor Day. The next day they both returned to work, and Howard Unruh, a former war hero, went berserk in Camden, New Jersey, and shot 13 people to death in 12 minutes, saying later he would have killed more but ran out of ammunition. Tim continued in his usual rounds, drifting and dreaming, but appalled, like most Americans, by this clear sign of moral breakdown in the world. On October 1, with the Nationalists fleeing to the island of Formosa, the communists declared the People's Republic of China under the chairmanship of Mao Tse-tung. Not to be outdone, on October 7 the Soviets, without benefit of elections, created the German Democratic Republic with its capital in Berlin. Bonn, the capital of the West German state, declared the East German regime illegal and claimed jurisdiction over all Germans. On October 10, in the new series *The Adventures of Philip Marlowe* on CBS radio, the actor Gerald Mohr, playing Marlowe, got involved in an impossibly complicated plot concerning a white Panama hat. On October 25, the first jet airliner, a British Overseas Airways Corporation de Havilland Comet, went from London to Tripoli, and the next day the minimum hourly wage went from 40 cents to 75 cents in the United States. And Upstate New York went toward yet another winter.

Tim continued to go out with both Peg and Lynn, and sometimes with other women. They both knew of his two-timing, though neither thought of it that way, since nothing "serious" had been declared between them, and they also, though less frequently, went out with other men. Lynn was going out, off and on, with a guy from Massachusetts, someone older than Tim who had been in the Navy. At this time, Peg sort of evolved, generally, into being his "inside girl"—they often would stay home, or go to someone else's house, to listen to the radio, watch television, or play cards or Monopoly or other board games, or just visit family—and Lynn into his "outside girl," for bowling, roller-skating, movies, and so forth. Lynn belonged to the Watervliet Young Republicans Club—a valiant stand, since Watervliet and all of Albany County were Democratic—and sometimes club members would do social things together, though Jim never formally joined the club. Why this inside/outside division happened could have been because of mutual family ties, throwing Peg to the "inside," but more likely it was just because things happen.

One of the most pleasant memories Tim could call up later, after he left New York, was of sitting in Peg's apartment on an unseasonably cold Wednesday night late in September, listening to *Escape* on the radio in the semi-dark and eating homemade popcorn. "We offer you *Escape*," the announcer said, "starring Van Heflin. *Escape*, designed to free you from the four walls of today for a half-hour of high adventure." And while Van Heflin ran around a remote island trying to escape a murderous madman in Joseph Hergesheimer's "Wild Oranges," Tim and Peg sat and talked and occasionally necked and speculated about the future. It would be one of Peg's nicest memories, too.

Memories feed on memories. Later, both he and Lynn would recall going to see Farley Granger and Cathy O'Donnell in *They Live by Night*, director Nicholas Ray's first film. To Lynn's thinking, Tim on this November evening seemed, strangely, more vulnerable and tender than she had ever before known him to be. Tim, for his part, was lost in thought of Cathy O'Donnell's fragile prettiness. Her perpetual air of sadness, like a nun committed to dolor, was terribly fetching. She looks like Aunt Eileen, he thought, except Eileen, despite her illness, smiles more. And then he remembered that he had once thought she looked like Helen.

The inside/outside split was not absolute. One significant departure was New Year's Eve, a Saturday, when Tim took Peg to a dinner-dance at the Guldwyck Eagles Club. Tim wore a sport jacket and slacks, and Peg a modestly cut, deep-blue satin, knee-length dress that displayed her figure nicely. Tim bought her a corsage, which got crushed a bit during their dancing. Despite his aversion to dancing, they did get out on the floor for a few of the slow ones. At close to midnight, when the band played "You're Breaking My Heart," which was currently popular in the Vic Damone recording, Tim thought it might be his own that would break, it was so full, and he came this close to telling Peg he thought he might be in love with her. But then it was midnight and the band began playing "Auld Lang Syne and everybody was singing and then shouting Happy New Year and the moment was lost. In the jostling of the raucous and drunken crowd Tim took tight hold of Peg and kissed her more fiercely than he had ever kissed anyone, so that it nearly frightened as well as thrilled her, and then he released her and she looked at him in wonderment, and then it was 1950.

\*        \*        \*        \*

In the new year Tim, who had been saving money regularly anyway, began putting away even more, sometimes as much as fifty dollars a week, in order to buy a new car. He had his eye on a 1950 Chevrolet convertible, which he had been admiring since the previous fall when the new models came out. It's the little things that catch your eye: He was inordinately taken by the speedometer, which, with increasing speed, turned a vivid red.

There were no draft inductions in late 1949 or early 1950. Seven men broke into the Boston Brink's Express Co. just after 7 p.m. January 17, tied up the employees, and made off with nearly three million dollars in cash and money orders. Four days later Alger Hiss, in the second of his trials on perjury charges, was convicted on two counts and, four days after that, sentenced to two concurrent five-year prison terms. On February 9 Senator Joseph McCarthy, Republican of Wisconsin, desperate to find a way to salvage his foundering Senate career, made the first of his communism charges. During a talk to the Republican Women's Club of Wheeling, West Virginia, he held up what he claimed was a list of 205 known communists working in the State Department. The next day, Tim got an income tax refund of $15.05.

On February 24, a Friday, Arlene and Dorothy—and their Grandmother Burnham, who had gone out to get them—came home from Arizona on the train. After a year and a half, the attempt to improve Eileen's health with the dry heat of the Southwest was over. It had not worked. Indeed, Eileen was on oxygen more often than ever. She and Dave were traveling back in the car by themselves so that they could make a stop at the Mayo Clinic in Rochester, Minnesota. Tim was happy to see the girls again, whom he loved more like nieces or even daughters rather than the much younger cousins they were. The weather all that month and into the next was bitter cold, often below zero. Late in the month he helped Peg's sister, Pat, and her husband, Bernie Pachowski, and their two young daughters move some of their belongings into Grandma Altschuler's house, the first floor of which they were renting with a plan eventually to buy the entire house. Tim told himself, well, I can't go back to rooming there now even if I wanted to.

✳    ✳    ✳    ✳

Mar 1 (Wed) Slept till 3:00. Got ready and went to work 4-12. A cold afternoon, 9 below, the radio said.

Mar 2 (Thu) Another cold day. Got a letter from Mother. Got my check, my pay was $67.76, banked $50. They want to know when we want our vacations. I want to go to Canada on mine.

Mar 5 (Sun) Church. That boy-crazy girl was after me again for a date. I went to Nichols for dinner. Boy, what a meal.

Mar 7 (Tue) 8-4 this week. I got up OK. The 14" mill has 2 25-men crews, not producing as expected. To Nichols for television. Milton Burrow was on vacation.

Mar 9 (Thu) Eddie H. owes me $1.00, Alvy 10 cents, Brody $1.00, Stanley 50 cents. These guys love to borrow and hate to pay back. Church, young people's meeting was a flop. Kids are to crazy.

Mar 10 (Fri) Got paid today. Made $101.48, net pay $88.40. Paid Aunt Cissy $6. Met Pam from Cohoes, told her to come down skating Fri nite 2 weeks away. She is small & cute soph. in school

Mar 14 (Tue) Beautiful day. Snowed hard last nite. A good nite, 4-12. I must get a haircut.

Mar 15 (Wed) Beautiful weather. Peg's back is a lot better now. This is 8 weeks she's been laid up with lower back pain. Poor kid.

Mar 16 (Thu) Planning on a new car by April or June. I see some Senator is going after Ingrid Bergmann for having an affair and a baby with that Italian movie guy but she's married to someone else.

Mar 17 (Fri) Happy St. Paddy's Day. Sun is bright, warm. Banked $100.00. Paid Aunt Cissy $6. Only owe $2 on Mother's vacume cleaner now.

Mar 21 (Tue) Got up without Aunt Cissy calling. Went to Nichols for television. The author of the Tarzan books died the other day. I liked them, I'll have to read some again.

Mar 25 (Sat) Went square dancing at Carrol's Grove. Met a Miss Bronson. All right.

Mar 26 (Sun) Was out till 4:45 a.m. last nite, with Paul M. to all the grills. I don't believe in that kind of doing so that's the last time.

Mar 27 (Mon) Gave Arlene $1.00 for dancing lessons. She and Dorothy are staying with their Grandma again. Got my registration for my Chev, $14.50. Wind was blowing today.

Mar 29 (Wed) 4-12. A good nite today. Was beautiful. Went to Albany to find out about Mother's compensation check she hadn't received and did some shopping.

Mar 30 (Thu) Went to Harriet's today. Got a letter from Jim Calder. He's sure stuck on that Denise and it's a shame. He's lowering himself.

*     *     *     *

Tim placed the order for his 1950 Chevrolet convertible on the first Monday in April. He ordered a tan car with a red plaid interior and a black top. The next day he went to the florist and ordered Easter corsages to be delivered to his mother and sisters in Black Run. He had continued going out, sometimes with Peg or Lynn or other girls, sometimes with Frank or just by himself, to the Nicholses, or to Dave's brother Henry, to watch television. He took Peg to see *The Third Man*, which he liked—especially the zither music—but didn't quite understand, and Lynn to see *Twelve O'Clock High*, about which he got very enthused. In his diary for April he noted that he went out with a girl he identified only as "Penny G.," whom he "necked" on one occasion "for five hours" and on another "till 4 a.m.," but was not more specific. He went to Easter church services, and the Tuesday night after Easter he took Arlene and Dorothy from their grandmother's over to Harriet's for a visit, but Harriet had to go to work so he ended up babysitting them and their energetic monkeyshines about drove him crazy. The next evening, April 12, Dave and Eileen arrived in Guldwyck in Dave's light green 1949 Ford—the model that, last year, Tim had salivated over—which he had bought in Arizona to replace the valiant but eventually gasping '40 Ford that had taken them westward. Their trailer they had sold in Tucson.

Eileen, Tim thought, did not look good. She was frequently, if not continuously, on oxygen, and definitely thinner than when he had last seen her in the summer of 1948. Yet, despite the signs of emaciation, the King female beauty would not be suppressed; she still seemed lovely to Tim, now almost ethereally so.

The Saturday after they returned—a gorgeously sunny and warm spring day—Tim went with Dave in Dave's car into downtown Guldwyck to price television sets for Eileen. As they rode down Raleigh Avenue and talked over recent events, Tim began to have one of those feelings of eternal recurrence, though he would never have put that name to it, that came over him at infrequent intervals.

"How's Eileen doing, then, Dave?" *Haven't I had this conversation before?*

"Oh, gosh, Tim. You've seen her. I—*we*—try to stay optimistic, and at the Mayo Clinic they said her condition was stable. But she's on oxygen almost all the time now. Fact, after we look at the TV sets, I should stop at the medical supply store and see about ordering some more."

"Arizona didn't do her any good?"

"No, not really. Even so, I liked it there—we all liked it there—but we decided we should come back here where family is, all other things being the same."

"I know my sister Connie enjoyed her time there with you."

"And we enjoyed having her. It was wonderful of her to help us out, and your mom for letting her. The King family is just plain wonderful any way you look at it. I sure lucked out when I met Eileen and her family."

Tim looked out his window at the people in light jackets or even shirtsleeves walking briskly down the golden spring sidewalk. From the car's radio, which was on low volume, Teresa Brewer began belting out "Music! Music! Music!" Tim reached over and clicked it off.

"You mind?" he asked, looking at Dave.

"No. I kind of like it. Bouncy. But I've heard it enough lately."

"You're going back to work at the Arsenal?"

"Monday. When I left I deliberately didn't burn any bridges. They liked my work and said if I ever wanted to come back, I could. And when we decided to leave Arizona, I wrote my old boss and he kept his word. Fortunately, we were able to move in with Grandma Altschuler for the time being. Can't stay there forever, of course, because she's going to sell the house to Pat and Bernie eventually. Oh, wait, here we are, Tredup's Appliances." Dave pulled into a parking spot about a hundred yards from the store.

In the store they were greeted jovially by a tall man wearing mismatched pants and sport jacket and a wide tie bearing a neon representation of a Hawaiian scene that barely reached halfway down the gut that hung over his belt.

"I'm Jack," he boomed, and extended his right hand, which until that point had been rubbing the left, apparently in anticipation of the sales riches to come their way. "What can I do for you folks?"

"We were interested in looking at television sets," Dave said.

"Then you've come to the right place," the man named Jack said, and spread his right arm out expansively toward a large array of television sets against the wall. "We've got more TVs than any store in Guldwyck. I doubt any store in the entire Albany area has more TVs. Were you looking for something in particular?"

"Well, I don't know," Dave said, in that purchaser's collapse all salesmen hope for. "Something not too expensive."

"Then you'll want to look at these table models here," Jack said, walking over and putting his hand down on one of them. Made of wood and covered with fabric in front, it looked like a large radio with a gray-green window. "This here's a Crosley. You probably know Crosley, good appliances, refrigerators, you know? This here's the Crosley 9-407. It's a 1949 model. They got a 1950 model coming out, called the 10-401, but I don't have any yet. Little more modern styling, kinda. I got a brochure around here someplace I could show you."

"I don't know," Dave said again. "What do they run?"

"Price? That depends on the set. Anywhere from two-fifty on up."

"Two hundred fifty dollars. Wow. Those screens sure look small."

"Most of these are seven-to nine-inch screens. 'Course, we got ones with bigger screens, floor models. Over there, you can see. But they start around three-fifty. Again, depending on the set."

Dave looked at Tim, who had hung back from the exchange. "I'd kind of like to have a larger screen. What do you think, Tim?" He moved toward Tim to talk privately.

Jack, fearing the private conversation that would lead to a decision not to buy that day or, worse, to check out other stores, piped up.

"Now, what I do have is a repossessed DuMont set. Guy couldn't make the payments. It's a handsome 1949 floor model, RA-108, seventeen-inch screen. Perfectly good set. Fact, it's still in mint condition. Here, c'mon, take a look at it." He led them down the line of sets and gave one a slap on its sleek mahogany veneer hide. "You know DuMont. No one knows more about television than DuMont. Heck, they practically invented it. Got their own network and all."

Dave and Tim looked at the set, visibly impressed with its design, with the screen set off to the left of the cabinet and the large dial to the lower right of it and the fabric-covered speaker area at the bottom.

"I can let you have that set for"—he paused a millisecond to make his final calculation as to what he could squeeze out of these two TV innocents—"two-eighty-five. And of course that comes with a ninety-day warranty 'cause that's how good we know this set to be."

And so Dave, after a quick, whispered huddle with Tim, and happy with the thought of how happy his housebound wife would be, let himself be led off to fill out the paperwork for becoming one of the 3.8 million Americans who owned television sets in 1950.

\*       \*       \*       \*

Less than two weeks later, on April 26, Eileen went into the hospital, Good Samaritan in Guldwyck. The girls, Dorothy and Arlene, went to stay with their grandmother. After a few days, Eileen's condition improved, and she came home again and continued to enjoy her new television. But the girls stayed with grandma; the care of them was too much for Eileen, and Dave was at work all day.

Tim's new Chevrolet was delivered to him in early May. He was so pleased with it, he took everybody everywhere in it, to his baseball games, to their baseball games, to miniature golf, anywhere he could drive with the top down. He taught Lynn, who did not have a driver's license, to drive in it. They went to the regional fruit and vegetable market, where there was open space, to practice. He and Frank Clay drove over to Saratoga Lake in it, sometimes looking for girls, though by this time it was mostly Frank looking, because Tim was going out almost exclusively with Peg and, to a lesser extent, Lynn.

One evening early in June his beloved tan Chevy sustained a ludicrous injury. He and Peg and Norm Artzahl and Norm's girlfriend had attended an Albany Senators baseball game at Hawkins Stadium. The weather had turned cold when they left the stadium, so Tim did not put the top down. As they drove through the streets, Tim and Peg heard sounds of increasing animation from the back seat, though they couldn't see the source of their emanation, because both Norm and the girl were out of sight. Tim looked at Peg, and Peg looked at Tim, and both grinned. All of a sudden, the girl shouted "Norm!," let out a screech, and her left leg shot up, sending her heel through the convertible's plastic rear window.

"Jesus, Sal!" Norm said to his girl, who was snorting with laughter.

"What the hell!" Tim shouted and quickly pulled over to the curb. Peg cautiously peered into the back seat, where clothes were swiftly being rearranged.

"Sorry, Tim," Norm said. "Guess we got carried away." His girl was laughing uncontrollably.

"Gah dam it, Norm," Tim said, twisting around and glaring fiercely at his friend. "This car isn't hardly a month old, and now look at it."

"Take it easy, Tim. I said I was sorry. It's easily fixed. I'll pay for it."

"That's not it. I mean, you get something new and look what happens." Tim looked dolefully at the rip in the window. He raised his hands in exasperation, and dropped them in resignation. "Oh, hell."

Peg, surprised at his unwonted outburst, glanced at Tim demurely out of the corners of her eyes with her head downcast, and smiled.

In the back seat, the girl couldn't stop laughing.

✳     ✳     ✳     ✳

Eileen died on June 20, a Tuesday, one day before her husband's thirtieth birthday. She was buried on Friday. The funeral was huge. Members of the Burnham and King and Altschuler and Davis families and dozens of their connections by blood and marriage from all over New York and Pennsylvania descended on the houses and apartments on Raleigh and Peach Avenues and elsewhere in the area for a place to light for the day while they attended the funeral. It struck Tim that his life was structured around funerals, he had been to so many, and that, though their purpose was sad, they were also festive occasions, being a chance for family to catch up on people they had not seen for years.

It was not a festive scene, however, on the crowded porch of Grandma Altschuler's house, where the main funeral cortege gathered, that brilliantly sunny June day. There is a photo of that scene that has survived, and not a person in it bears a smile, not even the pudgy little boy and girl in the center of the photo whom no one can identify anymore. Dave, who did not easily display his emotions, is sitting on the porch railing, sunk in despond, and his sisters, Peg and Pat,

their heads also lowered, are on either side of him, with their arms reaching consolingly behind his back. His brother, Henry, appears to be weeping. The two
girls, Dorothy and Arlene, cling to their Aunt Peg, sorrowful, confused. Tim,
propped against another railing, has his hands jammed into his pants pockets,
and his face is a map of dejection.

Later, just before the casket was closed to go to the cemetery, Dave lifted up
Arlene and Dorothy in turn to give their mother a final kiss. Both girls stiffened
as they realized what their father intended, but they did not refuse, and when it
was over they ran to Peg for solace. Tim, watching, thought it was both the most
awful and most heartbreaking thing he had ever witnessed.

✳    ✳    ✳    ✳

On June 19, the day before Eileen died, John Foster Dulles, an adviser to Secretary of State Dean Acheson, gave a speech to the parliament of South Korea,
assuring its members, "You are not alone. You will never be alone as long as you
continue to play worthily your part in the great design of human freedom."

# CHAPTER 12

▼

# THE BIGGEST BATTLE OF THE WAR

*Soldiers are citizens of death's gray land.*

—Siegfried Sassoon, "Dreamers"

Saturday Apr. 14, '51

Dearest Tim,

It's another Saturday and it's dragging by. Because you're not here, of course, but also because of the time of year, I think. It's kind of cold and not exactly rainy, or drizzly, but misty. The way it gets in April in Upstate New York. Misty, that's me.

But I need to cheer up. I'm sure where you are you don't need a "downer" letter from home. How are you, dear? I hope you are well and safe. That probably sounds silly, "safe," considering the things you've told in your letters, those patrols and all. It sounds very dangerous. Please take care.

Things are pretty good here. Work goes well. I can't believe I've been there over six years now. I also can't believe how old the girls are getting. Arlene turned 8 in February and Dorothy will be 7 in June. They're still living with me and Mom. Speaking of birthdays, she soon will be 61. She sure doesn't act it. Dave is still boarding with Uncle Merle and Aunt Virginia. I love having the girls here, and I think they like it. They seem to be coping well with the loss of their mother. That's another anniversary coming up—Eileen will be gone one year in June.

Oh, maybe I should just tear this letter up and start over, I keep coming back to gloomy topics. But maybe you don't mind, maybe any news from home is welcome. How do you get your mail? Do they deliver it every day? That must sound dumb too, doesn't it? I know you don't have mailmen. I mean do they bring it every day to your tent or foxhole or wherever you are?

Do you get the news? I'm trying to picture how you would get it, without newspapers or radio. But I guess you do have that army radio or whatever it's called, and the army newspaper. I'm sure you heard about President Truman firing General MacArthur, since MacArthur was your top commander. What an uproar that has caused here! People are furious. The Guldwyck paper is ready to lynch the president. I don't know what to think. Even though I'm more Republican than Democrat, my tendency is to say the president is the boss and his generals ought to do what he says, but I admit I don't know much about it all. How do you feel about the general who took his place, Ridgeway? Maybe you're not allowed to say.

I <u>try</u> to learn about it. You wouldn't believe how closely I follow the news now to see what's going on over there because it affects you. It's not like back in the war, when everyone followed the news daily, because I don't think people follow this so much unless they have someone involved. I hope that doesn't sound terrible but I think it's true. It sounds like things are going better for our soldiers, now that we've taken Seoul again. Do you ever see any foreign soldiers? That is, like the British or French? Not too long ago I heard that our armed forces have <u>doubled</u> since this war started, to almost 3 million men, I think it said. Did you hear about the Rosenbergs, those spies for the Russians during the war. The <u>last</u> war, I suppose I should say now. They've been given the death penalty. That seems terrible, they have two young boys, but I'm not sure how I feel about this exactly either.

Not much else to report. No social life without you. If I could smile and frown all at the same time and you could see it you would know what I feel like right now. I did go to see "Harvey" with Clara, that girl from work. It was at the Symphony in Guldwyck, that theater that shows second-run movies. I'm glad I got to see it because I missed it when it first came out last year. It's got that actress you said in one of your letters reminds you of me. I can't see it myself. I think it must be that we have the same first name, but it's dear of you to say it. Jimmy Stewart is terrific. He plays this sweet but kind of crazy guy, Elwood P. Dowd. I really liked the character. Do you ever get to see any movies?

Well, I've reported enough news and asked enough questions for one letter. No, I guess I haven't finished with the questions. Is it cold there now? You said in your last letter that it was bitter cold. What is the weather like there? The seasons, I mean—are they like here? Write soon and tell me everything.

Love,

Peg


"Hey there, Red Ryder," Warren said to Tim, who was sitting on an ammo box reading Peg's letter. The sky was blue, the air was warm, the day was calm and quiet. Tim felt as much at peace as he ever had since he'd arrived in Korea. *Please take care*, he read, and smiled, barely hearing Warren's greeting. "Whatcha got? Letter from home?"

"No, Goldfarb, it's a secret pirate map." Tim dropped his right hand, holding the letter, to his side and looked up at his friend. "You and I can be rich if we follow it, but I'm not sure I'm going to let you in on it."

"Who ever heard of a Jewish pirate, anyway? So who's the letter from? One of them Pennsylvania milkmaids? You were grinning awful wide."

"You're pretty nosy, you know that?" But Tim wasn't angry. He continued to smile at his friend.

"I hope that's not an ethnic slur. Is it that Ohio honey? No, you said that was long over. Must be that New York girl. One of 'em. Man, I'd like to know what she wrote to put that big stupid grin on your face."

"Yes, it's Peg, if you must know." And he explained the naïve remark Peg had made that caused him to smile.

"*Please take care*," Warren repeated. "Man, they don't know the half of it, do they? I guess they think as long as we don't forget to put on our overshoes, we'll be all right."

---

Thurs. May 3

Dear Peg,

I can't tell you how happy I was to get your letter. It made my day. Heck, it makes my week. I love to get the news from home. I've heard from Mom and my sisters too. Can you believe it, they made me a scarf? Hard to believe that they'll soon be going up to Lake George for the season again.

No, you're right, your mother sure doesn't act like she's 61. She's always so busy, it must keep her young. Please tell Dorothy I said Happy Birthday and that I wish I could give her a present, but that would be pretty difficult from here.

I don't know if you can tell it, but I'm still using the Paper-Mate pen you gave me. It is still holding up. I don't know if that means it's a really good pen or I just don't write much. It's probably the second. I'm not a very good letter writer.

Things are pretty quiet here now, at least compared to what I told you in my earlier letters. What they tell us is, we just went through what they call the Chinese Fifth Offensive. I don't know who's keeping track, it all seems like one big offensive to me with occasional lulls. We didn't get hit nearly so bad as some other units, thank God. I'll spare you the gory details, but I'll tell you a little about it—as much as I can, so you can explain to folks at home. I don't think most of them have any idea. I don't think it's anything like the last war.

We do most of our fighting at night, because that's when the Communists usually attack. Now it's almost all Chinese and only a few North Koreans. They have almost no artillery or airplanes, so they fight at night when it's harder for us to observe their troop movements until they're nearly on top of us. If we would shift our lines during the day, they would follow right along, no matter if we were pounding them with air and artillery assaults. They seem to have people to waste. They just throw people, thousands of people, into their attacks, and it doesn't seem to bother them to move past huge piles of their own dead and wounded. When night comes, we set up our defensive positions, and then it starts—the bugle calls and colored lights they use to signal an attack. No matter how long or hard we hit them with artillery or mortar or machine-gun fire, they still charge. There are so many of them compared to us, they break through more often than not, no matter how hard we resist. The Chinese hordes, that's what you hear talk of all the time. There's a joke going around, "I was attacked by two hordes and killed both of them." Another goes, "How many hordes to a platoon?"

It's not just us—the British and French and Dutch crack too under the pressure. There is a Dutch battalion attached to another regiment in our division. Usually the command posts of our battalions and regiments are safe from enemy attack because they are higher units and away from the fighting, but even they come under fire in this crazy war.

I hope that doesn't upset you. I don't know, maybe it bored you, going on like that, but you said you were interested. Maybe you shouldn't tell others like your mother or my mother. It might worry them.

We've been moving north and right now we're not far from a place called Chunchon. Oh yes, the firing of Gen. Macarthur caused quite a fuss here too I can tell you! And yes we get the news from AFN, that's Armed Forces Radio, and Stars & Stripes newspaper. And magazines, of course they're usually at least a month old. Boy that was some parade they gave Macarthur in New York, 3 million people I read. I wonder if he'll run for president, like some people say? I can't believe they'll impeach Truman over it. As far as Gen Ridgway is concerned we all like him. I haven't heard a bad word. Everybody likes Gen. Van Fleet too, he took over from Ridgway as commander of 8<sup>th</sup> Army.

Funny you should mention Harvey. We had it here a couple weeks back. I really liked it too and that Dowd character. I especially liked what he said, something about how in this life you can be oh so smart or oh so nice, and for a long time he was smart, but he prefers nice. Me too. Peggy Dow does too look like you, except you're prettier.

It's a peculiar war, but then I don't know why I say that since I have nothing to compare it to personally. What gets me is the children, so many orphans, on the streets, begging, not enough to eat. I see them and I think of Dorothy and Arlene and I get sad.

Well I really surprised myself how much I wrote. Probably you too, but I'd better cut this off now. Please write again, I love to hear from you and I miss you.

Love,

Tim


When Peg read "Love, Tim," in the kitchen while standing next to the refrigerator, she felt so light-headed that she instinctively steadied herself with her free hand on the kitchen counter. Her mother asked if anything was the matter, but Peg simply moved into the living room, saying nothing, and her mother went back to chopping onions.

*      *      *      *

The Fifth, or Spring, Offensive of the Chinese Communist Forces (CCF) turned out to be the biggest battle of the Korean War. The CCF threw 250,000 men in 27 divisions along a forty-five mile front north of Seoul from April 22 to April 30. When he wrote to Peg, Tim had no way of knowing that the offensive he spoke of was not quite over, nor had anyone else—except, of course, the Chinese, who had a Second Step, or Impulse, of the offensive up their sleeves. Later it was also referred to as the Second Spring Offensive.

Back when Tim and others were sitting around discussing MacArthur's departure, U.N. forces had indeed made significant progress. In early April the 88th Regiment was patrolling from the Cairo Line that started just west of Seoul, looped north of the capital and continued generally eastward to the eastern coast—part of an effort to check out air spotters' reports of increased vehicular traffic in North Korea. The 2$^{nd}$ Division, which had finally managed to build itself up to authorized strength after being continually depleted and never being able to recover because of the constant action it was in, was situated on the Kansas Line overlooking the Hwachon Reservoir. Advancing 8th Army troops met heavy mortar and artillery fire as they pushed closer to the Chinese forward supply area. Actions by many units, including the French Battalion, compressed the enemy into an area south of the reservoir, and when North Korean troops tried to escape across the reservoir in boats, they were fired upon by artillery and fighter strikes.

Though there was relative quiet in those early days of April, the 88th Regiment and other regiments of the 2$^{nd}$ Division and other elements of the 8$^{th}$ Army trained for what looked like a looming battle. Spearheads were made deep into communist areas of the Iron Triangle, a triangle-shaped area of relatively flat terrain 30 miles north of the 38$^{th}$ Parallel in the mountains of northeastern Korea. Its western base was the town of Chorwon, eastern base the town of Kumhwa, and the northern apex the town of Pyonggang (not to be confused with the North Korean capital of Pyongyang). An important North Korean rail and communications center, the Iron Triangle was also vital to the enemy as a staging area.

At midnight April 23 most of the U.N. line burst into a long, massive flash of flame as the Chinese attacked. The 2$^{nd}$ Division was spared the brunt of the attack. The ROK 6$^{th}$ Division caved, but British, Australian, and Canadian forces as well as 2^nd Division tanks plugged the hole that the Chinese tried to come through.

American and U.N. forces decided on a strong defensive line along a stretch of hills with a commanding view of the terrain to the north. Called "No-name Line," here the 2^nd Division and other elements of 8^th Army would stand and hold. It worked. On April 27 the 88th moved into position. It encountered light contact with the enemy the next day, and on the 28^th detected signs that the Chinese were pulling back. On the last day of the month the second battalion—not Tim's battalion, which was the first—of the 88th moved forward of No-name Line to set up an advance patrol base. From here they could see terrain dominated by a long, massive ridge running generally northwest and southwest, wrapping around the eastern rim of the Chunchon Basin. The slopes were covered with heavy timber and undergrowth, while the ridges were barren rock. The main peak in the ridge was Kari-san, which, at 1051 meters, looked down on two roads that looped around it, the Chunchon-Yanggu road held by the enemy and the Hongchon-Hangye road held by the U.N. What they could not see, or saw only sporadically and by accident, was columns of brown clad Chinese soldiers dog-trotting to the north, leaving behind thousands of their dead in graves hurriedly scratched out of the slowly thawing hillsides of west-central Korea.

✳     ✳     ✳     ✳

Yet in only a matter of days that relentless brown tide began reversing direction again. As the United States Senate swung into its month-long "Great Debate" on Korean War policy, the 20^th and 27^th Armies of the IX CCF Army Group swung eastward from their positions west of Chunchon. Under cloudy skies, the 12^th, 15^th, and 60^th Armies of the III CCF Army Group pushed southward from their encampments above Seoul. This massive flow of men and materiel moved into the country south of Chorwon, then east, then south again. For the battle ahead every soldier was instructed to husband his rations—dried corn, fried flour cakes, kaoliang or sorghum, and rice. When the soldiers looked back, they sometimes could see clouds of dust raised by trucks bringing in supplies.

It was a sight largely masked from American intelligence officers who were trying to puzzle out the reasons for the strange quiet along the 8^th Army battle front. Day and night the Chinese burned smoke pots whose haze blocked their activities from spotter planes. But from information divulged by captured Chinese and from occasional direct observation they learned that the enemy was repairing bridges and confirmed the general movement of the Chinese armies toward the southeast. They also learned that the enemy was gunning especially for the 2^nd Division and the ROK divisions to the east.

While Tim was happily reading the letter from and sending his letter to Peg, his division was establishing a special line, called the Roger Line, 4,000 yards in front of No-name Line, from which the 88th Regiment sent out patrols. Tim was not on any, but he learned that they met little resistance. Returning patrollers reported that the Chinks were acting funny: The slightest contact and they turned and ran. This reaction made some of them vaingloriously boastful of the obvious superiority of American fighting prowess, but others, like Tim, wiser and more cautious, found it unsettling.

Two battalions of a sister regiment, the 9^th, attacked forward of Roger Line and seized Hill 899, putting them within five miles of Chunchon. The second battalion of the 88th, still on Roger Line, was temporarily detached to become part of division reserve behind No-name Line.

Nighttime aerial reconnaissance now showed heavy enemy traffic, including signs of concentrations of soldiers and hastily camouflaged supply dumps. Around the 10^th of the month, 2^nd Division patrols began meeting stiff, even fanatical, resistance. Chinese were found where before there had been only North Koreans. On May 11 and 12, companies from the 9^th Infantry attempted to seize Hill 699 in the area of Chunchon, but were repulsed within 1,500 meters of the crest.

✳    ✳    ✳    ✳

A few days before that, soldiers of B Company of the 88th Regiment left the road near Chunchon and walked single file, rifles slung over their shoulders and weighed down by equipment, through the shrubbery and small trees by the rice paddies. The day was warm and intermittently clear and cloudy. During the brief clear patches it was indescribably lovely—sunny, gentle zephyrs, birds singing. Tim was not the only one plodding along that morning who was struck by the anomaly of such quiet, rustic beauty so close to violence. He looked around at the paddies and wondered how the Korean peasants could continue to pursue the cultivation of rice when they knew their efforts might be instantly and wantonly destroyed by foreign invaders, whether Chinese or American, or by their own countrymen. They got no other choice, he thought; what else are they going to do? He raised his left hand to his brow and with the back of it wiped off the beads of perspiration produced by the thick humidity.

"Jeez, it's hot," said Jansen, who was ahead of Tim.

"It's not the heat, it's the humidity," Tim responded. They were heading up a hill, and he was beginning to puff a little from the climb.

"You got that right, GI," said Caldwell, behind Tim. "Wisht I was back in Tucson. We don't have this humidity in Arizona. It's hot there, but it's a dry heat."

Tim inclined his head backward slightly to respond. "I've got an uncle used to say that all the time. He lived in Tucson a couple years. Said he loved the climate."

"A couple years? Why would anyone who ever lived in Arizona ever want to leave?" Caldwell said, his speech also labored by the effort of climbing.

Caldwell's remarks caused Tim's thoughts to turn to Dave Burnham, and Eileen and the girls, and then Peg and her mother, and then his entire family and everyone in Guldwyck and Albany, and he was overcome by a sadness heavier than any he had felt since he came to Korea. "It's a long story," he wanted to tell Caldwell, but it was indeed too long a story to tell anyone, even in a pleasant climate, and in any case they could never be made to understand about a beautiful, dying young woman with two beautiful daughters whom nothing, never mind dry heat, was able to save.

As they climbed higher they walked through scattered forests and the atmosphere grew cooler and less uncomfortable. The last part of the climb took them onto one of the highest outlooks in the region. Vines and bushes filled in spaces between the numerous trees. Some of the bushes were flowering, creating startling flashes of color in the overall dun landscape.

"Boy, those flowers are pretty," Caldwell said. "Wonder what they are."

"Trailing arbutus," Tim stated.

"Really?" Caldwell said, and then: "What's that?"

"I don't know. It's not really trailing arbutus. At least, I don't think it is. I have an uncle who used to say that any time someone would ask him to identify a plant he didn't recognize. It was his way of quickly getting rid of the topic."

"Really?" Caldwell repeated. "Not very sociable. Are you trying to shut me up? Is this the same uncle that couldn't stay in Arizona?"

"No, he was from New York. This one lives in Pennsylvania."

"You got a lotta uncles there, Davis, toksan uncles," Caldwell said, and then he, like the rest, gave himself over to the silent business of walking.

When they reached the lip of the hill they could see almost a half-mile to the left front and center front, but to the right front there was a rounded hill about a half-hour's walk away. Audible groans of pleasure and relief filled the air as the soldiers arrived at the top and shifted their loads from their backs to the ground.

"What's this place called, you know?" asked Clair, who had hurried over from his heavy weapons platoon's area to talk to Tim.

"I don't know the official name," Tim said. The Army identified every hill in Korea by its height in meters, Hill 770, and so forth. "I heard it's called Pear Hill, from its shape. You can see it from here when you look back down and to your right. Like a pear lying slightly on its side. From down below you can make it out even better. There's even a little knot of rocks here on the top—right over there—that looks like the stem."

"Oh yeah," Clair said, wonderingly, looking around the hill and down it.

"Hey, get this: I used to live on Peach Avenue and now I live on Pear Hill."

"And now you got a plum assignment."

Flashing a grimace, Tim took a swig of water from his canteen and wiped his lips with the back of his hand. As he finished, a soldier he recognized as being from another squad in his platoon but whose name he did not know, came up to him.

"Hey, buddy, you got a tombi?" he said, putting the first two fingers of his right hand to his lips to mimic smoking.

"Hava-no. Sorry. Don't smoke. I gave away the ones I had from my last C-rations." Tim looked at Clair, as if to push the request over to him.

"Me neither. Sorry."

"'S'all right. Thanks anyway." He scurried off to pursue his search elsewhere.

Once the entire company reached the top, Sergeant Paden pulled the platoon together to show them their sector. Tim's platoon took positions on the hill to their right front, with its heavy weapons squad assigned to give covering fire-power to the other platoons, which went forward, out of sight. Ahead of them were British units, and slightly ahead of them, South Koreans. Then Paden told them to get started digging bunkers. A universal moan went up, but it was only pro forma, as they all knew it was coming.

They began digging with their collapsible entrenching tools, which quickly had them bitching in earnest, because it was a pitifully slow and exhausting chore with such a small implement. But late in the day the A-Frame Army came crawling up the hill bearing not only timbers for the tops of the bunkers, rolls of barbed wire, and ammunition, but regular shovels and pickaxes for the platoons to work with. Many happy shouts of "our little friends" and "hey, Kim" went up. In gratitude some of the men passed out cigarettes to the Koreans, who accepted them, bowing and grinning gratefully.

"How do suppose the Army made this happen?" Tim said to Sbarra. "It's not that efficient."

"By me, Davis," the squad leader said, straightening up and running his right hand through his close-cropped black hair. "It probably happened something like this: Somewhere in Washington someone decided what we really needed was desert gear. Then somewhere else further along the line that got crossed up with—I don't know—maybe shotguns for riot duty. And then somewhere else still further along that got crossed up with shovels. And so by mistake we got the right stuff."

"That's probably it," Tim said. He spit on his hands and lay to with a pickax.

They spent the next few days preparing their bunkers, some two-and three-man, some large enough to contain a squad, depending on the situation. The day after their arrival on the hill, the battalion commander came by to inspect and exploded in anger. The bunkers were nowhere near secure enough; they needed more timbers, more earth on top. They had to be capable of withstanding artillery fire—maybe even their own, American, artillery fire. If the Chinese attacked in the numbers and with the ferocity that they did in April, it might be necessary to call in friendly fire on their own positions to get at the close-in enemy, and he wanted the bunkers to be able to hold up under that. Each day he came by, ripping into the company commanders until he was satisfied they and their men were giving him what he wanted.

Suddenly a huge project was in motion all over the hills, and Tim realized it was no accident they had been supplied with construction tools. He was impressed and concerned, impressed by its size and concerned with what it portended. Scores, even hundreds, of Korean civilian workers chogied up Pear Hill and surrounding heights, bringing wire, sandbags, and steel pickets for installing wire aprons, as well as regular supplies like water, rations, and ammunition. A herd of oxen was used to haul the heavy 4.2-inch mortars and their ammunition and the 55-gallon fougasse drums. So many "little friends" were making so many trips up and down the hills—soldiers were continually shouting "hey, Kim" to them—that buildings had to be set up at the bottom to feed them.

While some soldiers worked on the bunkers, others were stringing the barbed wire and sowing mines across the battalion's front. Men from an ammunition and pioneer platoon came in to supervise the work. Every section of the front had at least one wire barrier; most had two. For good measure, antipersonnel mine fields, fougasse drums, and trip flares were put in, telephone wires were buried, and communication trenches were dug.

They were loaded for bear. One day Lieutenant General James A. Van Fleet, 8th Army commander, and Lieutenant General E.M. Almond, X Corps commander, helicoptered in, looked around, saw that it was good, and said so.

After the generals flew off in their helicopter, Tim and Sbarra stood looking at the battalion front. Tim asked him about the drums.

"The fougasse drums? Didn't you ever see one of those babies go off? Man, wait'll you see it. It's like a big-ass, stationary flamethrower. It's filled with napalm and gasoline and you put in a charge of TNT or white phosphorous mortar shells, and when you detonate it, it sends out a ball of fire ten yards wide and maybe forty yards long. Instant incineration for any gooks in its path."

＊    ＊    ＊    ＊

The enemy, of course, was not idle. The Chinese sent out more, and more aggressive, patrols. Increased vehicular traffic pointed to intensified buildup. The trickle of civilian refugees from the Chinese side grew to a swollen stream. Late in the afternoon of May 14 air observers spotted masses of troops moving southeastward between Naepyong-ni and Sapkyo-ri, headed toward 2nd Division positions. The next day they saw more buildup south of Yanngu and movement along the south shore of the Hwachon Reservoir.

The second battalion of the 88th regiment was pulled out of division reserve and sent up on the line with the rest of the regiment. 2nd Division artillery and tanks pounded valleys and draws suspected of being Chinese assembly points. All units were told to hold their positions at all costs during hours of darkness.

In the early morning hours of May 16 the Chinese, knowing the ROK units were the softest, launched a preliminary attack against the 5th and 7th ROK divisions on the right flank of the U.S. 2nd Division. They pressed the attack across the entire ROK front all through the day, and by late afternoon forced the ROK units from their positions, laying bare the entire eastern flank of the 2nd Division. As this was going on, patrols from the 88th Regiment and from another unit called Task Force Zebra went out, and whenever they encountered the enemy they withdrew and called in artillery strikes to break up the concentrations of Chinese they had come across.

By dusk on May 16, U.N casualties were heavy and the situation on the eastern flank, where Tim's regiment was located, grew hourly more perilous. Through it all Tim's company remained mostly uninvolved and unscathed, as they heard mortar shells and larger explosives burst around them during the night, and heavy small-arms fire in the distance to the west, on their left. The next day they saw and heard exchanges of gunfire to the front and also behind the hill to the southwest.

Everything pointed to an imminent mass attack.

# CHAPTER 13

▼

# CALLED TO THE COLORS

*"I don't like wars, and I'm not crazy about armies, and I'm sorry
we're such barbarians that the men we love had to go out and settle
things with guns. But I'd be a lot sorrier if they hadn't gone. Now
you get out of here. The day you start behaving like a grown-up,
responsible man instead of a spoiled, dangerous infant, you can
come back."*

—Dorothy McGuire to Farley Granger, *I Want You*

On the morning of the Monday after Eileen's funeral, June 26, 1950, a bold,
72-point headline stretched across the top of the front page of the Guldwyck
*Standard*:

## RED ARMY STABS INTO SOUTH KOREA

To Tim, reading it at Jean's where he was having breakfast, its screaming significance seemed to pulsate above the gray columns of type. He lifted his coffee
cup to his lips and scanned the thicket of secondary headlines.

**U.S. Rushes Arms, Ammunition to
South; Truman Returns to Capital,
Calls in Defense, Diplomatic Aides**

A confusing welter of news stories on the same subject covered nearly the entire page. Dour, one-column photos of Truman, Secretary of State Dean Acheson, Secretary of Defense Louis Johnson, and General Omar Bradley, chairman of the Joint Chiefs of Staff, stared out at Tim. Still holding his steaming coffee cup in mid-air, he skipped what seemed to be the main story under a yet smaller headline—"President Explores Means of Aid to South; Weekend Missouri Trip Cut Short to Fly Back to Meet Korean Crisis"—to read one in the last column on the right side of the page. "North's Rush Reported Halted, Thrown Back," its headline said:

> Seoul, Monday, June 26 (AP)—Communist North Korean invaders today slashed to within 20 miles of Seoul, but a high South Korean military official said the rush apparently had been stopped and thrown back.
> (Korean Minister Kim Yong Ju said in Tokyo, however, that the invaders had reached Uijongbu, only 12 miles north of Seoul.)
> Cloudy skies, which checked the Northerners' superior air arm, brightened South Korean hopes of holding the estimated 50,000 Red troops who struck yesterday across the border.
> Maj. Gen. Choi Byung Duk, chief of staff of the South Korean Army, reported....

Tim read all of the story on the front page but didn't stay with it to its continuation page. Instead, his glance jumped around, taking in bits of the other stories: "Planes to Aid in Evacuation of Americans"; "M'Arthur Will Ship Munitions to South Korea"; "U.N. Security Council Orders Cease Fire in Korea War."

He put down his cup. This looked serious. He looked up at Jean, who was working at the sink.

"Did you see this in the paper?"

"Yes," Jean said. With a dishcloth she swept some bread crumbs from the counter into the sink. She wiped her hands on her apron and turned to face Tim. "It was all over the radio yesterday."

"Yeah, I heard something about it. I didn't pay that much attention. I guess I didn't think it was that big a deal. Just more communist shenanigans, like with Berlin."

"No, this sounds bad."

"Well, maybe we won't get involved. I mean, Korea? Where *is* Korea?"

"Oh, we *always* get involved, anymore, it seems." Jean twisted her hands together on her apron, and two ugly vertical lines split the lovely smoothness of her brow. "We're *already* involved, from the looks of the paper. Why should this country care if one part of Korea starts a fight with the other part? So that young men like you—" Jean broke off, not wanting to follow her thought where it was going, and turned around to face the sink and wash dishes. She reached over to turn on the radio. The discordant rhythms of "If I Knew You Were Comin' I'd've Baked a Cake" came out, and she angrily switched it off again, not willing to be jollied out of her current concerns.

Tim sat drinking the last of his coffee and skimming the news stories. Slowly it crept into his mind that something about the date troubled him. The Korea story said June 26. But *this* was June 26. How could the Guldwyck newspaper report a story from half a world away on the same day it happened? It must be the time difference. The events happened on June 26 *there*, and get reported on the 26th *here*. In Korea they must be at least 12 hours ahead of us, he reckoned. He examined the other stories for corroborating evidence of his calculations. The fighting had started on Sunday morning there, which was sometime Saturday night New York time.

He took a sip of his coffee. It had grown too cool for his liking, and he absent-mindedly set the cup down on the table while continuing to stare at the paper. No, he thought, it wasn't the time difference that troubled him about the date. It was something else, as if he already *knew* something about this date. It was too weird. This sort of thing is always happening to me, he told himself. He folded the newspaper and tossed it onto the table.

✳        ✳        ✳        ✳

When Rick came up to Guldwyck for Eileen's funeral, he did not go back home. He finally acted on his plans to move north to get work. He did not have a car, so he traveled by bus. He got a room in the Guldwyck YMCA, though Harriet had said he could stay with her and Freddie. She would have liked him to stay with her, in fact, because she could have used the rent money—Freddie's work, as usual, being inconsistent—but Rick did not want to get into that situation. He would have preferred to stay with Tim, but Aunt Cissy's place was already filled to the gunwales. Dave Burnham, though wrestling with his own bereavement, was as good as his word and got Rick a job in the Arsenal, as a tool grinder, thus proving himself to be as unselfishly helpful to the younger Davis brother as he had been to the older.

Rick, though now almost twenty years old, quickly fell back into the Little Brother role he had filled, and liked, when both brothers lived at home. He went where Tim went and did what Tim did—fishing, bowling, roller-skating. He usually attended Tim's softball games, and occasionally tagged along on Tim's dates with Peg and Lynn. Tim did not mind, usually, and, remarkably, neither did the women. It was a charmingly comfortable existence; everyone was used to each other, and all seemed content to have things go along much as they had been.

The thing that Rick really liked to do, though—in common with nearly all of America—was watch television. Television had so strongly affected national life that in the spring Film Daily, a Hollywood trade publication, reported that movie attendance had dropped from 90 million per week to 70 million in just two years, and 3,000 theaters had closed. In Rick's case the enthusiasm for TV could more readily be understood because he had hardly ever seen it. No one in their extended family in Pennsylvania owned a set, for the simple reason that television signals had not yet penetrated into that rural area.

Usually they watched at the house of Tim's friends, the Nicholses, or sometimes at Peg's, but on a Monday night in the middle of July they were at Lynn's, watching her parents' recently acquired set, from which came the smooth, rich, French-trained tones of announcer Andre Baruch:

"*Your Hit Parade* survey checks the best sellers on sheet music and phonograph records, the songs most heard on the air and most played on the automatic coin machines—an accurate, authentic tabulation of America's taste in popular music."

"*What?* The *Hit Parade?*" Tim protested, over the jouncy sounds of the "Be Happy, Go Lucky" theme song, "I thought it was supposed to be *Robert Montgomery Presents.* I like the Robert Montgomery stories."

"It's a summer replacement," Lynn said. "It started last week. They said it's a summer replacement."

"That's funny that it's on tonight," Rick said. "On radio *Hit Parade* is on Saturday night."

"They said it was a summer replacement, that's all I know," Lynn repeated.

"Well, I don't mind. I like *Hit Parade*," Rick said. "Hey, there's Dorothy Collins. And Snooky Lanson. You know, I don't think I ever saw what he looks like before. What kind of a name is that for a guy, Snooky?"

"I know. I wonder if he was in the Army during the war," Tim said. "Can you imagine a sergeant in front of a formation calling out 'Snooky'?"

Rick laughed. "I don't think I'd want to sleep in a bunk next to a guy named Snooky. I'd be too afraid I'd wake up *in* a bunk with a guy named Snooky."

"You guys," Lynn chided. "Be nice. He's cute. Besides, it's probably just a nickname."

"Hey, there it goes," Rick said. "I love to hear him say that. Every week, the same thing, just like on the bottom of the cigarette packs: 'L.S./M.F.T. Lucky Strike Means Fine Tobacco.'" He leaned conspiratorially toward Tim and whispered, "Back at Mott we used to say that meant Loose Sweaters Mean Flabby Tits." He sniggered. He felt as if he was back in school again, telling a dirty joke.

Tim, equally embarrassed but unable to resist responding, whispered back, "We used to say, Leaky Strippers Mean Fat Tummies."

Rick looked blank. "Strippers?"

"Yeah. Didn't you ever hear that? Strippers. You know. Rubbers. Prophylactics. Condoms."

"No, I never heard that. Strippers, huh? You sure you got that right?"

"That's what we used to say."

"What are you two being so secretive about?"

Rick looked up at Lynn. "Nothing. We were just wondering what the number one song will be." He scrunched himself more comfortably into Lynn's father's easy chair, "I'll bet it's 'Mona Lisa.' It's got to be. That's all you heard the last couple weeks, Nat King Cole and 'Mona Lisa.'"

"Tim and I saw the movie that's from," Lynn said, looking at Tim as if for corroboration. "*Captain Carey, U.S.A.* Alan Ladd. Good movie."

While the three of them watched *Your Hit Parade*, they discussed Tim's and Rick's plans to take a trip to Canada in Tim's convertible. Tim had put in for vacation in mid-August, and when he went to work at the Arsenal Rick had arranged to take that week off without pay. By the time Raymond Scott and the Lucky Strike Orchestra and the Hit Paraders Chorus swung into the weekly sign-off, "So long, for a while/That's all the songs for a while/So long to *Your Hit Parade*/And the tunes that you picked to be played/So long-g-g-g," their itinerary was firmly set.

\*　　　\*　　　\*　　　\*

The Canada trip never came off. Early in August, as the Army announced a call-up of 52,000 enlisted reservists for 21 months' active duty, Tim received his draft notice.

Events had not gone well for the United States and the United Nations since North Korea plunged into its invasion of the South on June 25. President Truman immediately ordered ground forces to Korea from Japan. The first advance contingent—a part of the 24$^{th}$ Division, known as Task Force Smith, under Lieutenant Colonel Charles B. Smith—landed there July 1 to try and stem the North Koreans' southward push. On July 8 General Douglas MacArthur, residing in imperial splendor as a kind of American viceroy in Japan, was appointed supreme commander of United Nations forces in Korea. In the ensuing weeks various other American units poured in—the 1$^{st}$ Cavalry, the 25$^{th}$ Infantry Division, more of the 24$^{th}$ Division, the 2$^{nd}$ Infantry Division, and the 1$^{st}$ Marine Brigade. The Selective Service Act, which governed the draft, had been due to expire July 9, but the House and Senate quickly approved a one-year extension, which the president signed June 30. At the end of July the Defense Department raised its conscription call for September from 20,000 to 50,000 men. And on August 4, the United States, through its emissary, the Somerton County draft board, said it required—out of its recently reported population of 150,697,361—the services of Timothy Arthur Davis to help meet that call.

Tim got the notice when he came home from work that Friday afternoon. The first person he showed it to was Norm Artzahl.

"Oh man. What're you going to do?" Norm asked.

"What *can* I do? Report. It says I have to report for my physical in two weeks."

"Maybe you could enlist. Join the Air Force or Navy instead of being put in the Army. Or the Coast Guard. The Coast Guard's part of the armed services."

"Really? I didn't know that."

"Not many people do. But it is. It was part of the Navy during the war."

"But I don't know if you can do that after you get your draft notice." Tim sighed. "Besides, what difference does it make—Army, Navy, Air Force? It's all the military."

"I don't know. Can't be as much marching in the Air Force or the Navy. And the food's supposed to be better in the Navy."

"No, I'll stick with this. See what happens with the physical. Who knows? Maybe I've got one nut hangs too low or something."

"Yeah, they don't want any dislocated nuts in the Army," Norm said, and smiled.

"Oh brother," Tim sighed. "Wait'll I tell Mom. Just what she's always fretted about."

He called his mother that evening to tell her. Long-distance telephone calls were not simple or inexpensive affairs in 1950. They were placed through operators, who connected with other operators, who connected with other operators, on down the line—cool, efficient, anonymous female voices talking to each other in the night. His call was all the more complicated in that Anna was working, as usual at that time of year, at a Lake George resort. Once he managed to connect with the resort's office, someone there had to go hunt down Anna to come to the phone. When he told her, she began weeping, and cursed "this damned war." The girls, Connie and Barbara, were working there, too, and had come with Anna to the phone, knowing that something important must be afoot, because a long-distance call could mean nothing less. As he talked to them, they began crying, too, and when he hung up the phone Tim did not see how he could feel any worse.

It struck Tim, as it had before, how important so many women were to his life. Anna and his sisters. His aunts Jean and Harriet—and Eileen, only recently gone. Arlene and Dorothy. Grandma Altschuler and Grandma Burnham. Aunt Cissy. So many other King family women still in Pennsylvania; so many "girls" he knew there and in New York. Helen. Lynn. And Peg.

He had gone to Peg's—to Grandma Burnham's—to make his telephone call. Aunt Cissy did not have a phone, and he did not want to trouble the Jenkinses downstairs. When he told Peg, she deflated as abruptly as a punctured balloon. Grandma, seeing Peg's distress, expressed her regrets and left them to themselves. While he was on the phone in the living room talking to his mother, Peg sat in the dining room trying not to listen and not to cry. When she heard him say goodbye and hang up, she went into the living room. They looked at each other in silence, and then she moved toward him. She put her arms around him and softly laid her head against his chest, and he put his arms around her, and they stood there in the middle of the room in the middle of the darkness and did not speak, knowing that the fear each felt was a strange expression of love.

*       *       *       *

But first the United States had to determine whether Timothy Arthur Davis was physically, mentally, and morally fit to be called to the colors. So, two weeks later he went, as bidden, to the Armed Forces Examining and Entrance Station in Albany, which was in the Post Office building on Broadway, along with the Selective Service headquarters. There, in the company of a couple hundred other naked and semi-naked "selectees" and enlistees, he patiently allowed doctors to thump his chest, peer into his ears and eyes, probe and palpate various parts of his body, ask him to stand on his left foot and then on his right, tell him to squat, and make him wave his arms about like a windmill. After these and other tests, the medicos in solemn consultation judged him according to the "Pulse" standard: P,U,L,H,E,S—P for pulmonary, U for upper limbs, L for lower limbs, H for hearing, E for eyesight, and S for psychological, probably because P was already taken and "psychological" sounds as if it begins with S. Given a range of clinical profiles to choose from that ran all the way from A to C—A for perfect, B for satisfactory, and C for unsatisfactory—they rated him a solid A. And so, at the very moment that President Truman in Washington, acting under a World War I emergency measure, was ordering the Army to seize control of the railroads to prevent a rail strike that threatened defense production, Tim officially became a United States soldier in Albany. After swearing to uphold the constitution of the United States against all enemies, foreign and domestic, he was given orders to report to Fort Devens, Massachusetts, on September 28, 1950, for initial processing.

✳    ✳    ✳    ✳

The testing had not taken a long time. Each exam was not terribly long, but the waiting in between them was. During one of the breaks, Tim and others sat on busted old fake-leather tubular-armed chairs and bitched and smoked. Bored, Tim began rummaging through a pile of old magazines on a nearby table. He picked up a well-thumbed copy of *Time*, which he took back to his chair. He flipped through pictures and captions until his eye was caught by an article on Korea, which he began to skim:

> "Six months ago South Korea, bedeviled by guerrilla raids, galloping inflation and the daily threat of invasion from the North, looked like a candidate for the same mortuary as Nationalist China. Now the Republic of Korea looks more like a country on its way to healthy survival.... It has trained and equipped a first-rate ground army.... our advisers have tried to give the Koreans Yankee self-sufficiency as well as Yankee organization and equipment.
>
> "The policy has paid off.... most observers now rate the 100,000-man South Korean army as the best of its size in Asia. Its fast-moving columns have mopped up all but a few of the Communist guerrilla bands ... and no one believes that the Russian-trained North Korean army could pull off a quick, successful invasion of the south without heavy reinforcements."

What the—? What in hell was this? Tim flipped back to the front cover and looked at the issue date: June 5, 1950. What was today? August something. 23rd? 24th? And when had the North Koreans invaded? He remembered it was June 25, because it was just a few days after Eileen died. He looked at the article again— "no one believes that the Russian-trained North Korean army could pull off a quick, successful invasion of the south"—and started laughing so hard that the sulking young man next to him asked, "What's so goddamn funny, buddy?"

*     *     *     *

Orderly chaos reigned in Grandma Burnham's living room. Kids ran crazily around the table, decorated for a party, and in and out of the other rooms, giggling and shouting, being restrained and calmed down by their elders, only to go running off crazily again. Arlene and Dorothy were there, of course—they lived with their grandmother permanently now, since their mother's death—and their many Burnham and King family cousins, children of Dave's and Eileen's brothers and sisters. Including their much older cousin, Tim.

The party was for Tim, a farewell party for his departure in two days for Fort Devens. It had been arranged by Peg and prepared by her and her mother. The table was packed to the edges with cake and other food and soft drink and coffee. The light from tall candles at each end winked in the curves of Grandma's best silver. Red-white-and-blue paper napkins, carefully fanned out at the four corners, bore the image of an eagle and the words "America the Beautiful."

With the living room momentarily devoid of the crowd and noise, Henry Burnham went around the table, picking up cold cuts and bread and vegetables and placing them on the paper plate in his right hand. He still had on the blue pants and white shirt with his name stitched over the left pocket that was his uniform at the Gulf service station he ran on Raleigh Avenue. A military-style cap with the Gulf emblem on the front above the visor was pushed back on his hair, which was already, in his mid-twenties, beginning to grow thin, as his midriff was beginning to grow thick. He took a cup of coffee and sat down next to Tim, who was sitting in one of the kitchen chairs that had been brought in and placed against the wall, holding Dorothy on his lap as she studiously ate a big piece of chocolate cake.

"So," Henry said, taking off his cap and reaching back to set it on one of the chair's uprights, "two more days of freedom, eh?"

Tim smiled. "Yeah, I guess so. Less than that, really." He gave Dorothy a little squeeze with his right arm. She turned her head and looked up at him.

"Tim, I'm going into the kitchen, OK?"

"Sure. What's the matter? Not enough cake in here?"

"No," Dorothy said. She slid off his lap and looked at him seriously. "All the other kids are in there. I just want to play."

"OK, kiddo. Seems reasonable enough."

Dorothy stopped and turned back in her progress toward the kitchen. "Will you come outside and play tag with us later?"

"Sure, if it doesn't get too dark."

"Good," she said. "No one plays tag better than you."

"That's quite a compliment," Henry said, as Dorothy ran off. "I didn't know there were levels of ability in tag."

"Oh, I play with them all the time when I come over. Hide-and-seek, too. They're great girls, her and Arlene. I'll miss them. It's such a shame about their mother. It's good they have your mother to look after them." Tim paused. "And your sister."

"And Uncle Merle," Henry said, referring to Grandma Burnham's brother, Merle Altschuler, with whom Dave Burnham was boarding. "I don't know what Dave would do if Uncle Merle and Aunt Virginia hadn't said he should stay with them."

"You have a wonderful family," Tim said. He stared at the floor, suddenly becoming a victim of the pensiveness he had wanted to avoid. "I'll miss all of them."

"Your family, too—Jean, Harriet—everything they've done," Henry responded awkwardly, in the hope that pointing out equality in familial helpfulness would somehow keep emotion at bay. "But I know what you mean. I guess you'll really miss Peg."

"I will. I will. I'll miss you all."

"Still," Henry said heartily, determined to fight off the descending pall, "might not be so bad. This thing in Korea could be over before we know it. Looks like MacArthur's got the Reds on the run now, with that Inchon landing a week or so ago. I heard just today that we're taking back the South Korean capital from the Reds. Seoul—that's it, isn't it? Seoul is the South Korean capital?"

"Yes, Seoul. Funny, three months ago I'd barely heard of Korea, much less its capital."

"Heck, you might not even go to Korea. This fighting will probably be over before you're done with your training and all, anyway, but chances are you won't even go there. You're more likely to be sent to Germany. We got a lot more troops in Germany than we do in this Korea."

"Not for long."

"Well, maybe," Henry conceded. "I don't know why we have to have troops anywhere overseas. What are we, the world's policeman? But I'll bet you don't even serve your two years. It'll be over and they'll be looking for guys to let out early. That's what the enlistment term is, two years, isn't it?"

"About that. Unless they pull that 'for the duration' thing they did during the war."

"Nah, they won't do that. The public wouldn't stand for it."

At that point Harriet Farrell stuck her head around the archway from the kitchen into the living room, looked at Henry and Tim, and said, "Hey, what're you two looking so glum for? This is a party, isn't it? C'mon here into the kitchen. Bernie's telling about this guy he works with at Niagara Mohawk, a real jerk. It's so funny."

Later, when the party was over and all the guests were gone, and Tim had come in from playing with Arlene and Dorothy and the other kids, he and Peg sat on the couch in the darkened living room. They didn't speak, just sat close together, her head on his shoulder, and listened to the plaintive sounds of "Good-night, Irene" coming from the radio. They could not have chosen a song better suited to deepen their mood of dejection, and of course they did not choose it, as it was immensely popular and hard to avoid. And so they listened and wallowed in its and their woe.

"I've got a little going-away present for you," Peg said, when the song ended.

"What? What did you do that for?"

"It's not much, but I wanted to give you something." She lifted her hand from where it was resting near her right thigh and handed him a small thin package wrapped in red-white-and-blue paper.

"You shouldn't have done this," Tim said, taking the package. He quickly unwrapped it. "It's a pen. Thank you. Oh, wait, it's one of those Paper-Mate ballpoint pens I've read about. They're supposed to not leak or smudge." He examined it admiringly. "I'm surprised you could get one. I understand they get gobbled up as soon as they hit the stores."

"It took some searching, but I finally found one. I figured this way you'd have no excuse not to write me, even when you're out in the field or on bivouac or whatever you call it."

Tim looked at Peg. He thinks she looks beautiful, in her sad softness, beautiful enough to be an actress. Who does she make him think of? Rosalind Russell? Yes, the face is similar, but Rosalind Russell is too big, too expansive. More like Judy Garland. Peg is small like that, fine. He leaned over and kissed her, almost chastely, and on her heated lips the kiss was cool, dry.

"I'll write you, honey. I'll write you all the time."

"Honey," Peg thought, opening her eyes from the kiss and studying his face. Had he ever said "honey" before?

The next night, the night before his departure, Tim said goodbye to Lynn and her family and Aunt Cissy. The parting from Lynn was muted. She knew about the party the night before, and was not exactly offended, because it was, after all, his family—even Peg was, by lengthy extension. But in the intensified emotional circumstances Lynn found the unstated competition of Peg less tolerable than usual. She and her parents fed him supper, gave him a toiletry kit as a present, and they all watched *Arthur Godfrey and His Friends*. When the program was over, Tim bade them a discomfited farewell. He spent his last night, not in his room upstairs, but at Jean's, and the next morning departed from there for Fort Devens.

# CHAPTER 14

▼

# YOU'RE IN THE ARMY NOW

*Every man thinks meanly of himself for not having been a soldier,*
*or not having been at sea.*

- Samuel Johnson

Row after row of uniform, two-story, flaking, cream-colored barracks swooshed past the Army-brown school bus carrying Tim and a couple dozen other—uniformly silent if not indeed sullen—recruits into the heart of Fort Devens. Tim stared out the windows, gritty with ancient rain-streaked grime, at the buildings lined up along the paved roads, scruffy with incipient vegetation trying valiantly to survive in the dirt and sand. That was something Tim would marvel at later: sand. Other Army bases he would come to know, all in temperate climates, were covered with the kind of fine sand normally found in warmer regions. Why, he never learned. They must truck it in, he thought.

The bus lurched to a stop in front of a huge Quonset hut with a massive door that opened and shut on a track, above which was a large sign: Initial Receiving Point. The bus driver, a pimply-faced PFC with a thatch of straw-like hair bursting out from under his fatigue cap, killed the engine, swung out of his seat, and looked back at the two rows of nervous and wary faces.

"All right, gentlemen. Here we are, Devens Hotel and Military Resort. Please step into this building and the personnel inside will see to your accommodations.

If you don't see anything you need, please ask. Enjoy your stay at Devens Hotel and Military Resort." He turned around and dropped back into his seat, tugged the bill of his cap and faced the windshield, already clacking the shift lever through the gears preparatory to departing. "You'll be *sorr-reeee.*"

That was another thing Tim was to discover in his military sojourn: Everybody was a comedian. If he had known the German word *Schadenfreude*, he would have said that was it exactly: delight in another person's discomfort, especially discomfort that one had gone through oneself. It had started already at the Examination and Entrance Station in Albany, and was expressed through sarcasm, most of it obvious but some quite pointed and witty. But what was going through his mind as he got off the bus, other than a spurt of hatred for the driver, was surprise that no one met them at the bus. He had expected a screaming sergeant to be at the bottom of the steps.

With the others, Tim filed tentatively into the Quonset hut and up to a scarred wooden counter a few steps inside the door. The counter ran out from the curved wall for about twenty feet, then took a right angle to run to the front wall, thus blocking off the entrance area from the rest of the huge room. A half-door cut into the right-angled section of the counter provided the only access to the room, around which desks were scattered higgledy-piggledy. Tim could see several men in faded green fatigues, and many men in civilian clothes. No one seemed to be doing much of anything. The smoke from countless cigarettes floated up to the ribbed metal roof, and from somewhere in the back Tim could dimly hear the Ames Brothers' "Rag Mop" playing, presumably from a radio. Tim turned and looked questioningly at the recruit on his left, a tall, thin fellow in a frayed brown tweed sports jacket, who returned Tim's glance wordlessly with raised eyebrows and shoulders. Just as he did Tim noticed a soldier get up from one of the nearer desks and walk toward them. Two stripes on his sleeve, Tim could see—a corporal. When he got to the counter, the corporal—a pleasant-faced man of medium height in his early twenties—placed both hands on it, leaned forward, and said:

"Gentlemen. Welcome to Fort Devens."

*Gentlemen*, again? Tim said to himself. And *welcome?* This was the Army? Tim shot another questioning glance at the fellow on his left and received the same response.

"Pay attention, gentlemen, because I have here some paperwork for you to fill out and I don't want to have to repeat the instructions more often than absolutely necessary. Most of it is simple and self-explanatory and should be manageable by even those of you from the less-enlightened regions of these forty-eight states.

Line up here at the left of the counter and I will pass the materials out. Wherever it asks, enter your name and service number *exactly* as they appear on your record jackets. You will notice that there is a postage-paid postcard with the materials. Do not—I repeat, *do not*—fill out this postcard until I instruct you. There are pencils here and clipboards for you to write on. You may sit on the bench behind you and when you run out of bench you are free to sit on the floor. When you are done, bring the completed paperwork up here to me with the pencils and clipboards. The pencils and clipboards are property of the United States government, and theft of government property is a crime punishable by imprisonment in the stockade, which is not a nice place."

Tim received his pencil, paperwork, and clipboard and, being one of the first in line, found a seat on the bench. He tucked his carryall, containing the few items he had been instructed to bring with him to basic training, underneath the bench between his legs, and began filling out the papers. As he did he heard the corporal answering, remarkably patiently, the inevitable silly questions—"What does it mean by 'home of record'?"—that even fully functioning, intelligent people ask when they are extremely anxious and seek reassurance, and, less patiently, chastising one person for prematurely filling out the postcard they had expressly been forbidden to fill out ("You aren't from Alabama, by any chance, are you?").

"Everybody done?" the corporal asked, when he could see that the scribbling had mostly stopped and faces were turned up toward him. "Good. Now we will fill out the postcard, with the exception of the gentleman from Alabama or wherever it is he's from." Not everyone was able to resist looking at the unhappy soul.

"Listen carefully to how I tell you to fill out this postcard," the corporal continued, "because it is your first contact with the outside world. If you screw it up, the outside world will not know what happened to you, assuming that it even cares. If you cannot read it—well, God help you, if you can't read, you shouldn't be here, but the Army desperately needs men—but if you can't read, get the guy next to you to read it for you.

"The postcard says you have arrived safely at Fort Devens, Massachusetts, and you will be here several days for processing before being sent someplace for basic training. That place will not be here. Basic training is not conducted at Fort Devens. This is only a reception station. This card will allow you to have two visitors to come see you. Please spare me the comments about 'like in jail'—we have heard it before. On this card you will see two blank spaces. In the first blank you put your name. That's your own name, the one your mother gave you, not the words 'Your Name.' In the second blank you put Saturday, 7 October 1950, 12 noon to 4 p.m. Let me write that down on the blackboard for those of you with short attention spans."

And he did. He waited. Then he said, "On the front of the postcard you put the name and address of the person you want to visit you. It can be anyone— your mother, father, wife, girlfriend, parole officer, anyone—but whoever it is can only bring along one other person."

Tim thought a long time about whose name he should put down. He couldn't make up his mind. Finally, when the corporal sharply began to call for the cards and other papers to be passed in, he quickly wrote down Peg's name and address.

After that they were given chow in one building, a large concrete mess hall, and in another—a barracks building that had been set up as a quartermaster's store—a bored supply clerk threw sheets and blankets down on the counter as they filed by.

They all made their beds—not in the precise Army fashion they would be instructed in during basic training—and bedded down just before 10 p.m. Tim went to the latrine at the end of the barracks to brush his teeth and take a pee. When he came back into the barracks bay, he heard from the two flanking rows of double-decker bunks snoring, wheezing, sighing, farting, and a whimper or two. His first full day in the Army had come to an end.

✳    ✳    ✳    ✳

The next day when Tim woke up, the barracks stank. God, how it stank. Actually, he did not awaken so much as be awakened—by a corporal, a different corporal, dressed not in fatigues but in a brown uniform, who hurried down one line of bunks and up the other, rattling and rapping a baton against the metal frames of the double-decker bunks.

"Get up! Get up!" he cried. "The rest of your life awaits you." Tim, fuddled with sleep, stumbled out of his bottom bunk in his shorts and looked at his watch: 4:30.

Slugabeds who remained lying in their bunks had their blankets rudely ripped off them by the corporal. And when one of them angrily and sleepily gave him lip the corporal told him, "The correct phrase is, 'What in hell do you think you're doing, *corporal?*'" To those who remained recalcitrant and unmoving, the corporal went back down the rows of bunks, ruthlessly pulling their mattresses out, so that they lay half-in, half-out of their beds, dazed.

He strode deliberately to the center of the barracks, his brown combat boots thudding on the floor. Planting his thick fists on his hips, baton still in his right hand, he faced his groggy charges.

"My name is Corporal Renfrew. I'm here to get you through the initial phases of your processing at Fort Devens. I am not a babysitter. Which means you've got two minutes to get dressed and fall out in formation, in four ranks, in front of this barracks. Anyone who isn't out there, his ass is gonna be in a sling." He turned smartly on his heel and stormed down the barracks and out the door.

Two minutes later they were all outside, clothes half-on or haphazardly tucked in, shivering in the autumn chill in front of the corporal, who eyed them with displeasure.

"That is without doubt the sorriest-looking formation in the history of the United States Army. But what can you expect? You're not in the Army, not really, not yet. Experts will work on that with you. Today you are going to get your initial clothing issue and go through processing and other good shit designed to set you on your way to becoming a United States soldier, if that's humanly possible."

He paused to glance at his watch, and someone from the raggedy ranks dared to pipe up.

"Sir? Corporal? If you please?"

The corporal glowered at his bold interlocutor with gimlet eye rare in one so young. "Did I call for questions?"

"No, sir. Uh, corporal. But I was wondering if we could take showers. It stinks in that barracks. Some people I think don't have very good personal hygiene." He glared around him, accusingly.

"Sure you can take showers. I was about to say, before I was so rudely interrupted, that it is now oh four fifty-two. You have until oh five thirty to shit, shower, and shave, and fall out here again in formation to go to breakfast."

"But there's no hot water."

"*And?*"

The appellant opened his mouth to reply, but quickly snapped it shut. Somewhere in the ranks someone sniggered.

"I suggest—*if* there are no further questions—that you do not waste any more time. Anyone not back in formation by oh five thirty is shit out of luck for chow. *Fall out!*"

And so Tim and his new comrades slowly adapted to this first, lightly regimented week of Army life. They learned to sacrifice some of their individuality for the common good. They quickly discovered on their own that each of the old barracks was heated by its own coal-fired furnace, and if they wanted heat and hot water they would have to set up a rotation for tending it. The Army, at this point in their enlistment and this season of the year, apparently didn't care. They learned that forty men into fifteen sinks do not go, and so if they wanted a shot at the latrine they had best get out of the sack pronto. Tim, extremely sociable and far from shy, got along well with nearly everyone, though he did find it disconcerting to be brushing his teeth or shaving and look up into the mirror to see someone sitting on the toilet behind him, legs splayed, trousers down around his ankles, and reading a comic book.

They received their initial clothing issue of brown uniforms and stuffed them into their olive-drab duffel bags: two Class A uniforms with an Eisenhower jacket and overseas cap, four sets of fatigues and two fatigue caps and one field jacket, an overcoat that seemed to have more green in it than the other pieces and that Tim thought was smart-looking, two pairs of combat boots and a pair of shoes, called low-quarters. Tim was impressed by the care with which their boots and shoes were fitted, and as they were trying things on and storing them away, he mentioned it to Rudy Ditzen, the tweed-jacketed fellow who had been in line next to him at the receiving station and who happened to have gotten the lower bunk next to him.

"I mean," Tim said, standing up from the edge of his bunk and stamping his feet into the boots, "the rest of the stuff they practically throw at you with almost no regard to size. My field jacket, for one thing, is too tight on me. I'm going to try and swap it with somebody who maybe got one too big."

Rudy looked up at Tim through his pale-plastic-rimmed glasses. "The Army is profligate, Tim, but not stupid. Not completely, anyway. Your feet are going to be your main means of locomotion for the next two years and it wants them well and truly shod. A soldier with blisters on his feet is a soldier who can't get close to the enemy."

"I guess you're right." Tim sat back down on his bunk and began pulling off the boots, looking at Rudy. "Did I hear you got drafted through Albany, too?"

"Not drafted. Enlisted."

"Enlisted? You're RA?"

Rudy nodded.

"Huh. That's interesting. Not me, I'm US." Tim pushed his boots underneath his bunk. "What'd you do? I mean, what'd you work at before this?"

"Nothing, really. I graduated from Syracuse University in June and was planning on teaching high school English, but then this thing in Korea came along."

"Yeah, but you didn't have to enlist. Maybe as a teacher they'd never even draft you."

"Maybe, but I think they'll get down even to the teachers before this is over. Anyway, my brother was in during the war, and I thought I should be in, too. Especially with this." Rudy waved his hand vaguely, as if Korea was just outside the barracks walls.

"What was he? In the Army?"

"Yes. Rifleman. Well, actually, he was a bazooka man. In the 102nd Division. He was killed shortly after the Battle of the Bulge."

"Oh. Sorry." Tim stared at the floor through his laced fingers in a respectful moment of silence, then looked up again. "I was working at Allegheny Ludlum. I can't say I'm thrilled to be drafted, but in a way I'm not sorry to be out of there. It was a good place to work, good pay and all, but I was getting restless. I had—I have—this idea I'd like to be doing something else. Something different. Something that means something."

"Well, you will be now. This'll be different. And I think it will mean something."

"It's not quite what I had in mind. But then, I admit I didn't have anything definite in mind." Tim sighed. "What about you? With a college degree, you could be an officer, easy. OCS, maybe?"

Rudy smiled. "The recruiting sergeant tried hard to sign me up for OCS, but I said no. Infantryman was good enough for my brother, and it's good enough for me."

For a week they did more processing and got their shots. They got their dog-tags. They filled out yet more forms and questionnaires. They took tests, psychological, mental, and emotional, designed to determine what jobs they could do for their Uncle Sam and how well they might do them. They attended lectures moral, legal, military, and venereal. They met with the chaplain, who told them what a vital mission they were embarking upon and had them fill out index cards listing their religious preferences and spiritual concerns that were then filed away and never looked at again. And then their orders were posted, for places all over the map of the United States. Tim and Rudy were among those posted to Fort Dix, New Jersey, for Basic Infantry Training with the 9th Division, which had been deactivated in 1947 and then reactivated later the same year at Fort Dix to serve as a training unit.

*     *     *     *

Tim wasn't at all sure Peg would make it. But she came, that Saturday afternoon of the dying year, with Rick, in Tim's car, which Tim had turned over to Rick "for the duration." Rick had also taken over Tim's room at the Jenkinses', continuing his Little-Brother-Follow-the-Leader role that suited him so well.

They met at the mess hall that had been designated on the postcard and turned into a kind of guest reception center for the occasion. Hundreds of soldiers and family members were milling around, hugging, kissing, crying, laughing. At first Tim did not see them, and began to despair, but then he a spied a fire-engine-red coat coming across the parade ground from the parking area and his heart leaped. When he saw the little matching red beret-like hat, he was sure it was Peg, and then walking next to her he saw Rick. He half-ran to meet them. They were at the trees that lined the street across from the mess hall, looking around for him, and crisp dry leaves were drifting down around them, one of them landing on her hat. When Peg caught sight of him, she darted forward into the traffic-less street and with a couple of steps they were in each other's arms.

"Oh Tim." She pulled back her head, looked at him, and gave him a demure little kiss on the lips. She hugged him again, pressing her head against his chest. "Oh Tim."

"Peg," Tim said, as they pulled apart. "Peggy, Peggy, I'm happy you came. I've really missed you."

"Really?" she asked weakly, her voice breaking, and with the knuckle of her right forefinger wiped a small tear from her cheek. "Really? Oh, look at us, in the street, like fools. And here's your brother, we're completely ignoring him."

Rick hung back, a couple paces away from Tim and Peg, inspecting his shoes, almost shy. At Peg's mention of him, he looked up. He took Tim's proffered hand, shook it, then they gave each other brotherly hugs. "Good to see you," Tim said.

"Same here. Say, you look good in that uniform."

"Yes, you do, very nice," Peg said, brushing her hand fondly across Tim's lapel.

"So, how was the trip over?" Tim asked.

"Pretty good," Rick said. "Traffic wasn't bad at all."

"How's the Chevy doing?"

"Great. It's really a sweet car. I'll take good care of it for you, I promise. How's the Army treating you so far?"

"It's not so bad. I've met some great guys. The guy in the bunk next to me, his name's Rudy, is from Albany. Some of the others—let's just say they're, well, interesting." Tim smiled and looked first at Peg, then Rick. "You want to walk around a bit? I can show you my barracks, some other things."

"Sure," Rick agreed. "I'd like that. Say, did you hear? The U.N. forces are crossing the—what do they call it?—the 38th Parallel into North Korea. That's the dividing line between North Korea and South Korea. I think they'll have this thing licked soon." The forced hopefulness in his voice was evident to both Peg and Tim.

"Oh, let's not talk about that." Peg hooked her right elbow through Tim's left. "Let's just enjoy this beautiful, beautiful day. Show me where you live. Is that the right way to say it, 'Where you live'? It doesn't sound very military," she said, exaggerating the sense of feminine ignorance. And they set off, three cheerful souls, into the delicate wheat-hued afternoon. Tim took them around all the points of the base he could, showing them among other things his barracks and the dozen other mess halls. Peg wanted to know why all the mess halls seemed to be at unnecessarily great distances from the companies they served, and Tim said it probably was just the perversity of the Army. After about an hour they ended up at Tim's car.

"You want something to eat or drink? We could go over to the PX."

"No, not right now." Peg shot a covert glance at Rick.

Rick caught the glance. "You know what, I think I'll make myself scarce. You two probably have a lot to talk about. Maybe I'll go to the PX myself, get a Coke or something."

"You won't be able to get in without me. Civilians aren't admitted unless they're accompanied by a military member."

"With this crowd?" Rick indicated the clumps of people in sight all over the base. "I'll attach myself to somebody at the PX. You just point it out to me." He started to leave, then stopped and said, "Wait. Here's the car keys, case you need them."

"I'm not supposed to drive. I can't leave the base."

"Just in case." Rick handed over the keys and he went off in the direction Tim indicated, not at all planning to act on his brazen suggestion that he would enlist a total stranger's help in getting into the PX.

As Rick walked off, Tim and Peg turned toward each other, joined hands, and, in the silence of the dying afternoon, drank each other in. The sun was low in the sky over Tim's shoulder.

"God, Peg, you look so pretty. That red really suits you."

"You really think so? Thank you. I hesitated about wearing it, it seems so bold. But I have to admit, I do think it's not bad with my coloring, if that doesn't sound too vain."

"You couldn't be vain if you tried."

Silence.

"You want the radio on, some music?" Before Peg could answer, Tim opened the car door and slipped onto the front seat. He turned the key, clicked on the radio, and twisted the tuning knob. Out of the cacophony of audio swirls and crackles came Guy Lombardo's "Enjoy Yourself, It's Later Than You Think."

"Oh God, Tim. Turn that off. It's such a stupid song. Besides, I don't want to be reminded at this moment that it's later than I think. I'm not in the mood for music anyway."

"I guess you're right," he said, and clicked the radio off.

"I called your mother when I got your postcard," Peg said, after Tim had climbed back out of the car. "I told her I was coming to see you."

"Did you? I'm glad. I hope she's not upset that I didn't send it to her, but Black Run is just too far to come for a few hours on a Saturday afternoon."

"Of course she's not upset. And I told her I'd call again when I get back and tell her how you are." Pause. "But she may wonder why you didn't send the postcard to Rick." Pause, then, slyly: "Or Lynn Jenkins."

"Lynn Jenkins?" Tim said, immediately sensing the lack of conviction in his own voice. "Why would I send it to Lynn Jenkins?"

"Why Lynn Jenkins?" Peg's mock bewilderment was gentle but thick. "Oh, I think you know."

"No, I don't know."

"You don't? Well, how about this? Maybe because she has been your mother's overnight guest in Pennsylvania? Maybe because you have been known to—how shall I say this?—*consort* with her?"

"Consort? That's ridiculous." And Tim was aware not only of the lack of conviction, but that he kept repeating what Peg had just said. "Of course I would send the card to you. You—you're practically family."

Peg, startled, rolled her eyes. "Family? Let's see. My older brother was married to your aunt. Why, we must be kissin' cousins, at least. That is the *lamest* justification of anything I've ever heard in my life. And, under the circumstances, almost cruel. Why couldn't you just say you sent the card to me because I was the one you wanted to spend these precious few hours with?"

"That's the truth. That's why I did it. Why did you have to bring up Lynn Jenkins?"

"I brought up Lynn Jenkins"—her speech was accelerating with every sentence—"because I was happy you *didn't* send the card to her and that probably meant you care more for me than for her. And because ... because I *love* you, Tim. I shouldn't say it. I know that even in this modern day and age well-brought-up young women aren't supposed to say that to men, but I just have to. That's why what you said seemed almost cruel, because I thought, well, family ... you and I, we might—." She broke off, weeping softly.

Tim's heart was rent. He folded Peg into his arms and felt the gentle staccato of her sobs against his breast.

"And I think I love you, Peg."

And with that the floodgates of his mind and memory opened, overwhelming him. He remembered Helen saying she *thought* she loved him and he had said nothing, and here was Peg saying she loved him, unreservedly, and he could only respond that he *thought* he loved her. Lynn had chided him about Peg, and Peg about Lynn, and both had made oblique but inquisitive references to Helen. Everything seemed to remind him of something else, though never very clearly, and things seemed to keep recurring, though not exactly, and it all seemed to be aiming someplace, though where exactly had not been revealed to him, and it was all terribly confusing.

Peg pulled her head back from his chest, sniffed, scrabbled in her purse for a handkerchief, and dabbed at her nose.

"You *think* you love me. Well, that's something, I suppose " She gave him a wan smile. "Look at me. My nose must match my coat now."

"No, you look at me," Tim took her chin in his right thumb and forefinger, and in the act of doing so thought, *This seems so phony. This is like some movie.* But it wasn't phony, it was real. "Peg, I *do* think I love you. I'm sorry, that's all I can say now. I'm all confused. I'm going off soon to I don't know where for I don't know how long. It's just all so uncertain." From somewhere in his mind those sentiments came welling up from the past to meet the present. *And all that sounds like movie crap, too.*

Peg opened her purse, stuffed the handkerchief back in, and clicked it shut. "Well, it's just as uncertain for me. People have been walking into a future they couldn't be sure of for as long as there have been people." She smiled at him again, this time more brightly.

"But I'm not angry at you Tim, really. You want to know why? Because I not only love you, I admire you. I admire almost everything about you. And you know why? Oh, I just said that. Because you don't take advantage of women. Wait a minute, you think I mean sex. I don't mean sex. You're probably just as—

excuse me, I've got to use the word—*horny* as the next guy, and believe me, I've met the next guy. And it's not just opening doors and holding chairs. It's a basic decency, like you understand that women are people, too. Oh hell," she concluded, inconclusively, and began twiddling with his tie, trying to straighten out the rumples her weeping had put into it.

She looked up at him. "Other women have told you the same thing, haven't they?"

Tim grinned and looked embarrassed. "Yeah. Not exactly, but sort of."

"Why are you grinning? Is this funny?"

"It's more complicated than what you just asked. Someone even asked me once before if someone had told me that before. If you can understand that?"

"I understand that. And you're proud of yourself, I suppose? Don't get a swelled head. You're not that great." She gave his tie a final pat. "So where are we?"

Tim put his arms around her waist and drew her to him. "We're in Fort Devens, Massachusetts, and I'm about to go off to Fort Dix, New Jersey, where you will still be my girl."

"'Your girl.' There's a first. Not exactly a diamond ring, but I'll take it. It's progress, of a sort. We've known each other about two years now. Another two years and we'll probably advance to being business partners." Off to her right she could see Rick approaching in the distance. "Now, I'm not the sort of girl who usually necks in public, but give me a good smooch to cover up all this bawling, because your brother's coming. Besides, the sun's going down and I'm getting cold."

*     *     *     *

The screaming sergeant Tim had expected to greet his bus at Fort Devens materialized at Fort Dix the following Monday. Their bus was met by a sergeant, three stripes up and two down, who shouted at them to get out: "Move it move it move it move it!" Dragging, pushing, and falling over their duffel bags, they rushed down the aisle and down the steps, where he screamed at them to fall in in four ranks in front of him and square it down. There followed another scene of confusion in which the unorganized rabble tried to form an organized rabble, while each of them sought to avoid being in the front rank. After a short period of pushing and shoving and muttering, the four ranks fell still and silent, facing the fierce glare of a dark-faced man about thirty years old and six feet in height, light brown hair under his red helmet liner, and of trim build. On his chest was the Combat Infantryman's Badge, which Tim knew was one of the Army's most-prized awards, since it designated service under enemy fire. Elsewhere, around him, Tim was aware of other buses and other recruits stumbling off them while being yelled at by other sergeants.

The man continued to look at them without saying anything. When, after a few moments, he did speak, it was only to say, quietly, "What a train wreck." He turned to his left, as if hoping that help might come from that direction. Then, with an attitude of summoning reserves of strength and conviction he himself did not know he had, he squared his shoulders, faced them again, and, with a hint of steel in his voice, said, "We'll soon get that straightened out." He paused, then commanded:

"A-ten-*shun*."

The four ranks struggled to pull themselves up to an approximation of the military posture that had been provisionally taught them at Fort Devens.

He observed their efforts and said, "I guess that will have to do for now." His words formed puffs of smoke in the chill air as he spoke.

"My name is Sergeant Rogers. Sergeant First Class Richard Rogers. I know, some of you may have heard of another person out there who has the same name as mine, except he spells his with a 'd,' which is tacky. He is the *lucky* Richard Rogers. He gets to write songs and hang out with pretty showgirls while I am inflicted with the chore every few weeks of trying to turn a ragtag-and-bobtail bunch of lunkheads into American fighting men. It is not fair. Anyone given enough time could eventually write *Oklahoma*, but even with all the time in the world imagine trying to turn"—he walked up to the first rank and placed his face directly in front of that of one of the men—"what's your name?"

"Stevens," the man said, bracing still more stiffly.

"Stevens, *sergeant*."

"Stevens, sergeant."

"Imagine trying to turn Stevens here," the sergeant continued, "into something approximating a United States soldier. It is an impossible task. God himself has barely managed to turn him into something approximating a human being."

From somewhere in the center of the ranks came a brief snorting sound.

"There is no talking in ranks unless I tell you to speak," the sergeant said. "In the ranks there is no talking, laughing, giggling, belching, weeping, or farting unless I tell you to, and if I tell you to, then you *will* talk, laugh, giggle, belch, weep, or fart. On command."

He waited for another involuntary response from the ranks, but none came.

"I will be your chief platoon sergeant during your period of basic infantry training here in the 9$^{th}$ Division. "I will be responsible for the training that may save your lives in Korea—me and the rest of the cadre of this company."

Sergeant Rogers began to pace slowly back and forth in front of the men.

"Now, you probably have heard the fighting in Korea referred to as a 'police action.' I don't know what that means. What *is* a police action? As far as I know, there are no cops in foxholes and bunkers over there arresting people for mugging or speeding or holding up liquor stores. There are American soldiers, fighting and sometimes dying. Our goal is to prepare you to do the former and avoid the latter.

"No, what is going on in Korea, I am here to tell you, is a war and nothing less. You may also have heard people—politicians who know nothing and newspaper columnists who know even less—say that it will be over by Thanksgiving, or by Christmas. Every war I have ever known of, people have said it would be over by Thanksgiving or Christmas, and every one lasted for years. This one will, too, believe me. Which gives me heart, because that gives me a chance to get into it if I can ever get shut of having to play nursemaid to a bunch of Sad Sacks.

"But that makes my responsibility all the more awesome, because, with my luck, I may end up serving over there with one or more of you. So how well I train you, and how well you absorb that training, may save not only your life but, what is more important, mine.

"First thing, then, I want you to count off by fours, starting at my left—that's your right—in the front rank and continuing through the second, third, and fourth. One, two three, four, one—and so on. If you can manage to do that without totally fucking up, we'll be off to not too horrible a start."

\*       \*       \*       \*

More by accident than by alphabetic proximity of their last names, Tim and Rudy were placed in the same squad in Sergeant Rogers's platoon. When they discovered this, they raced to claim lower bunks next to each other, since each was the only friend the other had in this brave new world. They were sitting on their bunks in the late afternoon of that first day, discussing their new sergeant and agreeing that he looked like being a real hard-ass, when they heard an oddly accented voice from the bunk above Rudy's:

"Ah, he's a pussycat, compared to some."

Tim looked up and saw the head belonging to the voice stick itself out over the edge of the bunk. Thick red hair topped a long bony face with a thin bony nose and a smiling mouthful of irregular teeth.

"Compared to who? Whom?" Tim asked.

"Compared to the average bastard sergeant in the British Army," the stranger said, sitting up in his bunk.

"You're English," Tim said more than asked.

"I am that," the man agreed, and dropped to the floor. He thrust out his right hand. "Adrian Tomlinson."

"Tim Davis. This here's Rudy Ditzen." Tim and Rudy took turns shaking hands with the tall, extremely thin newcomer, who said, "Pleased to meet you both."

"If you're English, what are you doing in the American Army?" Tim asked.

"Well, they drafted me, so they did."

"Can they do that?"

"Actually, it seems they can. The law seems to reason that if you are a resident of these United States and enjoying its bountiful blessings, then you ought to be subject to its obligations, too. I have to admit, that's hard to argue with."

"But how did it happen?" Rudy asked. "Were you on a visit, or a student or something."

"Oh no. I've been here since 1948, came over when I was twenty. I was living in Schenectady and working at a coil company. I don't mind it that much, actually. If I was back in Blighty I'd have to be doing my National Service anyway."

"But now there's Korea," Tim said.

"Well, as to that, we—sorry, the British, that is—seem to be as much in the thick of it as you Yanks, with 27 Brigade coming over from Hong Kong and apparently more to follow."

"But wouldn't you rather be in the British Army?" Tim found this young man and his situation tantalizing. "This must seem so ... strange."

"Not really, not after two years in the States. I reckoned on becoming a naturalized citizen, anyway, and this will only aid the process. Besides, your lot pays sixty-eight dollars a month. Do you know what a British private gets? Bugger all."

"Sixty-eight dollars a month." Tim sighed. "I used to take home more than that in a good week."

"So did everyone, mate. I recently read where the average weekly wage in industry is something like sixty dollars, or a few cents more—the highest ever. I was doing all right meself. But as to the British army, there's also, as I said by way of introduction, the sergeants. They'd have had us square-bashing all day today till our back teeth jarred out. They're a terrible hard lot."

"Square-bashing?" Rudy asked.

"Oh, you know, pointless and endless marching and drilling about the barracks square. The parade ground, I believe you call it."

"I imagine that's coming," Rudy said. "Where are you from, by the way? I mean, what city or county or whatever it is? Not that I'd know where it is."

"From any number of places, I suppose you could say, but Carlisle is as accurate an answer as any. That's where my family lives now, though we moved around a fair bit when I was a kid. Carlisle is an army town. That's how I know about the sergeants, because me Dad is one, you see. He's a sergeant-major now, not far from retirement. He's a tremendous fella and I like him and all that, but he's right hard on the lads who come under his scrutiny."

Adrian was about to climb back up to his bunk when they heard the tremendous *clap* of the barracks door being slammed open.

"And speaking of sergeants, here comes ours now, and he's got blood in his eye. Hmm, I wonder if he might have done a turn in the Border Regiment?"

\*     \*     \*     \*

Tim and Rudy and Adrian became fast buddies—"mates," as Adrian said—and, after being shorn in their first "GI haircut" and going through processing, the three cheerful musketeers soon fell into the routine and rhythm of basic training. Tim learned that a basic training company was essentially an oversized version of a regular infantry company made up of four platoons. Whereas the infantry platoon has four squads of eight or nine men each, his training company—C or Charlie Company—had four platoons of ten or twelve men to each squad. Each barracks had two floors, with one platoon to each floor, which meant that more than forty men lived on one floor in double-decker bunks. The barracks next to theirs, with its two platoons, made up the rest of Charlie Company. Their company commander was a captain, standard for an infantry company, but they did not have, as an infantry platoon does, an officer—a lieutenant—as platoon leader. They were led and instructed instead solely by a cadre of non-commissioned officers like Sergeant Rogers and other sergeants and corporals. The cadre chose squad leaders from among recruits who had some sort of military experience, whether ROTC, previous active duty, Reserve, or even military school.

From the mess hall in the morning they hurried back to the barracks, gave it a quick sweep and clean-up, put on their brown helmet liners and their cartridge belts and the rest of their gear—including, as the weather turned colder, their field jackets—and fell out in front of the barracks to face Sergeant Rogers or one of the other cadre, or often both.

"Dress ri-i-i-ght, *dress.*" The men wriggled this way, then that way, lining themselves up. "Red-*dee* ... front!" Sergeant Rogers looked at them, then, "Puh-*raid* ... rest!" They were introduced—had been, already—to the concept of "pushing New Jersey away," or the basic push-up, which was invoked for the slightest infraction: "Drop and give me fifteen!"

Protest: "Aw, sergeant, I was just—"

"Did I say fifteen? What was I thinking of? I meant twenty."

They would form up with the rest of the company for the day's training. "Com-puh-*nee* ... ah-ten-*shun.*" Then, "Com-puh-*nee* ... at ease!" Then attention, right face, sling arms, forward, march. If they were not being bused to a distant training site, such the KD (known distance) rifle range, they marched along with a man bearing the guidon in front, in columns of twos or fours, in their green fatigues, field jackets, and helmet liners, with rifles slung over their shoulders, singing cadence:

> *I had a good home but I left*
> *You're right!*
> *I had a good home but I left*
> *You're right!*
> *Sound off, one two*
> *Sound off, three four*
> *Sound off, one-two*
> *One-two, three-four!*

The NCO marching along beside them, ramrod-straight, shoulders thrust back, chin tucked in, proud as a peacock, bellowed at them while never shifting from the eyes-front position:

"Sound off like you got a pair!"

And they went through it again with greater spirit and volume, ending the dying fall with an enthusiastic:

> *Sound off, one-two*
> *One-two, THREE-FOUR!*

Tim occasionally pulled guard duty, sometimes guarding an ammunition dump, sometimes a building, sometimes demonstration tanks. He learned how to operate the 57 mm. recoilless rifle and the 60 mm. mortar. Most of all he and his comrades learned their basic weapon, the M1 rifle. They learned it inside out and backward and forward, how to take it apart, clean it, and reassemble it in the dark, always being exhorted to improve their time. The NCO who instructed them was a pudgy sergeant first class of many years' service, every year worn on his lined and creased face:

"This is your rifle. It is not your gun. Your gun is that thing you got between your legs. Some of you got a bigger caliber than others. You do not shoot your rifle, you fire it. You fire your rifle, you shoot your gun. Remember that: This is my rifle, this is my gun; this is for fighting, this is for fun. This rifle weighs nine and a half pounds, except at the end of a twenty-mile march, when it weighs sixty pounds. It is the best military rifle in the world. It is the thirty caliber, clip-fed, air-cooled, gas-operated M1 Garand rifle. The taxpayers of the United States have been good enough to pay for a bayonet to go with this rifle. It weighs only one pound, except at the end of a twenty-mile march, when it weighs fifteen. Most likely when you get to Korea you will have occasion to introduce this handy device to the guts of a gook, for the bayonet is far from being an obsolete weapon."

They received training in that bayonet. "What's the spirit of the bayonet? To kill! On guard position, yah! Short thrust and hold, yah! Recover. Long thrust and hold, yah! Recover! Vertical butt stroke and hold, yah! Kill! Kill! Kill!"

When they went out to the range to qualify with the M1, Tim always thrilled, for some reason, at hearing the range officer's spoken-by-rote command: "Ready on the left, ready on the right, ready on the firing line. Lock and load one clip of ball ammunition." The flag down the range went up, waved briefly, and went down, and the trainees blazed away at two hundred yards until the range officer shouted over the PA system, "Cease firing! Cease firing!" Tim eventually made Sharpshooter, the skill level most trainees achieved. He was a little shocked when he saw that those, known as "bolos," who failed to qualify at even the lowest level were got through by the cadre, who simply picked up the bolos' rifles, fired at the targets, and qualified for them. Everybody *had* to qualify on the rifle to get through basic training, no matter how.

Besides standing guard, other extra duties they pulled included KP (kitchen police)—which could involve washing pots and pans and trays for eighteen hours straight and was generally exhausting—barracks guard, furnace detail, and CQ runner. Tim didn't mind the last, because it only meant having to be in the company orderly room for a stint of two hours or so to run errands for the NCO who was on duty as charge of quarters. Aside from the interruption in sleep, he especially liked it late at night or in the wee hours, because at those times usually all he had to do was answer the phone, which rarely rang. It gave him a chance to read or to write letters. But one night while he was CQ runner he gave Peg a running commentary on a situation in progress:

> About half an hour ago there was a hell of a ruckus in our platoon's barracks. And I can hear one going on now in the next barracks. The sergeant who is on CQ (Charge of Quarters) duty tonight walked through. Everyone but the barracks guard, of course, was asleep. The sergeant isn't one of ours, he's from a different platoon. He went through our barracks, ripping open the lockers that were unlocked and throwing the contents on the floor, also taking the money out of the pockets of the guys whose lockers were open. The sergeants had warned us and warned us to keep our lockers locked for our own good, and that they wouldn't give us any more warnings. So he hit us with a raid tonight. Of course, everyone will get their money back alright, but they'll have to go to the sergeant to get it, and you can be sure that he'll give them some kind of detail (dirty job) to pay for it. I'm OK; my stuff was not hit, I had it all locked up. And do not think that what he did was terrible, because, after all, they have warned us about it for 2 weeks, and he is right: it is only for our own good to lock our things up, for no one can tell who might be a thief in the barracks.
>
> However, here is another thing: The sergeant is more than half-gassed. That's right: pickled, loaded, drunk. I could smell it on him from 5 feet away when I reported for CQ duty. Besides, he kept getting people mixed up, and couldn't pronounce correctly. He has been "under the influence" other times, too, when he has been in charge of giving a "class" to us in some "subject" or other, like hand-to-hand combat.

Another night when he had CQ duty Tim was flipping through copies of magazines lying on a table and came across an August 7 Life with an actress on the cover he had never seen before. He was attracted not just by her name but her looks. Peggy Dow, it said on the cover, and underneath that "Camera Chameleon." That night he wrote Peg, telling her how he had read about this actress in a new movie called "Harvey" and that she reminded him of her. That wasn't strictly true, as he guiltily admitted to himself. It was simply the shared name, Peggy, that prompted him to say it. It was really her looks that struck him, because her surface demureness seemed to him like that of another actress, Cathy O'Donnell. And she, as he even more guiltily told himself, reminded him of Helen.

Basic training, Tim learned, was more than training. Sometimes it was the "details (dirty jobs)" that he mentioned in his letter. "Details" like raking the lawn of the post commander's house, or clearing debris from a lot. Sometimes they weren't even that logical or rational or, seemingly, necessary, like digging a ditch whose purpose Tim could not figure out. Maybe the Army didn't know itself. Maybe the Army just liked to have spare ditches around. But not all details were totally unpleasant, as Tim explained in a letter to Peg he wrote after being out on one on an unseasonably sweltering late October afternoon:

> Yesterday was great day for me. It was a "detail day," which means everybody in the company is sent out to various places on the post to do crumby jobs. The place I went to didn't work us very hard. But better than that: In the afternoon, the sergeants and NCOs there were getting ready for a party they were going to have that night. They'd bought enough cans and bottles of beer to almost fill a garbage can. Then we (another guy and myself) had to chip ice to place around and on top of the beer. And, <u>then</u>, they invited us to have some of it. I had four cans of beer on that extremely hot afternoon. Man, that was great!

*       *       *       *

Mail call" was the highlight of everyone's day. People, if they could get away from what they were doing, went galloping toward the soldier distributing the mail. "Smith?" *Here!* "Jones?" *Here!* "Mac—Mac—shi—shillo—oh, what the hell." And everyone laughed, even the guy with the hard-to-pronounce name, because they were so happy to receive mail. It was just like in the movies. Lots of things were like in the movies—the stereotypical Italian and Jewish guys from New York City and the shy farmer boys from out in the sticks and the Mama's boys who cried in their bunks at night. And just like in the movies, the other soldiers laughed and ribbed the guy who got too many letters at one mail call. Tim got his fair share. Peg wrote just about every other day.

Oct. 28, '50

Dearest Tim,

Here it is Saturday and it's raining and I'm feeling kind of low. Not so much because it's raining, but I'm sorry to have to tell you that my grandmother passed away yesterday afternoon. It's probably not good to burden a soldier with sad news, not when he has so many pressures on him already, but I know how much you cared for your "Grandma Altschuler" so I was sure you would want to know.

She went yesterday afternoon. Pat found her in her rocking chair when she came home from grocery shopping. She was 79, almost 80, her birthday would have been Nov. 23. Thanksgiving this year, I just looked on the calendar. Not much to be thankful for, is there? I guess I shouldn't say that. She had a good life. My mother is okay about it so far, a little weepy, but you knew Grandma had a bad heart, so this isn't totally unexpected for Mom. The funeral will be Monday. First Eileen, now Grandma. Funny thing, Pat and Bernie had just completed their purchase of Grandma's house a couple weeks back. It's almost like Grandma was saying, Everything is done and in place now, it's time to go. But I suppose it's foolish to think that way.

That's not the only reason I'm feeling low, of course. I miss you, We all miss you, but I'll bet no one does more than me. I think of you often, wondering what you are doing at that particular moment. You have told me so much about your training that I can call up pictures in my mind of you down there. The pictures are probably not very accurate, but I enjoy them. Then I go and compare them with your photo. (I wish you could see me smiling here)

Well, that is about all for this time. I'm not in much of a mood for trying to scratch up news to tell you, and news like this is enough for one letter, anyway. When I think of you, I also think of our last day together there at Fort Devens and all that we talked about. That's why I hope you take it in the "spirit of understanding" that we had that day when I end my letters with

Love,

Peg

Peg always ended her letters with "Love," hoping, as she tried to tell him, that he understood the carefulness and tentativeness with which she did so. Tim never used "Love." Sometimes he signed his letters baldly "Tim," and nothing else, and sometimes he used tortured phrases like "With Deepest Affection." When she read the latter, they seemed to be such a transparent avoidance while at the same time trying to mean something, that Peg wished he would stick with just "Tim." But she smiled at it, too, because she realized it meant that he was trying, that he hadn't given up.

*       *       *       *

The weather turned much colder and they donned their long, heavy woolen underwear. They were growing more adept at soldiering and earning occasional respect from Sergeant Rogers and the other cadre, who made them conduct fewer "GI parties," in which they had to throw their entire energies for entire nights into communal cleaning of their quarters. They went on bivouac, sleeping two to a pup tent—each man carrying one "shelter half"—in the freezing cold. It was a tactical bivouac so they had to keep their weapons with them at all times, even in the chow line and the latrine.

They went on night firing exercises, and on a night "problem" for which they blackened their faces with coal dust. That caused them to laugh bitterly, because it snowed and their black faces showed up more starkly against the white snow than they ordinarily would have.

Fortunately, when they ran the infiltration course the weather was relatively mild, and they didn't have to negotiate its eighty-yard length in the cold and the wet. Tim found himself exhilarated as he crawled his way through its hummocks and dips in the ground with the .30 caliber machine guns, mounted on sandbags, spewing red tracer rounds over their heads. The guns sounded almost musical to him with their rattata-tattata. Sometimes the course forced him to turn over on his back to wiggle under barbed wire, a delicate maneuver to pull off underneath the constant stream of fire overhead. Every so often a fixed explosive went off next to him, simulating an artillery hit. When they first arrived at the trench by which they approached the infiltration course, the NCO who was the range instructor in charge of the problem had given them a grim warning.

"You men, you keep your ass down when you're out there. You've been told it, but I mean it. Those guns are set not to fire lower than a certain level, but you stick your ass—or your head—up and they *will* shoot it off. I seen it happen on one of these courses. It was down to Benning. Guy got his ass *all* tore up. Had to shit through a hole in his side from that time on. 'Course, it got him out of the Army, if that's what you're thinking."

They looked at the NCO, not knowing how to respond.

"And remember to stay off the mounds, that's where they got the fixed charges," the sergeant added.

"Everybody's a comedian," Tim said to Adrian after they had moved further into the trench, close to the low flight of steps leading up to the course.

"Didn't sound so flamin' comical to me," Adrian said, rolling his eyes up to look at the red-streaked night and tugging on the lip of his helmet to give it an unneeded righting.

"Ah, they're always doing that, exaggerating the difficulty by pretending that the danger you're in is humorous to them. Oops, hey, they're giving the signal. Here we go."

"Oh well." Adrian sighed and scrunched up close behind Tim, preparatory to moving forward. "As the mother said to her daughter on her wedding night, close your eyes and think of England."

✳     ✳     ✳     ✳

Sergeant Rogers was right. The war was not over by Thanksgiving. Nor was it over by Christmas, for which basic training at Fort Dix shut down. Much had been happening in the world, and most particularly in Korea, while Tim and his comrades were in training, most of which they had no time or inclination to pay attention to. The "Chinese People's Volunteers"—so-called in a pretense that China was not in direct confrontation with the United States—had entered the war against the U.N. forces, dealing them several reverses that also reversed the hopeful signs many in the United States had been pointing to early in the fall. In late October the U.S. 8th Army's northward drive in northwestern North Korea, and that of X Corps in the northeast, was halted by the Chinese. General George E. Stratemeyer, commanding general of FEAF (the Far East Air Force), describing the beginning of this "new war" to a congressional committee, said U.N. forces had been moving ahead unopposed, "But then, lo and behold, the whole mountainside turned out to be Chinese." The first Chinese MiG fighters appeared in the skies over the Yalu River that was the border between North Korea and China's Manchuria. General MacArthur charged the Chinese with unlawful aggression, while President Truman assured them that he had no intention of carrying the hostilities into their country, which they did not for a moment believe because they knew that was exactly what MacArthur wanted to do and what they had entered the war to prevent. By early December, shortly before President Truman declared a state of national emergency, X Corps and 8th Army were both withdrawing in the face of the Chinese offensive.

Some of it, however, Tim and his comrades were definitely aware of, and followed in the news as much as their constrained circumstances allowed, most notably the Battle of Chosin Reservoir. Elements principally of the U.S. 1$^{st}$ Marine Division, but also of the U.S. 3$^{rd}$ Infantry Division and 7$^{th}$ Infantry Division and of the British Royal Marines engaged in a harrowing effort to break out of Chinese encirclement in the frozen desolation of northeastern North Korea in late November and early December. They fought against overwhelming odds— seven, eight, even ten to one, a company against a Chinese regiment, a battalion against a division. By the time Tim arrived home on leave, morale in the 8$^{th}$ Army was on the verge of collapse, as was the 8$^{th}$ Army itself, and its commander, Lieutenant General Walton H. Walker, had been killed in a vehicle accident. By the time Tim returned to Fort Dix from leave, Lieutenant General Matthew B. Ridgway had succeeded him and was preparing to turn things around.

*        *        *        *

"Oh God, Lynn. Not that song. Anything but that. Turn it off. Please."

Tim's leave had begun at 5:00 p.m. Friday, the 22$^{nd}$. He managed to get a ride with another Pennsylvania soldier to Altoona, where Rick, who had driven down from New York, picked him up well after midnight. Rick had made the trip especially so that Tim—and he—could spend at least part of the holiday with Anna, Barbara, and Connie before heading back up to Guldwyck. It was a hectic time for Tim, and it left him almost as tired as in Basic. After an "early Christmas" of opening presents with his mother and sisters, and having a big "Christmas dinner" in the middle of the day on Saturday, he and Rick headed north in a light snowfall. Fortunately the roads were not too bad, but even so they did not arrive until midnight. Tim fell into bed, exhausted, at Jean's apartment and Rick continued on to his room—formerly Tim's—at Aunt Cissy's. And now, at 10 o'clock Christmas Eve, Tim was almost directly below that room, in Lynn's living room, begging her not to play "The Tennessee Waltz."

"You don't like 'Tennessee Waltz?' I love it. Everybody seems to love it. You hear it all the time."

"You're telling me. That's all I've been hearing the last few days at Dix. On the radio, in the jukeboxes. There's some guys from the South there, maybe they're from Tennessee. I swear they'd take a record player on bivouac with them to play it if they could. I don't know how they got there; most of the recruits at Dix are from the Northeast. But they're there and they listen to that damn thing every chance they get. So does everybody else, though at least they take a break now and then."

"All right, I'll take pity on a poor soldier." She got up from the couch and went over to the record player. She lifted the needle from the record, cutting off Patti Page in the middle of "my friend stole my swee—." Lynn sorted through a stack of records. "I'll put on some Christmas music."

Unlike the season, their reunion was proving less than festive. Tim was tired, and a little irritated over somehow having been shanghaied, by Lynn and her mother, into "agreeing" to go to a candlelight Christmas Eve service at their church, Jermain Memorial Presbyterian on Fifth Avenue in Watervliet. Sitting there, waiting to leave for church, he still was unclear how it had happened. And in a few hours he had to get up and go to a Christmas morning service with Peg at Raleigh Avenue Methodist in Guldwyck. Lynn knew about that, which only added to her simmering resentment over feeling that Tim had failed to write to her often enough while in Basic. Goaded by her twin discontents, and thinking that it might tweak him a little, she mentioned that the man from Massachusetts she was occasionally dating had been called back into the Navy.

"He thinks it's really unfair. He complains about it in *all* his letters."

"It *is* unfair," Tim said, Lynn's jealousy-tipped shaft missing him completely. "You know what they're doing? They're calling up guys from the inactive reserve, who weren't being trained and weren't being paid for their reserve status, and *not* calling up the guys in the active reserve, who *were* being trained and paid. Yet most of the guys being called up from inactive have already done their part— they're veterans of the last war. A lot of the active reservists were never even in the war. It's screwy. In a way the call-ups are paying a penalty for being veterans. They have skills and experience that the Army—or Navy—needs, which the active reservists don't have. They're being made to do their duty twice, while others aren't doing it once."

"Sorry. Didn't mean to get you upset. I didn't think it would affect you that much."

"It's just that I'm seeing it all the time—officers and NCOs that are being called back in. They're not the least happy. They're—oh, here's your Mom. I guess it's time we thought about going to church."

Peg wasn't happy about the dueling Christmas services, either, but she was less miffed than Lynn. She knew it was largely a case of impressment and not really his fault. He was simply the victim once again of his innate agreeableness.

Besides, in her corner she had the bonds of family—Tim was naturally going to spend the bulk of his time with his family, linked to hers—and of affection, if perhaps not quite love. All in all, Peg was quite content that Christmas morning after the church service as they walked up snow-clump-spattered Raleigh Avenue toward her mother's apartment.

"Just think, two whole days yet together. This *is* a nice Christmas." Tim had to be back at Fort Dix by 11 p.m. Wednesday, the 27$^{th}$. She squeezed her right arm, hooked through his left, tight against her side in a spasm of happiness. She looked up at him as they almost loped along in idleness.

"You look tired."

"I *am* tired." He wanted to say, "All this church-going," but thought better of it.

"You can take a nap before dinner. No place to go, nothing to do."

"I plan to. It was nice seeing everybody at church again, the kids especially. It's funny, it's only been a couple months, but it seems like I've been gone a couple years."

"They were happy to see you, too. They're all proud of you. *We're* proud of you. *I'm* proud of you." She squeezed his arm again.

"Proud? What's to be proud of?"

"For being in the Army, silly. For serving your country."

"I don't know, I'm just doing my—" Tim slid past the word "duty" as too high-sounding—"what you're supposed to do. When you think of what the guys did during the war. I have to admit, though, I do wonder what my Dad would think if he could see me now."

Peg looked up at him again. It was the only time she had ever heard him speak of his father.

"Do you know yet what you'll be doing after basic training? Your job? I'm sorry, I don't know the military term for it."

"My MOS. Military Occupational Specialty. I don't know yet. I'll probably be put in the infantry. That's what they need right now, badly."

"Oh dear," Peg said, and thought, "That probably means Korea." But she was determined not to be downhearted. "That's a long way off, and there's a terrific Christmas dinner in between, cooked by my mother, the best cook in Upstate New York."

\*          \*          \*          \*

But it wasn't such a long way off. Tim went back to Fort Dix exhausted, and more confused about his romantic entanglements than ever. Shortly before completing his remaining weeks of training, Tim received his MOS: 1745, rifleman. Early in January he received his orders to report to Fort Lewis, Washington, for transportation to FECOM, Far East Command. Upon graduation from basic, he was given two days to clear post and three days' leave. There was time only to rush over to Pennsylvania to see his mother and sisters. From there he called Peg, who was so distraught she could barely speak. He reported back to Fort Dix. And, while the United Nations was debating resolutions over a ceasefire and Chinese aggression, Tim was riding a troop train to Fort Lewis, home of the 2$^{nd}$ Infantry (Indianhead) Division, which, hastily ordered into action after the outbreak of hostilities on June 25, had begun departing for Korea from Seattle on July 17. Tim would catch up with it in about a month's time.

# CHAPTER 15

▼

# SECOND TO NONE

*In the name of the President of the United States as public evidence of deserved honor and distinction the $2^d$ Infantry Division is cited for extraordinary heroism and outstanding performance of duty in action against the armed enemy in the vicinity of Hongchon, Korea, during the period 16 to 22 May 1951.*

—Distinguished Unit Citation

*"WHAT?!"*

"I said, I don't see how we can hold here any longer!" Sbarra crouched in the cool dirt next to Tim and screamed into his right ear, trying to make himself heard over the cacophony of screams, bugle calls, explosions, and bursting and whizzing metal that rent the early morning darkness. The chaos had Sbarra frightened nearly out of his mind, but he retained enough self-possession to move along the line of his squad members, urging them to hold their positions. "Christ, this is fucking insane. I don't know why battalion doesn't pull us back. We're no good here. The whole fucking Chinese nation is out there."

"Maybe it's not up to battalion," Tim screamed back. "Anyway, they probably forgot about us. God, this mess, I don't think even company knows what's going on here. Where the hell is Paden?"

"I don't know. I think maybe he bought it. I haven't seen him I don't know how long." Sbarra flinched as a mortar round slammed into their right front and sent a spray of shrapnel that chewed up the dirt ten or twelve feet away. He tapped the back of Tim's helmet encouragingly and inched his way to Tim's left, where Jansen was positioned.

"Jesus jumping Christ, corporal," Jansen shouted, hunching down while trying to peer over the lip of his position. "Lookit them Chinks out there. There's thousands of 'em. Thousands. Whyn't they bring in more artillery on 'em?"

"They're firing a Van Fleet load now, looks like. It's coming down in curtains," Sbarra said. One of General Van Fleet's innovations during the Spring Offensive had been to order a massive increase in the rate of artillery fire, sometimes five times as much as had been normal in Korea, which became known as the Van Fleet rate or Van Fleet load. Later it was found some batteries had burned up their gun barrels attempting to achieve the daily rate of 250 rounds for a 105 mm. howitzer. "I don't know how they could do more. They can't bring it in any closer. I heard they already hit some of our guys in the 9th, and the ROKs."

Though Jansen and Sbarra were shouting, Tim could make out only snatches of what they were saying, so overwhelming was the enveloping noise of battle. He was aware of Sbarra's moving again to the left, away from Jansen to buck up Caldwell, who, Tim could see in the occasional flashes of light, was shaking. The tip of the barrel of Caldwell's M1 was bumping up and down on the mound of dirt in front of him. This was by far the worst that Tim had faced in Korea, and for the first time he wondered if he was going to die.

A bullet thwacked into the sandbag just above his head to his right, sending a trickle of dirt skittering down the descending edges of the stacked-up bags. He turned his attention back to his immediate front, and he experienced one of those strange, almost peaceful states of involuntary activity combined with clear thought that sometimes descend on people under extreme stress. The moonlight and the mortar and howitzer explosions and the red tracers and the occasional flares created enough light for him to be able to make out dimly what was in front of him. Smoke drifted about everywhere. Was it smoke or was it morning fog, or both? Could fog even materialize in—hold its own against—such a violent, heated atmosphere? The earth trembled with each artillery strike, causing his whole body to bobble. It made it hard to aim his rifle. He could see brown mounds of Chinese soldiers, some only yards in front of him. Sometimes the mounds moved, and the movement was always toward him. He was aware of sighting the rifle and shooting at them, but not of hitting anything. He thought he did, but he wasn't sure. Spent shell casings were scattered around his right thigh. He wondered how the Chinese could keep moving, keep coming forward. He could see that the artillery rounds were coming in, as Sbarra said, like a curtain of steel, and they were having a devastating attack on the enemy.

Tim, who was anchoring the right end of his squad's sector, heard far off to his left a scream so piteous that it rose above the foundry-like deafening madness. Someone had been hit. It wasn't Jansen or Caldwell, he could see that; it was someone beyond them, but he couldn't tell who. He heard someone call "Medic!"—probably Sbarra—and it came to him that that was only the second time he'd heard anyone do that in combat. The first was during that first fight in which the Mailman had been killed. But this time it was someone he knew, really knew, except he couldn't tell exactly who it was. It bothered him that he couldn't concentrate enough to figure it out. He cudgeled his brain to recall who else was out there to his left, but all the names had left his head.

He tried to snatch another view of what was going on to his front, but the incoming fire was too withering to get more than a glance at the menacing, moving mounds. What the hell, Tim thought, and took hold of one of his grenades. He didn't like hand grenades; he thought them too unstable. They weren't controllable like his M1, or a carbine, or even a BAR or machine gun. He always feared the pins might somehow come loose on their own; it was unreasoning, but he couldn't help it. But he took the grenade, pulled the pin, waited barely a second—he never could bring himself to wait longer—and tossed it stiff-armed from his semi-prone position into the darkness before him. He thought he could distinguish its explosion from the generalized fireworks, but he was unwilling to risk a look to see whether he had done any damage.

Tim marveled that amid all the thunderous noise and carnage and human bodies, enemy and comrade, he could feel so isolated. He continued firing his M1 and changing clips and firing and changing. No one, beyond Sbarra, seemed to be in charge. Shouldn't generals be down here seeing what was going on? It was all too appallingly magnificent to be the domain of a mere squad leader; surely it demanded the attention of no one less than presidents and four-star generals. But then he realized that this was going on everywhere, not just in his little patch, and probably for not that long. He had completely lost all sense of time; what seemed like hours had probably been but a few minutes.

Like everyone else he was frightened—he could even appreciate why it was said that people sometimes shit their pants with fright—but it also thrilled him. The realization he had had that he could die here did not worry him, strangely. Not because of all those years of comforting assurances from dozens of evangelical pastors that he would be with Jesus, though he thought he would be, if it came to that. It just seemed a pointless worry to have in the face of this enormity. He wished now he had gone to that church service last Sunday, not to top off his tank of salvation or anything like that, but just to go. Church itself, aside from anything ethereal it might represent, comforted him, and he liked to go. So when the Methodist chaplain showed up in the battalion area Sunday afternoon he should have gone, but he had sacked out instead, and now the regret over a missed opportunity, though a mundane one, pained him.

His mind had begun to drift back almost serenely to memories of church in Guldwyck and church in Black Run, when all of a sudden the entire front was ablaze with light as bright as noon. Tim's body jerked in astonishment. Searchlights had been turned on to aid in locating the onrushing Chinese. Forgetting his earlier caution, Tim looked out, and he could see Chinese soldiers everywhere, piles of dead ones but even more of them alive, crawling, leaping, running, and—in the glare of the lights—seeking to hide. Just as he was beginning to adjust to the new situation, he heard someone come running into the platoon area behind him and the rest of the squad. Sbarra came scurrying over.

"What in hell's going on?" Sbarra shouted at the man, a corporal whose face in the residual light showed pain and dirt in equal measure. "You from battalion? Why in hell hasn't battalion pulled us back? I know the old man's asked for us to pull back to battalion forward. I mean, he did till both the phones and the Prick-6 went out."

"That's why I'm here," the man said, gasping for breath. "Communications are out almost all over. You're supposed to get out. Blow up as much ammo as you can, but get out! Pull out now."

The man turned to head back in the direction he had come, but Sbarra grabbed him by his right arm.

"Wait a minute. Pull out? Where we supposed to pull out to? Back to battalion forward? C'mon, you got to tell this to Captain Freitag. He's got to hear this, not just me." Captain Freitag was the commander of Company B.

The man ripped free of Sbarra's grasp. "Jesus Christ, there's no time. I got to tell the others. Just pull outta here. The goddamn Chinks are all over the place. Able Company on your right's got it worse than you, they're all chewed up. The Chinks've come through Able Company. They got into battalion forward and killed a couple officers. Shit, a couple of them even got into battalion rear and killed the colonel. Right in his goddamn tent."

And there, in the midst of one of the largest and most ferocious battles of the mid-twentieth century, Corporal Sbarra stood stock still, stunned at the news and unable for the moment to move, and watched as the messenger took off. Tim looked first at his squad leader and then at the departing messenger. Then he turned his head back to the line and saw a ragged line of Chinese relentlessly pressing forward in the bright light.

✳        ✳        ✳        ✳

Approximately thirty-one hours before those Chinese soldiers padded, blinking, into the glare of their enemy's searchlights—that is, by nightfall of May 16—it had become clear that the long-expected offensive was under way. Four Chinese armies representing twelve full-strength divisions rammed into the U.S. 2nd (Indianhead) Division. The 12th CCF probed ROK positions on the right, then sought to get behind the Indianhead Division and envelop its right flank. The 15th CCF made the frontal assault before splitting and moving along the Indianhead's flanks. The 60th CCF was used as an assault force that hammered the 2nd against the enveloping 12th CCF. And the 27th CCF Army along with the 12th was to follow up north of Pungam-ni.

Early in the night the 2nd Battalion of Tim's 88th Regiment beat back repeated attacks. Tim's 1st Battalion escaped much of this early fighting, except for Able Company, which shared Pear Hill, a vital link in the chain of positions along No-name Line, with Tim's Baker Company. The enemy's persistent attacks were made at horrific cost. The barbed-wired minefields and the Van Fleet loads of artillery fire left thousands of Chinese soldiers groaning and dying, as the screams and bugle calls of their comrades coming after them filled the night air.

Shortly after midnight on May 17 No-name Line was declared secure, though despite that the 2nd Battalion of the 88th Regiment was ordered to pull back due to continuing Chinese pressure. On its left, the 9th Regiment was also being battered, but managed to hang on.

As daylight arrived the U.N. forces could see the staggering losses that B-26 bombers, artillery and their forces' coordinated fire had inflicted on the Chinese, who lay in their hundreds if not thousands on the inclines, saddles, and hollows in front of them. French troops were ordered out of division reserve to plug the hole left open when the 2nd Battalion of the 88th withdrew. But Able Company, virtually surrounded by the swarming Chinese, was in danger of losing its tenuous grip on its part of Pear Hill.

Throughout the day there was no letup in the battle as more than 137,000 Chinese and 38,000 North Korean troops threw themselves against the 10,000 men of the Indianhead Division. American artillery worked the Van Fleet load to its maximum: More than 30,000 rounds were fired in the first twenty-four hours of the attack. In one eight-minute period more than 2,000 rounds were dropped in front of one company's sector alone. In a later twenty-four hour span more than 44,000 rounds were expended. In mid-afternoon the 2nd Division commander, Major General Clark M. Ruffner, went up in his helicopter to view what was happening on the vitally important nearby Hill 1051. The motor failed and the helicopter crashed, slightly injuring Ruffner and his driver, but Ruffner was able to confirm reports that the hill had fallen to the communists. The situation grew hourly more desperate. The South Koreans had already fallen back. The success of the attack by his attached Dutch Battalion that Ruffner had ordered was in doubt. If the 2nd Division did not hold, the Chinese might outflank the entire 8th Army line.

It did not take a general to understand what was happening. About 1 p.m. that May 17 Tim and his platoon mates saw the South Koreans falling back, followed by the British. Then word came to them that the other platoons of Baker Company were to pull out and they were to hold to cover their safety. From 3 p.m. until dusk it was fairly quiet. But just as the last traces of sunlight filtered through the twilight, they heard bugles blowing. Then they saw the first large mass of brown-uniformed soldiers come charging over the crest of the small mountain to their northeast.

\*     \*     \*     \*

Looking back, Tim calculated that they had less than thirty minutes before the ragged line of Chinese advanced to their position. Once again he was amazed at his own coolness. GIs were running here and there, piling ammo and weapons, on Sbarra's instructions, for destruction. Some soldiers had already panicked and taken off, and Sbarra was powerless in the circumstances to prevent it. Tim wondered if he should keep any weapons himself. He asked Sbarra, who told him to do whatever the hell he wanted, he didn't know. Tim thought that his M1 and some grenades might give him a fighting chance if he came across any Chinese. But then he figured that nothing would be of any use against their overwhelming numbers, especially if the Chinese caught him alone, and that if he faced capture he might have a better chance of not being shot if he was unarmed rather than armed. So he stripped off his grenades and ammunition and with his rifle threw them onto the pile. Sbarra nodded at Tim, wished him luck, told him to haul ass, and said he was going to take off himself in two minutes.

Tim looked at his watch. 0252. What was the date? He couldn't remember. But it must be May 18. Yes, May 18. At three o'clock in the morning of Friday, May Eighteenth, Nineteen Fifty-One, I personally fled, on direct orders of those placed over me, from the advancing enemy. A flicker of uneasiness ran through him. He thought of Peg. He thought of Helen. He thought of his mother and sisters, and of his Aunt Eileen. And then, with the voice of Sbarra in his ears telling everyone to get out, "I'm going to blow this bitch," he took one last look at the Chinese, who were noticeably nearer, and ran. Ran.

✳     ✳     ✳     ✳

A moist and clammy dawn was breaking when Tim ran into Clair Kasten and another man from Clair's platoon that he knew later only as Alan. He had been running and hiding for a little more than two hours and beginning to feel terribly alone and naked in the world. He wished Warren was with him. He hadn't seen Warren since the squad's defensive position had been set up before the Chinese offensive. At first he thought Clair and Alan were Chinese. He had already skirted a large group of maybe forty Chinese soldiers hunched down under cover of tall grass. He couldn't be sure in the semidarkness, but their sitting attitude seemed to project misery and some of their arms and legs looked to be wrapped in blood-soaked bandages. He waited until the Chinese got up and moved on. When he saw the two men scuttle from one clump of bracken to another he knew they were Americans on the run, and he recognized Clair. If he had been Chinese he could have shot them, if he'd had a weapon. Instead, glancing left and right to make sure no one else was around, like a man about to cross the street, he called to them from the small mound of earth behind which he was hiding.

"Clair! It's Tim. Tim Davis."

He saw Clair's head jerk back.

"Clair! Kasten! It's Tim Davis."

"Tim. That you?" Clair's head peeked back out around the bracken. "Holy Christ, boy, where you at? You OK?"

"Yeah. I'm right here." Tim repeated his man-about-to-cross-the-street glance, then hurried, crouched over, to where Clair and Alan were sitting.

"Tim, boy, good to see you." Clair hugged Tim's shoulder. He inclined his head toward Alan and introduced him to Tim, saying he was in his platoon and from Missouri, as if it was important to clarify his origins. Tim nodded and Alan nodded back.

"Boy, ain't this something?" Clair's voice radiated fear and excitement and worry. "This is some pickle we got ourselves in. How in the name of the sweet lovin' Jesus are we goan to get out of it?"

"I don't know, but we can't stay here." Tim hugged himself and shivered. A hint of rain was in the air. "It's just luck we haven't been caught yet." He told them about the platoon of Chinese he had come across. "Maybe if we could find a place to hide, we could ride this out. The Chinks might move on. One thing, we can't go wandering around in the daylight, especially when we don't know where we are."

The Missourian cleared his throat, softly. "I seen some houses off to the east there, less than a mile, I figure. A little village, I think. I only seen 'em in the dark, so I don't know, but maybe they might be abandoned. A lot of the gooks scattered when this big fight started up. Or maybe they's an outbuilding or something we can hole up in for a little while till we can get back across our lines. If we can ever find 'em."

Tim looked at Clair. "Whattaya think?"

"I got nothing better," Clair said, and looked at Alan who, not wishing to seem forward by pushing his own idea, stared at the ground.

"Let's do it," Clair said to Tim. "You got any food? I got some C rations and a canteen of water." He jiggled the canteen as proof. Tim and Alan also had remembered to bring along C rations and water. So, after carefully looking around, they stood up and walked off eastward into the brightening day.

The village, if such it could be called, consisted of no more than six or seven houses and even fewer outbuildings. All seemed to be abandoned. They chose a likely looking one with the usual thatch roof and forced their way in, an easy task. It had three small rooms, flooded with the morning's sunlight.

"Looks good," Clair said, turning in a circle in the main room, nearly empty of furnishings. "But there's no place to hide. What if the gooks—or the Chinks—come back?"

Tim looked around, then up at the ceiling, which to him looked to be made of mud or some such compound.

"We could hide up there. Then if someone came along we'd be safe until we could figure a way to get away."

Clair looked doubtful. "I don't know. Pretty obvious, ain't it?"

The Missourian spat. "Hide in plain sight, I've heard is the best trick."

Clair brightened. "You could be right. And I still got nothing better. But will it hold us? And how do we get up there?"

"If there's a ceiling there's got to be rafters of some kind up there," Tim said. "We just punch a hole in the ceiling. What's another hole in a war-torn build-ing?"

They found an old, broken idiot board—the A-frame pack that Koreans used to carry enormous loads on their backs—and by propping it up against a wall and standing on it they were able to reach the low ceiling and bang and knock around until they found a likely spot near a corner in which to poke the hole. Then they drew themselves up, lay down, and, exhausted from more than twenty-four hours' warfare with and evasion of the enemy, promptly fell asleep.

*      *      *      *

They were awakened a few hours later by voices downstairs. Who it was, Chinese or Koreans, they could not know. Each was afraid to speak, even whisper, to the others, for fear of giving themselves away. It was not quite pitch dark in the space they considered to be an attic, but too dim to see each other well, even in day-time. By twisting his arm to catch a thin, diffuse shaft of light, Tim could read his watch. Just before noon.

They stayed like that for more than two hours, listening to the men move around and talk, taking in the odors from the cooking fire they apparently had built on the floor below. They had to be Chinese, each of them decided for him-self; the Koreans, whether owners of the house or not, would not have started a fire like that.

After a time the house grew quiet. When they heard no sounds for more than a half-hour they assumed the Chinese had left and felt emboldened to talk, in whispers. They discussed what they should do. Clair was for taking off, but Tim and Alan thought they should remain. Tim said they had no way of knowing where the Chinese might be right now; they could be nearby and if they left they would be caught. He tried to scout around by looking through openings in the thatch, but his field of vision was too small to be of any use. Alan argued that probably the Chinese would not remain long; they should just wait it out. They took advantage of the soldiers' absence to relieve themselves in the farthest corner of the roof, away from the main room. Not long after that the Chinese came back, talking and laughing, and the three men fell silent again.

For another day and a half they remained like that, with the Chinese going in and out. During the brief absences they quickly and hotly debated their options. They couldn't stay there much longer; the cramped situation was growing impos-sible, and their food and water were running low.

Finally, Alan's snoring decided their fate. They had stayed awake as long as they could, and then tried to coordinate their brief sleep interludes with the Chinese soldiers' activities, but eventually the sheer demand of sleep overwhelmed them. Tim and Clair were immediately alert upon hearing the snores, and they punched Alan softly to wake him up. It was early morning again; the dampness and a slight lessening of the inky blackness told them that. But had the Chinese heard? They held themselves stock still and listened to the sounds below. The movements of the Chinese were clearly more jerky and energetic than usual, and their conversation more querulous. Soon they were aware of a questioning voice—despite the language barrier, they could discern the rhythms of a question—directly below the hole in the ceiling, and right after that a thick stick being poked around vigorously in all directions above the hole. It didn't take long before it found Alan's left calf. He instinctively jerked his leg back, causing what seemed like a hell of a racket, and not totally successfully tried to stifle an "Ow!"

Immediately the noises below grew louder and more insistent. The Chinese were scrambling around, obviously grabbing weapons. They could hear more questioning tones. The distinctive snickety-snick of the weapons being cocked whipped up to their ears.

"Jesus. What'll we do?" Clair whispered.

"We've got to do something fast," Tim replied. "They'll start shooting. They won't risk checking us out first."

"I'll go down," Alan quickly decided. "They know I'm here." And before Tim or Clair could say anything more, he slid over to the hole.

"Don't shoot," he shouted, pointlessly, and dropped down.

As soon as his boots slammed to the floor, the insistent gabbling intensified. The soldiers descended on him with kicks and cuffs and slaps and more futile questions in Chinese, to which Alan responded "Me give up" and "It's just me" and "No one else, just me." A short period of less angry questioning followed, and then the room below grew silent. Someone walked over and stood under the hole.

"Might as well come down, guys." Resignation filled Alan's ceiling-directed voice. "They know you're up there."

\*　　\*　　\*　　\*

"What do you suppose that stuff was?" Tim asked. He and Clair and Alan were sitting on the ground outside the house an hour later, licking their fingers after having consumed a soupy grain that their five captors had given them to eat.

They had no bowls or other dishes, so the Chinese simply poured it into their cupped hands. The Chinese stood a few paces away, earnestly talking and gesticulating while keeping a close watch on their prisoners. Obviously they were discussing what should be done with them. The day was gorgeous: bright, sunny, warm, and breezy, with just a few streaks of clouds in the dazzlingly blue arc of the sky.

"Millet," I think," said Alan, whose father was a farmer. "Sort of looked and felt like corn meal mush going down, but I think it was millet. Tasted all right, too. I'm surprised they gave us it. Didn't exactly fill me up, but tasted better than the bullet I was expecting. I really was."

So were Tim and Clair. Tim was grateful at this point to still be alive. Coming down from their hiding place, he had expected every second to feel the shattering blow of a Chinese bullet in his chest. When the Chinese did nothing more than shout at them and yank them around a bit, and then gave them something to eat, he was astounded. All sorts of thoughts swirled through his brain. Once again he missed Warren. He wondered where Warren was and what he would say about, and maybe to, these Chinese if he were here. Probably ask them if this stuff was kosher. Tim smiled, in spite of the situation. He was glad he was with somebody he knew well, Clair, a friend from his home, and this Alan was an OK guy, too.

The Chinese kept them there that day and the next. They marched them a couple of miles to a bunker, one of the bunkers that American troops had occupied during the offensive but that the Chinese had overrun and taken over. The first evening two of the Chinese left, then came back the next morning. The Chinese, who remained curiously aloof from them, nevertheless gave them some of their provisions to eat. They allowed him and Clair and Alan to talk to each other, as long as they did not become too animated and did not go on too long. All of them, Chinese and American, slept at various times during that day. The second night, as soon as darkness was complete, the Chinese roused them and indicated they should leave the bunker. Once free of the bunker's fug, Tim drew in great drafts of the cool night air. His gaze swept across the blue-black deepness of the sky and he thought how much it looked like it did at home. He wondered if he would ever see it there again. It struck him that for the first time since their capture he did not hear sounds of warfare, near or far. The guns—for now, anyway—had fallen silent.

＊          ＊          ＊          ＊

Thus began their trek northward with, eventually, about 2,100 other prisoners of war to a POW camp along the Yalu River. It took four months, including several stops of varying lengths at different places. During it, all grew weak, most became ill, and many died.

Tim, Clair, and Alan began the trek by being made to walk and then run in an easterly direction. After an hour or more they came to a valley about a half-mile wide and two miles long, north to south. In the dark they could make out more thatched-roof buildings. They were led to what looked like a large cattle shed and thrust inside, to join several other Americans already sprawled around. Throughout the night and day more and more prisoners were brought in, among them Captain Freitag, their company commander, who had been wounded by shrapnel in his left arm.

They stayed there no more than two days. Freitag was growing feverish from his wound. A medic from South Carolina, a friend of Clair's, said the shrapnel would have to come out or the infection would certainly cause him to lose the arm; moreover, in the absence of any medical care, most likely he would die. So, without painkillers or surgical instruments, and with Clair and two other men holding the captain down, the medic cut out the shrapnel with a highly honed pocket knife. Someone contributed a fairly clean Army handkerchief to wrap around the arm. By the time they left the shed, the captain was in better shape to go on.

They left on an evening with just an hour of daylight remaining. They were lined up along a dirt road, approximately four hundred Americans and six hundred South Koreans, with a Chinese guard to every third man or so. It was a long column.

The guards, a small number of whom spoke limited English, gave the order to begin walking, this time in a northerly direction. They had been on the road only a few minutes when they heard explosions behind them. Slowing down and looking back, against the urgent protests of the guards, who prodded them to keep up their pace, they saw artillery shells dropping, in almost a straight line in the direction of the buildings that had sheltered them.

"Kee-rist," said Clair.

"Amen," said Tim. "Looks like this is our lucky day," and he gave a bitter laugh.

As night fell the dirt road led into the Chinese MSR—Main Supply Route. As the prisoners walked north they passed a steady stream of traffic headed in the opposite direction—a few slow-moving trucks, many heavily laden bicycles, and seemingly thousands of foot soldiers, nearly all of whom seemed in a happy mood.

"What in hell they got to smile about?" Clair wondered.

"They smile," the guard next to them answered, surprising them with his English, "because they fight for Chairman Mao and the glorious People's Republic of China. They know socialism will bring them peace and prosperity."

"Oh yeah? Ain't that something? Peace is kinda elusive right now, though, ain't it?"

"You see slate each soldier has on backpack?" The guard tapped Clair on the shoulder, then pointed. "Every day, during breaks in march, they listen to lectures, then chalk lessons on board. What you fight for? Cap-i-tal-ism?" The guard got the word out with difficulty, then snorted.

Clair did not answer. Tim thought, once again, that if Warren were there he would have come out with some smart retort. "Not me, Wun Lung, I'm fighting for Harry Truman. He's the one who got me this marvelous opportunity." Or maybe not. The circumstances were not conducive to humor. Tim plodded onward.

They were in the upper end of a large curve in the uphill-tending road in the moonlight when they heard the distant sound of aircraft. Just as they were bearing out of the curve, the planes came over, dropping flares that momentarily bleached the landscape white. Everyone, guards and prisoners, dived for the side of the road. To Tim, viewing the scramble as he scrambled himself, the running men caught in the illumination looked like a huge photo negative, herky-jerky as in an old-time silent movie. Several large bombs fell, injuring no one. After the excitement was over, the guards ordered everyone out of the ditch, and they began walking, and sometimes running, again.

At daybreak they veered off onto a tree-covered hillside to spend the day. Just as they had been too weary to talk on the march—which the guards actively discouraged, though not quite prohibited—so were they too weary to do so on their breaks. Most dropped to the ground, exhausted from traveling and, in increasing cases, illness. Some, however, went on a futile scrounge for something to smoke. By then all cigarettes that hadn't been taken at capture were gone, but some men still had matches. A few, to appease their craving, tried to smoke dried vegetation found along the road. Despite his gloom, Tim had to laugh as he watched them. Into his mind came the Lucky Strike tobacco slogan, "So round, so firm, so fully packed, so free and easy on the draw," and then a memory of that night he and Rick had watched *Your Hit Parade* and sniggered over the smutty meanings teenage boys gave to "L.S./M.F.T." What might it be now, he wondered. Loser Soldiers Make Funny Tobacco? The memory of that night and Rick and Lynn made him so melancholy that tears came to his eyes.

Twice a day the Chinese brought them food and hot water. The food was a cereal, grain of some kind, usually sorghum, or so the farmers among them reckoned. Most accepted the steaming hot ball of the mixture right in their hands. Tim looked around and found an empty C-ration can, with which he scraped a flat piece of wood into a spoon-like utensil, so he had something almost no one else had: a tool to eat with.

One night they forded a small river. As they got to the far side they saw a tipped-over sign, placed there by the U.S. Army Corps of Engineers, informing them they were now crossing the 38th Parallel. Around midnight—the Chinese had taken Tim's watch from him, so he wasn't sure of the exact time—they came to what looked like the entrance to a cave in a hillside. Tim and about fifty or so others were motioned to go inside. It seemed to be some kind of level mining shaft, possibly for coal, Tim thought. They had to bend over to negotiate the low ceiling. Tim wondered what was happening to the other prisoners who were not ordered in. He walked to the rear, about seventy-five feet, where he saw a Korean family huddled, man, woman, and two small children. An inch of water covered the floor, but they were so tired they eventually sat down. Those who had matches lit them now and then. The Chinese placed a heavy barrier over the entrance and posted a guard.

Anyone who was able to sleep that night slept only fitfully. The atmosphere grew warm and heavy as the air grew so thin that a lighted match went out almost immediately. With each passing hour breathing became more and more difficult. Men were covered with sweat and their lungs became sore from gasping for air. Some grew hysterical. The officers told them to remain quiet to conserve the air, but by daylight they too were pounding the barrier and yelling.

The barrier was removed at midmorning. The men clambered to get out. Tim stepped from the suffocating darkness into the blue-vaulted sunshine and breathed in great lungsful of sweet air. Birds chirped somewhere. He thought back to that first night in the bunker with the Chinese, and felt resurrected. None of them ever learned why the Chinese had put them in the cave.

*     *     *     *

About the time the Chinese felt it was safe to walk in the daytime, Tim and Clair became separated from Alan. It's possible he was still in the column, which was growing larger as they went along through the addition of more POWs. But it also lost a few through the dropping out of the dead and dying, and it's possible Alan was one of them, because they never saw him again. No longer did they follow a fairly direct course northward, but were being detoured through villages where the residents lined the streets—perhaps on orders of the communists—to jeer and throw stones at them. As he paraded by the villagers, Tim thought, Well, maybe I'm fooling myself, but not all of them look like they want to be doing this to us.

One morning they walked into a fair-sized town with possibly two-hundred-fifty to three hundred houses, most of which looked empty. The houses facing the street they came in on appeared to have a wall in front, but upon getting closer it proved to be boxes of ammunition stacked wall-high to give the appearance, from the sky, of being a wall. That must have some advantage, Tim told himself, but I can't figure out what. He and Clair and a half-dozen GIs were herded into one of the abandoned houses.

"What's that, you suppose?" Clair asked Tim, and pointed to a hole about three feet square and two feet deep in the center of the main room.

"Don't know. Looks like it might be a place for a charcoal brazier." Tim cocked his head, listening. "What's that?"

"What's what?"

"That noise. I think it's airplanes."

Clair strained to listen, too. "You're right. It is. Prop planes, too. Bet it's Corsairs from some carrier. We close enough to the coast for Navy planes to reach us?"

"You got me. I have no idea where we are, other than in the asshole of the universe, which may be that hole right there. I—"

At that moment the ground began to shake, and the sound of explosions reached them from a distance.

Tim looked at Clair, Clair looked at Tim, everyone looked at everyone else, and at the same moment all eight men leaped for the hole in the center of the room. Only four of them, including Tim and Clair, fit, and not very well. When it became clear that the planes were limiting their bombing to the other side of the town, the men sheepishly got up and quickly looked for other places of safety.

The planes circled for about fifteen minutes, looking for more targets, then flew away.

By this time they were well into their second week of captivity, and some of the men were failing noticeably. Though the Chinese captors provided water, it usually wasn't the freshest and it wasn't plentiful. Some began drinking whatever water they would get, from dubious wells or even standing pools, and quickly developed painful dysentery. Some refused to eat "that poor excuse for food" the Chinese gave them, and were beginning to look thin and haggard. Others who hadn't taken care of, or had lost, their combat boots were reduced to hobbling around on feet bound up with grass. Tim felt relatively lucky, when he looked around him. He had his health, a tolerance if not an appetite for the food, and a pair of boots still in fair shape.

✳      ✳      ✳      ✳

Early in July, not long after General Ridgway offered to meet with communist commanders to discuss armistice, Tim and his fellow prisoners arrived at what later became known as the Mining Camp. Some sort of mining once was carried on there, but just what was never firmly established in the prisoners' minds. Some said gold, some said silver, some said other metals. A high cable with steel buckets on it ran from the town below to a mountaintop, but they never saw the cable in operation.

They came down a high mountain road and as they rounded a bend they saw Chinese army women washing clothes in a river far below. Reaching level ground, they passed rows of occupied houses, the first they had seen of all-wood construction. They went past a town well where women were waiting to draw water. They turned west and in front of them was a flight of wide concrete steps, with several landings, going up to a wide, flat earthen area. Beyond that, against the side of a steep hill, was a line of houses. Tim and Clair and several others were marched there and led into one of them, which had four large rooms. They went into one of the empty rooms and sat down.

After a few minutes a Chinese officer stepped in.

"Don't you men have enough training to stand up and salute an officer?" He was angry. His eyes glared and his cheeks flushed.

Tim and the rest stood, but they didn't salute. The officer glared some more and fumed in silence, then quickly outlined the rules they were to follow. He left, and two soldiers came in. They took the GIs' names and service numbers and made them empty their pockets. Everything of value was taken and a record of it entered against their names. They were allowed to retain their dog tags, military scrip, and pocket New Testaments given out by the chaplains. The soldiers went out of the room, leaving the men alone again.

"Look, guys," one of them said, turning around to the others and waggling seven or eight limp, dirty scrip notes in the air with his right fist. "First time the Chinese first sergeant gives us a pass, I'm going into that town down there and get me moose with a hooch and screw all night long."

Some of the men laughed at the man's bitter humor, knowing there was for them no first sergeant, no pass, no Korean woman with a house, and the scrip was all but useless. Besides that, none of them had the stamina, much less the desire, for sex. The laughter was anything but hearty. Food was all they thought of.

"You'd do better with this," said another, who held up his New Testament and solemnly and lovingly caressed its worn leatherette front cover with the tips of his fingers. He was known as a Creeping Jesus who always kept to himself, and the men, ill at ease and not knowing how to respond to his lugubrious admonition, looked down or away from him.

*        *        *        *

Each of them was given a tin cup and bowl and spoon. It wasn't much, but more than enough with which to eat the meager provisions they received. Chinese soldiers brought in two shiny buckets. In one was another cooked cereal or grain, red in color. In the other was watery vegetable soup with a little vegetable oil floating on top. Once again there was a guessing game as to exactly what they were eating.

"What's that, then?" Tim said, looking askance at the steaming grain.

"Damned if I know. Sorghum, again, you suppose?" Clair peered into the brackish-looking mixture and pointed with his newly acquired spoon. "I *am* sure those are bugs in there, but don't ask me what kind." He skimmed his spoon across the top, catching some black specks.

"Eeuww!" Tim's stomach threatened to come up to his throat, and the look of disgust on his face intensified.

Another prisoner dipped up a scoop of the mess, swished it around, and examined it.

"Be fair to the Chinks," he said. "Some of 'em ain't bugs. Some's just little bitty stones." The man then waggled his spoon in the direction of the soup. "That soup, there, now. It's got some vegetables in it, that's good, and they're only the littlest bit moldy."

Tim and Clair, not getting the man's sarcasm, looked at him as if he were insane.

"Well, hold your nose and eat up, boys," the man said, his grin revealing gapped and brownish teeth. "Could be a long time before you get anything else. Besides, bugs is protein, so I've heard."

That the food was not at all seasoned was the least of their deprivations. The Chinese assigned GIs to cook the food, and rumors quickly started that the cooks divided the vegetable oil among themselves and poured only a small amount of it into the soup for the rest of the camp. Later, another, less credible, rumor started to the effect that they were deliberately being starved to make them weak and thereby more susceptible to communist indoctrination.

After eating they were assigned rooms to live in. Tim and Clair became separated. They struggled to be allowed to remain together, but the guards had made up their minds who was going where, and that was that. Tim and seven other men got a room in the center of the building. All of the rooms led off a long hall on one side of the building, and Clair got put into a room further down the hall. There was no glass in the large windows on the other side of the building that faced the courtyard.

To sleep on the men received straw mats, which were simply the bags woven of rice straw into which about two hundred pounds of rice was packed. When cut open the bag was about five feet long and a little wider than a man's body. Tim used his boots as a pillow and slept with his field jacket covering his head and chest.

Their primitive latrine was behind their rooms in a stretch of ground about twenty-five feet wide, just below an almost vertical hill. Soldiers stepped up onto vertical poles inside and squatted over a deep pit. Soon it was stinking and swarming with green-and-blue flies.

One room was set up as a classroom with a chalkboard that spanned one wall. Sometimes they heard informal talks on communism by an English-speaking Chinese officer who had studied in the United States. Occasionally the walls were decorated with pencil or pen-and-ink cartoons or political drawings by soldiers in other camps. Tim was shocked at what seemed to be American soldiers' aiding the enemy's propaganda efforts.

There was no water to wash with nor any soap if there had been. Everyone quickly became infested with lice, which lay their eggs in the linings of their clothing. Once their clothes were taken to be boiled in water in an unsuccessful attempt to kill the vermin. In any case, the rooms were never cleared of the lice so they never disappeared.

The first ritual of the day was to sit in the sunlight and inspect their clothing seam by seam.

"Kind of gives new meaning to 'little friends,' doesn't it?" Tim said to a gaunt teenager sitting next to him on the stony bank near their building one morning. "Little friends" was the derisive term the soldiers sometimes applied to South Koreans.

"Oh, man, this is the most sickening thing yet," the young man said, and scraped a deposit of eggs out of his filthy, tattered shirt. "I'm sorry I ever left Sleepy Eye, Minnesota." Weary of high school, which for its part had indicated it was weary of him also, he had lied about his age to get into the Army and now was barely eighteen.

"Ah, I got one!" Tim shouted, a note of triumph in his voice. He crushed the live louse between his thumbnail and fingernail. "Send that little bastard to Buddha. That's what the Chinese believe in, isn't it? Buddha? Or they're communists, atheists. Maybe they don't believe in anything?"

"Heck, don't ask me, I'm Foursquare Gospel. I don't have any truck with this heathenish stuff."

"Really?" Tim said. "I'm Church of the Brethren. I mean, I was, back home in Pennsylvania. Lately I was attending a Methodist church."

The young man looked up from his labors. "Church of the Brethren? Ain't that a peace church or something? Don't believe in fightin'?"

"Yes, I suppose so, officially speaking."

"What you doin' here, then? You belong to a church that's got rules against fightin', you shouldn't never have gotten drafted."

"Well, when it comes right down to it, a lot of people don't really hold with that. The church's got rules against adultery, too, but I think people break those maybe as much as the ones against going to war."

"You got that right," the young man said, and turned back to probing his clothing.

The conversation transported Tim back to his arrival in Korea and a similar conversation with Warren. He thought of Warren every day and eagerly looked for him when fresh contingents of POWs came in to the camp. He questioned all the newcomers about him—many of whom he knew from his battalion and even his company, including Jansen and Caldwell—but no one had any information. He hoped that meant his friend had survived the fighting and had escaped capture.

＊　　　＊　　　＊　　　＊

Before long burial details were being carried out at least every other day for those who had died the night before. Tim never went on one, but he knew how they were conducted. Because of the prisoners' weakened conditions, there usually were two details: one to dig a trench a couple of feet deep, another to carry the body or bodies.

Exactly what they died of was, in most cases, anybody's guess. A lot of the men thought the lice introduced viruses into the bloodstream, which then got passed from person to person. Malnutrition, filthy conditions, and lack of medical attention killed the most. There was an American medical officer in the camp, living in a building on a lower level, but he had no medicines or equipment to work with, though he tried. One day the prisoners were forced to attend a mock trial, his "crime" being that he practiced medicine without the permission of the camp authorities. His fate was another of the many things Tim never learned.

Bodies undermined on the marches or from other causes succumbed rapidly. Those who were not sick—or, more accurately, less unwell—soon grew familiar with the symptoms. A man would lie down and not want to get up or eat food. He would turn his face toward the wall, lie quietly as if in sleep, gradually lose consciousness, and usually within a week be dead. More than once Tim woke up late at night to see someone crawling about looking for a helpless person in the final stages of death, or one already dead, and going through the pockets looking for anything of value. Tim and anyone else who saw it protested, but it was futile. Anyone who had the moral, or amoral, audacity to rob the dead was psychologically strong enough to stand down his accusers, and the argument that "he can't use it anymore" was hard to rebut. And with each passing week the physical strength to put up a protest grew less and less.

＊　　　＊　　　＊　　　＊

Tim grew thinner and thinner, less able to perform chores or indeed any activity. He was not alone in this; a haggard, drawn, listless, weak demeanor was the norm. He watched four occupants of his room die, to be replaced by others, two of whom also died. For the rest, life, such as it was, somehow went on.

In the first week of September the Chinese fed them good white rice and added canned pork to the soup. It tasted wonderful but was too rich for their shrunken stomachs and brought further distress to already wracked digestive systems. Two days after that they were ordered to line up for the march to the permanent camp. The Chinese said that anyone unable to walk would be put aboard trucks. No one in the camp believed that; they were certain that anyone who didn't make the march would be left to die. Tim was both glad and troubled to be going. He was glad to get away from the scene of so much misery and death where every day seemed like a week, but worried that his increasingly fragile condition would not stand the march. In any case, would the new place be any better? Only home would be better, home with Peg and his mother and his sisters and everybody in Somerton County and in Guldwyck. Standing in the stinging chill of a late-summer predawn darkness, shifting from foot to foot to keep warm, Tim looked up at the sky peppered with stars. He imagined it as an immense navy-blue blanket with pinpricks in the fabric through which tiny, intense pulses of the dazzling light of the universe beyond managed to escape. He knew nothing of the heavens, beyond the North Star and the Big Dipper and commonplaces like that. One star, a shimmering silvery blue specimen slightly larger than those around it in the northeastern sky, transfixed him. Its sight pleased him; he stared and stared at it, and when it seemed to wink out he felt somehow diminished. But just then the Chinese ordered them to get ready to move out.

✳     ✳     ✳     ✳

The march north took twenty days. The Chinese did not hurry them, but let them walk at a casual pace. They passed the North Korean capital of Pyongyang, where people continued to live in the mounds of ruins, albeit underground. When rain came down they continued walking though soaking wet; later the sun would come out and dry them again. A couple of times they stopped near railroad towns, in one of which Tim and others were put into a house occupied by an older Korean couple. The house contained useful items the POWs could have taken, but no one wanted to take advantage of the kindly couple. Besides, the Chinese sense of propriety was strong: If they learned about the theft, the consequences could be severe. But their resistance to thievery was not total. Near a window stood several large pottery jars. That night they silently removed their lids and discovered within a fermented brown sauce, into which they dipped their tin cups. For several days thereafter they had flavoring for their rice. The red peppers were hard on their delicate stomachs, and they had to dig out a few dead bugs, but neither was a real detriment to their enjoyment.

# CHAPTER 16

▼

# VOICES

*I never saw a man who looked*
*With such a wistful eye*
*Upon that little tent of blue*
*Which prisoners call the sky.*

—Oscar Wilde, *The Ballad of Reading Gaol*

### Gerald Christian
### Manitowish Waters, Wisconsin
### Formerly rifleman, 23rd Regiment

I remember it all very well, getting to Korea, the capture, the march, the Mining Camp, the Main Camp at Changsong, called Camp One. I've made kind of a study of it, not like a professor or some other scholar, but probably more systematically than my fellow ex-POWs. I don't mean to put them down by saying that. And I don't mean my memory is better. We all have our memories, and they differ. We're all obsessed by the POW experience, and will be till our dying day. It's just that I've tried to straighten out the contradictions where I can, reconcile conflicting stories. And at this point the conclusion I've come to is that it's impossible. Too many stories have been floating around for too many years for much of anything to get set in concrete, as you might say. Why, some of us—former POWs, I mean—can't even agree, for instance, on whether the Mining Camp and the Bean Camp were the same place or different places. Little things. At

POW Association meetings, I've heard people say that few Chinese spoke English, yet it seems to me I remember a remarkable number who could speak at least a few phrases in English.

Well. I remember Camp One. There were high rugged mountains to the southeast and sloping farmland to the south and west. We arrived in the afternoon on, I think, the last day of September and were assigned rooms in houses right at the southern edge of Changsong. Beyond these last houses were the guards' walking posts, and then open fields that weren't farmed while we were there.

Our sector had two rows of houses. The outer row faced the main road through the town. The inner row faced scattered buildings used by the Chinese—cookhouse, infirmary, living quarters, and so forth. I'm not certain, now—their living quarters might have been on the other side of the road.

We were put into squads of ten men, each squad having one room. The houses had a kitchen on the north end with a flue running under the floors of the rooms to a chimney on the south end. This is how they heated the houses. The Koreans call it "ondol." When the houses were occupied by Koreans, normally the housewife would start a fire in a lined hole under a large circular pot where the rice was steamed. The hot air from the fire heated large, flat heat-conducting stone slabs set on a platform under the floor. Over this was a thin layer of cement for a smooth surface, and on top of that were layers of a shiny yellow material, cut to size and fixed in place. The rooms would be heated from the warmth coming up through the floor.

That first day they gave us POW ID numbers and a thin wash towel and a bar of soap. We might also have gotten toothbrushes. We received one set of clothes, just like the Chinese had, except theirs were tan-colored, ours were blue. A long-sleeve shirt, a pair of pants, sneakers—also blue. Did we get underwear and socks? Funny, I don't recall. You can imagine what our uniforms looked—and smelled—like by then. We had been wearing them, most of us, from the middle of May to the end of September with never a change or a bath.

They told us to take off our Army uniforms and change into the blue clothing and then come back out and line up on the road in formation. As we stood in place, some red flags and banners with writing on them were handed to the guys in the front rank, who refused to take them. Someone said, "Let's go back and change into our uniforms again." This made the Chinese angry, and apparently broke up plans for a staged demonstration or march.

The usual day started with a roll call outside at 6:00 a.m., with a Chinese sergeant in charge. One person from each squad went to the kitchen to bring back a bucket of steaming milk-like liquid made of soybeans. This was poured into individual cups and we could sweeten it with our sugar ration. Our main food was white rice. Later, anyway; at first it was kaoliang, which is like sorghum and I think more nutritious in vitamins and minerals. We also got sliced turnip soup twice a day.

For the first week or so we had no electric lights. This was because the Chinese feared air attacks. They bragged that they had air superiority in the north, but that was a lie. On one of the first nights we were hit by bombs, killing several Chinese and possibly some GIs. I know for certain that some GIs were wounded.

So before the lights came on we ate supper in darkness. The first couple of nights we got pieces of bread and fried whole fish about three to four inches long. I bit on something hard while eating the fish, and since I couldn't see, I stepped out into the moonlight. It was the fish eye. I gagged and then threw up.

When they installed lights they also put loudspeakers on poles throughout our sector. In the evenings we'd hear patriotic Chinese marches, or sometimes songs by Paul Robeson. Worst of all were the Chinese operas.

Also about this time the Chinese began separating us. They came to rooms at night and took away individuals, either to isolate them or to remove troublemakers or potential leaders. Blacks and Puerto Ricans were segregated from whites, sergeants and officers from enlisted men. The British and Turks, of course, had their own areas. They tried to get the blacks worked up about their treatment in America. I don't know how well that went over, but they also tried to pit Americans against British and that wasn't at all successful.

Not long after that we got our first haircuts and shaves. The barber's razor, like one of those old-fashioned straight razors, had a tough time of it with our four-month-old beards, so the shave was painful. I believe they took individual photos of us to turn over to the U.S.

There wasn't much work to do. When it started to get cold we were sent into the forests, where they had cut trees into ten-foot-long logs. Despite the cold and the snow, most of us liked that, because it was a chance to get out and do something. We would balance a log on our shoulders and walk the two miles back to camp. Soon we had a huge pile of firewood for winter. At this time we were issued thick winter clothing, padded with cotton, and one blanket to be shared by every five men.

If we were ill or in pain we could go to a small shed to be examined by a Chinese who knew next to nothing, including English. But he had a variety of colored powders in individual folded paper packets that were doled out according to supposed symptoms. For example, if you had a stomach ache you would grab your guts and moan, and supposedly he would understand. So far as I know, no one died from this.

The hospital was a separate place, and basically it was to segregate the dying from the well. No one really wanted to go to a place with the reputation of death. I didn't know Tim Davis, but if he was in the hospital ... well, the best I can say is, people *were* known to survive and return from there.

✳      ✳      ✳      ✳

### Robert W. La Claire
### Du Bois, Pennsylvania
### Formerly rifleman, B Company, 88th Regiment

We just got out of our positions, our foxholes and bunkers, and the Chinese just moved in. Had us surrounded. Captured twenty-one hundred of us at one time.

When we were captured, there wasn't a lot of fightin'. There was at Able Company, but not to us at Baker. There was just so many of them. They just came in and surrounded us. And you didn't shoot back, because you knew if you did you were going to be shot.

I know my directions well. I could tell where we were by the North Star, which way we were traveling. They took us north, they took us west, they took us east, they took us back south. It took us from May the 18th to the end of September to get up to our camp. Camp One, that was, at a place called Changsong. I think it went by different numbers at different times—Camp Three, maybe Camp Five, too—but it was Camp One when we first got there. Right up along the Yalu River.

At first, I think they were frightened of us. They thought we were bigger and stronger. I think they were afraid of us. I saw them hit some guys in the back with a rifle butt, but not too many. If the guys tried to keep up, they did all right. After a while they learned we weren't that mean, we got along all right. But like I said, they were showing us off. They were showing us off to their troops to build their morale. We only marched at night, because they were afraid of our planes. I'll tell you one thing. I don't know how those little Navy—what were they? Corsairs?—I don't know how they did it, but they followed us every day, and they *found* us every day, too. The Chinese'd *hide* us. One day we hid in a big pine thicket—and I mean it was thick, you could hardly tell if it was daylight—and those Corsairs were there, and they just kept circling. After a while they'd flap their wings and take off. They knew where we were. *Every* day they knew where we were.

The Incorrigibles. That was us, the company I was in, in the POW camp. We were—well, we weren't *bad*, but we pushed 'em just as far as we could and not get ourselves in trouble. So they called us the Incorrigibles. One time they had a Mayday celebration in this town. Everybody, all the POW companies, were supposed to march down carrying a red flag in front of them. We decided we weren't gonna march behind no red flag because we're not communists. We fell out in formation in the street, the red flag was there, so we just fell back out of formation and went back into their houses. The Chinese wanted to know what was wrong. We explained we wouldn't march behind a red flag. They said, "All the other companies did and you will too." We said, "No, we won't." So they said we had to get down there, everyone else was down there in the square. So we fell out again, started marching down. So pretty soon down between two houses comes a guy—I don't know who it was, a Chinese or North Korean—carrying a red flag. We just did an about face and came back to our houses again. Then they really gave us a talking to. We said, "We don't care. We're not communists and we're not marching behind a red flag. We don't care what everybody else did." Finally we went down there without the red flag.

Yeah, Tim Davis was in my Army company *and* my POW company. So was Clair Kasten, though neither one was in my building. Tim was in my company until he went into the hospital.

There were fourteen hundred in the camp as I remember, eight hundred Americans and six hundred British. We were separated from the British only by a street, but we weren't allowed to cross the street.

Our rooms were about seven by nine, eight by nine, something like that. Ten men slept in there, imagine that. Helped us keep warm, though. It was cold in winter. We slept head to toe. There wasn't room to sleep on your back. We slept on our sides. If one person turned over, we all turned over. I hope never to get that close to another man again. We were segregated by rank. Sergeants on up were in separate buildings. Officers too. The Chinese had machine gun nests out on the hills. No fences.

Heck, they didn't need no fences. A couple guys tried to escape. They caught them and brought them back. And they laughed. They said, "You guys are crazy." They said, "Your fair skin and light hair, everybody else has got black hair, even the Koreans—you can't get away."

I never went up to that so-called hospital. I don't know what Tim was in there for. Whatever it was, being there couldn't've done him much good. What *didn't* he have wrong with him? Or three-quarters of us, for that matter. Dysentery, probably, and malnutrition. The Chinese gave dysentery sufferers rice starch to try and dry them up, but it didn't work.

We all had beriberi, too. Look at my shins here, if it's not too disgusting. See those long red marks? Lingering effects of beriberi. Hell, I had malnutrition, beriberi, pleurisy, dysentery all at one time. *Most* of us did.

And then too, Tim helped too many other people. He helped people when he should have been helped. He was that kind of guy. He would do for somebody else. That place brought out the best and the worst in people, and I'll tell you, Tim was the best of the best.

What I saw of him, that is. From what I'm told he went downhill pretty fast. Why? Well, one thing, the transition from our type of diet to their type of diet was drastic. I mean *real* drastic. It didn't happen to two persons in the same way. For some it was too sudden a change and others could compensate, could make it a little longer. Myself I went down to ninety pounds from one hundred eighty.

People ask me if I have any animosity toward the Chinese, and I don't have, because they treated us as good as they could. They didn't have much. They didn't have refrigeration, this is why we got beriberi. They couldn't freeze vegetables and bring them to us. We ate rice all the time. It was polished rice. It would have been better if it was whole rice, because of the vitamins.

The rice had weevils in it. Those weevils were black, and the polished rice was white. They cooked it all together, you know. Each squad had a wash basin, and that's what we took our baths in and that's what we went and got our chow in, too. I know that sounds repulsive, but we washed it up afterwards, the basin. Whoever had the detail that day would go get the basinful of rice and come back and divide it into ten equal portions.

Guys would sit around, they'd pick out a couple weevils, set them over there. Eat a spoonful of rice, pick out some more weevils. Then those guys would get sick, throw up the rice they did eat. Other guys would just eat everything, talk about girls, talk about steak, talk about cars, and just *eat*. We're the ones who came home. If you just didn't think about it, then you didn't throw up what you ate. I don't know if Tim had any eating difficulties like that.

I think the only time we had meat after we were captured is when planes would strafe a mule train or something. I ate mule and I ate horse. If I had my choice I'd eat mule, it's sweeter.

Except just before the truce was signed we began to get canned meat. By the time I was released I was up to 138 pounds, a gain of 48 from my camp weight.

One thing, though, I don't remember exactly how we learned they had potatoes, but we told them to bring us potatoes. "Ah," they said, "you don't want potatoes. Potatoes are hog feed." Yeah, they eat polished rice in China and feed potatoes to the hogs. We said, "You bring some." So they did, and we devoured them.

I've been hungry in my life and I've been cold in my life, and I don't ever want to be hungry or cold again. It's a hell of a feeling going to bed hungry and there's nothing to eat. And it's a hell of a feeling to be cold and know that there's not a damn thing you can do about getting warm.

I didn't think much about the war before I went over. But I didn't dread going, for the simple reason that I knew that other guys fought for this country, a lot of them gave their lives. 'Course, I had been in a little while before that, not much more than a year, starting in '47, and they let me out early. Then I got called back in in '50, like a lot of guys. But I thought our country had a reason for sending me over there, so I didn't dread going. I didn't want to *go*. I was married, to my first wife, and she was pregnant with our first child. But I went. I don't have any bitter feelings against this country, nor do I have any bitter feelings against the Chinese.

I can't say for sure, but I think Tim felt the same way. Tim, well, it was just his demeanor, I would say. He didn't have anything against anybody. He'd help you before he'd hurt you. He had no animosity about going over. He was just a heck of a good guy, I'll tell you.

I was interrogated by Army officers at Panmunjom when they released us in Operation Big Switch in August of 1953. Then on the ship back home me and the others were interrogated by the FBI. They were interested in collaboration with the enemy, and I have to say there was.

There were guys who maybe thought they'd get extra favors by cooperating excessively with the Chinese. Couple of the worst ones were right in my company. Far as I know they never got any favors because they weren't any better off than we were.

The Chinese gave us lessons in communism, usually in winter. Gave us stuff we had to read, then discuss it. But we'd sit in a room and talk about cars or girls—like I told you before—and never read it. One time the interpreter handed us something to read and discuss and stood outside the door listening. When he discovered what we were doing, he ripped the door open, ordered us on our feet, told us to get outside. Sat us on the ground outside with a guard on. We *had* to read it then.

It's funny when you think about it, all that indoctrination and our side never did anything along the same lines. I can't really remember the Korean War breaking out. When I got called back in, I can't recall being given any instruction or classes in what the war was supposed to be about, or why we were fighting in Korea. I think that was the case with most of the servicemen: They didn't know. You went because the government sent you there to do a job. Maybe that says something good about us, that we trusted our government enough that we didn't need all that propaganda. Wonder if we'd feel that way today? Wonder if the *young* people feel that way today?

You know, once we got into what you might call the swing of things at the camp, we didn't have much to do. Our main job was to cut firewood, but that didn't take long. We made playing cards out of the boxes that tobacco came in. Played just about any card game there was. Even canasta. I learned to play canasta in camp.

Now you talk about health and dyin', it was the younger guys died first, I don't really know why. As for Tim, he wasn't ill on the march. He got weak and rundown, but not really sick. On the march, Tim's attitude was good, and like always, he always tried to help someone else. I can't get more specific than that: Just helped those that were too weak to eat.

I'd see Tim in the camp every once in a while. Whenever they'd march the POW companies down to this big square for a talk by some big-shot Chinese, I'd get to see Tim that way from time to time. He used to play basketball, or anyway fool around with a basketball. I didn't know Tim was bad off until they told me they took him to the hospital.

Before I got called back into the service, I was working for the Pennsylvania Railroad in Altoona. I got military leave from the railroad to go back into the service. After I got discharged, I went back to work the next day, and they handed me furlough papers because my job didn't exist anymore. That was November 1953. They didn't need me.

✳    ✳    ✳    ✳

## Mark Savage
## Tucumcari, New Mexico
### Formerly platoon leader, B Company, 88th Regiment

I don't recall Tim Davis, but I remember few of them because as a first lieutenant, I was a brand-new replacement officer, as were most of the others, except the captain. The indoctrination began almost immediately, and they didn't have to torture us, because the lack of food was such that we became skeletons in little over 30 days. When I say skeletons, I mean *exactly* like those men in Buchenwald that you see pictures of. We looked exactly like that. My thumb and finger went all the way around my bicep. Try *that*.

I was in the officer squad. After about a month we were divided, and the officers were in a separate group. The officer squad was fifteen officers, but only half lived. And the man who could survive in this thing here was the guy that lived during the Depression. I was a boy in the Depression, and I was well-equipped to live through a thing like this. I was also a paratrooper for three years in World War II. I can tell you that the food was absolutely terrible in the beginning, and we just went down quite rapidly. By the time those men died individually, they didn't even know what world they were in. It was that bad.

I was captured May 19th, one day after most of the others. We got bumfoozled by higher headquarters, if you want to put it that way. I might as well tell it straight. Because what they did, they communicated down to us by phone and said there's been a small breakthrough over on the right. Now, I'm not running down the South Koreans at all. The Chinese could have attacked us just as easy as they could have attacked the Koreans. A lot of guys run down the Koreans, but that's not right. The Koreans had pretty good divisions. But they did break through over there. But they told us that they penetrated 1,500 yards, and instead it was five-and-a-half miles. So they made a great arc, if you know how this is done in war. They go straight through for quite a ways, and then they start arcing around in a big curve. And then they come up behind the next outfit that's on the line. What they did with ours is they came up behind and burned the motor pool and we didn't even know it. Regiment wouldn't give us any information. We couldn't get any artillery. We had this artillery all planned to where we wanted to fire, and they were so damned busy moving this artillery back that they wouldn't support us and they wouldn't even tell us why.

I've heard it said it was every man for himself. Let's compare our Army to the British. The British have long-term unit solidarity, men and officers serve together for a long time. The British have esprit de corps. They're just like brothers, fathers, everything. Whereas we were strangers thrown together to fight a battle. Now, there's a big difference there. Those people knew each other for years, those British, and they took a lot better care of each other when they were captured, too. We were like a disorganized mob. Because as prisoners, it *was* sort of every man for himself. But it got better once we got to the main camp. Conditions got better, too, in the main camp. We got sugar, clothing, soap, and later toothpaste.

Officers were treated the best, because they offered the most resistance, and the sergeants were better in that regard than the enlisted men. We were called "reactionaries." All the ones that resisted the propaganda were called reactionaries. And the point of it is, the more reactionary you were, the more respect they had for you.

Respect ran both ways. I had considerable respect for the people, especially. The people were absolutely honest. They were rather naive. A guard told me about the peace talks—told me *twice*—though he should have known he might get in trouble. No, the Chinese people were very friendly people. It was the commissars we didn't care for, the people who were doing the propagandizing.

Why did some survive and some didn't? People have been trying to figure that out since the fighting stopped. Attitude had a hell of a lot to do with it. I was a guy who got up and carried water or whatever else needed to be done. I got up and did something every day. Every day, see? I did not lie down and—well, we called it "giveupitis."

There was another officer in our battalion, a lieutenant brand-new out of ROTC. He came from a wealthy family so he didn't have near as good a chance of surviving in conditions like that. That's the reason he died.

Unless they died right in your own hut, you didn't even know it unless you seen 'em carrying their body by. That's the only chance you had. Unless they called on you for burial detail, you didn't know a damn thing about it.

I'm originally from Nebraska. I don't mind saying I was angry about being recalled. I thought I had pretty much done my part. I *was* bitter. But after Korea was over, I wasn't bitter any more, because I knew why I went there. See? But I was bitter up to that point.

I was automatically in the Reserves by virtue of being an officer. The point is they needed these officers and they needed them quick. So they ran down their records real quick and said, "Hey, look at all these airborne guys here. We'll get some of them."

\*        \*        \*        \*

### Claude S. Bauer
### Emporia, Kansas
### Formerly C Company, 88th Regiment

I was a squad leader, though when I got to Korea my MOS was machinist. When things got tough, they grabbed everybody they could, and I was one of 'em. I was captured about the 23rd of May. I got hurt the 18th and managed to evade the Chinese until then. I was just out in the mountains. I didn't have no house to get into. Rainy son-of-a-bitch, I'll tell you. A member of my squad, a guy we called Bud, was with me when I got captured.

That night we got overrun, the first lieutenant, the company commander, got it between the eyes, just before dark. I heard it estimated that there were 110,000 Chinese right out in front of our little ol' company there. So we didn't have much of a chance. I can't recall much artillery support, but shells fell around me and Bud where we was hiding out. Friendly fire—that I didn't appreciate. They didn't know I was still there, I don't guess. If they'd listened they'd probably heard me hollerin' at 'em.

We just got overrun. There was just more of them than there was of us, and they broke through the ROK Army on our left and come down the ridge top right down on top of us. I was out on the flank. After the Chinese broke through, I took my BAR man and his assistant and went to the left flank, trying to keep Chinese off of us. But, hell, that whole hillside just turned yellow, and here they come.

That's when I got hurt. Broke my back. They told me I was supposed to have died over there, I wasn't supposed to come home. But I fooled 'em. I had a compression fracture, is what they called it. It busted a vertebrae and shoved it in and put pressure on my spinal cord. I didn't get it fixed until a few years ago.

After about four or five days they pulled me and this Filipino out of the march north and took us another way from where the main group was going. Took us up into the hills where there was this big bunker. We stayed there for six months—me and the Filipino and eleven to fifteen Chinese. If you ask what were they doing with me, I'd have to say that's a good damn question. I wish I knew. I don't know yet. I didn't have anyone to talk to. The Filipino didn't speak English.

Then they took me to Changsong and treated me like I'd just been captured. Put me through the severe interrogation you get when you've first been captured. I got to Changsong sometime in November.

After they finished interrogating you and found out you weren't going to tell anything, they gave up on you. But if you gave them a little piece of information, why, they'd keep after you and keep after you and keep after you. A lot of the POWs, they couldn't keep their mouth shut, I guess, and they'd keep at them continually—take them in night after night after night and talk to them.

I don't know, I guess they were looking for better treatment. Some of them would try to suck in and get a little something extra. 'Course, them we didn't have much use for. They got their asses kicked and got throwed in the shit-can, and everything else.

Some of them went just whole hog their way, the communist way. 'Course, if you hadn't had anything when you went over there, they'd get to brainwashing you about how good you'd have it if you was a Chinaman and shared in everything. A lot of them were swayed by that, by them preaching to them. Poor boys come from the back sticks, never had nothin' and never were gonna have nothin', they kinda fell for their line of bullshit. If you ever had anything or wanted to be your own man—well, they didn't sell me nothin'. They washed my ol' brain, but it didn't come clean.

The food, if that's what you want to call it, sometimes you'd look at it and you'd say to yourself, "Hell, I can't eat this." And then I'd think, "By God, I'm gonna eat some of it, maybe it'll get better tomorrow." That was my theory. "Hell, I'll try it today, eat whatever I can, maybe it'll get better tomorrow." Took a lot of tomorrows for that to happen, till the peace talks got to goin' pretty good. You could tell how the peace talks were goin' by the way we were treated and the kind of food we were given.

The ones that I knew personally that didn't make it were an only son or a child that had been born after their parents were old and they were given everything. Treated like they were carried around on a pillow. When everything got rough, they just couldn't hack it. From what I've heard, that wasn't so with Tim Davis. He just took sick. Or so I heard. I can't say from my own knowledge.

I enlisted right out of high school, after World War II. Went to machinist school in El Paso, Texas. I was in the first guided missile regiment. Stayed in the States. I put in my hitch, got out, went into the Reserves, and about eight months later they called me back. There was a lot of us over there that way.

I tried to read a number of books about the Korean War. I'd start through one, then think, why, hell, that's a foreign country to where I was at, so I'd lay it down.

\*    \*    \*    \*

### Roman Cardinale
### Pascagoula, Mississippi
### Formerly platoon sergeant, 23rd Regiment

Am I a prince of the church? Yeah, I get that a lot. Roman cardinal. It doesn't bother me anymore. I just go along with it.

Well, the last I remembered was the officers saying, "Don't leave any of the wounded behind." And the Chinese were already behind us. We tried to get to the high ground to get out of there, but we got cut off, surrounded.

On the 23rd's right was a division of ROKs, that's where the Chinese went through. When we started pulling back we were up one hill and down another hill, till a group of us got cut off carrying our wounded. We were fighting a rear-guard action, is what we were trying to do.

Down in the valley there were tanks trying to give us fire support to pull back, but then the Chinese just swarmed all over those. They had all they could do— they were shooting Chinese troops off of each other, the tanks were. And it's a sickening feeling when you see the last vestige of your American support going on down the road and you're surrounded. But we held out till the end till the ammunition ran out, and then there's not much more you can do.

After we were captured the Chinese tied us up with communication wire, which was all over the battlefield. They kept guards on us from up on a hill. In the morning they marched us to this washed-out place in the valley where there was a gathering place where they kept bringing others in. They didn't feed us for three days. Probably a couple of hundred POWs there.

I think officers were in Camp Two and the NCOs in Camp Four, but I'm no longer certain of that. I stayed in Camp One despite being a sergeant because nobody ever squealed on me. I had been in the Army at the end of World War II and was in the Enlisted Reserve. And when you come in as a fill-in you don't wear rank. I mean, you're going to live with the same guys in foxholes and stuff, they know who the sergeants are, they know who the top sergeant is.

They gave us the full treatment of indoctrination, that's for certainty. They had you write your autobiography. "You're the aggressor in Korea, and why are you?" All like that.

You can't really generalize about who died first, what sort of person or personality, I mean. But I'll tell you, they died of common things that a little bit of medication would have cured them—dysentery, all kinds of things.

∗        ∗        ∗        ∗

## Richard Sipel
## Tucson, Arizona
## Formerly BAR man, B Company, 88th Regiment

I was a corporal when I got captured, but when I got released I found out I'd been promoted to sergeant, backdated to date of capture. I enlisted in 1949, when I was 17, and I didn't get out until 1953, in Operation Big Switch. I hadn't planned on staying that long, I can tell you. I got to the 88th in December and spent Christmas on top of a hill. That's all they got in Korea, is hills.

All the fighting I was in was below the 38th Parallel. In February the regiment was in a couple of firefights, one in a place called Massacre Valley, I think they called it, that I think only thirty enlisted men and one officer were all that got out unhurt from my company. Then in March the company was in another firefight where I got wounded. They sent me to the Swedish Hospital in Pusan, but they seen to it I got back to the company at the beginning of May in time for the big offensive. Tim Davis most likely was a replacement for casualties we suffered in February and March, but I couldn't say for sure anymore. It was like this: When I first got there we were going through platoon leaders pretty quick. We went through about three of them in three months. You couldn't keep up with their damn names.

Our company commander, he always wanted us to call him Pappy. If we'd salute him, he'd read the riot act to us. Because we was in combat. He didn't want to be known as an officer, because officers and NCOs were targets for snipers. And after he was captured, he didn't want the Chinese to know he was an officer.

The night of the attack, you could look down in the valley and see Chinese coming four abreast as far as you wanted to look down the valley. Word was more or less passed on from one to the other to give up, lay your weapons down and give up, because there was just too damn many. I field-stripped my weapon and buried pieces here and there. Then the Chinese got us grouped together, ordered us to strip off our watches, wedding bands.

Then they started moving us north, so they did. We traveled mostly at night. Some nights we'd go north, some nights we'd go east, maybe the next night we'd go west, then maybe the next night we'd go north, then maybe the next night we'd go south. I don't know why we zigzagged like that.

We stopped at the Mining Camp maybe a month. Quite a few died there. I got to know this big, tall, strapping fellow from Texas. He got sick, three days he was dead. Now what from, I can't tell you. I don't know. If you got sick, you could figure, you're done.

I've heard of the Bean Camp, but I wasn't there. When we were at the Mining Camp, some groups came in and merged with us, and I think some of them were from the Bean Camp. And from my understanding it was rough, so it was.

On the march north, if you started lagging behind, they boosted you along a little bit. But they weren't as brutal as what the Japanese were in World War II. I think it was more for propaganda reasons, or how do I want to say it? Because they tried to educate us on communism, so they did.

They—what we called instructors—would come into your room. Maybe there were ten, twelve to a room. They'd come into the room and they'd sit down and start in on this American imperialism, you know, and all this communist crap, and how good communism was. And it didn't work. Not on me, anyhow. It worked on some, though. There was twenty-one who stayed behind when they released us. There was at least three or four that I knowed personally that stayed.

Why some of us made it and some couldn't, some died and some didn't, honestly and truthfully, I don't know. It just seemed that the guys gave up, they didn't care. I just made up my mind I was coming home. I didn't give a damn what I had to do or what I had to eat, I was coming home. But I never got very sick. There was some kind of building or facility for medical treatment at the main camp, but I never was in it. Once I had two back teeth that were giving me trouble. There was this old boy, I don't know where he came from, if he was a Chinese horse doctor or what, but he pulled 'em. With nothing, no pain-killer. He had trouble pullin' 'em, but he worked till he got 'em. That was rough, and no mistake.

If you behaved yourself, they left you pretty much alone. If you caused trouble, you were going to get into trouble. If we'd got caught at some of the shit we did, they'd still have us over there. I don't know who did it, but someone set their warehouse on fire. And of course there were some of us in the back takin' out sugar and tobacco. Now if we'd got caught, we wouldn't be here today, so we wouldn't.

All these years later, I don't know how to explain it. It ain't that I'm really mad at the Chinese. I don't know, maybe you'd call it a grudge. What really burns me up is that we fight these countries—Japan, Korea, China—and then we build them up and give them all our jobs. I'm bitter. I ain't afraid to admit it, I'm bitter. I can say I forgive them, but I'm still bitter. Right, wrong, I can't help it.

But I can truthfully say I didn't mind going to Korea, and I didn't mind being in the infantry. To me, I was protecting my country. I'd do it again if I had to.

*     *     *     *

**Alan Labuschagne**
**Bend, Oregon**
**Formerly B Company, 88th Regiment**

I was a PFC. I entered the Army in October 1949. After basic, I was sent to Guam and was three months in an engineering company. Then we were sent to Korea and I pulled guard duty for about six months in Pusan before being sent to the front lines as a replacement. That was February 1951. I think during the attack that about 130 were captured and about 70 were killed from our company.

The Mining Camp and Bean Camp were different. I was only at the Mining Camp and Camp One. I believe the people captured before us and later sent to Camp One were at the Bean Camp. In the Mining Camp, every two or three days someone died in the building we were kept in, and it probably ran true in the other buildings. There were no athletics or games in the Mining Camp. In any case, no one was in any shape to play. Everyone was pretty weak and lethargic.

I don't have any hard information on it, but I have a feeling that the withholding of food while on the march was planned in order to weed out those too weak to survive, and to make people more pliable when the indoctrination started. And to make it easier to control the POWs. None of the American doctors were allowed to help sick POWs in any way at Camp One, and there was no medical care at all at the Mining Camp.

Actually, I was kind of fortunate in that the group I was put in right after capture was comparatively small. The Chinese knew which plants along the way were edible. Before each meal they would forage along the roadside and pick the ones they wanted to eat. With that and other stuff they would cook the meal. Each Chinese had a flask of oil and some kind of frying pan. They also carried a larger utensil for cooking the rice. We ate the same as they ate, which was the white rice and the fried greens. I think probably we ate better than some other groups that were captured. For a time we ate a greenish-yellow meal that came in long bags. It didn't look very appetizing, but it was a very nutritious meal that the Chinese used to supplement when they couldn't get other supplies.

Another thing, I don't have any hard information about this, either, but there were rumors of strange, experimental operations conducted by the Chinese at Camp One. I don't know whether anyone died from them, only what I heard from POWs who came back to the squad rooms from the hospital and mentioned what had been happening. These were both POWs who had been operated on and who had seen what was going on. Maybe it was a crude method Chinese used to drain wounds, or treat sicknesses. I can't say. But the rumors were widely known. The hospital at Camp One was more or less a sick room where the desperately sick were taken and no one would go there of their own free will because it was known as a place to die in, not a place to live.

I wouldn't say selfish behavior was exactly common. I would say ten percent of the people become nasty and self-centered and would crawl around at night trying to steal something from someone. Of course the dead don't talk, and things robbed off the dying people wouldn't be seen by anyone else as a general rule, because all shoes looked the same and all jackets looked the same and all shirts looked the same. This was in the Mining Camp. In Camp One things got relatively better.

I imagine those who were captured in the winter or the late spring before us probably had a greater bitterness because they were on death marches, and also those captured by the North Koreans would be more bitter because the North Koreans had a very base nature and a low opinion of life.

For the most part we didn't have any interaction with Chinese because very few Chinese, usually officers, spoke English and none of us spoke Chinese. We didn't get into personal conversation with them until the Mining Camp, where the Chinese assigned political officers to POWs. All the time I was at the Mining Camp, I didn't see any brutality. At Camp One there were instances where people would be put into so-called hot boxes as a means of punishment. I never saw it, but from what I heard they were wooden boxes with metal roofs that got extremely hot in the summer.

*       *       *       *

### Harrison E. Whitelaw
### Candor, New York
### Formerly platoon leader, B Company, 88th Regiment

I had been a combat officer in World War II. I spent a year in Japan after the war ended. When I came home, I ran a dry cleaning business. That's what I was doing when I was called back in in 1950. The recall was rapid. They didn't have combat unit leaders. My MOS is what got me—1542, which is a combat unit leader. And they called back a number of reservists in my category when we weren't supposed to be recalled. But 1542 was a critical MOS. They didn't have combat unit leaders. It was just bad.

There was a lot of combat action going on with B company on May 17$^{th}$, don't let anyone tell you different. Though the action actually started on the 15th, and it was sporadic, across the whole front. The first and third platoons came under the heaviest attack on the left flank, and on the right A Company left their positions first. I don't know whether they just ran, I don't know what happened, all I know is they left, and I was not aware of it until later when battalion informed me. It was a tremendously heavy attack all along the front. The 23rd Regiment had been committed over on the right flank about seven miles from us, and they were pretty well wiped out. Our 3rd Battalion on our left flank held, but they were under attack until they were authorized to pull back. The attack was extremely strong. Seeing this mass of Chinese troops struggling along the road at night under the flares. It was *unbelievable,* that crowd of 10,000 men in view at one time. The attack was a concentrated effort to break the front at that particular time at the 2nd Division. The Chinese told us that was their specific target. They wanted to annihilate the entire division.

Tim Davis, now, he might have been in Savage's platoon or one of the other two platoons, but I don't think he was in my platoon. In all probability he was with us on the march, because most of the people captured then in that position were taken in the same column that I was in, all the way to the prison camp in North Korea.

After we got to Changsong, food was regularly available—what they *called* food—and most of our deaths occurred on the trail or at the Mining Camp. That's an interesting thing: I don't know and I don't think the military knows precisely where the Mining Camp was. In the 1970s someone from the Army contacted me trying to establish the location.

It has worried me ever since it happened, why some men, seemingly strong and capable, simply could not make it. I don't know why. One young fellow—I can't think of his name now, but I can see his face plain as day—was one of the strongest-looking men I met in Korea. He died. In perfect health and good spirits, it seemed, until suddenly in July he just wilted and died. It—well—it's beyond description. But seeing what we had to eat, of course, it may have made a difference. People that had been accustomed to having about everything they wanted, much less needed, maybe couldn't stomach it, because we had worms and bugs in the food. It was not a matter of looking for them, they were there, you couldn't avoid seeing them. And the food that we had, the grain, was indescribably bad.

I'll never get over my disappointment at the way American prisoners of war acted. Total lack of consideration for the fellow man. It was survival, period. It was almost universal, though there were exceptions. The veneer between civilized man and the primitive man is so thin it can be removed overnight. And it was.

My knowledge is limited by what I experienced or saw myself, but I didn't observe nearly as much sickness, ill health, or death in the services of other countries as I did in our own. But the problem is that ninety percent of the prisoners were Americans, and maybe among the other ten percent you wouldn't have noted as much. I'm just not sure. In other words, the sample, as the social scientists would say, was not large enough to make accurate projections. But their courage, their morale, seemed to be much better than ours, as a general rule. It just seemed that way to me. And of course the British stuck together. The Gloucesters that were there in camp with me were almost an intact unit, and that makes a difference, too, when you're associating with people you know.

As for the Chinese, I felt sympathy for them because they were, like us, soldiers ordered to do a job. They did it with remarkably little support. Their armament was poor, their food was poor, their clothing was unbelievably sparse. I mean, you wouldn't think people could live in temperatures like there with as little clothing as they had. And they continued to fight. While we were told they were fighting using drugs, et cetera, I never saw any evidence of that. None. They were very young, the ones that I encountered, or appeared to be very young. Our own people seemed to look on the Chinese as inferior people, and they weren't. They really had a lot of consideration for us and tried to show it. But instead of us being receptive and trying to do things to improve our own conditions, there was an antagonism. Maybe that's the way the military's supposed to be. But I don't think it is. I don't think it's the way *men* are supposed to be.

I have no way of knowing precisely whether conditions were the same for enlisted men as for officers in the main camps. As long as I was with the enlisted men—in close proximity to them, I should say, because they separated us—when I was in the same camp area, there was no difference there. The officers were perhaps not as receptive to the propaganda, and when I say propaganda I don't mean necessarily that they told us falsehoods, because they seemed to believe *completely* what they were telling us.

The Chinese separated officers, NCOs, and EMs early in the march—in two weeks. We could see the enlisted men, but weren't allowed to talk to them. When we got to the Mining Camp, they moved the officers down into the village, maybe 150 yards from where the enlisted men were kept, but we all ate out of the same pot. When we got to Changsong they moved the officers out of the camp altogether and put them in Camp Two, though in Camp Two there also were enlisted men. I would venture that basically there was no difference. Now, the propaganda may have been different that they fed us. But as far as the food, clothing, shelter, this sort of thing, I don't think there would have been any difference.

Those struggles up those hills on the march were almost impossible. And we had to walk in the dark, sometimes holding on to the person in front or to a rag or something to keep contact, because you couldn't see them. And we'd walk ten to twenty miles in every twenty-four-hour period. And the food was almost no food. The Mining Camp is where they really began carrying them out. There'd be four, five, six bodies a day dragged past our room down on the road in front of the big building.

I wish there was some way for us to siphon off the false from the truth and see really what happened there, because we don't know. We'll never know. But it was a horrible experience for everyone who went through it. And still, it was a learning experience.

You take the Tiger Group, now. That's the men of the 24th Division who went to Korea early, July 1950, and a number were captured in late July and August by the North Koreans. They don't want the truth told, I don't think. The way they try to paint it, you couldn't make it harsh enough, because they want it to appear that their group had a worse time than anyone else. When in reality all the men who were captured, no matter where they were captured or how long they were kept, had a pretty horrible experience.

\*     \*     \*     \*

## Walter C. Sheridan
## Mt. Airy, North Carolina
## Formerly B Company, 88th Regiment

Harrison Whitelaw was my platoon leader. He liked to be called Harrison, not Harry. 'Course, we called him "lieutenant," but I remember he didn't like to be called Harry.

I was in Japan for six weeks recuperating from a broken foot I got while on patrol. I had been back in B Company only five days before we got captured. I joined the Army August 6, 1950. Enlisted. Trained at Fort Knox, Kentucky. I was an assistant BAR man. I can't remember the name of the BAR man anymore.

We were definitely on what they called Pear Hill when it happened. I wasn't far from Whitelaw. The Chinese surrounded our whole outfit. I think the Army—division, regiment, whatever—used us as bait. They claimed they got about 90,000 of them by using us for bait, while we lost 2,000. Which it looked pretty dirty. Now I used to like to play checkers. You can't win a game if you don't give one for two or three in return. So that's what they was doin' with us.

There was nothing but Chinese as far as the eye could see. Oh, man, they just come in droves. And a lot of them didn't even have weapons. They just picked up the weapons of the men who died before them.

It was so quick that, really, it didn't bother me. I tell you, I was scareder about a year later than I was then. This was when the guards came in the middle of the night and got us up and I thought they were taking us away to execute us. I couldn't figure out what was going on. So I thought, well, they're going to take us all down here and kill us all. I really got scared. I mean, that's the scardest I've ever been.

When we were being marched down the street, about six abreast, I was on the outside. Eventually I just weaved my way and got in the middle, you see. And I said, if they go to shootin' and any of them guys go to fallin', I'm goin' to fall with them and try to play dead. Because I don't care what nobody says, you're number one. You're going to fend for yourself before you do for anybody else. Turned out it wasn't nothin'. Just one of their damned assemblies.

Now, my outlook might sound terrible, but things was the worst you ever seen. It was dog eat dog. It sounds bad, but then if you think about it, there'd be a guy who couldn't move—he'd be in a coma, rattlin' somethin' or other but you couldn't understand him—knowin' he's goin' to die within a few hours. We got so we could tell for sure, because there was lice all over us. And when your temperature went to runnin' up, you could see the lice leavin' the body. And when you did, you knew that man wouldn't be alive twenty-four hours later. So we could predict pretty well when a man was goin' to die. And so maybe he'd have a pretty good pair of combat boots or a pretty good pair of pants. Because all of us had messed in our drawers and everything else, and we couldn't take a bath. So one of us would say, "I knowed him. I'm gettin' his boots." Another'd say, "I'm gettin' his pants." It'd remind you of a vulture settin' there waitin' for somethin' to die. But really, he wasn't going to need them boots where he was a-goin', if you think about it that way. But still, it looks cruel.

You could get so sick, you didn't *care*. One time in the Mining Camp I got sick, I figured I was going to die. Couldn't walk, messed all over myself. There was an American doctor with us. He didn't have any medicine to give, other than APCs. I had heard that if you got a bubble of air in your veins from a hypodermic needle, you would die when the bubble got to your heart. I asked the doctor to give me a shot like that, since I was going to die anyway. He refused. Said it would be murder. This doctor died a short time later. He was put to hard labor for doing forbidden or illegal things. Once we got to the Main Camp, very few died.

Life don't mean nothin' to them, the Chinese. In fact, one night in the Mining Camp I had to go to the latrine. Don't know why, really, because I had just messed all over myself. But we had these old slit trenches, and it was drizzlin' rain that night, just one of them dreary nights. And this little guard was out there close to the latrine, and I hollered, "Chow bien," because I had to you know what. And he says, "Okayla, okayla." So I got on there and he was nervous. He had to be, because I had no more than dropped my pants and started and my stomach hurtin', and he started shoutin'. And I said, "OK, OK." He kept wantin' me to talk to him, see. He thought I was tryin' to slip up behind him, I reckon. So I finally got through, and you know, everybody was passin' blood and mucus. You'd feel like you was gonna do a pig, and about a spoonful would come out. I just got back in. His relief come around from the other end of the building to relieve him. And he had an '03, it looked like, or it could have been a Japanese rifle, looked like our American '03s, old bolt action job. He come up to relieve him, and a little crack of lightnin' flashed up, and he got a glimpse of him. And he hollered, "Halt!", and just as he hollered "Halt," he shot at the same time. And killed him, hit him right in the chest. And you know they killed him for killin' his relief? They had the trial that night. Well, when they first called for him they took the rifle away from him. See, we was right there within ten feet of it. They hit him upside the head with his own rifle, and they took and carried him off down in the village, and some of them down there in them buildings, in the village, said they shot him. Now, that was the last time I seen him, but they said they killed him. They 'bout beat him to death with that rifle butt before they ever carried him off.

There's another thing. They say they brought back to the States the bodies of the men who died there. *There ain't no way in hell they coulda done that.* I'll give you the example of a guy I took basic training with, a guy from Massachusetts. He was in the 3rd Division. I saw him again about two, three weeks after we were captured. He was shot in the arm with a .25 caliber burp gun, though he didn't lose much blood.

We didn't have much to eat, but they kept tellin' us, "When we get to the rear, you'll have better food, good medical attention," and all this old junk. Which we did, it was a little better, but it was still bad. But he says, "I ain't goin' to eat that old kaoliang, I'll wait till we get to the rear." I says, "You better keep your strength up." I don't know whether he thought he was too good to eat it, or what, but he died. And that's the only person I've ever put the dog tags in, but I rolled the dog tags in his mouth, you know, and we buried him out there in a little field. We dug with old sticks and stuff. He wasn't covered up six inches deep. They could take me within a hundred yards of that place and say, "Find it," and I couldn't remember it. There ain't no way they got those people back, and we had literally hundreds of bodies go down the Yalu River. They buried most of 'em in the snow and ice, and quick as it thawed, they went right down that Yalu River.

That's what makes me mad, too. There wasn't but two thousand two hundred and seems like thirty-five MIAs in Vietnam. That's all you hear, all them Vietnam MIAs. We have *eight thousand one hundred and seventy-seven* still unaccounted for from Korea, and you ain't heard nothin' said about it.

\*         \*         \*         \*

## Kenneth Smith
### Binghamton, New York
### Formerly squad leader, B Company, 88th Regiment

I was a squad leader in the second platoon, a sergeant. I'd been in the Army since 1946, right after high school. I started out in armor, but eventually got into the infantry. I'm what they call a lifer. I stayed in after being released from prison camp. Retired in 1966.

At the time we got captured I'd already been on the front lines for nine months. I landed in Korea August 4, 1951. Basically the reason we got captured was because this one lieutenant surrendered us. He believed it was a hopeless situation, so he surrendered, and I was in the group that he was in charge of. I was very angry and upset, because I believe we should have fought it out. I always regret that. Even years later, I tell myself, "What if I'd done this or that?" Hindsight's better than foresight, though. What if I'd said, "Hey, let's stay here and take on these guys? We got a whole platoon here, practically." If I'd said to myself and my squad, "C'mon, follow me." That's in my imagination now, you know. I think we'd have been a lot better off. But you don't know.

As soon as the group I was in was captured the Chinese started marching us to their rear areas. They took our personal possessions—watches, and so forth. We were attacked by some of our own planes, who didn't realize we were American POWs, though no Americans were hit. We traveled basically at night. It rained a lot, so that made it pretty miserable, too.

They were more or less like death marches, you know. A lot of the men succumbed on those trails. Couldn't keep up. They were too sick or too weak to do so. Most of them died on the march or in the Mining Camp. Food was what we called cracked corn or bug dust. Bug dust was the shavings off of sorghum kernels, I think.

On the march, there was no medical attention whatsoever. If a man got bitten by lice, and it became infected, his leg would swell up and he'd get gangrene from the infection because there was no way to stop it to begin with. Even in Changsong the medical attention was still so very, very poor. The food got a little better. Little bit of rice, little bit of sorghum, little bit of goat's meat, things of that nature.

After the peace talks started our aircraft were able to identify POW camps so they wouldn't bomb us. When we first reached Changsong we got strafed and approximately fifteen POWs got killed because the Chinese fired at these planes at night, and of course the planes didn't know who they were so they came down and riddled the whole camp.

The Chinese weren't brutal, but outside of the death marches they didn't have to be. There wasn't anybody left who could resist them too much. If you didn't keep up they'd just leave you on the trail and let you die.

Now, about "giveupitis": I think it was just the simple fact that a man gets so damn sick and tired and physically worn out, he doesn't want to struggle through it any more, so he doesn't try to continue to live under those circumstances.

The mind's got a lot to do with it, it really does have, especially mind over matter. And those men that were born during the Depression, those men who probably did not have a real good home life but had to rough it, maybe born in poverty and lived in poverty all during the Thirties, even up to the Forties, they seemed to be able to hang in there much better than men who'd perhaps just been drafted and had excellent conditions and excellent home life. Not in all cases, now, though. And the ones that had a high degree of built-in patriotism in them. Like when I was a kid I didn't believe that America could do anything wrong. But I found out later on that that wasn't true.

What killed most of the men was things like lice infections and diarrhea. Men would defecate in their pants, and these flies would lay maggots and things like that on you. That was a pretty horrible situation. A man's too weak to clean himself up and the other fellow's too weak to even help him, then they would spread more disease. There were really no toilet facilities. You'd just defecate in a hole out in back of the building.

All in all I'd advise anybody if possible not to be captured by any Asiatic army, because their culture and style of life is so completely foreign to a Westerner. Conditions they could live under, you can't.

They had what they called the Lenient Policy. You had to listen to these communist lectures every day on how great communism was, how great Stalin and Lenin were, and how great their society was compared to ours. They said we were the aggressors and would show propaganda pictures of Dulles overlooking the 38th Parallel, planning his invasion of North Korea. They started this indoctrination right away.

Letters going out were censored but I don't remember incoming letters being censored too severely. I'm still a little bitter that so many people back in the States knew I was in POW camp, and only one person wrote me.

I always wonder sometimes what Americans think about. See, to me, Vietnam and Korea were two wars the American people didn't have guts enough to complete it or finish it. Especially Vietnam. Vietnam was a war where the American public just cut and ran.

\*      \*      \*      \*

### William Ellsworth
### Naugatuck, Connecticut
### Formerly 5<sup>th</sup> Regimental Combat Team

I was in the 5th Regimental Combat Team, 24th Division. I got drafted Aug. 21, 1950. Took basic at Fort Meade. They sent us to Fort Jackson first, but it was closed or something, I can't rightly remember. We hung around there a couple weeks doing fatigue details—mowing grass, things like that—and got our shots, then they shipped us up to Fort Meade. After that to Fort A.P. Hill. I got to Korea March 25, Easter morning. I was captured April 22, 1951.

I remember we spent four days in this cave. One morning we surrendered, walked down to this valley and surrendered. We didn't have any food. And those Chinese soldiers, they were as much scared as what we were. We said

"Too-shawn," which means I surrender. Right away they fed us. They didn't have much to offer. They give us some rice and sorghum. During May we were on the march. They marched us at night, because our planes were in the air every day, bombing and strafing.

You could escape if you wanted to, but where would you go? On the march north soon after we were captured, the roads were so crowded with Chinese going south that we just had to push our way through. I remember there were only four or five of us, they were taking us north. And these old Chinese they were a-chuggin' down this ol' road, you know, carrying pots and pans and bags of rice. They didn't have trucks and jeeps like we had, only what they captured from us. And there wasn't any fat ones, either. They were in good shape.

I can't recall much about the Mining Camp. Except I saw a man shot there, after a so-called trial. He tried to escape and he killed two Chinese soldiers and they caught him again. They gave him a chance to run, and they shot him in the back. I saw that. The Mining Camp seemed to be kind of a receiving station. The Chinese kept telling us we'd be marched north to a main camp. I was surprised the Chinese could speak English. Not a lot, and not all of them, but more than you'd think.

I have to laugh. At the Main Camp they made us take part in filming a propaganda movie. The Chinese were on one side and we were running toward the Chinese and they were shootin' us down. I wonder if they showed that in their theaters, or was it just for the soldiers? We'd have these indoctrination classes. They'd tell us that DuPont and Rockefeller and the big wheels in the United States run the country. Which I sometimes think they were right, when it comes to these wars.

If you done what the Chinese told you to do, why, they left you alone. I was never beaten by them. I didn't see any brutality on the march. If you were too weak to walk, someone would have to carry you. There was never a time when I thought I might not get out, not really. I always had faith. Yep. Someday the war would be over and we'd get out.

In summer we could go to the river and swim. In winter we would go to the mountains and carry wood back to heat the buildings and cook food. I liked that, though wintertime was rough. There was a kind of recreation room where we could go play cards. Play Chinese checkers with the Chinese. They'd always cheat. Some guys could play guitars, the Chinese give 'em guitars. We could keep fairly warm in winter.

What made us mad was at Christmastime people at home would send you a Christmas card, and they'd just put their name on the back. They just couldn't take a couple of minutes to write a few lines. That made me mad. And as long as it took to get 'em, too.

The food on the march was the worst. I remember eating that stuff at night so you wouldn't see the damn bugs and worms. You had to, or you died. I had a damned old tin can and a GI spoon, that's all I had. I remember the first day we got in camp. Everyone was hungry. The Chinese brought out two big wooden boxes filled with cooked sorghum and rice. And those GIs went at that stuff just like a bunch of starved hogs. I can still see them rushing forward. I remember sometimes at night I'd be so hungry it was hard to fall asleep, because you'd think about food. I didn't think about sex too much.

I got to know Tim Davis in the Main Camp, but he wasn't in my POW company. I just met him one day, you know? He came there after I did. I liked him a lot; wish I'd known him before. He was a great guy, one of the best, one of the best. I saw him go downhill. I couldn't tell you what from. Could have been a dozen things, probably *all* of them. Bob Karns and Clair Kasten knew him better, they might know. I think they were both from his hometown, or from around there. In fact I think Bob Karns visited Tim in the hospital. A so-called hospital. It was a hogpen. They just laid people in there to die.

Clair told me Tim was always playin' with a danged basketball. He was always dribbling, playing with it, you know? He says he thinks that's what run him down. I remember Kasten tellin' me that.

# Epilogue: Changsong II

… It had to be Tim because there was nobody else in the room. He was lying on a wooden bed on top of some straw and had nothing on him but his blue prisoner's uniform, not even a blanket. He was deathly still. Bob approached the bed gingerly, his heart in his throat, because he was afraid Tim was, in fact, dead. But then he saw faint movement of the chest and closed eyelids.

Drawing to the side of the bed, Bob dropped to a squat alongside it, his greatcoat's skirts splaying out around him, and looked at the still form. There were flies crawling over the straw and on Tim's face and forehead! Flies, in the dead of a North Korean winter! Bob could not believe his eyes, but there they were, moving slowly and lethargically, but flies all the same. With his left hand he brushed them carefully off Tim's face. For the rest of his life he would tell of seeing flies on a desperately ill man's face in one of the harshest climates inhabited by man, and his hearers would be skeptical, but he knew that they were there.

For a couple of moments he could not accept this as his friend Tim Davis, this motionless, silent, monstrously gaunt thing with dark and sore-covered face. But it was momentary only. He knew him enough from boyhood on to know that this was Tim Davis.

Bob took hold of Tim's right hand. "Oh Jesus. Oh Christ. Oh Timmy."

There was no response.

"Oh God, Tim. It's me, Bob. Bob Karns, remember? From Repringer. From West Linton. Remember? Oh God, Tim, don't die."

There was no response. Bob had seen death many times over in his months in Korea as soldier and prisoner, but his mind scrambled to think of words for his mouth to form that might push death or the thoughts of it away.

"I didn't even know you were in here. Kasten told me. I mean in the camp, not here. I didn't know you were in here either, of course—this, this hospital, I mean." Bob threw a glance contemptuously into the dim reaches of the room, as if to dismiss any idea that it had any connection with a hospital. "He said you were captured together. It was just chance, me running into Kasten. Jeez, I wish I coulda got to see you before. Clair told me you was always playin' with that blamed basketball." Bob stopped, realizing he was rambling. He tried once again to organize his thoughts, but nothing came to him but a tumble of trivialities from their past.

"Hey, Tim, remember Sunday nights down to Bagtown? Roller-skating? Oh, Sunday night, that was a big thing down there, roller-skating, a big thing. All the gals, they always liked you, Tim. You was always a great hand with the ladies. I wisht I had your luck with the ladies."

The prone body before him moved. Whether it was in response to the noise of talking or to the change in air pressure in the room caused by the entrance of a third person, or mere happenstance, Tim raised one clawlike hand three or four inches off the bed, turned his face infinitesimally toward Bob's, and opened his eyes. The movement was enough to cause Bob's mind to race even more frantically in search of words that would evoke further indication of life.

"And the movies down in Horton? You and Jim Calder and Herb Wentley, you run around together. But sometimes you and them and me and a whole bunch of us, we'd go there. And we'd get up in that balcony and just laugh and carry on. We wouldn't get home till about three o'clock in the morning, but we'd have a good time."

Bob stopped. All the while he had been gabbling he was watching Tim, and now he realized that the blank blue eyes saw no one and the dirt-encrusted ears heard nothing. But then the lips began to move, ever so slightly, trying to form a word, a sound.

Bob bent closer to Tim's face and said, "What, Tim? Did you want to say something?" Tim's almost motionless lips gave a soft expiration of air, hardly a sound, and Bob bent still closer, asking again, "What, Tim? I didn't catch that. What did you say?" And there was another push of air, a bit more forceful, a bit more breathy, and Bob thought it sounded like "Helen." But that meant nothing to him. He knew plenty of Helens, but none that he could connect with Black Run or Somerton or Tim. And then Tim's hand fell back on the bed.

Bob became aware of the guard standing next to him, and looked up at him. The guard nodded solemnly again. It was time to go. A nod to come in, a nod to go out.

He rose and faced the guard. He felt the ache of squatting, made worse by insufficient exercise and food, spread up his thighs.

"Tim wasn't a hell-raiser or anything like that," Bob said, as if the guard could understand, though he knew he was talking only for his own benefit. Probably he had been all along. "He just liked to have a good time. I never saw him drunk or nothin' like that."

Tears welled in Bob's eyes. The guard stared at him, not unsympathetic, non-committal. Bob turned swiftly and walked to the door.

At the door he turned back for one last look. The guard had gone back to his corner. Tim lay on the bed, his face toward the roof. His eyes were closed again, and in this gloom, where the shadows were deep and unearthly, his eye sockets looked like those of a skull. If he still breathed, Bob could not tell from this distance. He turned and pushed out into the arctic cold.

# Coda: Beloved Son

*"Where did we get such men?"*

—James Michener, *The Bridges at Toko-ri*

The day they buried Tim Davis in Horton Cemetery—July 7, 1955, a Thursday—was stunningly beautiful. As people say there, they couldn't have ordered up more perfect weather. The sun shone brightly and steadily from the moment it slipped up from behind the low mountains east of the cemetery, which sat on a low ridge overlooking the broad valley cut by Hacketts Creek. A few streaky clouds drifted imperceptibly westward through the azure of the sky. It was a large cemetery, and its emerald greensward swept down and continued into the variegated green carpet of the Point Deadly Golf Course below it. The temperature was in the low 70s and an occasional breeze ruffled the longer tufts of grass around the bases of the cemetery monuments and, stronger at higher elevations, caused the American flag to snap briskly—though soundlessly—from its distant flagpole.

How much everyone had moved on, particularly in the matrimonial direction! Peg Burnham had married a career Navy NCO the year before. She was pregnant with her first child, which is why she was not there this day. Both of Tim's sisters, Connie and Barbara, had married. Dave Burnham was soon to be wed again, to a Roman Catholic woman, an eyebrow-raising development for Burnham family and their friends. And Anna had remarried and moved to Florida.

That is, most people gathering this day thought they were burying Tim. Some, including his brother Rick, weren't so sure. Rick was home on leave from the Air Force for the funeral. No one could believe that a family in which one son was a prisoner of war would have to give up the only other son to the armed services, much less a son who was blind in one eye. But such is the maw of conscription in wartime, and under pressure of the draft Rick enlisted in the Air Force in late February 1952. That was, though no one knew it until months later, only one month after the official date of his brother's death in Changsong.

It was odd. The way Rick puts it, he was actually drafted into the Army—for a day. Then he got the opportunity to change services.

"I was living in Watervliet. I called mother in Pennsylvania, I'll never forget it. I said, 'You know, I'm in the Army.' She said, 'Oh, God!' I said, 'They give me another day to join another branch. What do I do?' She said, 'Get in the Navy or Air Force.' So I said, 'OK. Bye.' So I went over and walked across the hall there and told the Air Force guy, 'How do I get in the Air Force?' He says, 'No problem.' I entered the Air Force on the last day of February 1952—February 29, it was a leap year."

Rick was stationed at Mather Air Force Base east of Sacramento when he learned of Tim's death.

"Mother called me and told me what happened," he said later. "She told me that she got word that he had died in the prison camp. Boy, I felt so lousy when she told me that. I went downtown and I walked the streets all night. Walked up and down. 'Course, I had to be back at the base for duty the next day. I was all by myself. I felt so bad. I didn't know what to do. I had no one to talk to. I'd just walk the streets. I'd go along and I'd kick the buildings and the trees."

It wasn't long after that phone call that he met Bob Karns, who was among the 12,773 U.N. POWs repatriated in Operation Big Switch between August 5 and September 6, 1953. He had heard from his mother that Bob was coming in, and the newspapers were filled with the news of the imminent arrival of the released POWs. Rick saw Bob get off the ship in San Francisco, but couldn't meet and talk to him until later. When he did, he asked him about Tim's dying. Bob told him what he knew, but said he never saw Tim buried.

"After a death there'd be a burial detail, you know?" he told Rick. "Guys come in and carry them up to the graveyard, throw 'em in a big hole. I hate to say it, but the dogs got some of the remains. I'm sorry to say it so crude like, but you asked and I figured you wanted the truth. Don't ever tell your mother."

Much later, when Rick had a chance to talk with Clair Kasten, he heard much the same thing.

"I don't see how they could ever have located his grave, Rick. So-called grave, I should say. That's what makes me wonder, when they bring a body home, if it *is* the body. But don't ever tell your mother or sisters, because that's neither here nor there. If they believe those are his bones, that's good enough."

They were there at the cemetery, of course, Bob and Clair, along with dozens of friends and family members from Pennsylvania and New York. Yet another funeral for a member of the extended King family. There had been Anna's husband Hugh; Clyde Friedle, husband of Anna's sister Cassie; Grandma Naomi King; Eileen Burnham, Anna's younger sister; Grandpa Lawrence King, who died at age 86 in September 1953, not long after Anna received official word of Tim's death. The irony was that the Horton *Express*, the weekly newspaper, carried Grandpa King's obituary and the announcement of Tim's death in the same issue, on different pages, without making a connection between the two.

And now the cemetery service for the youngest family member yet. All had gradually moved toward the site, and silence was settling on the open grave. Anna stood there, in black dress and veil, holding tremulously with her right hand the forearm of her second husband, Del Frace. The girls were there, also in black, Connie with her husband, but Barbara was there alone, her husband being in the Army in West Germany. Rick stood next to his mother, in his Air Force uniform with black band around his upper sleeve. The rest of the crowd fanned out and around the grave site, their proximity to the grave being in general relationship to their degree of affinity or consanguinity to the deceased. Everyone looked expectantly at the minister, who seemed to be waiting for a pair of nearby bluebirds to cease their cheerful chatter.

He was the Rev. Carlton Riemenschneider, youngest son of the now-retired Church of the Brethren pastor, and a curious successor to his father's calling. A notorious hell-raiser in his teenage years, as preacher's kids not infrequently are, he had got caught by World War II. Despite his church's historical peace stance and opposition to all war, he did not contest his conscription. The war made him a hero—winner of the Silver Star for saving the lives of six men in his infantry squad while personally overwhelming a German machine-gun nest—and also taught him a thing or two, one of them being that heroism doesn't matter, at least not in the way it seemed to him that heroism generally is perceived. It also turned him into a person of faith with a thirst for knowledge, neither of which had been noticeable in him as a preacher's kid. After the war he went to Penn State on the GI Bill and then, breaking further with his father and his church, to Princeton Theological Seminary for eventual ordination as a Presbyterian minister. But the theological and personal breach with his father healed, to the extent that he had taken as his first pastorate the small Presbyterian Church in Horton. When news of Tim's capture and then death became known, he went out of his way several times to speak to Anna and her daughters about it, because of the near-obsession with war and its emotional and spiritual consequences that his combat experience had instilled in him. Because of this peculiar understanding, Anna had asked him rather than the Brethren pastor to speak at Tim's services. This had caused a minor stir among the faithful, but as Anna and Del had been living in Florida for a year, and would be going back there soon after the funeral, local denominational squabbles could not stop her from giving her son the burial service she thought most fitting.

The Rev. Riemenschneider raised his arms and pulled the Bible in his hands to his black-clad chest, as if to say to his audience, Come unto me. The gaping ends of his robe's sleeves slid down his arms, revealing the sleeves of a gray suit jacket. Anna let her gaze sweep across the assemblage. She knew nearly everybody there, though her eye was caught by a couple she did not recognize, a woman, who looked to be in her late twenties, and a boy, about seven or eight, standing at the edge of the crowd a couple of hundred feet away. The minister cleared his throat.

"Dear brothers and sisters in Christ.

"The service for the dead is an Easter service. It finds all its meaning in the resurrection. Because Jesus was raised from the dead, we, too, shall be raised.

"The service, therefore, is characterized by joy, in the certainty that 'neither death, nor life, nor angels, nor principalities, nor things present, nor things to come, nor powers, nor height, nor depth, nor anything else in all creation, will be able to separate us from the love of God in Christ our Lord.'

"This joy, however, does not make human grief unchristian. The very love we have for each other in Christ brings deep sorrow when we are parted by death. Jesus himself wept at the grave of his friend. So, while we rejoice that one we love has entered into the nearer presence of our Lord, we sorrow in sympathy with those who mourn."

Smiling, comforting, the handsome young minister looked directly at Anna. She returned the gaze, biting her lip, until her eye was caught again by the sight of the unfamiliar young woman, who was having to struggle to hold on to her hat in a sudden strong breeze. The little boy, holding the woman's hand, looked up at her.

"Timothy Arthur Davis," the minister continued, "whose body we commit today to his native soil, was a soldier for Christ as well as for his country. Most of us here know what a dedicated adherent he was of his boyhood church. Indeed, many of us attended that very church with him, though some of us have strayed from that path—in various ways."

The Rev. Riemenschneider smiled again, broadly this time, encouraging response to this little joke at his own expense, but no one wanted to risk even a hint of humor at a solemn occasion.

"When he left us to seek his fortune in the wider world, as so many from these mountains have had to do down through the decades, we know that he remained true to his Christian upbringing. He was an unusual young man in that regard. A kind, helpful, genial, faithful young man. And impossibly likable. There is no one who met him who did not like Tim Davis. Our Lord can hardly ask for a better modern disciple than that.

"Nor can our country. Timothy Arthur Davis was also true to his country. When it called, he answered. Perhaps no more gladly than we sometimes answer the hard calls our Lord sometimes issues to us, but what is important is to answer, and he answered. He did not count the cost, and ultimately the cost was of the highest. He became a brave soldier, and died a terrible death while—to use that strangely poetic phrase of government documents—'in the hands of the opposing forces.' From there he passed, we are assured, into the bosom of our Lord."

The minister paused briefly and looked around him, before beginning again.

"He also passed into the pantheon of heroes. 'Hero' is not a word we should use lightly, but we do, every day. Because of that overuse it loses some of its meaning and impact. Thus many heroes get lost to us. Heroes like Tim, and the thousands who are still missing in action, and the tens of thousands of others who died, and the soldiers and sailors in their hundreds of thousands who braved enemy fire and, thanks be to God, came back to us. We take their lives and expend them so freely, so thoughtlessly, as if they were coin with which we can do what we will. And we forget that through their sacrifice—in too many cases, what we call the ultimate sacrifice—they have become heroes. Invisible heroes.

"There is a bit of wisdom from the fourth century B.C. Chinese philosopher of war, Sun Tzu, who writes in his *The Art of War*:

'Regard your soldiers as your children,
'And they will follow you into the deepest valleys;
'Look on them as your own beloved sons,
'And they will stand by you even unto death.'

"This, then, is how we remember Tim Davis—as our beloved son. The beloved son of his parents—his dear mother Anna, here, and his deceased father Hugh—and of his family and of this place, his native ground. The beloved son of the church. We hope that that is how he will be remembered by his country—the country he stood by as a soldier, even unto death. From those whom our heavenly father sets above us we can expect no more, and Tim—our beloved brother, our beloved son—deserves no less.

"We are saddened, of course, by Tim's death, that it came at such an early age and in such a brutal manner to one of such great promise and personality, and we wonder: Why? We must not ever think he died in vain. To the contrary, he put his body in the way of one of the world's great evils. Today we are too caught up in it to understand, but decades on the magnitude and necessity of the struggle may become clear to us.

"We take comfort, as I am sure Tim with his faith must have, in knowing that God has a plan—for him, for us, for all of creation. We cannot fathom it with our inadequate comprehension, but it is enough to know that there is one. Its healing powers are expressed in an even greater bit of wisdom from Julian of Norwich, the 14th century English mystic: 'All shall be well and all shall be well and all manner of thing shall be well.' That is the greatest comfort."

The minister paused again. Some were snuffling, some were dabbing at their eyes and noses with handkerchiefs. Anna had her right hand underneath the veil of her hat, pressing hard against her mouth. Del Frace looked as if he had just come in from another planet and did not comprehend these strange rites. Connie and Barbara were shuddering with sobs. All knew what was coming.

The minister raised his right hand as if in benediction and darted a glance in the direction of the pallbearers at the edge of the grave, who, at that fleeting signal, tightened their grip on the straps running underneath the coffin. Then, grim-faced and sweating in their unaccustomed suits, they slowly lowered the coffin into the ground as the minister spoke.

"Hearken unto these words of Scripture:

"'I am the resurrection and the life, saith the Lord. He that believeth in me, though he were dead, yet shall he live. And whosoever liveth and believeth in me shall never die.'

"And these:

"'I know that my Redeemer liveth, and that he shall stand at the latter day upon the earth. And though worms destroy this body, yet in my flesh shall I see God, whom I shall see for myself, and mine eyes shall behold, and not another.'

"And these:

"'We brought nothing into this world, and it is certain we can carry nothing out. The Lord gave, and Lord hath taken away. Blessed be the name of the Lord.'"

Soft weeping took over the crowd. Bob Karns and Clair Kasten were grateful for the cover that their positions in the second rank of mourners gave them; even as it was, they dropped their heads to their chests and struggled for composure. With the coffin resting at the bottom of the hole, the Rev. Riemenschneider took a tiny shovel and dribbled earth down upon the coffin, intoning:

"In sure and certain hope of the resurrection to eternal life though our Lord Jesus Christ, we commend to almighty God our brother Timothy, and we commit his body to the ground. Earth to earth, ashes to ashes, dust to dust. The Lord bless him and keep him, the Lord make his face to shine upon him and be gracious to him, the Lord lift up his countenance upon him, and give him peace. Amen."

After that it was quickly over. "Taps" was played, an honor guard from the VFW fired three ragged volleys, the military escort gave the U.S. flag to Anna, and the service broke up. Mourners paying their respects came by where Anna, Del, and Tim's brothers and sisters were sitting. As they did so conversation picked up throughout the crowd and the mood slowly but surely grew lighter.

✳    ✳    ✳    ✳

Most of the mourners had left the cemetery. Only immediate family members remained—Rick, Connie, and Barbara, Anna's sisters and brothers and their spouses, a few others—discussing what was next on the agenda. Bob Karns and Clair Kasten were gone, as were other boyhood friends, and more distant relatives from Pennsylvania and New York—all had said a few words to Anna and made good their exit. But Anna noticed, lingering outside the invisible ring of this family circle, the youngish woman and small boy she had wondered about earlier. They had not come through the line of mourners paying their respects. The woman looked as if she was trying to get Anna's attention now. Anna excused herself and walked toward her.

"Did you want to see me, dear?" As she got closer Anna saw she was wearing a dark gray suit and a hat that did not quite match but was suitable for the occasion.

"Yes, thank you, Mrs. Davis."

"Frace, dear. I remarried last September."

"Yes, I know. I just forgot there for a moment." The little boy, still holding the woman's hand, looked from her to Anna.

"Pardon me, but do I know you?" The woman was quite pretty, in a soft and accommodating way. Yes, she looked late-twentyish, but lines of life were already beginning to etch upon her brow.

"Well, yes, in a way. Oh, dear, I'm forgetting myself. I wanted to say how very sorry I am for your—for your loss."

"Thank you. It is still hard, after all these years. We've known of Tim's death for two years now, of course, and feared it long before that, even. But still, this is … final." Anna's voice trailed off as she looked at Tim's grave, now filled in.

"It was a beautiful service. Just beautiful. Very moving."

"Wasn't it? I'm so glad I asked Rev. Riemenschneider to do it. He seemed to understand Tim so well. Of course, they knew each other when they were younger, but even beyond that. His war experience, I suppose." Anna turned to look at her family, who were deep in conversation. She turned back to the woman. "But you said we've met?"

"Not exactly. Oh, I'm keeping you from your family. I'm sorry."

"Not at all. We have nothing very pressing right now." Anna's smile was not completely successful in suppressing a note of impatience.

"I won't take much of your time. I'm Helen Sheaffer." She extended her hand and Anna shook it. "And this is my son, Andy." The little boy stepped forward, solemnly extending his hand, which Anna also shook.

"A handsome young fellow, Mrs. Sheaffer." This time Anna's smile was genuine. "How old is he?"

"Seven. He was seven in May. And please call me Helen. You may remember me as Helen Booth."

Anna's eyelids batted involuntarily in an effort of remembrance, and after about three beats the light went on over her head. "Helen Booth! Of course, you were the girl Tim was—Tim was sweet on. But that was so long ago. And weren't you from Ohio? Surely you didn't come all that way. Do you live around here now?"

"No—oh, it's difficult to explain. Andy"—she knelt and placed her hand on her son's shoulder, turning him to look toward the honor guard, who were completing arrangements to leave—"why don't you go over and watch those soldier men put away their guns and things? Don't bother them, but if you're quiet, I'm sure they'll let you watch." With her right hand she gave him an encouraging little boost on his rear. His face registered an initial impulse of resistance, but then he slowly walked off in the direction indicated.

"He seems like a nice boy," Anna said, watching him stroll off in his miniature man's suit. "Do you have other children?"

"No, just Andy. He is. He's a wonderful boy. Mrs. Frace—"

"Anna. Please call me Anna."

"Anna. You asked if I was from around here. No, I still live in Ohio. Oh, it's hard." Helen was flustered and her voice anguished. "I probably shouldn't have come."

"Then you *did* come all that way. But why? Surely not because—I mean, Tim, after all these years? And how did you know about the funeral?"

"I knew about it because—I don't think you knew her, Francine Avitek, she lives over in Frawleysburg. I worked with her at Beech Haven that summer. Francie, we called her. She's married now, her name's—it doesn't matter. But we were really good friends, and we've always stayed in touch. We've visited each other a couple of times. She told me about the funeral. She saw it in the paper, the Horton paper."

"Still, I have to ask, all that way for a youthful romance of—what?—eight years ago? What—?"

"Mrs. Frace, Anna," Helen broke in, rushing her words, "I came because Andy is Tim's son."

Anna stood, thunderstruck, in the silent dazzling sunlight. She looked at Helen's pale, frightened face. Her trim body seemed to have lost fifteen pounds in the last few seconds, expended with the effort of making her startling revelation.

"Tim's son." It was not a question.

"Yes. Oh, Anna, please don't be angry with me." Helen reached out with her right hand to touch Anna's left arm. "I know you must be confused. I'll try to explain. I came because I had to come."

Anna stood looking at this woman, and instantly knew that what she had said was true. This was a solid, honest woman, and whatever her motives for being here were, Anna knew in her bones that they were not venal.

"That means he is my grandson." Anna looked over at the boy, standing next to the men gathering up their equipment.

"Yes."

"From—from that summer at Beech Haven?"

"Yes."

"Did Tim know about him—about Andy?"

"Yes."

Anna, in shock, could think of nothing more to say. She sighed. Then: "It makes me sad to think that my son did not meet his obligations to you and to your—*his*—son."

"Anna, don't think that. Don't ever think that. Tim *tried* to, more than once. I wouldn't let him."

Rick broke away from the group he was talking with and approached his mother and Helen, who, he thought as he drew nearer, looked somehow familiar.

"Mother, excuse me, I think we should be going now."

"Not just now, Richard," Anna replied, half-waving her hand backward in dismissal. "In a moment. This lady and I are talking."

Rick pulled back at the snappish sound in his mother's voice and the use of his formal name. He looked again at the woman, and went back to his sisters.

"You wouldn't let him," Anna said, and again it was not a question. "You didn't love him?"

"I loved him fiercely, Anna, so much it hurt. He was a wonderful boy. I wanted us to marry—that is, before ... before Andy."

"But Tim didn't love you, that was it?"

"I think he did love me. No, I *know* he did. But he was so confused. He wanted to do so many other things, so many things he didn't know what they were. Or maybe he didn't have anything he really wanted to do then, except *not* get married. So we broke up. That is, *I* broke up with him."

"I remember how terribly upset Tim was then. We could hardly live with him." Anna paused. "You didn't know you were pregnant then?"

"No."

"When you found out, did you tell Tim?"

"No. Not till after he had moved to Upstate New York. I didn't know his address, so I wrote to you, enclosing a letter to him and asking you to send it on. I was deathly afraid you would open it up and discover everything."

"I vaguely remember that. No, I didn't think anything of it. I just sent it on as you asked." Anna sighed again. "Why did you tell him then, if you were set on not marrying him?"

"I thought he should know. I didn't want to make him feel bad, or guilty, or even responsible. I mean, he was, of course. He was the father. He was responsible for creating my—*our*—son. But not legally or financially responsible. I didn't want him to feel that. I just thought he should know."

"And is that when Tim tried to convince you to marry him? I'm sorry, I seem to be badgering you with questions, but they just keep coming to me."

"That's all right. I knew something like this would happen when I decided to come here. Yes, he did try to get me to marry him. It was awful. He called and called. From pay phones. I can still picture the poor guy, in the train station, in the bus station, trying to talk with the PA system going off in the background. I had to beg him not to come out to Ohio. It would have been just too embarrassing."

"Embarrassing? You mean, your family didn't know about … about the situation then?"

"No, because by that time I had a solution to the whole problem. That sounds calculating, and it was nothing like that. I was going to marry another man, a guy I had gone out with in high school. He was two years ahead of me, but we had been an item for a long time. He was home on leave from the Army, and he asked me out again. Back then, in high school, I think he loved me as much as I loved Tim at Beech Haven. But back then, I guess I was acting like Tim. I didn't know what I wanted, or I wanted too many things."

"That's right, you did say your name is Sheaffer."

"That's right, his name was Andy Sheaffer, too, just like his—just like his son's. Andy—my husband—was going back to the Army in a couple of weeks. He asked me to marry him. I explained the situation to him. He said it didn't matter, the child would be his. He had wanted to marry me out of high school. And I said yes."

"So you *could* marry Andy Sheaffer but you *couldn't* marry Tim." It wasn't quite a question and it wasn't quite an accusation.

"Anna, Andy really wanted to marry me. Tim didn't. Not really. Nothing against him, but he simply didn't." Helen smiled. "And you know what? I loved Andy, I did. Say what you will, I've been blessed with some pretty terrific guys in my life." Her smile grew broader. "Including my son."

"So now you all live there in Ohio."

"My son and I do. Andy, my husband, is dead. He was killed in Korea, too."

"Oh my God, child!" Anna's hands flew to her breast. "What are you telling me? In a POW camp?"

"No, in combat on Bloody Ridge in September 1951. Heartbreak Ridge, I guess they call it, also. Andy was planning on staying in the Army. But it was not to be, I guess. Another invisible hero, like the minister said. I liked that. It seemed right."

"Oh," Anna groaned, and tears welled up in her eyes. "These wars. These wars. I am so sorry for you, child. Please forgive anything I've said that may have sounded harsh."

"Anna, there's nothing to forgive. If anything, I should apologize for placing another burden on you on a day that is burden enough. But, I can't tell you why, I simply had to do this."

"I'm glad you did, Helen. What you've had to endure. I think—" Anna scrabbled in her purse for a tissue to wipe away tears—"I think, oh, I don't know. I think Rev. Riemenschneider should have spoken about invisible heroines."

"No, he was right, Anna. And what has happened to me is nothing compared to you—a husband lost in a horrible accident and then your son … and to live in uncertainty for so long. I—" Helen paused to regain composure. "Besides, well, life goes on. I'm seeing someone else, now. Another terrific guy, you might say." And Helen smiled that soft smile that had melted Tim Davis's heart and haunted his memories.

Connie came up to the two women.

"Mother," she said, a note of crossness in her voice, "we *really* have to go now." Connie looked at Helen, questioning, Who are you?

"Connie, you and Barbara and Rick and the rest go along to the cars. I'll be along shortly, as soon as I finish talking to this"—Anna looked Helen directly in the face and smiled—"old friend. Come, let's go get your son."

Slipping her right arm through Helen's left, Anna led her up the gradual slope to where Andy was playing by himself. As they walked Anna told Helen about the young woman Tim had been seeing in Guldwyck, Peg Burnham, who had since married and was expecting her first child. She asked Helen whether she would ever tell her son the truth about his father, and Helen said she had often pondered that question, and what did Anna think about it? And into the bright green-and-gold shimmering sunny afternoon two women whom life had made so unhappy and so happy walked arm in arm, dropping burdens as they went.

✳          ✳          ✳          ✳

"Who's that woman with Mom?" Rick said to Barbara. They were standing at the foot of Tim's fresh grave, reluctant to leave. "Seems like I've seen her someplace before."

"I don't know. Mom said she's an old friend. I've never seen her, I don't think. Maybe it's someone from Florida. I don't know what's so important she has to talk to her about that she can't leave with us now."

Rick squatted down. He picked up some of the loose earth and let it sift through his fingers.

"You know," Rick said, looking up at his sister, who could see that he was growing weepy, "the reverend there said Tim was a beloved son. I suppose he was, to Mom, and to the country, and to everything and everybody that the reverend said. But he was a good brother too. He enjoyed life. It's a shame he was killed, he would have enjoyed his life. Such a nice guy. Everybody liked him. I really looked up to him. It really hurt me when he, when he ..." Rick's voice trailed off. "Even when he was up in New York he thought of Christmas and our birthdays in Pennsylvania and would send you something. It's not fair. You don't find too many brothers like that."

978-0-595-46183-7
0-595-46183-2

Printed in the United States
96133LV00004B/112-138/A